Cover design by: Neil Kilby

To Joan with Love

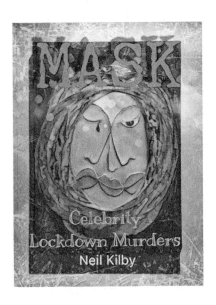

MASK

Celebrity Lockdown Murders

By

Neil Kilby

1.

Cecilia had got to a certain age. She knew psychobabble wouldn't work for her. Even so, she had tried it when a part of her life was crashing to the ground. The thought of being regressed again would only mean the pain would get worse, not better. It was built into the fabric of her being. To share such things with a total stranger would only serve to destabilise her more.

None of what she was thinking was relevant to the moment, but it consumed the time. Waiting could be a pleasant thing to do in the right surroundings, but the cold dark night that was accompanied by a fog that permeated her bones was not the best place to do it.

Strange shadows were faintly created on the floor, as a warm glowing mist hung around a streetlight. It was adorned by a halo in an almost perfect circle that was wrapped around it, which made it look like an angel patiently waiting to collect a soul who might pass that way. A conversation continued inside her head as she decided whether to move or to wait a bit longer. She used the time to reminisce. Her life had spread over seventy years. She enjoyed these moments; they were a backdrop to her whole life, having been an actress for most of that time.

......

Cecilia was in a theatre, in the wings, about to go on stage. It was the first time, her first time in front of a live audience. She could feel the nerves again, her blood charging through her veins, so much so it made her perspire. Her words were stuck in her throat, she knew they would not be said. Someone was saying go, but her feet were rooted. At this moment she knew what it was like to be a tree, until she was pushed. On stage, the darkness of the wings was a memory, the safety net had been withdrawn. It brought about a fist in her stomach. Adrenalin launched her into her lines, as her body settled to the part, which was all of four lines and no more. She realised at once that it was the best feeling she had had since the day she started acting.

Cecilia was lost in this memory. She could smell the theatre again, the expectation, the excitement, the body heat heightening the creative process, as mist drifted off the stage into the audience.

A passing car snapped her out of it. Her thoughts then slipped away, joining the fog that surrounded her. This waiting was as if she was back when nerves overtook her before a first night. Here, like then, she stood slightly hesitating, before she knew she had to go on.

The memory, like many others of her past, had been a constant of late. It seemed with great age, came a myriad of happiness, coupled with sadness, which somehow drowned her when she looked back over her life.

She moved. Her joints cracked. She needed to get on with it. The 'it' was to visit someone, someone whom she hardly knew at all.

Lockdown was continuing due to the outbreak of Covid 19. Everyone was taking precautions. Even so, most people were still ignoring its dangers. Cecilia stood outside a luxurious apartment building. Only one of the apartments was occupied at the time. The others had also sold quickly and were awaiting their buyers. She made her way up to the top floor of the three-storey executive accommodation. Security as yet was almost non-existent. She admired the décor as she went; tasteful framed prints adorned the walls, with strategically placed pot plants to soften the corners. Overall, it was impressive. She lowered the hood of her coat, to reveal slightly greying hair, which she tidied with her free hand. She knocked on the door, even though there was a buzzer. Her eyes widened in expectation. They were a clear piercing blue.

Although she was elderly, it could easily be said she looked younger than her years. Some would say she looked beautiful; others might say she was past her prime. These were the kind of things that ate at the heart of Cecilia. Her view of the world had become jaundiced as she got older. Maybe it was the fact that her acting career had shone. Trouble was, she wasn't ready to shuffle off quietly into the sunset. After all, she had been a successful actress.

She had a small bunch of flowers in her hand. She knocked again. She could hear movement and assumed that she was being spied upon. After a few seconds, a face appeared, as the door slowly opened. The face had a mask on. Not a paper one, but a beauty mask applied to help erase imperfections. A woman stood there wearing pink satin pyjamas, as well as an Asian dressing gown. Her appearance appeared almost comical to Cecilia, but silence hung in the air as these two masked people seemed to have a face-off. To be more precise, they both kept their masks on.

"Hello," said Cecilia, "you don't know me but I'm a big fan. I have always liked what you do on social media and l follow you avidly."

Something inside Cecilia squirmed at her own words, as she said them, then she continued to issue more flattery. Immediately, the woman smiled and cracked the perfect smoothness of the cream-coloured face mask. Cecilia presented her with the flowers.

"Oh, thank you! They're beautiful! Can you come in while I sort this out?"

The words were tight and quiet as she pointed to her face which cracked even more. Cecilia looked around the apartment from where she was standing. It was a large open space, airy and brightly lit. Immediately, Cecilia thought it seemed minimalist, then realised there must be more furniture on the way. In one corner, looking lonely, there were two very large cream leather sofas facing each other; a coffee table sat in between them. A widescreen TV framed the wall behind. An expensive oriental carpet covered a large part of the floor. On the walls hung a couple of chintz paintings that Cecilia thought looked cheap.

The young woman came back, bright-eyed and make-up-free.

"I'm sorry, I never see anyone without my make-up on, only I wasn't expecting any visitors. I'm Tracy, Tracy Bowman, but you know that anyway! Silly me!"

As she said it, her happy 'like me' face shone through. She had an innocent charm that immediately made people like or hate her. Tracy was a constant on all social media platforms; some might say, too many. She was one of the originals. Trailblazer was a word that was in her profile. Cecilia had no love for any of them, but she was there for other reasons.

"You don't need make-up! You're quite beautiful without!" said Cecilia. They went to shake hands. There was a brief hesitancy, to which they both smiled, then shook hands anyway.

"I'm not sure we should have done that," said Cecilia.

Cecilia continued to talk about how much she liked the things that Tracy did. More praise hit all the right spots. Then Tracy asked Cecilia if she would like a drink. Tracy moved towards the kitchen which was to one side of the large room. It was clinically spacious, neat and tidy. She went behind a large counter area, where she touched a cupboard with the end of her finger. A door opened. It was certainly a high-end designed kitchen. Cecilia was impressed.

"Would you like tea, coffee, or something stronger?"

She smiled at Cecilia. "I'm sorry, but you still haven't told me your name."

"Oh, how remiss of me. It's Cecilia. Coffee would be fine."

Tracy paused, as Cecilia proceeded to take off her face mask, then said,

"It's strange, but you look familiar to me."

Even though she was in her seventies, her eyes and her face structure were almost perfect. Tracy stared at her.

"Yes, I know your face! Don't tell me! It will come to me!"

She continued to make the coffee, as Cecilia looked around the room. Tracy was babbling to herself, to which Cecilia wasn't really listening. As she was waiting for the coffee machine to do its job, Tracy organised a vase for the flowers which she then cooed over. Cecilia was beginning to have second thoughts as to why she was there, let alone what she was hoping to achieve. It was as if a life in films, fantasy and made-up stories, (which most of the acting profession was about), had brought on some kind of madness in her head. As far as she was concerned, she had been given a wonderful part in a drama and she was actually living it.

Tracy brought around the coffee and asked Cecilia if she would like to sit on one of the sofas. Tracy placed the coffees on the table, then made a point of saying how big the coffee table was and, more importantly, that she had had it specially made. Cecilia looked at it. She wasn't sure, but thought it to be too large and top-heavy. Of course, she was no expert, so she merely smiled, then sipped her coffee.

Cecilia felt ill at ease, as Tracy made herself comfortable by pushing her legs under herself, then pulling her colourful dressing gown around her body, as if it was a blanket. She then sipped loudly on her coffee. Immediately, this grated into Cecilia's psyche. Her whole life had been about good manners, especially in company. It was the little things that tipped Cecilia over the edge. She felt mesmerised by these moments, feeling alien to why she was entertaining the idea of being in the company of someone like Tracy.

Tracy was curious to know why Cecilia was there but had convinced herself that one of her fans, of which she had many, wanted an insight into her lifestyle. Normally, this was a dangerous thing to do, but up to now, she felt no threat from Cecilia. Anyway, she was enjoying entertaining the stranger.

"If you don't mind me asking, how did you get my address?"

For a second or two, Cecilia hesitated. She wasn't thinking of the bigger picture. When she acted on stage or in a film, the script was precise. She was making this up as she went along.

"I googled it."

These words were foreign to her, but she'd heard them over and over again from other people, as well as the media. So much so that it irritated her.

"Oh," said Tracy, "It's amazing how quickly modern technology can catch up."

Cecilia was amazed. She was surprised at how she was reacting to a situation that was foreign to her. What she didn't say was that she had been following Tracy on and off for the last few months.

Although, initially, Cecilia had strong inner resentment towards her and many others like her, she felt it was softening, the more she talked to Tracy. Even so, Cecilia felt the bile inside turning over. Her years of being passed over for young celebs had left a rage in her body that she had found almost impossible to control. Hence the reason for being in the company of Tracy. Fortunately, it wasn't the only one. If it had been, then she would not have been there at all.

Since Cecilia had had a breakdown, many years previously, she had only acted in bit-parts on TV and film, occasionally working opposite celebrity types who were given roles for their ability to attract a younger audience. In Cecilia's opinion, this didn't mean they had any kind of skill whatsoever.

"Oh my God!" said Tracy, "I know who you are! You're the Agatha Christie actor, the one from years ago! Cecilia Walters!" Cecilia felt a warmth inside for being recognised, but resentment at the 'years ago' applied to the statement. Tracy put her hands to her mouth and let out several expletives, then laughed, wide-eyed and happy to be in the presence of such a famous person. Tracy reached for her phone, but before she did, Cecilia got up.

"I'd better go, I really need to be somewhere else."

"Can I have a selfie of us together, before you go?"

The very thought of it angered Cecilia. One thing she vehemently hated about modern life was the mobile phone. She moved quickly towards the door. Tracy got up hurriedly to follow her. In doing so, the belt on her dressing gown got caught around her foot. Cecilia heard a cry of anguish, looked back and saw Tracy fall forward onto the large glass table. It was as if it was in slow motion. Cecilia stood helpless, as Tracy crashed to the floor, then the large circular glass panel stood on its end like a ballet dancer. It spun mesmerisingly, then, with all its weight, fell on Tracey's head. It only took seconds, but Cecilia took it in as if it was a performance piece. If the result had not been so graphic in every way, she would have been compelled to applaud, then shout for more.

This was a tiny thought that then got lost in the far reaches of her mind. She saw Tracy lying face down on the floor. She went closer to see if there was anything she could do. It was clear to her that the glass table had caught Tracy's head, blood had run down across her forehead onto the polished oak flooring, some of it slowly moving towards the oriental carpet.

One thing Cecilia was familiar with was dead bodies, having acted most of her life in detective dramas. Obviously, they would have been actors playing the part, but the premise was just the same. In her life, she'd seen a lot of things, but this was truly shocking. It took all her self-control not to panic. Fortunately, her acting ability kicked in to keep her calm. This experience, however, was testing, to say the least.

She stood perfectly still, knowing that this could be very messy in more ways than one. Lots of things went through her mind. Firstly, being there at all would be seen as illegal under present guidelines. Then there was the fact that Cecilia had been stalking Tracy on the internet for the last few months. The police would surely find out things that may involve her deeply in what had happened.

Cecilia quickly covered her tracks. There was no CCTV outside the building. She'd made sure of that. The place had only just been finished and it wasn't connected. She knew this because she'd come there with an ulterior motive, which now would not be activated, although the outcome was just the same. She took out plastic gloves from her pocket, then cleaned away any traces of her being there. As she finished, she felt relieved, but somehow on a high. Cecilia saw herself as an actor who was second to none. As far as she was concerned, she wanted to be at the centre of every scene, taking the applause.

She paused momentarily as if to double-check her tracks. After looking back across the room, she felt satisfied she had done a good job. She closed the door carefully, then made her way out of the building.

2.

Carne Woodthorpe was entering his cocktail bar at the edge of the city, but not by the front door. The lockdown was in full swing. People had been told to stay at home and keep their distance. All bars, restaurants and meeting places were closed until further notice. Carne and many of his friends were conspiracy theorists, who were flouting the law. He had a big following on social media. He was famous for being famous. The cocktail bar was a plaything for him, but also a hub for other things that he liked to keep quiet about. He called the people who followed him his friends. In fact, they were just hangers-on. He was no stranger to using his fame to vent his opinions, although he was always careful to play the devil's advocate. He used his social media channels to peddle his thoughts. Carne was a man of today and, like many others like him, he was followed religiously.

He checked himself just before he walked into the bar, using his phone as a mirror. He was good-looking with film star-like dark hair and a permanent shadow on his chin. It was almost as if his beard was impatient to appear. This he kept under control by occasionally leaving it for a few days. It seemed his fans loved it when he looked a little rugged. What's more, he had a body to match.

The bar wasn't full; after all, there was a lockdown. None of the clientele were wearing masks, most of them well on the way to getting drunk. It was a small back room, so no light or music could be seen or heard from outside the premises. High fives went around the room as he entered. He enjoyed the adulation. It wasn't long before Carne was drunk like the others. If only his many thousands of followers could see him now, but this was only the tip of his iceberg. After snorting a line of coke, he made his farewells, leaving the running of the bar to his second in command.

"I'm off home now," said Carne, "but I'll be in early tomorrow morning to accept a special consignment."

His barman gave him a knowing wink.

Carne hit the street. There were puddles everywhere, the streetlights creating crazy pictures in the reflections. Carne was well on the way to being out of it but knew his worth, happy to sober up a little on the short walk home. The city centre was deadly quiet; not a soul to be seen. He approached his apartment building. It was six floors high, plush and expensive. A covered vestibule was at the front of the building, then double security doors with a code to punch in. By the doors, a woman was trying to put in her PIN to get in.

"Oh dear," she said.

"Have you forgotten the number?" Carne asked.

She looked around at Carne.

"Yes, silly of me!"

"That's ok, I'll let you in."

They both walked into the open hall area. Post-boxes hung in rows on one wall, with big pot plants placed against the other. Carne, in his semi-drunken state, leaned against the one wall. The woman was wearing a black mask and a long grey coat with a hood up over her head. His first thoughts were, what beautiful eyes.

"I haven't seen you here before," he said.

"I could say the same about you, apart from the fact I think I have seen you on the internet."

Immediately, Carne felt pumped up that his fame went before him.

"I must say you're more impressive in the flesh."

The flattery was music to Carne's ears. He put out his hand to shake hers, but she refused.

"Oh yes, the virus."

He placed his fingers in the air as if to suggest a quotation, then he laughed.

"Are you an unbeliever?" she asked.

"You could say that."

"I'd be interested to hear your thoughts on that," she said.

The cogs in his head were slow to connect. As he moved off to the lifts, she followed. They got into the lift, in which there were mirrors. He asked her what floor. She looked at the panel and was hesitant, but quickly said,

"Five."

He then pressed five and six. He looked at her in the lift mirrors and was curious to see her face. He knew she was getting on, but she had looked after herself.

"Would you like a drink of coffee or something stronger?"

She seemed unmoved. Her outward sophistication fascinated him. He waited for an answer. She looked at him with her piercing blue eyes. He felt as if she was undressing his soul.

"Why not! The night is young," she answered.

They went to his penthouse apartment on the sixth floor. He opened the door and beckoned her in. Immediately, she was presented with floor-to-ceiling glass windows, the lights of the city brightly shining like a carpet of pretty dancing flowers. It was something to behold. There was a lot to take in, but she could see he had expensive tastes. Large easy chairs, which seemed to dominate the main living area, were set before the panoramic windows.

"You're a very lucky man to afford all this."

"Call me Carne. By the way, what's your name? You never said."

"No, I don't believe I did."

There was a pause, as she thought it through.

"I'm Cecilia."

It was in Cecilia's mind to use a pseudonym, but she didn't want to complicate her thought processes. After all, this was her story. She was writing it as she went along.

"Cecilia, what would you like to drink?"

She took off her mask. Carne looked at her. It might have been the drink or the drugs, but he thought this woman was quite beautiful. He was in his mid-thirties. He guessed she was in her sixties, but he felt an almost electric sexual attraction to her.

"I'll have whisky and ice please."

She removed her coat and placed it on the back of a chair, then waited there as he came over to her. She was dressed impeccably in a smart navy-blue trouser suit with a lacy white shirt which complimented it.

"Cheers," he said.

He seemed to leer at her, which made her feel uncomfortable.

"Bottoms up!" she said with a smile. She was a great actress.

A wry smile came across his face. She could see what he was thinking. She could feel a stirring inside for this virile young man, whom she would like to kick where it hurts. He moved closer to her, imposing himself on her space. She could smell a mixture of alcohol as well as expensive aftershave as he ran his finger down her cheek.

"Tell me about your work," she said, "and why you feel the coronavirus is a sham."

The complete gear change surprised him.

"Why do you want to know?"

"I don't know, just call me curious."

She turned away from him with an air of superiority as she said it.

"Well, Curious!"

He seemed to somehow purr the words, then he smiled. "Why don't we go to my bedroom, and we can talk about it?"

She felt slightly sick. She wasn't certain how long she could play this game. She had a plan, but to apply it she needed time and another drink. She downed her whisky.

"Would you like another?" she asked.

"Why not?"

"I'll make it," she offered.

He relaxed onto the sofa and lifted his empty glass. She took it. It was an easy thing to do, she had turned the tables. She was now in control, making the drinks, playing her part brilliantly. A few minutes later, she sat down next to him on the sofa.

"Tell me," She said, "what do you think you'll achieve by lying straight-faced to all your followers?"

"What makes you think I lie?"

He sipped his whisky.

"Look at you, you're a mess, an alcoholic drug addict and yet you sell yourself as a healthy young man on social media."

He looked annoyed, took another swig of his whisky, then he got angry.

"Who the hell are you to ask me questions like that?"

His demeanour turned nasty, his face turned red.

"I'm your conscience. I want you to be honest with yourself and the people you sell lies to."

He laughed, then got even angrier, lashing out words that he knew would hurt.

"What do want, you bag of bones?"

"No need to be obnoxious, although I know it's in your nature. I'm also pretty sure you can be violent. Of course, there are also the drugs you peddle. What's worse, your involvement in sex trafficking. Your bar is a nice front for so much depravity, yet you come across like a goody two shoes on the internet."

His face was in shock, his mouth open.

"You're crazy, you old hag!"

"Tut, tut! Sticks and stones, young man, will never hurt me. All of this, though, will hurt you bad. You deserve it!"

He moved towards her. She was quick to get up and move away. He stumbled to the floor, garbled a few words, then managed somehow to scramble up. For a moment, she was scared. He went for her throat. She lost her balance and they both fell on the floor. His hands were still around her neck. They lay there briefly. Cecilia stared at the ceiling. A cold realisation ran through her mind, which made her think this was not acting. This was real and quite terrifying. He released his grip as it seemed he wasn't quite able to hold on. She scrambled up, breathing heavily, then sat on a chair. He managed to pull himself up, then looked at her and stuttered a few words.

"Who the hell are you?"

"I'm a nightmare you're so welcome to. I'm here to deal out retribution for the lives you have ruined. This is where you pay for it all. Why? you ask. Because, Carne, you picked the wrong people to hurt!"

She told him the reason for wanting him dead. She wasn't certain how much he understood, but she felt better for telling him.

He was in great pain and was lost in her words. She then added, "Of course, you most probably helped to spread this hideous virus with your irresponsible actions as well."

His eyes blurred.

"What did you put in my drink?"

"Something that you can maybe sleep off, Romeo, but then again, maybe not. It might be that you have taken a few too many tablets. That plus the drugs and alcohol."

"But....?" he spluttered.

That was his last word on the matter, as he fell flat on his face. It was in her mind that she had someone's life in her hands, but quickly thought this was part of a bigger picture. Unlike all the parts she'd ever played, this was for real. Even so, it felt like power to Cecilia.

She proceeded to eradicate any trace of her being there, then went back to Carne. She took his pulse. He was dead. She didn't feel sorry. In her mind, the justification far outweighed any guilt. As she was leaving, she put on her coat, pulled up the hood over her head, then put on her mask.

As she stood at the door, she looked back. She thought as an actress, *I'm also a brilliant murderer*. She didn't know why, perhaps it was all the parts she'd ever played, but she felt a kind of thunder running through her veins and, even though there was no audience, she was ready to take the applause for what she had done.

As she slipped out of the building, she made sure it would be impossible to recognise her on CCTV. After a long walk at the edge of the city, a car sat waiting in the darkness.

The next day, it was all over the news that Carne Woodthorpe, social media personality had died. At that time, the police were uncertain as to how.

3.

Detective Inspector Ella Askew was taking a long deep breath on her e-cigarette. A large cloud of cranberry-smelling vapour almost enveloped her. She had just been promoted and was starting her first case. She was nervous, having given up smoking over nine months ago, but she still couldn't escape the need to have something in her mouth when she was on edge.

During the Coronavirus, crimes had dropped to an all-time low, because people were told to stay at home, which, in some ways, was fortunate for the government who had made big cutbacks to the police force. Even so, the pandemic wouldn't last forever. One day, the situation would come back to haunt the authorities.

To Ella, none of this mattered. She had a job, a good job, and she had convinced her bosses that she would be great at it. The truth was, she was overdue for promotion. The pandemic had conveniently opened the door, because illness had hit the force.

She was standing outside in a small area designated for smokers. No one else was there. As she was finishing smoking, she turned and looked at herself in the glass entrance door. She used her hands to tidy herself. Not that anything was out of place; her immaculate dark grey suit and white blouse looked perfect. She had shoulder-length auburn hair, which had a slight curl to it, something that often irritated her when she was busy. So, she often tied it back. The face she saw in the reflection was kind to her. She was in her mid-forties. Life plus two marriages had worn her down. She had one child from her second marriage, a daughter, who was in her teens. Ella thought about her for a moment and tried to rationalise why she was such a pain in the arse. She then quickly realised she needed to just think about the job in hand. She looked again at her reflection.

"C'mon girl, you can do this! This is your time!"

As she walked back into the station, she slipped on her face mask and then sanitised her hands. The feast of cranberry smoke had given her an artificial high to face her first case and her team. She walked into a large office with three people, socially distanced, sitting at desks, working on their computers. She exchanged pleasantries with them, introduced herself, then set out her thoughts.

"As you know, I'm Ella Askew. New to this job, but I have over twenty years' experience in the force. Due to the Coronavirus, we find ourselves having to solve crimes in what only can be described as very difficult circumstances. So, let's start, as we are all new together. We'll have to play everything by ear and also have a mask attached to both of them. By the way, unfortunately, we have the window open for obvious reasons, although I can see we are all dressed for it."

A smile of sorts came to their faces. Ella continued.

"When a crime is committed, someone has to solve it, even if it seems difficult to do so. We are indeed in a position where our lives are in danger, so we must be careful at all times. Where possible, we will tackle our enquiries remotely. If we can't do that, we must always follow government guidelines."

She looked at her very small team of three and, without prompting, they introduced themselves.

"I'm DS Nigel Faron. Call me Nige, everyone does."

Nigel Faron was a very experienced DS who had no ambition to go higher, but he was great at his job.

"DS Amber Katz. I have also recently been promoted."

Amber Katz was very ambitious. She wanted to be a DI like Ella one day. Her enthusiasm made her very keen to impress.

"DC Ethan Jackson."

He said nothing else. He was still finding his feet.

"So, what do we have?" asked DI Askew.

"Little at the moment, ma'am," one of her team answered.

"Right! From the offset, I want to play this differently. No ma'am, guv, boss, or whatever. Although I am the boss, I am also someone to whom you can talk. After all, if we are a team, let's act like a family of sorts."

"Do you mean Liquorice Allsorts, boss? Sorry, Ella?" The joke hung there like wet washing.

DC Nigel Faron's attempt at humour was poor, to say the least.

"Although that's not that funny, Nigel," said Ella, "I'm happy that we look at what we do with a certain amount of humour. It's either that or we'll all go mad, kill each other and of course, that would be counterproductive."

This was the first day, so everyone smiled at the thought of this approach. A few moments seemed to skip by as they took in what Ella had to say. DS Faron informed them of the details of the Carne Woodthorpe case.

"It's maybe nothing," said DS Faron, "but I think there's another case that overlaps this one."

"What other case is that?" asked Ella.

"Well, they are both celebs, high up in social media."

"Sorry, I thought we were just looking at the case of Carne Woodthorpe, who it appears could have died suspiciously. Who else are you looking at, DS Faron?"

"A woman called Tracy Bowman. Apparently, she died when a glass table crashed on top of her and struck her head."

He showed the report to Ella, who said,

"It says here it was accidental, so how can it be linked?"

"The two of them are about the same age," he replied, "and are high-profile media types. I've looked at their backgrounds and their paths cross."

"That could be said about everyone on a media platform," said DS Katz.

"These people also live in the same city and died only three weeks apart," DS Faron added.

"You're clutching at straws, Nigel," said Ella, "but get Ethan to look into Tracy's case to get more details. I want to know everything about her."

Ethan nodded his head like a mechanical dog at the back of a motor car.

DS Faron had hoped he had his colleagues in the palm of his hand, but they just looked at him questioningly. Ella was intrigued and happy that at least someone was thinking outside the box.

DS Katz looked at the case files of Bowman and Woodthorpe, then said,

"There's no sign of any fingerprints or DNA of any kind at either of their apartments."

"How about CCTV?" asked Ella.

DS Katz continued,

"The Tracy Bowman case was returned as an accident, but there was no CCTV nearby anyway. At Carne Woodthorpe's there was just one CCTV camera outside the building, but it wasn't very clear. Within hours of him dying, several people came in and out, but none are recognisable."

"What about neighbours?" asked Ella. "What of other CCTV? Check it out! Also, check out any car movements. One thing is for sure, there aren't many cars on the road at the moment. We might find someone who shouldn't be there! I think at the moment we'll treat Carne's death as suspicious. Leave Tracy's as an unfortunate accident till we have something more significant to go on."

"Excuse me!"

Ella looked at DC Ethan Jackson.

"You don't need to put your hand up, Ethan."

"Ma'am, sorry boss, sorry Ella, I, I, feel strange calling you Ella. In my training we were always told to be respectful, calling those above us by an appropriate name. I find it difficult to stop doing that."

Ella thought for a moment.

"Ethan, do you think you would be disrespectful to me if you called me Ella?"

Ethan sat up straight, almost like someone had told him to.

"No!" he said, "Ma'am."

It was as if he was at training school.

"For God's sake, Ethan, if you feel that uncomfortable, call me what you feel happy with."

"Yes! Ella, ma'am, boss!"

He went bright red, as Katz and Faron burst out laughing. Ella smiled and joined in the fun. She walked towards Ethan, then presented her elbow. After a second, he did the same. The effect of the conversation brought about a feeling of camaraderie, which they all enjoyed.

"Another point I'd like to make," said Ella, "is that working remotely from home is impossible when it comes down to investigating a murder or any other serious crime. However, it may be that some of us will have to work from home shortly and communicate via our computers. Well, I don't suppose we've solved any crimes, but at least we've paved the way to move forward."

4.

A familiar sound could be heard, as the man on the TV plied his muscles to the camera. Many welcomed the sound of his voice, although there were those who hated it. He stood there in his multicoloured spandex doing everything with ease, not seeming to use a breath of air to complete each task. He did this most of the day, every day, no matter what. His programme, his blog, and his internet site had grown tenfold during the pandemic. It was known as Flex with Ferdinand. He, like many other people, had filled the internet and TV channels with their thoughts on how to beat the void that lockdown had given them.

Cecilia had stumbled onto Flex and his twitching muscles. They stirred something inside her body although it wasn't her need to exercise. She then found a Midsummer Murders she had not seen before, however, this did nothing for any part of her body, so she turned the TV off.

After her experience with Carne Woodthorpe a month earlier, she was taking it easy. She had convinced herself, after talking to Rupert, her one-time lover and fellow actor, whom she had known for over forty years, that Carne's demise was inevitable, due to his lifestyle and, more importantly, because of the terrible things he had done over the years. She then sat back and listened to a play on the radio four.

Antonio De Leone was better known as DJ De-Le. He had been popular on Radio One. However, he was also responsible for many number-one hits, mainly in collaboration with other artists. He was in his late thirties, a diminutive figure with a big personality. He had been quoted saying he was proud of his Spanish roots, although, in interviews, he was careful not to divulge much of his history. Antonio had an air of mystery about him, which somehow made him more appealing to his public. He had made a lot of money, moving from DJ to agent, with at least fifteen artists of all descriptions in his stable. He was ambitious and, on the way, to being one of the top agents in the country. He achieved it in super quick time, by being in the right place at the right time. He did have his detractors who believed he had been involved with hard drugs for some time. That being said, it added to his charisma in some strange way. Whichever way you looked at it, he wasn't even forty and was a millionaire several times over.

Antonio De Leone owned a big pile of expensive stone that was called El Castillo. The once dilapidated castle he had rebuilt, then renamed it. Many locals in the area complained at the time, but the council agreed that the millions spent to put the castle right, gave the owner the right to change it. He was famous for his parties, which he had at the castle as often as there was a good reason to have one. They were always select affairs with many of the celebrity elite being there. It was also known that he was very relaxed about low-category drugs being used. This being the case, there was always a lot of secrecy attached to each party.

Not long after Boris Johnson, the prime minister, had eased the guidelines midsummer, Antonio decided to give a party in celebration of that fact. A personal invite went out to some of his clients and friends.

A car made its way up the country lanes towards El Castillo. The castle was not far from a big city but seemed in the middle of nowhere. At nearly ten o'clock in the evening, the car stopped in a large round drive-in front of the castle. Cecilia got out of the car. She could immediately hear music vibrating from inside the castle wall and thought this could be a long night. The car pulled off, then disappeared down the drive. Subdued lighting complemented the walls of the castle. It looked impressive.

She rang a bell outside the large oak front doors, where there would have been a drawbridge over the moat, which was no more than a dip in the grass. A young woman, who looked slightly worse for wear, came to the door. She stared hard at Cecilia.

"Hi, are you here for the party? You do know it's not fancy dress?"

Cecilia was dressed no differently from any other time. She wore a long dark coat with the hood drawn up over her head. On her face was the obligatory mask.

"Yes, I have an invite."

The young woman didn't look at her invitation.

"Come in, then and party!"

Cecilia walked into a hall the size of most people's houses. It was beautifully transformed. Whoever had done the work had kept most of the original fixtures, only adding sympathetic changes. As the woman walked off to where the music was coming from, Cecilia asked,

"Can you tell me who you are and also where are the lavatories please?"

"I'm Phe, Phoebe Wilson."

She turned, then did a sort of dance move, then made peace signs with her fingers.

"The Teen-Tings. We've had four number ones."

Cecilia looked at her blankly, then said,

"Oh, l didn't recognise you without the other members of the band."

It was a shot in the dark, but it might have eased any suspicions Phoebe might have had.

"The restrooms are at the top of the grand stairs," Phoebe said, "I'll tell you now, they are impressive."

At that moment, the Americanism restrooms irritated her, but the thought quickly passed. She walked towards what were truly grand stairs. The whole place was palatial. She found the lavatories; they were more than impressive. She thought it would be just as easy to have a party there as anywhere.

She immediately tutted at the extravagance. Floor-to-ceiling marble with gold fittings everywhere, no expense had been spared. She was beginning to think it was all too much and over the top, maybe even in bad taste, but then she realised she had a job to do and wasn't there to give a critique on home improvement.

She had a mental plan of the castle that Rupert had provided her with. She made her way through a couple of large rooms that had paintings hanging on all the walls. They were modern art. Strangely, they blended in perfectly with all the ancient oak panelling around them. She paused to take them in. Eventually, she came to what she thought was Antonio's bedroom.

Years ago, her nerves would have affected her performance, indeed sometimes, even for the better. Her worries about being caught were not a problem. She thought she was invisible at this moment in time, her confidence being quite high. As she opened the bedroom door, she wasn't expecting what she found. The room was enormous. It was obvious that this was an add-on, an extension, a modern slab on the back of the castle, befitting a modern man. The ceiling was black as was the floor. One wall was just one sheet of glass overlooking what she assumed were gardens. A bed, bigger than any bed she had ever seen before, sat squarely in the middle of the room. It, too, was entirely black. She touched the sheets. They were pure silk. "Tony, you have expensive tastes indeed."

Rupert had acquired the plans for the house, which she had seen, but the décor was out of this world, even for someone who had spent a long time on the planet. In front of the wall of glass sat a couple of modernist chairs that didn't look particularly comfortable. Cecilia tried one and was surprised at how nice it was. She sat in the dark, looking out at the black sky. The gardens below had subdued lighting dotted here and there. The view was magnificent, made all the better by a moon that seemed to play hide and seek with the patchy clouds.

Cecilia was feeling her age. Maybe if she'd been at the party, she might have been able to keep her eyes open. She must have drifted off. People talking or maybe just one, seeming to shout, getting irate, woke her. She looked at her watch. It was nearly two o'clock. Panic went through her body, because she had it in her mind to find somewhere to hide, but there was nowhere to do that. She considered just walking out of the room, acting as if she was lost or pretending, she was drunk. After all, a well-known critic had remarked on one of her performances. *'Cecilia Walters was the best actor I've ever seen, in my opinion, playing a drunk person whilst not being inebriated.'* She could see the review in her head as clear as day. Of course, she had had a couple of drinks beforehand to get into the part she was playing. Nevertheless, she always saw it as a standard to live by. The problem at that moment was it was too late for that.

The moon had given enough light to see, so she moved towards the wall to get nearer to the door. As the voices got nearer she stopped and waited. She was leaning against a wall. A door, that must have been concealed, opened. She slipped inside. A light came on automatically. The door closed behind her. She immediately had respect for the designers, for being imaginative enough to use such an idea.

She was faced with a well-lit corridor which seemingly had no doors. She was wise enough to realise there must be doors somewhere, so she touched the walls to see if anything would happen. By the time she got to the end of the corridor, she had found two dressing-rooms, a bathroom and a shower-room. Finally, another door opened up to a large bedroom, not unlike the previous one, but entirely different in design and decor.

This room had a feminine touch: pastel colours on the walls, more furniture, but still ultra-modern. A wall to wall window allowed the moon to brightly shine in. She felt grateful there was no automatic lighting. Strangely, there were places to hide in this room. In one corner stood a large ornate dressing screen, that Cecilia was drawn to. She could see that it was painted in the style of Klimt, one of her favourite Art Deco artists. Even in this light, she thought it could be original. It was in front of an even more ornate 1920s dressing table. She felt an immediate affiliation for the woman who slept here, if indeed it was a woman. Cecilia ran her hand over the screen and felt weak.

"This is divine," she whispered to herself. She was almost fawning over the furniture, when a burst of light hit the room, only to be immediately dimmed. She hid behind the screen.

"You silly cow, why the fuck did you drink so much? As for sniffing the coke, you must be mad."

Cecilia heard a man's voice chastising someone who seemed to just murmur back words that made no sense. She assumed it was a woman. The voice of the man continued to complain, then he left the room. As he went, the lights went out.

Cecilia questioned her ability to carry on. She was hot, exhausted. It was way past her bedtime. She took off her coat. It wasn't thick, but moving around with it on made her hot. She was on medication, prescribed and otherwise. Her prescribed tablets helped with ongoing health problems, the un-prescribed was something that Rupert had acquired from people he knew. It wasn't legal, but he'd told her, "If you take a couple of the tablets when you're feeling weary, it will stimulate your heart to get you through."

She moved from behind the screen to see what looked like a young woman sprawled face down. Her small figure seemed lost in the oversized bed. The young woman groaned. Cecilia thought it best to leave her to her slumbers.

She went back the way she came, being as careful as possible not to make too much noise. Her hand was placed on the wall, the door opened, and a light came on in the bathroom. She was faced with a figure standing there. She quickly raised her hand to her mouth, before sucking in air to suppress any scream she might have made. She saw herself in a glass mirror that covered the whole wall. Her coat was draped over her arm, she still had a mask on her face. White gloves on her hands, a black figure-hugging body suit completed the picture. She looked like an extra from a James Bond movie. Inside her, there was a panic that wanted to overtake the calm.

The toilet in the corner seemed the ideal place to ease the pressure, mental and otherwise. Her ability to control her bladder had always been sacrosanct when it came to acting, but now she had to go. She knew she had underestimated the part she was playing. Maybe it needed re-writing. She thought about it. Usually, in her job, that would be done by someone else, but she knew this was down to her.

Suddenly the bathroom door opened. A man stood there in boxer shorts and a T-shirt looking slightly blurry-eyed. He saw Cecilia on the toilet, then looked horrified.

"Who the hell are you, and what are you doing in here?"

Cecilia, although she was surprised by the sight of this man, she didn't want to be shouted at.

"I'm sorry," she said, "I'm having a pee. Do you mind?"

She waved at him to leave the room. He was speechless from her response but retired without a word. She made herself presentable. He knocked on the door, then entered again. She was as calm as the day was long and felt she had the upper hand. After all, this sort of situation was meat and drink to her. He wasn't fit or in the right attire to match her. She knew him to be Antonio de Leone, but it wasn't his real name. She had seen photographs of him, but the ones she had seen were of when he was in better shape.

He had dark hair, shaved high at the side of his head, then a longer piece at the top which was tied up into punk spikes. He had the look of a Casanova about him, that's if Casanova was five foot six and overweight. She knew him to have been a lady's man at one time, but it would seem that they had lost interest. At least he had someone who was fast asleep in the next room.

He got angry because she wasn't responding to his previous questions but, just as she was going to speak, he grasped his chest and his eyes seemed to glare at her. He left the room quickly. Cecilia followed him, as he seemed to be in terrible pain. She found him sitting on the edge of his bed still holding his chest. He slumped to one side, gasping for breath. She knew, now, he must be having a heart attack. She pulled him up, which was no easy task, then he slid onto the floor, but was still leaning against the bed. She got down on her knees.

"Come on, Tony! Don't die on me. I'm not going to let you steal my thunder."

She slapped his face. He was still trying to catch his breath, then he opened his eyes.

"That's better Tony, you can do it."

"My name is Antonio."

"There you are, Tony! On the edge of death and still, you're trying to pull the wool over everyone's eyes."

He looked lost in her words, but his breath evened out.

"Good, well done, Tony! Deep breaths!"

He gathered himself as best he could, staring carefully at Cecilia.

"I think you have me confused with someone else. Who are you anyway?"

The words were weak and uneven.

"My name is Cecilia, Cecilia Walters. You don't know me, but I know you. Your past is common knowledge to me, although you did your best to change it."

She then laid out the story, why she was there, in such a dramatic way, that she knew it was having the optimal effect.

"I don't get it. Even if this is true, what's it got to do with me?"

She told the story, while sitting a few meters away, on the thick, black, luxurious carpet. She had already cast off her shoes and was now sitting cross-legged in a lotus position. She pushed her hands into the carpet, then cooed at how it felt.

"This is wonderful, Tony! How lucky you are! A bit luckier than Susan and Carne, I would say. Of course, they didn't change their names, but their past and their present had a say in their lives or should I say, deaths!"

His silence, as well as the story, had made him breathe heavily again.

"I believe that if you take aspirin, it may thin the blood and so control the flow of it into your heart. Would you like some, Tony?"

He nodded. She got to her feet, a few bones clicked and she groaned slightly, but the yoga position had made her feel quite good. In the shower room, there was a wash basin. Above it, was a mirror in the wall. She guessed the mirror would open if she touched it. It did. Inside, there was an array of medication, everything you would need in a bathroom cabinet. All she needed was a glass. She filled it with water, then went back and gave it to Tony. She handed him two tablets. He swallowed them then drank the water. Cecilia assumed the same yoga position. She was enjoying herself. The part she was playing was perfect. What's more, she had all the best lines. Tony looked at her. He had gathered his thoughts.

"You're stark staring mad! Who cares? It's all in the past! It has no effect on my life. I'm far more important than any of that shit."

"That shit was someone's life, Tony."

"So, why should I care?"

"Everything has consequences, as you will find out, like your friends have and will."

"Look, Cecilia, whatever your name is! I don't care! I've moved on, that's the past! My future is in other things. So, why don't you get your holier than thou crap out of my house, or I'll call the police."

It was as if the tablets had had a miraculous effect on him. Colour returned to his cheeks. He stood up, moved off towards the wall, then touched it. A door opened. In a shallow wardrobe, a dressing gown hung. He put it on, then walked back purposefully towards Cecilia.

"Get up, get out, take your fucking story with you!"

Cecilia got up slowly, picked up her coat, then put it on. She then walked towards the door. He guided her forcefully, without touching her, through the castle, down towards the entrance hall. They ended up by the big front doors. As they stood by them, she looked back into the castle.

"This is an amazing place. I hope you enjoy it for the short time you have left to live."

She looked at him enquiringly, as if she was waiting for the words to sink in.

"Nothing you can say or do can do me any harm, unless you had some crazy idea of killing me. But that's unlikely, as you didn't do it when you had an opportunity."

There was an air of confidence in his voice, an almost obnoxious attitude that angered Cecilia.

"You should pay attention to detail, Tony. Are you sure I gave you an aspirin?"

She opened the door, then held it ajar, as she looked at him. She could see on his face the words had hit home. His face immediately went red, his hand went to his chest.

"Goodbye, Tony Lee. It's been a pleasure meeting you. By the way, I think you'll find, within a short time, the tablets I gave you will send your blood pressure so high that your heart will be unable to cope with it."

Cecilia walked away. It was still dark. She put up her hood, her mask already in place. She felt good inside.

5.

There was a hiatus, as it seemed that the virus had been tackled, but still, there were warnings it was coming back. Despite the guidance that was given by the government, many people dropped their defences. Of course, many hadn't put up their defences in the first place.

Cecilia had become something of a tour de force, her art was being put to a good cause. Her good cause was her need to put right the wrongs of the past. This meant some would fall by the wayside, mainly the rotten apples which were being thrown out of the barrel.

Cecilia had taken it into her mind to visit Rupert. The semi-detached house in a nice area of town looked like a picture, with its roses climbing up the outer wall and a small flower garden to the front of the property. It had been a while since she had visited him. It was a miserable day, but no rain had been predicted. As usual, Cecilia wore her big coat and hood. She was not one for being recognised wherever she went, unless it fitted the occasion. It helped her anonymity to be wearing a mask.

Rupert was expecting her and welcomed her in. The old friends greeted each other, both commenting on how well they looked. Rupert had an air of the distinguished actor about him. He still had all his hair. Although well-kept, it was very grey. He was a good-looking man, tall, sophisticated and lean. Like Cecilia, he was always aware that the right part might be offered to him any day, so he was always ready.

Cecilia removed her mask. They hugged warmly, neither of them thinking twice about the pandemic. The house, which looked small outside, seemed much larger inside. The hall led to a comfortable living room, almost wall to wall with books, some of which were quite valuable. There were many first editions. Like Cecilia, he had a penchant for things that were precious to him. He also loved art, as she did. In fact, they had spent hours, weeks, maybe even years talking of such things. These days it was mostly on the telephone, as they lived on opposite sides of the town. Even though Rupert was into technology, he knew his dearest friend and one-time lover would not stoop so low as to communicate via email.

Rupert made them coffee, as it was quite early. They sat in the room amid thousands of pounds worth of treasures. Not that they thought of such things. What surrounded Rupert and Cecilia were things that were loved and would never be parted with. The feeling was comfortable, warm, hard to define, as they talked about the old days at length. It was at least an hour or so before they spoke about things in the present.

"How are you feeling about your visits to the people we have talked about?"

Cecilia, after a few minutes of reflection, replied,

"Oh, you mean Tracy, Carne, and Antonio."

She said the names without a thought as to what had happened, almost like she was reading out a shopping list.

"Yes, tell me, Cecilia! How did you feel about what happened?"

She thought for a moment. A very noticeable dramatic pause followed. This was a well-worn path between two great established actors and friends, almost as if they were discussing a play they were in together.

"I can't say that I'm proud of my actions. It seems to me that life has a way of levelling up. I think sometimes that I am a messenger. A messenger that has a role to play in the retelling of someone's life."

She paused as if she was looking for justification in the words she was saying. Rupert sat there like a psychiatrist, saying nothing, waiting for Cecilia to finish. She looked thoughtful, as if searching for the real reason she had visited these people. The puzzlement hung there between them. No words seemed to fit the conspiracy that they shared.

It was like a game of chess, as they both changed positions. Cecilia looked at him with a stare of concern that he was not taking her side, even though he had always agreed this was the right route to take. The truth was, they had talked it out, finding it to be the only way forward. He was never one to be at the sharp end. His thoughts were more on how to plan an operation for Cecilia to carry it out, or, as he liked to think of it, he was the director in the play. Rupert was a hundred per cent behind her. He told her so.

"You do realise, Cecilia, if you are caught, you will go down for murder."

The words rang in her ears. She had heard them so many times playing detective parts in TV and film. She smiled.

"Maybe we could share a cell, Rupert. Maybe a threesome if it's a crowded prison."

The thought amused them both, they laughed together. In both of their lives, there had been many other relationships, many highs, many lows that had punctuated the passage of time, but they always generated back together. They were constant, like the moon going around the earth. They could depend on each other.

A more relaxed feeling settled between them, as it went quiet. She asked him about his hearing because he had told her he was finding it more and more difficult to hear properly.

"You could hear a pin drop in two inches of snow, Cecilia, whereas I would find it difficult to hear a plane crash."

They both laughed. Feeling perfectly at home with the best friend she could have, they drank their tea. It was almost as if things that needed to be said had been said, but both of them knew they were not taking it as seriously as they should. It could be said the rarefied atmosphere was laced with an artificial feeling of detachment, but somehow, they both seemed unrepentant. The truth was they were as guilty as each other and knew there was no going back.

6.

Fitzroy Agole was moving back and forth to the music. He was a rapper in his thirties, rapping words like a gun that had an endless supply of bullets. The words were attached to the continuous beat. Fitz, as he was known, had a large following, some of whom had become so taken by him, that they found it difficult to turn him off. Young people, older people, some who said they never liked rap. Somehow or other, he had a hypnotic voice to go with his personality. Others watched him morning, noon and night. When he wasn't rapping, he was selling something or other that contributed to his ever-growing fortune. Needless to say, he had his detractors, but he was more loved than not, mostly by the younger generation, but, as always, the older generation or media types wanted to plug into his selling capacity. He found himself sliding more and more into other media formats. He was small in height but had a very large ego. His trademark designer glasses dominated his face, selling his brand as much as he did. Like Elton John before him, he wore different styles nearly every day. Fitzroy had spent some time researching his heritage, because he knew someday he would hit the big time. The blurb on his media page said he was proud of his Afro Caribbean/ Asian background.

Fitzroy had an entourage of people who made his life easy. At one time, not long ago, he would have done everything for himself. However, since his success, he had had a string of personal assistants, but, one after another, they had left, because he was such an unpleasant character to work for. He was a notorious sexist bully, but money talks, so he got his pound of flesh.

He was known by those who worked for him to also lash out when he lost his temper. Up to now, in his short career, no one had exposed him for it. His newest and longest-serving personal assistant was Debbie Stone, better known as Debs. She was a professional. She was patient, very loyal and took his rants easily in her stride. She was always super cool under pressure, so she seemed able to cope with his occasional loss of control.

In a world that had come to abolish all forms of isms, Fitzroy Agole was an alpha male. Debbie, however, had learnt otherwise; not that it mattered, but Fitzroy was interested in all forms of sexual activity with either sex. Debbie had no argument whichever way his sexuality lay. She just couldn't understand why he lied about it. Debbie lived in a small flat in the basement of Fitzroy's large, modern house that he had recently acquired. After a long day spent following Fitzroy around town doing promotional work, Debbie found herself relaxing behind closed doors, while Fitz, as he liked to be called, relaxed three floors up in his specially built home studio.

In her cocoon, she turned everything off, so she could relax in a long, hot bath. Meanwhile, Fitzroy made a call to a private escort company. While he waited, he looked down from a balustrade on the third floor, where he had installed a studio. The vast space below, his living area, was perfect. The back of the house was mainly glass, which allowed him to look out onto a private garden from nearly everywhere in the property. He was more than pleased with himself. He spread his arms and did a little dance.

"I'm the king!"

He shouted it for all the world to hear, but no one could. The house was sealed like a drum. It was the main reason why he bought it.

Not long after, a face appeared at the intercom. Normally, it was channelled to Debbie, so she could filter out unwanted visitors but, as it was after hours, Fitzroy let in the visitor.

Fitzroy was excited. Nothing did it for him more than meeting a new sex partner, and then smoking dope. He had enough cannabis to last a month and sex was coming up the stairs.

He leaned back in his expensive, black leather chair, blowing cannabis smoke towards the open roof windows. A dark figure appeared at the top of the stairs. He stared at first, open-mouthed, then said,

"Who the fuck are you?"

"I would just like to say," said the figure, "why is it that people don't have more imagination when it comes to greeting someone who is a surprise to them?"

It was as if someone had spoken gibberish to Fitzroy.

"Who the fucking hell are you? I asked for someone tall, dark and handsome. I've been sent a witch."

"Oh dear, this is going to be a difficult night. My name is Cecilia Walters."

Cecilia spoke from the darkness of the hood. The room was brightly lit. She looked foreboding as she stood still at the top of the stairs, her hand resting on the rail that ran across to a wall, five meters away.

"This is impressive, Fitzroy."

She looked down to the floor below then up at the skylights above.

"I believe this is what they call a minstrel's gallery, the perfect place for a studio."

Fitzroy was spooked by her but thought it to be an elaborate joke to frighten him. However, he immediately pressed a panic button, which was fed down to Debbie in her flat.

Debbie was in her bath enjoying the relaxing sounds of mindfulness. A red light was blinking peacefully away in another room, out of the line of her eyesight.

When no one came, Fitzroy was almost in panic mode, although he quickly got it together, realising he only needed to talk his way out of the situation. After all, he was a man of the street and he knew how to look after himself, but something was beguiling about the stranger. She lowered her hood slowly and her sallow but beautiful face was revealed.

"As I said before, who the hell are you?"

The fact that he didn't know Cecilia meant nothing to her, because she was a character that she was playing. She was playing it with aplomb.

"Do you think you are worthy of all this?" she asked. "After all, what have you done apart from tell lies, hurt people?"

Fitzroy was having none of this. What he thought was a joke was now turning into something more serious, so he picked up his phone and tried to call the police.

"I think you'll find your phone has no signal."

Cecilia was enjoying her role, having found another stage to shine on. She had an inner power that befitted her, and she believed she was doing good. Fitzroy had had enough He moved towards her at the top of the stairs, then went to push her to one side. Unfortunately for him, in her roles as detective and police officers over the years, she had learnt how to defend herself, so he found himself flat on his back, dazed and confused.

As he got up, he moved away from her, looking fearful as to what might happen next.

"Look, if you want cash, I have loads in the safe. I've got drugs! You can have them. Just leave me in peace, please."

Cecilia had been hardened to most things in her life, so some jumped-up noise-maker wasn't going to make her leave now.

"What makes you think anything you can offer me will make me want to leave you alone?"

"So, what do you want?"

"There are a few people like you who become famous, then become obnoxious, thinking they can treat people like dirt. Although that's not why I'm here."

"The public loves me, my team love me."

"Do they? Do they love the liar? The hypocrite? The bully? The drug pusher? No, they love the plastic version you sell to everyone who follows you."

"Yeah, like so many others in this business, that's what they want."

"Really, so they want to be lied to, to be fooled, to be hurt. The truth is, Fitzroy, you are part of a group of brutal, selfish people who would sell their mother into slavery."

He looked at her. He knew he was losing the argument.

"So, what the fuck you gonna do? Put everyone like me to rights? Will that make it better?"

"Maybe, maybe not. I leave it to you to make your mind up, I'm nearly done here. Oh, by the way, I'm not sure if you keep up with the news, but your former friends from Spain are dropping like flies. They have met with their maker. That's if any of them believed in God. Do you, Fitzroy?"

"What the hell are you talking about?"

"Tracy, Carne, Antonio."

The names hit him, though he said nothing.

"Yes, you remember. You, like them, were bad then and you're bad now. Things that go around, usually, if I'm not mistaken, come back around. In all of this, someone is pulling the strings and dealing with the rewards. I won't be happy till I find him and tell him what I think."

"Good luck with that! You're dealing with someone with so much power you'll be wiped up with a rag and thrown in the trash."

"Argh," she said, "don't give me your Americanisms, please, they are so unpleasant here."

Cecilia put up her hood. Her long dark coat seemed to swish, as she turned to go down the stairs. The stairs jutted out into the large open space. As Cecilia walked down, Fitzroy stood against the balustrade, leaning on them as he shouted angrily at her.

"Go on, leave! You're out of your mind! You must be fucking crazy coming here, selling your stupid fucking stories!"

A few seconds later, Fitzroy was heard screaming, as he fell from the floor above. Cecilia watched, almost like it was in slow motion, then he crashed onto the floor below. He died instantly, making a terrible mess of the beautiful Greek mosaic floor. She reached the bottom of the stairs, looked at his broken, bloodied body and felt nothing. She had seen a lot of blood in her time, playing parts in detective series on TV. Mostly artificial, but it was always messy. She stopped for a moment, then she carefully avoided leaving any sign she'd been there by not treading in the blood.

The words Rupert had said rang in her head.

"You can't always predict what people might do, but one thing's for certain, everyone wants the last word."

If only Fitzroy hadn't wanted that last word, maybe he would still be alive. Of course, he didn't know the railings had mysteriously become loose.

7.

DI Ella Askew and DS Nigel Faron arrived at Fitzroy Agole's house after his body had been found by his assistant, Debbie Stone, early the next morning. The first police officer to attend informed Ella and Nigel of what Debbie had told him, that when she got up and came into the main part of the house, she found Fitzroy lying dead in a pool of blood. She then immediately called the emergency services.

"Where is Ms. Stone now?" asked Ella.

"She's in her flat in the basement. She's obviously in shock."

Ella and Nigel went to interview her. She was only able to answer a few questions, as she was feeling quite sick. They decided to speak to her when she was feeling better. One of the forensic team attending informed Ella of what else he knew. He speculated that it could just have been a nasty accident, as it didn't look as if anyone else was involved. Forensics were already all over the scene and, up to this point, nothing seemed suspicious.

Later that afternoon, Ella and Nigel visited Ms Stone at her sister's house. She was sitting on a sofa, sipping a hot chocolate, with a blanket around her shoulders.

"How are you feeling, Ms Stone?" Ella asked.

"Call me Debs. I'm feeling better now. It was a terrible thing seeing Fitz just lying there. He looked so white, like a ghost."

There were tears in her eyes.

"I know this is all very upsetting, but can you tell us anything about the last evening?"

Nigel made notes as they talked.

"I went to my flat, I had a bath, I went straight to bed. I heard nothing. The flat is completely soundproofed. I woke up this morning, saw the alarm flashing on the wall. I must admit to having turned the sound off, then I came into the main part of the house and there he was."

She put her hand up to her face as if to hold onto her emotions. Ella continued,

"At the moment, this is open to interpretation, but could you tell me whether Fitzroy was happy, unhappy? What was his mood? Could he have been depressed? We have to have an open mind about these things, until forensics have gone over everything. Till then all theories are on the table."

Debbie looked as if she was trying to find answers to Ella's questions.

"No, he had the world at his feet. If you're asking me if he killed himself, I would have to say no."

"So, how did he treat you and anyone else that he worked with?"

Debbie laughed. It was a welcome relief from the tension that surrounded them.

"That's simple," said Debbie. "He was a wanker, a total wanker that paid well!"

Ella and Nigel were surprised by Debbie's very honest reply.

"Let's say, then, if this was a suspicious death, would you say someone may have murdered him?"

Her honesty continued.

"Yes! He could be a very cruel and vindictive man. He used his power and his money to manipulate people."

"This does put you in the picture, if it looks like he's been murdered," said Nigel. Debbie thought for a moment, as she realised what she'd said.

"That might be the case. I might have good reason to, but I didn't."

The interview continued. Debbie showed them a bruise caused by Fitzroy after he'd hit her in anger a week before. In her honesty, Debbie had put herself up for prime suspect without thinking. Ella was no fool. Nobody with an ulterior motive would be so foolish.

Back at the station, the need to be socially distanced and masked up continued. Working in such conditions made the environment hot, annoying and, most of all, difficult to communicate. It was in their interests to be as professional as possible. Ella and Nigel were looking into Fitzroy Agole's past. Amber and Ethan were busy researching his more recent history. After a few hours of looking, one thing was certain: that Fitzroy was not a nice person and he certainly had enemies. Up to this point, however, it looked like a strange, unfortunate accident.

"I don't know why," said Nigel, "but something's niggling at me about this guy and our two other high-profile deaths."

"What is that?" asked Ella.

"It's a gut feeling that there's a link."

"You mean you have no evidence whatsoever, but your gut's groaning. Ok, Sherlock, explain. We are waiting with bated breath."

The others turned and stared as they sat on their socially distanced chairs. Nigel dropped his mask off his face to speak.

"I think it's the social media side of it. It just seems peculiar to me that three high profile media stars have died strangely in fairly quick succession."

He said nothing else.

"Is that it, Nigel? We need more than that, for Christ's sake! Next, you'll be saying you can feel it in your water!"

She was being hard, but Nigel was giving her nothing.

"Right," she said, in a very business-like way, "what we have is a lot of ifs, ands and maybes."

"No, I think it's straightforward," said Nigel.

Ella shook her head.

"You're clutching at nothing, Nigel! I want evidence. Something that can link them if there is any. Till then, the jury's out, so, let's make a point of getting Debbie back over to Fitzroy's house. Ask her if anything looks unusual."

8.

There was a gap in the market and, like many others, Celeste Garnier was happy to take advantage, having moved to the UK prior to the pandemic. She had already been extricating money from people who were willing to invest in bogus ideas. She was beautiful, slim, multilingual, intelligent and most of all, charming.

Celeste had a history in France she wanted to forget. She wanted to start again, so she moved to Britain where she built up her mindfulness and revitalisation web site, which had everything, from sex toys, creams, even DVDs on how to get the best out of a relationship. She did have a female clientele, but her target was men and women who wanted to discover themselves. In many countries, people will talk about most things, but sex, depending on where you are, can sometimes be taboo. Celeste had it in her mind to push her thoughts via her web site.

It was early days, but the Coronavirus had found an awful lot of people twiddling their thumbs and other things. These were who Celeste was trying to capture. She balanced it well and tried to inform the public about everything to do with getting the best out of their sex lives. The back story, however, went somewhat deeper. Celeste sat meditating in her all-white living-room.

She had made a good job of turning her whole house into one of Feng shui, the mood where she believed sex was best delivered. Large double doors were opened wide onto a patio area, a soft breeze blew through pure white net curtains as the sun danced on the hard wood flooring. She was preparing to start her yoga programme, which she was recording on her computer. Her perfectly formed body was relaxed. She'd tied back her long, blond hair into a ponytail and she was comfortably attired in a loose, white shirt over her all-in-one body-hugging yoga suit. She then proceeded to go through her routine. The atmosphere was one of peace and tranquillity, essential to what she was trying to sell. When she had finished, she sat motionless, as if she was continuing to meditate. A shadow cast across the room. She felt a shiver go through her bones. Her eyes were half open, as a dark figure stood just inside the doors. It seemed unworldly with the white nets flipping back and forth, caressing it. She went to scream, then a voice stopped her.

"Please don't make a noise or you'll attract too much attention, which may be dangerous"

For Cecilia, this was the best bit: enter mysterious woman, looking threatening, delivering powerful lines. The stage was set. Her cool voice was somehow shielded, muffled, but still overpoweringly convincing. Celeste moved her body to look towards the voice. Cecilia stood there in a dark full-length coat with a hood over her head, part of her face covered by a black mask.

"Oh, Mon Dieu!" Celeste's voice cracked, then strained to speak. "Who are you?"

Cecilia was pleased with her entrance. All she needed was applause to go with it.

Celeste reached for her phone, automatically.

"I don't think you want to do that. If it's the police you're going to call, they might find out something you don't want them to know. It might be better if we just talk."

Celeste said nothing but rose from the floor and then sat very correctly on an easy chair. She was calm, cool, collected.

"Look," said Celeste, confidently. "I'm not shockable. In my life, I've seen it all, most of it has happened to me."

Her French accent was there, her control of the English language perfect.

"So, who are you and what do you want?"

"I'm Cecilia Walters."

"Am I supposed to know who that is?"

Up to now, Cecilia had commanded respect, during her lifetime, regarding her performances. This was in some ways an extension of that. In this part she was playing, she had become something of a spirit to equal out good and evil. However, this was not the only reason. She was also out to deliver a form of retribution, but for now that was by and by.

"I am here to put you in touch with your conscience."

Celeste was quick to assess the situation. She looked at Cecilia, who had moved into the room and looked less threatening.

"Is this a joke?" she asked. "It seems to me that you are like a character from A Christmas Carol, a spirit yet to come. One of many English traditions of which I am aware."

The role that Cecilia had played so far had filled her head and heart with a certain amount of satisfaction. Although in some ways Celeste was right, Cecilia didn't want to be questioned about it. After all, this was Celeste's comeuppance. The two women, one standing, one sitting, seemed to have a moment, which neither wanted to move away from. Cecilia removed her mask, then made herself comfortable opposite Celeste.

"From what I have learnt, you have two stories, one in France that gained you notoriety, but under a different name."

A look of surprise darted across Celeste's face.

"Marilyn Doucette, I believe."

Celeste looked dumbfounded. Up to now, she was a match for Cecilia.

"It would seem, Celeste, that you were the manageress of a high-end brothel. You were no stranger to using your clients' liaisons with your ladies to extort money from some important people. One of them being a prominent politician. The only problem was he called your bluff. You then exposed him; the news became public. To cut a long story short, your scam was uncovered."

Celeste sat open-mouthed, as her life was laid out before her.

"So, I suppose," said Cecilia, "if you play dirty, you get dirty. The only problem was the politician hanged himself, leaving three young children, a wife, and a government in tatters. Who could they hang all this on? Nobody! Because you had an escape route, one that no one would uncover. That was unless you have the help of the dark web where all things can be found if you know where to look. Fortunately, I know someone clever enough to do that. That someone also found your plastic surgeon. I must say, Celeste, he did an amazing job. I don't think anyone would guess that you were once Marilyn Doucette. The other thing that I've found out about you is your part in trafficking young girls for sex. Overall, Celeste, you're not a very nice person, are you?"

Celeste sat head in hands, caught somewhere it would be impossible to escape from, it would seem.

"Who and what are you in all this?" she asked.

Cecilia thought for a moment.

"That question will take you back to when you were living in Spain, just twenty years old, the leader of a gang of teenagers."

Cecilia told the story that she had told her now-dead friends, Tracy Bowman, Carne Woodthorpe, Antonio de Leone, Fitzroy Agole.

"And, of course, you. Marilyn Doucette, alias Celeste Garnier."

Celeste looked as if someone had stolen her soul. Her face was ashen. Surprisingly, after a few minutes, she started to laugh, which threw Cecilia.

"So, what's funny?" Cecilia asked.

"You! What do you think you are? The grim reaper? Someone who can right the wrongs of the past for everyone, then dispose of their soul?"

That question had not really come into Cecilia's mind. All she thought she was doing was using her considerable abilities to place the facts before those that had done wrong, then maybe deal out retribution. In her mind, she was doing the world a favour.

"Whatever I am doing, I think people like you deserve your just desserts."

"Trouble is," said Celeste, "if I can quote the words of Ebenezer Scrooge, you may be an undigested piece of beef, a blot of mustard, a piece of cheese, a fragment of underdone potato."

Cecilia was appalled. She believed in herself ultimately. The very thought that her captured audience might use a classic writer to poke fun at her, made her very annoyed. Up to now she had proceeded in a calm, thoughtful way. She was never one to get angry easily.

"I see," she said, "do you think this is all a game, or maybe a play within a play? One that you and I can act out, then we both go on our merry way?"

Celeste looked thoughtful.

"Yes, something like that. I read about Tracy, Carne, and Fitzroy, but I know nothing of Antonio. He, like me, wished to move on with another name obviously."

Cecilia thought that Celeste was a cool customer, so guessed this was no pushover.

"Coffee, tea?"

Cecilia paused her pacing, then sighed.

"Black coffee, no sugar!"

The silence seemed welcome to them both. As Celeste made the coffee, Cecilia realised the caffeine may help her keep on top, but she needed to compose herself.

"Can I use your lavatory?"

"Why, of course! Upstairs first door on the right."

She left the room. Five minutes later, she returned, then removed her coat and sat down. Coffee was placed on a small table between them.

"I haven't been truthful," said Celeste as she sipped her coffee, "I do know you, I've seen you on TV and in films. That's why I quoted Dickens. I thought it might amuse you, as it seems to me that you might enjoy the game."

"The game?" said Cecilia.

"Yes, you love this thing that you do, this role you're playing. To tell you the absolute truth, I was warned I might be visited by a stranger."

Cecilia was now definitely caught unawares. At first, she'd had the upper hand, then she was equal to the task, but this statement had put her on the back foot.

"By whom?" she asked.

"That would be telling, wouldn't it?"

The element of being dramatic had been stolen away from Cecilia, but she needed to finish off her task.

"I see! It seems that the one who controlled you has intervened."

Cecilia knew, by saying this, that she had hit the right spot as to who had forewarned Celeste.

"I think we have stalemate. It would seem, Cecilia, you have managed somehow to dispose of four irrelevant people who I had known years ago. However, the power is now on my side. I think you should leave and take your ideas of restitution with you. You're a has-been with strange thoughts about putting the world to rights. If I were you, I wouldn't speak to the police, because it might be the last thing you ever do."

Cecilia stood up, slipped on her coat, her mask, then moved towards the patio doors.

"I think," said Cecilia, "you are mistaken as to what's happening. I am on a journey to inform those that have done great wrong, to place the facts before them. Obviously, my words can be ignored, but for my part the ending will be the same regardless. I'm guessing, by this time tomorrow you'll be long gone. and have another name. You may run, but you will never escape your past. In fact, I think I will have the last word."

The words hung in the air as they both thought they had the upper hand. Celeste smiled broadly, her face triumphant. At the door, Cecilia looked back.

"I would never use the police to do my work. Where would the fun be in that? Goodbye Marilyn Doucette."

With that, she left the house.

Celeste sat there for a moment, basking in her own glory, then felt uncomfortable, as she thought about her confrontation with Cecilia Walters. This was followed by an urgency inside to get away as soon as possible. She left the room, then went upstairs, where she contemplated having a shower, but thought it would take up too much time. So she quickly filled her suitcase with as much as possible. She wasn't panicking, but she couldn't be absolutely certain Cecilia would not go to the police. She washed and changed quickly, brushed her hair then applied makeup. Although the plastic surgeon had done a brilliant job, she still needed to cover up a few very fine scars here and there. She stared at herself in the mirror. This sometimes made her feel strange. After all, when you have looked at the same face nearly all your lifetime, having a new one took some getting used to.

"Never mind," she said out loud, "maybe South America will be the best place of all to start again."

She traced the bright red lipstick across her lips, then pushed them together to get an even coating. The unusual bitter taste didn't trouble her at first, then she felt strangely feverish, as she stared at her reflection in the mirror. Celeste then knew that Cecilia had indeed had the last word.

Cecilia walked in the dimming light, making sure to use the back streets. She was used to it by now. The Coronavirus had left most places deserted, so walking was a pleasant experience. She had never been stopped or asked why she was out; if she would have been, she knew she was a good enough actress to convince the police she had a right to be there.

Cecilia got home in the dark, let herself into her apartment, then drank some expensive brandy. She downed a couple of glasses, before even thinking of taking off her coat. As she did, she pulled a beautifully engraved silver container out of her pocket. She opened it, then looked at the empty Hypodermic needle inside.

"Well, Marilyn Doucette, alias Celeste Garnier, you will never have another life to spread your evil ways. It would seem that this actress picked up a few tricks during her acting career. Now who's smiling all over her face?"

The truth was, Cecilia wasn't smiling, she was exhausted. The last few months had taken their toll. She needed time to recuperate, but she had one more part to play.

9.

Ella and Nigel had decided to do some reconnaissance after Celeste Garnier was found dead, as it was thought that someone might return to the scene of the crime. It was clutching at straws, but another high-profile death deserved further commitment on behalf of the police force. They had gone to Celeste Garnier's house in different cars, but then decided to sit in Nigel's The streets were deserted. Ella and Nigel had struck up an understanding and relationship in a short time. Although they were pushing the boundaries of the regulations, they were willing to do it to be together.

"I miss this," said Ella.

"You miss surveillance?" Nigel scoffed at her comment. "You must be mad. Tell me why!"

They were both eating a takeaway burger and fries.

"I guess it's the grubbiness of it, but it's what police work is all about. Of course, the junk food is an added bonus."

He laughed, then pondered her answer.

"Truth is Ella, you don't have to be here. You could have said no."

"That's not true. With staff levels low, with the pandemic, I have to set an example. Also, it's dangerous not having a partner for back-up."

He shrugged his shoulders.

"I doubt if there'll be any danger tonight," said Nigel, "it looks dead as the grave. I think we probably stand more danger of contracting Coronavirus than catching any villains."

"Do you mean you have no confidence in track and trace and wearing masks to keep us safe? And, of course, being inoculated?"

A silence hung there for a second.

"I think the reality is," said Ella, "this Coronavirus has certainly changed the patterns of crime. Looks like the low-lifes want to stay healthy till the good times come back. I suppose the other thing about doing this line of work is it does give the mind room to think things through, which is a bonus."

"On that note, Ella, have you thought anymore about the link on these celeb cases?"

"I didn't think we'd come to the conclusion that they were related. Or had we?"

"No, no, that's true, but in my mind, I still see them as linked, especially as, after looking over Fitzroy's place again, it was discovered that some nuts were loose on the railings that he fell through."

"Yes, but that could be bad workmanship or even poor maintenance. It doesn't prove anything. There's no sign of anyone else, apart from his assistant being in the property."

Ella finished her last chip.

"Why is it the last chip, like the last sweet, always tastes the best?"

Nigel had finished his chips way before Ella, but thought about it.

"It's as if you haven't really appreciated what's gone before," he answered.

"I'd love a jelly baby now," Ella added.

The two of them seemed to gaze into the windscreen, lost in sweet heaven.

"Sherbet lemons."

They both joined together in the moment.

"Mmmmmmmm!"

After what seemed like an eternity, Nigel looked at his phone.

"Apparently Celeste Garnier died from poison being syringed into her lipstick, the autopsy report says. Also, her real name is in fact Marilyn Doucette."

"That name rings a far-off bell. Isn't she that French sex worker that disappeared after being embroiled in a French minister's death?"

Nigel thought about it for a while.

"Yes, I think I recall that information as well. Congratulations, Ella! Well done, but it's not what I would readily call to mind."

She looked pleased with herself and said.

"I've always kept my eye on international notifications on criminals via our internal computer. You never know when one of them might land on our shores."

He then sketched her in on the details he had just received.

"I think, Ella, we should have another look at her house. See if anything is suspicious."

"Overall, I'd say it's good that we are in a bubble, or we couldn't do this at all," she said.

He looked at her.

"That sounds so cosy for a car that smells of burger and chips."

They laughed. A moment passed between them, a look in the eye. The conversation seemed to hang on more than just the memory of sweet things.

"Let's call it a night. I guess it's been a nice bit of overtime, Ella. I've enjoyed it."

"Don't mention overtime," she said, "that's red rag to a bull to the superintendent, Coronavirus or no Coronavirus. And, yes, I've enjoyed it as well."

As Ella was getting out of the car they shared a brief kiss.

A week later, at the police station, Ella's team were looking into links between the recent suspicious deaths. The office had all the windows open, which was fine on a good day. Obviously, because of Covid, masks were obligatory. The whole task of gathering information about any investigation had been a trial of perseverance. The very fact that they were there at all showed how dedicated they were to the job. Even so, they did put themselves at risk of catching the virus every day.

"So," said Ella, "Celeste Garnier what was she like."

Ms Garnier was hot-tempered and abusive, not at all like the persona she put across on her website and blog."

"We spoke to her neighbours" said Nigel. "It seems to me that one thing we've learned about all these people is that they are not nice at all."

"Bit of an understatement don't you think?" said Ella.

"We've gone through her computer," said Amber, "Apart from normal stuff, very little to help us."

Nigel butted in.

"Doesn't it seem strange that we've turned nothing up that links her to her past in Paris?"

Ethan put his hand up. Ella gave him a glare. He put his hand down quickly.

"This morning," he said nervously, "we had a long communication from the French police. They have sent details about Marilyn Doucette's misdemeanours."

"Excellent," said Ella. "Let me see it."

She walked around to Ethan's desk. He got up and stood to one side, so they would be a safe distance apart.

"This is all in French," said Ella.

Ethan spread his hands as if to say *of course it is, it's from France.*

Nigel and Amber smiled. Ella was out of the loop for a moment.

"Ok, ok, French is not a subject I'm up in."

She turned, looked at Ethan, then said,

"Can you translate it?"

He did. He was precise and didn't falter in any way whatsoever. Ella was impressed.

"I did A level French when I was at school. Also, my mum and dad have a property in France."

There was a small hand clap of appreciation from Nigel and Amber.

"That's enough, for God's sake!" said Ella. "He's not a performing seal!"

Ethan had a smile from ear to ear. He felt as if it was the best day ever. The information from the French police was long and damning. Ella continued,

"It seems to me that there's going to be a lot of people in France who will be happy to hear of the demise of Celeste Garnier, or should I say Marilyn Doucette."

10.

The virus was picking up speed again, after being pinned back. A new variant had given it a new impetus. The public, however, were still confused. The government, after eighteen months, were still unable to manage the problem correctly. The NHS was bearing up well under the circumstances, but people were dying unnecessarily.

The leaves on the trees were turning. Autumn was on its way. A large houseboat sat on the river. One of half a dozen or more, they had the best spots along the bank. These were expensive homes on water, owned by people who had plenty of money. The cost of the moorings alone could keep some people alive for a year. The river footpath usually had many people jogging, cycling, or walking their dogs. However, the pandemic had cut these down to a masked few. Unlike some places, here people were observing the rules, staying at home.

Of course, there were always the exceptions. One of these was Falcon Diaz, a young man with one foot in the future and another in a murky past. He had, over recent years, ventured into forming a social media site, which had become quite successful. FiF, Friends in Focus, was his brainchild. He had managed to garner people who were fed up with the current social media platforms. His idea was to aim at people in their twenties to fifties. Up to this point, he had nearly two million on board. He had little to do with the running of the brainchild; other people did that for him. The truth was it was a great place to invest his laundered money.

Known as Birdy to his friends and acquaintances, he was at the top of his career. He was in his late thirties, tall, good-looking and something of a ladies' man. His Spanish heritage gave him the look of a Latin stallion. He had had a string of short-term relationships, which all ended badly with his attitude towards women. He was a modern-day chauvinist who had no desire to change. Falcon had been cooped up on his boat for months. He was beginning to feel like a rabbit in a cage. Zoom, at this point in time, was for many the only means of communication. As for Falcon, he found escape through drug-dealing, something that helped his growing fortune. However, like so many others, the present circumstances had made a big hole in his income. He alleviated his boredom by moving back and forth to his luxury flat not far away, but he preferred his riverboat lifestyle. He was on his mobile phone, after taking a line of cocaine. He was frustrated and wanted sex. After looking at a few sites on the internet, he contacted one. He knew he would have to pay a premium, because of lockdown. Even so, he was aware of a few who were still operating, although it was considered dangerous. An hour later, someone tapped on the window of his boat. He opened the door. There stood a young girl in a leather coat, scarf over her head, mask on her face. He ushered her in. It was warm, cosy, and very modern inside. Lots of white, but tastefully wood-panelled to soften the atmosphere. The furniture was complimentary to the surroundings. The girl looked around but said nothing.

"Drink?" he asked.

She shook her head. Her eyes were stunning. They looked like those of an angel.

"Why don't you take your mask off?"

She shook her head. He took a sip from his vodka and coke.

"How do we get to know each other if you don't speak? Or do we just have sex and you leave with the cash?"

She nodded.

"For fuck's sake, I'm bored! I haven't spoken to a living person for days!"

She looked uncomfortable. He then told her to sit. She took in the luxurious interior of the boat.

"It very expensive, all of this?"

Her accent was foreign, which was not unusual to him. Many of the sex workers he'd had were often from another country. He smiled at the way she was speaking.

"Yes, amazingly so," he said, "but I wouldn't have it any other way."

"What do you want? For me to suck or fuck?"

He laughed at her matter-of-fact way of talking.

"Yes, and everything in between!"

She looked puzzled.

"In between, in between what?"

He laughed.

"No, I mean, everything else as well."

"Oh. You know that is more money?"

"Why, of course. You don't think I'm hard up do you?"

"What is hard up? Is that your cock?"

If nothing else, he was amused by her lack of understanding.

"Let's just have a few drinks, then we can have sex."

She reluctantly took a drink from him but refused to take her mask off. She slipped it down, then took a sip. He looked at her youthful, soft-skinned face as she did so. He couldn't help being captivated by her beautifully shaped lips. He immediately wanted to kiss them.

"Where are you from?"

She slipped her mask back on.

"Albania. Kruje."

He continued his small talk; his initial annoyance having abated. He desperately wanted this young girl.

"What is your name?"

"Suzy."

"Is that your real name? You don't look like a Suzy to me."

She looked a little hesitant.

"My real name is Flutura. I was told I should use another name, more sexy."

"Flutura is a beautiful name, really sexy."

He came towards her, then sat down. He ran his hand along her fishnet stockinged legs, then up underneath her leather coat. She shivered.

"How long have you been doing this for, Flutura?"

She didn't answer, but looked nervous.

"Is this your first time?"

He was leaning across her undoing her coat. She was wearing very little underneath. His excitement could be seen in his loose-fit trousers.

"Relax!" he said, "Let's have some fun!"

He tried to remove her mask, but she pushed his hand away.

"No!"

She then turned her head to one side.

"Ok, have it your way!"

He climbed on top of her. His hands were everywhere, his legs pushing hers apart. He then had his hand on her throat. Her eyes were full of fear. The angel had gone from them. He dislodged her mask, then stuck his tongue into her mouth. It was all going so fast. She wasn't certain what to do, but she felt like her life was being taken from her. He managed to release his erect penis and was about to enter her, when she managed to lift her knee, then hit his testicles, simultaneously biting into the end of his tongue. He fell to the floor holding his groin with one hand and holding his mouth with the other. Blood dripped onto the thick lush carpet from his mouth.

Flutura stood up, pulled her coat back across her body, while wiping the blood from around her beautiful red lips. She stood over him. He was in considerable pain, his vision blurred, a combination of cocaine, vodka and fear making it difficult for him to see clearly. Flutura looked down at him. Her mask was back in place, she pulled it to one side, then spat on him.

"You are a kafshe! It is an animal in Albanian."

She kicked him in the stomach. He blacked out.

Half an hour later, he was sitting up against the sofa where he had been earlier. A different figure was sitting opposite him. He groaned. He thought everything would hurt but it didn't. However, the end of his tongue was very badly swollen. He was going to speak but wasn't sure if he could. The figure spoke.

"Hi Birdy! Or should I say Falcon Diaz, as we haven't been introduced? You will probably not feel too much pain at the moment. I thought it might help you to have a bit more cocaine to ease it. I can't have you groaning all the time when we talk. Correction, when *I* talk."

His face was distorted and confused.

"You want to know what happened to the beautiful Flutera? Now there is a story. It would seem that the young girl would rather have money off me, than a kafshe like you. As you know, Falcon, money talks. To tell you the truth, I think she would have been happy to do it for nothing. She left with a smile on her face and your blood in her mouth."

He tried to speak, but mangled words came out and she could see that it was painful.

"Who am I, you ask? I'm not sure that's what you said, but I'll furnish you with it anyway. I'm Cecilia Walters. You won't know me unless you watch tv or films. I'm pretty certain none of those things are your forte. Why am I here?"

She paused, as she could see he was confused by all of what was going on. Cecilia, who was in her long coat and hood with mask across her nose and mouth, got up and reached for water that was placed on a table next to her. She held the glass near his mouth. He then took a sip. He looked a little better. The rest of the water she emptied over his head, which made him more alert. As it slipped down his back, he shivered.

"I believe you have Spanish roots. Do you remember some friends in Spain years ago?"

She continued to read out the names of the people she had already visited. He looked horrified.

"I can see by your face that I have hit the spot and maybe you have heard that the rest of those friends are no more. Of course, that leaves you, and the one who controlled you all, but he's something for another day."

She sat back, feeling relieved. Falcon stared at her.

"Wwhhhyy? "

The word was garbled and hardly discernible, but she got what he meant.

"I've had a long life. It's been a joy, and, I might say, sometimes very difficult. The good things always overshadowed the bad. Let me just say you and your friends laid a shadow over my life, maybe an indirect shadow, but a shadow all the same. Perhaps there are things a long way back that have got all mixed up in this story. There are no punctuation marks left. All I want now is a full stop to end it."

He was lost in her words. She wasn't certain if he got what she was saying. She didn't really care. She walked across the space between him and her, then held his nose and poured cocaine into his mouth.

"Bye bye, Birdy."

There was a stillness hanging over the city that was haunting. Flashing shop and bar signs looked forlorn, almost as if an expectation of normality was just around the corner. It didn't seem that long ago that boozy revellers would be punctuating the night, as they moved from bar to bar, but now, street after street was empty. Only the sound of neon lights clicking and humming could be heard. Cecilia's nerves settled, as rain started to fall.

The sound of her shoes seemed almost deafening, as they tapped on the footpath. The rain got heavier while her mind drifted off to when she was younger. She used to love being in productions where she could use her talent as a singer and dancer. At this moment, she harked back to it. It was a cornerstone to her art, one that she had used sparingly. However, deep inside, she wanted to dance more than ever. She stopped walking, then pulled back her hood. The rain hit her face. She felt good, so happy to be alive. The things she had done were more than justifiable in her mind. After all, it was just another part she had played to the best of her ability. All she wished for was that she could have good reviews. She hummed to herself, then looked up and down the street. Like any street in the rain, it looked drab, but somehow the odd shop light or streetlight gave it a warm glow. She tapped her feet to the sound of her voice at first humming the tune, then she sang it.

"Singing in the rain, just singing in the rain, what a glorious feeling, I'm happy again."

It was like a stage set just for her and not a soul to be seen. She undid her coat, then moved her body from side to side, slowly at first, speeding up to keep in time with the music in her head. While chorusing the words she dipped and twirled through puddles that had got deeper in the road. Unlike Gene Kelly, she had no umbrella, so she made up for it by using her body to exaggerate her movement. The rain continued to fall. She was saturated, but, inside, her heart and mind were caught up on the sheer joy of being at one with nature. Above all, there was a feeling that she was a young woman again, on a stage in front of an audience and she was the best dancer in the world.

Suddenly, she stopped dramatically in the middle of the road. A fox was sitting below a streetlight staring at her. She stared back at the fox. It seemed to Cecilia her audience might be puzzled as to what was going on.

"Mr fox," she said, "or is it Mrs fox? You are my audience. Am I to be applauded or booed off this stage? I'll leave it up to you?"

The fox just stared back at her.

"I will take it then, that you think it is the best performance of Singing in the Rain, since Gene Kelly."

She curtsied, then bowed. The fox then got up and disappeared into the night.

The rain had made her sodden, the cold had permeated her skin. She continued to walk home. Although she was perishing, her heart and head were full of sunlight. Whether it was for a fox or a thousand people, she was a consummate performer. The headline flashed in her head, a smile was on her face. The only problem was that her mind felt fuzzy, and she was pretty sure she had a temperature.

11.

Cold air circulated the office. Both Amber and Ethan had their coats on. The heating wasn't adequate to keep the room warm enough with the windows open.

"Amber?"

She looked up. Ethan was twiddling a pen as he was scrolling through his computer. His eyes wandered around the room as if he was looking for something. Like his eyes, his whole body seemed to fidget.

"Amber?" he said again.

"Yes!" she said impatiently. She saw him looking up into the room, staring at the empty space.

"What are we looking for Ethan?"

Ethan looked quizzical.

"Well, I was watching the news last night. There was a report on about the Coronavirus. I don't usually do that, because my parents are obsessed by the news at home. There was nothing else to watch, so I listened to this professor talking about the virus. He was speaking over an animated film about it. It showed you if someone coughed or sneezed, black clouds filled the room."

He waved his arms around as if he was directing the movement of what he saw. Amber patiently listened to Ethan, although she somehow knew it was going nowhere. He stopped and continued to look above him.

"What are you trying to say, Ethan?"

"Is it possible, do you think if one of us had the virus, then sneezed, would we see the germs floating around up there?"

He pointed his pen up towards the ceiling while dipping his

head. Amber looked up.

"For God's sake, Ethan, get a grip! Do you know for someone who is really intelligent, you do talk daft sometimes!"

Ethan's crumpled face looked dejected and confused.

Ella entered the room, followed by Nigel. A flurry of good mornings followed.

"Nice and warm in here today."

Amber and Ethan looked at each other, then pulled their coats closer. Ella smiled.

"Please close the windows. We have all been jabbed and we are in a bubble anyway.

Ethan jumped up, closed the windows and immediately looked happier but, as he sat, he looked upwards towards the ceiling.

The phone rang.

Amber passed the phone to Ella.

"For you."

"Hello... yes... no... when? ... who? ... where?"

The other three knew this was another case. They waited as she continued to talk in shorthand.

"Ok, we'll get onto it."

She put the phone down.

"We have someone who has died on a houseboat. Looks like an overdose, but with suspicious circumstances. A guy in his late thirties. The boat was moored not far from the centre of the city. His name is Falcon Diaz."

She looked over at Amber and Ethan.

"Ok, you two, find out everything you can about him. C'mon Nigel. We're off to look at a boat!"

"Hang on," said Amber. "I know him! He's the guy who started up FiF Friends in Focus."

"Oh yeah, I know him too!" said Ethan. "It's a fairly new social network site. I'm on it."

Ella wasn't into social networking. Nigel and Amber said they had recently joined it.

"Delve then!" said Ella, "Dig up what you can about him and FiF."

The boat had crime scene tape around it, with a police officer standing nearby. Ella showed her card, as did Nigel. No one else was on board. Due to the current restrictions, everyone who may have been involved in the investigation attended in stages.

"Wow, this is nice," said Nigel, as he climbed on, "plenty of dosh has been spent on this place."

"Not done him any good though has it?" said Ella, as she looked down at Falcon Diaz's body.

"Seems strange to me, if you're going to overdose, that you shove cocaine down your throat like that."

She stared into his mouth.

"I'd say someone's done something to his tongue as well."

Nigel took a look.

"Oh yeah, you're right Ella! Looks like a rat's been nibbling at it. Nasty!"

"I think," she said, "our Mr. Diaz has had more than his fair share of attention from someone who wanted him dead!"

They continued to look for any clues that might help them with the investigation, then left the boat. On the way back to the office, Nigel said,

"Oh, by the way, Ella, the media have come up with a headline!"

Ella looked at him with narrowed eyes and a feeling that this was going to annoy her.

"Go on, tell me, what is it?"

"The celebrity lockdown murders!"

Her head dropped. She then sighed.

"That's all we need. TV news all over it and a frenzied battle for the front page. And what have we got, Nigel?"

"An awful lot of questions and very few answers!"

"I wouldn't mind," she said, "but none of them are real celebrities!"

12.

Eighteen months later.

A young freelance investigative reporter, who worked for the local paper, had been looking for different stories, other than those about Covid 19. Jeremy Bakshi was finding it difficult, as it seemed the world didn't want to let it go. It was almost twelve months since all the restrictions had been lifted and people were trying to move on. Even so, Covid 19 was still making people ill.

As far as Jeremy was concerned, he didn't personally know of anyone that had died. During his investigations, he had heard of a few who had. Of course, he had also investigated the conspiracy theorists. He could write a book about them alone. Indeed, he had many notes to back up the idea. At the moment, though, he wanted to deal in facts. The everyday reporting was his bread and butter, whether it was burglaries or an industrial dispute. He would be there, phone in hand, to record the words or take photographs.

Jeremy saw himself as ambitious. Being half British, half Asian had brought out the best of both nationalities. His dad Sidu, having lived in Britain since he was in his teens, had had an arranged marriage, not long after he arrived from India. Over the years, he and his wife had worked hard, had two children, and had become a cornerstone of the community. Unfortunately, his wife died in her early forties from a heart attack, leaving Sidu heartbroken. Five years later, with the help of family and friends, he managed to keep his life together.

Sidu worked as a taxi driver. He had the required knowledge. He knew every nook and cranny of the city and was a valuable employee of A2Z&BACK. So much so, that the owner at one time was in need of more capital to improve the company.

Sidu had built up some savings, so he offered to help with an injection of money, but only if he could become a partner. Sidu became a part owner, then didn't look back. In fact, he had fallen for a woman called Florence. She worked as a dispatcher for his company. The only problem was, did she feel the same way about him. It took a conversation between Sidu and his daughter Maya, to bring it to a head. She was trying out some of her cooking skills on Sidu one night, as she was keen to become a chef when she got older.

"Aba, have you ever wanted to marry again?"

Sidu, who was sitting at the kitchen table, looked up from the local paper he was reading and didn't know what to say. Maya's mind was on her cooking, so she didn't see the look on his face. He looked at his daughter, saw how confident and independent she had become. A feeling of pride ran through his mind. She stopped, caught his eye, they smiled at each other. It was if they both understood what they were thinking, then he let it slip. Almost like his inner thoughts had found a space to occupy at the end of his tongue.

"Florence."

As soon as he'd said it, he wished he hadn't. He felt it was a sign of weakness to even think of another woman. Especially in the company of either of his children. Maya immediately stopped cooking.

"You mean the woman with the lovely voice at your work?"

He'd said it now. He had to explain. After eating, he talked to her about Florence. She listened carefully.

"Why haven't you asked her if she would like to go out for a meal or anything?"

Sidu was shocked and felt uncomfortable. He asked her not to talk about it anymore.

"Ok," she said, "but don't leave it to stew, Aba, none of us live forever."

He realised for someone so young, Maya had a wise head on her shoulders.

Sidu took the bull by the horns. One late night, while he was waiting for a fare, he asked Florence to go out with him. It was a clumsy affair, but he found out that she felt strongly about him too. Before long, they consummated their relationship, then got married. A bigger surprise came nine months later, when Florence gave birth to a baby boy. To her, it was life changing, because she'd never thought she was able to have children, having been married before. She was told her age might make her pregnancy difficult but, in the end, she had no problems whatsoever. Both she and Sidu were gleefully happy. Maya also shared their happiness.

However, Kazi, Maya's older brother, was not. He resented his father for not marrying someone of the same faith that they had been brought up in. In some ways, this made life uncomfortable at times for Florence, but she weathered the storm.

Florence had a name for their son. It was a name she had always loved. Sidu put up no resistance. He had learnt that Florence got her own way in the end.

Jeremy, like all young children in families, got all the attention. He became something of an entertainer, at school and at home. He was pushed by his mum into all the musical instrument experiments that most children go through growing up. The piano was one of them. He showed some promise by passing a few exams but, after a while, he felt helplessly out of his depth. At school, he found acting to his taste. Especially, as it meant being involved with the opposite sex. The school plays quickly became the centre of his universe, but the prettiest girl in the school was just too far above him, in age as well as in height. So, eventually, he grasped at the opportunity to write in the school publication, which had been organised by a keen English teacher. His love for certain writers and poets helped him to hone his style. As yet though, he was unaware of that. At this point, it was just the thoughts of a teenager and all the things that got under his skin. Of course, he was seen as a nerd, like all the other kids who did well.

Where he was educated was like so many other inner-city schools, full of a cosmopolitan mix of races, colours, and sexual diversity. So there was much to write about. He did well, enjoying his time there. Before going to university, he got a part-time job on the local paper. It was a fairly easy thing to do at the time. The wage was a pittance, but he was there at the beating heart of what brings the news to everyone's doors. Most of the time he spent there, he was fetching coffee, sandwiches, moving paper and post. Computerisation had all but killed off the buzz of newspapers, but Jeremy didn't care. He was happy as a kid who had been asked to make paper aeroplanes.

His time at university was patchy. He stuck to it but longed to just write about things he cared about. So, he wrote articles, stories, sending them off to magazines. He was lucky. Every now and again, he got something published, which bolstered his bank balance. On his twentieth birthday, he turned away from his university course and got a job with a big newspaper in the same city. It was a baptism of fire, unlike his own city. This one was bigger with in-your-face stories and people to match. He did six months learning at ground level. Only problem was, he wasn't ready for it.

He went home for Christmas, a time he loved. Even though his dad wasn't into it, his mum was. As far as she was concerned, it was all about family, turkey and all the trimmings, not to mention presents.

After the New Year passed, he stayed at home and reconsidered his future. His dad, as well as his mum, were very understanding, happy to have him living with them again. Sidu had tried to heal his differences with his son, Kazi, over the years. A fragile peace had settled between them, in so much that Kazi had offered Jeremy a job in his warehouse. Kazi had now got a wife, children, and his own business. He considered himself to be a man of the world. Jeremy declined his offer.

Maya backed him up by saying why would Jeremy want to waste his life in a warehouse, when he had such a creative talent?

Sidu often had people in his taxi that he had got to know. One day, he was having a conversation with a regular fare. His name was John Scotland, the editor of the local paper, the same local paper that Jeremy had worked at before going to university. During the conversation, Jeremy's dad brought up his son's writing background. One thing led to another. Before long, Jeremy got a job at the newspaper. This time with a proper wage.

13.

Jeremy was now twenty-five, having worked on the local paper for nearly four years. Because of restructuring cutbacks, he was now mostly self-employed. It seemed to him, even though it could be precarious at times, the industry had now given him other avenues to explore. As far as his writing was concerned, he was always keen to find other stories, whenever he could. He still lived at home with his mum and dad. His dad was still doing the odd taxi run for his business, even though he was in his late sixties, and was also a constant source of information for Jeremy, which he often acquired from people who frequented his taxi.

It had now been three and a half years since the Coronavirus had overshadowed the world. People who had been trapped like canaries in cages, were now glad to see the back of Covid 19.

Jeremy had learned from a friend on social media about someone who used to be very famous, who now was in hospital with long Covid complications. Never one to stand on ceremony, he went to the local hospital the next day. The pandemic was all but a thing of the recent past. People could now visit hospitals, albeit one to a bed.

Jeremy had a name, although he knew little about the woman, apart from the fact she was an actor called Cecilia Walters. He wasn't familiar with her work. He didn't think it would be easy to get to talk to her, but he was more than willing to try.

At the reception, he pulled out his journalist card, then thought better of it. When asked, he said he was a relative. The receptionist helpfully instructed him to go and sit in a waiting area, as it wasn't visiting time yet.

He used this time to swot up on Cecilia Walters. He was transfixed with his phone, as he learnt more about her. At one time, she had been the ultimate actor, famed for her many roles in film and theatre. She was well known for her eccentric behaviour. However, over the last ten to fifteen years, her light had dimmed.

He made his way through the hospital, via lifts and corridors. He had the feeling he had been lost in a rabbit warren, by the time he got there. His shoes somehow found the floor not to their liking, constantly squeaking on the shiny floor. He did his best to ignore the irritation. Nurses, one after another, looked at him as if he needed to be oiled. He was considering whether or not to take them off, when he reached a desk.

"Can you tell me where Cecilia....?"

Before he could finish her name, the auxiliary nurse pointed him in the right direction. He came to a side ward, where the door was slightly ajar. The room was like so many others, two beds, one opposite the other. One bed was empty, the other had a very pale long-haired woman in it. She had an oxygen mask over her face, seeming to be asleep. He went in, looked at the bottom of the bed to make sure it was the right person. It was. He noticed a few cards on the cupboard and a bunch of flowers in a vase. He went to pick up one of the cards.

"And who are you?"

The voice that came from behind the oxygen mask was almost like a stabbing, the words slightly muffled, but perfectly clear.

"Er..." he uttered.

"Er, what's er? That's not an acceptable way to converse."

This shocked Jeremy. His nerves were very good normally. In fact, he had reported on violent demonstrations in his time. Manhandled, kicked, and even bitten, but this caught him unawares.

"I'm Jeremy Bakshi. I work for The Record, the local newspaper."

The words were decanted, as if he'd said them a thousand times before. Cecilia eyed him, then slipped the mask from her face.

"I see," she said clearly, with more of a soft edge to her voice.

"What, may I ask, do you want?"

She waited, with a question in her clear blue eyes. He fought hard not to say, er,

"I'm looking for stories on how the Covid virus has affected people."

"So, you would like a story about me, would you?"

Her voice was slightly mocking, which made him feel uncomfortable.

"Yes, that's if you want to talk to me. As a journalist, I think the government is desperately trying to air-brush all of this away. Especially the way they handled it. Maybe what you have to say might be of interest to the general public."

Cecilia smiled.

"I was a communist once, you know. It was a long time ago, at the beginning of my career. I was red-haired, carefree, in love with a man who was passionate in more ways than one. The two of us were like a burning fire of words and deeds. Do you think they might be interested in that?"

She spoke with a far-off look in her eyes.

"If you are a writer, why aren't you writing this down?"

She stared at him. Already, he could feel her eccentricity. "Sit!"

Jeremy sat, just like a dog would do if its mistress had told him to do so.

He took out his phone, notebook and pen. He wanted to establish a dialogue straight away to report how Covid had affected her. From what he had heard so far, he knew Cecilia was going to be in charge.

"Could you get me some water, please," she asked, then paused for a second, looked at him, then, as if it was gifted to her, she added, "Jeremy?"

He left the room to find water. An attractive nurse gave him some with ice in it.

"She must have it very cold," she said, as she handed him the jug. "Are you a relative?"

"No, I'm a journalist."

"She's very grand," the nurse said. "I think you could say that Cecilia Walters is a national treasure."

"Yes, I think she commands a certain amount of respect," answered Jeremy. Whether she was a national treasure or not was something he would try to find out for himself.

Minutes later, he was back in the ward with the water. He poured it. Cecilia drank it in sips.

"It's so hot in these places."

"How long have you been in here?" he asked.

"Too long, in my opinion. They say I might not survive at home without help. So that's it. It's here or the end."

The dramatic words had gravitas. A short silence followed. It was if an imaginary cortège was passing by. Cecilia held the moment in her eyes. Jeremy saw her eye lids slowly closing. He wasn't an aficionado by any means, but this was the perfect moment to pass away. He rested his hands on his knees, the need to write any more placed to one side. He then rose to move towards her. In his mind he thought he should summon a nurse, but she opened one eye.

"I'm good, am I not?"

Jeremy was a little shocked, but tried not to show it. She laughed heartily, then started coughing. He moved towards her, but this time she put her hand up as if to stop him. She then reached for the ventilator. A look of ease came over her face. Without another word, she slipped off to sleep. Jeremy, now keen to continue the conversation, didn't know what to do. There was still an hour of visiting time. So he slipped out for a coffee. Jeremy found his way to a small seating area with a coffee machine. He looked out of a window at the backstreets and the hospital car park. For a few moments, his mind slipped away. He tried to think of the last time he'd been in a hospital. He vaguely remembered having his tonsils out when he was a child. He then recalled his father breaking several of his toes, when one of the taxi drivers drove over his foot by accident. His thoughts went back to his mother, who picked him up from school.

"Your father's had an accident," she'd said, "we have to go to the hospital."

She had seemed a little flustered, but took it in her stride, as she told him what had happened. In the hospital, they'd found his father in a little cubicle, his foot being attended to.

"It's nothing, Florence," he'd said, "it's just a few broken toes."

As his mother had hugged his father, he'd felt a warm feeling inside, even though his father was in a lot of pain.

"Hi!"

The attractive nurse was suddenly at his side.

"You seemed far away," she said, "was it somewhere nice?"

He was surprised by the interruption, somewhat confused, as his thoughts seemed lost. He hesitated for a moment.

"Sorry, yes, miles away!"

There was a silence that was filled with the hospital's forever sounds. He stood opposite her, for a few seconds, as they looked into each other's eyes. He was dumbfounded by how beautiful she was. No words came to his mouth.

"I'll maybe see you another time, then?" she hastily said, "I must dash."

She was gone.

"Fuck! Shit! What a tit I am!"

His angry words echoed in the waiting area.

"What am I thinking? She's beautiful and talking to me like a friend."

He was beating himself up verbally, as a couple of people approached the coffee machine. They looked at him strangely, then turned and walked down an adjacent corridor.

"For fuck's sake!" he said quietly to himself, then threw his empty coffee cup in the waste basket and made his way back to the ward.

In Cecilia's room, there was another nurse attending to her. Jeremy stood to one side, as she took her temperature.

"Have you met my young man, nurse?" Cecilia asked, "He believes he's a writer of sorts."

The nurse was very young and inexperienced, it would seem, in most things, as she coloured up quite red.

"Don't worry, he won't eat you. He's only a few years older than you, still green behind the ears."

Jeremy also looked embarrassed, as the nurse slipped from the room quickly.

"I am a qualified journalist!" he said, with an air of confidence. She stared at him with her steely blue eyes. For some reason, he felt as if he was at school and the teacher was calling him out.

"I'm sorry! What I said was uncalled for, Jeremy."

Her attrition soothed his annoyance, not that it was much to speak of. She continued,

"I observe, digest, then, if appropriate, I comment. It has sometimes been said over my career, that I was difficult to work with. The truth is, I was just too honest. Honesty can sometimes be seen as ignorance but, in my personal opinion, there is not enough of it about. So, I'm not being rude, I'm just telling you how I see it."

Jeremy was aware he was still a young man and, in many ways, inexperienced. One thing he was certain of, he was eager to learn.

Jeremy had already found out that Cecilia liked the sound of her own voice. Why wouldn't she? After all, it was wonderful to listen to.

"I've watched a few of your old films on You Tube. I must admit you were really good. Do you miss those days?"

She caught his eyes, as he said the words. He felt as if he might have put his foot in it straight away, but she laughed. He liked her laugh. It made him feel closer to her.

"Honesty. Yes, I like it Jeremy. You were listening. I hope when you've seen more of my performances, you may feel they were better than good. Yes, those were great days indeed. Everything was simpler, none of this social media rubbish we have today. In my personal opinion, I think it erodes the soul. Back in my day, we had a certain amount of privacy. Now, a person's life is like dirty washing hanging on a line, for everyone to see. In my opinion, it's all in bad taste."

Jeremy made notes, but also had his phone on to record the interview. It was in his mind to buy a more expensive digital recorder, because something inside was saying he might need it. Cecilia went quiet. She seemed to be studying him.

"I hope you don't mind me asking," she said, "can you slip off your mask?"

He obliged her without question. She studied his face for a moment.

"You seem to have perfect skin, Jeremy, the tone of it is quite perfectly olive in colour. Your bone structure is beautiful. Do you have Asian heritage?"

The focus was perfectly switched around to him. He felt a little embarrassed, but he was eager to create a cordial atmosphere between them.

"My mother is British. My father was originally from India."

"Yes," she said, "you have gained the best from the mix."

Her words sounded tired. The visiting bell could be heard. Cecilia looked exhausted, but just as he got up to go, she said, "Good night, good night! Parting is such sweet sorrow, That I shall say good night till it be morrow.
Romeo and Juliet."

He knew the quote well. He had done the play when he was at school, but to hear it from a professional actor was a privilege. She had said it in hushed tones, then blew him a kiss. He knew, then, that Cecilia was so much better than good. Hypnotised by the interview, Jeremy went home. Much of the journey he couldn't really remember.

14.

For Jeremy, there was joy to living at home with his mum and dad. For many reasons, one being the love of food. Both his mum and dad loved cooking. So much so, they alternated most nights. His dad liked it hot, so he was into curries. His mother was more the traditional English, with a splash of Mediterranean. Jeremy loved it all. His tastes, like his upbringing, were eclectic. In the kitchen, his dad was cooking rogan josh. Jeremy's tastebuds were dancing. He realised he'd been so wrapped up in Cecilia's story, he'd skipped lunch. The kitchen, which was part of the living room and dining room, was extensive. Jeremy sat opposite his mum on a bar stool, while his dad cooked. His mum asked about Jeremy's day.

"Actually, it's interesting. I'm interviewing someone at the county hospital about long Covid. Her name is Cecilia Walters."

"Do you mean the actress Cecilia Walters?" she asked.

"Yes! Do you know of her?"

"Oh my God! She was a big name in films and on TV! To tell you the truth, I thought she was dead."

Jeremy's dad only half heard what they were talking about, because of the extractor fan.

"Who did you say, son?"

"Cecilia Walters," he repeated.

His dad echoed his mum.

"I thought she was dead."

"No, she's alive and kicking!"

Jeremy then corrected himself.

"Sorry, she's not kicking. In fact, she doesn't look well at all, but she is mentally very alert."

His mum looked as if she was trying to remember something,

then recounted.

"I'm not sure, but I think I remember seeing her in the film, Death on the Nile in the eighties, also Shoestring, later on in Silent Witness. She's been in loads of things."

Jeremy was impressed by his mum's memory.

"I remember Silent Witness," said his dad, "she was one of the lead investigators." He thought for a moment, then said. "Pathologists."

His dad looked pleased with himself for remembering. His mum and dad were keen TV watchers, so Jeremy wasn't surprised they knew of her. However he did realise that he needed to research Cecilia more.

"Jeremy, I think if you use your laptop, I'm sure you could see some of these things on that."

Jeremy smiled, ever patient with the input from his parents.

At that moment, Jeremy's half-sister Maya came in. She was hugged by her mum, dad, then Jeremy. She worked at a top restaurant in the town as a chef. Tonight was her night off.

"Wow! That smells gorgeous, Aba!"

Maya was vibrant, breezy and had an infectious sense of humour. Her appearance though casual was smart and understated. She was never one to conform to type. A quote from John Lennon's lyrics could relate almost perfectly to her. *She's so good-looking but she looks like a man.* Jeremy and Maya high fived each other.

"Jez!"

"May!"

"What have I missed?" she asked.

"Your brother has been interviewing a top film and TV actor.

"Do I know her?" she asked as she filled her mouth with naan bread.

"Cecilia Walters," said Jeremy.

"Isn't she dead?" asked Maya.

"If she is, she is doing a good job as a talking corpse," answered Jeremy.

She punched him in the arm in response, her mouth still full of naan bread. She then closed her eyes, lay across the countertop pretending to be dead.

Jeremy laughed, then tickled her. She immediately started laughing, then bits of naan bread shot from her mouth like a volcano. There was nearly thirteen years between Jeremy and Maya, but sometimes, in each other's company, they acted like children. This was mainly because Maya had not wanted any long-term relationships, so had always generated towards home.

"For God's sake!" said their mum, "Behave! You're supposed to be grown-ups now!"

They both stifled their behaviour, but proceeded to nudge each other under the counter. Maya was in her late thirties, but still a child at heart. Her career was the thing. She had thrown everything into it. Nothing was going to get in the way.

"So, when are you taking your new girlfriend out for a meal, Jez?" asked Maya.

"So funny," answered Jeremy. "She's very sophisticated."

"Does that mean she said no to your advances, then?"

She continued to have a dig at Jeremy.

"Ok, you two," said their dad. "Stop it! Time to eat."

The rest of the evening, the banter continued between the siblings, so their mum and dad went to bed.

Maya used the sky controls to find a Cecilia Walters film.

She found One and put it on.

"Research for you, Jez! See if you can revive the corpse!"

She laughed. Maya fell asleep, Jeremy watched it right the way through. He was captivated, not only by her acting, but also by Cecilia's beauty.

Jeremy woke early the next morning, keen to get to work. He had a few appointments at the local paper about new stories, plus ongoing ones. His intention was to clear everything, so he could visit Cecilia. Being part self-employed meant he had a free run most of the time, but to have an income, the work at the local paper was necessary for his lifestyle. He sat eating cereal, his mum busying herself around the house. Mum stopped her work to sit and take a breather. She watched him affectionately as he ate.

"Well, son, are you seeing her today?"

Jeremy half smiled, pretending not to understand what his mother was on about. She stared into his eyes impatiently. He knew she knew him too well to play silly games.

"Yes, of course I am! She possesses a certain aura that's somehow captivating."

A dreamy look came over his face.

"If I'm not mistaken, you may be falling for an elderly woman, who, for all intents and purposes, is old enough to be your grandmother."

He laughed, took it in good measure.

"Yes, I'm sure I could be her toy boy, Mum!"

15.

Cecilia had somehow recovered enough to be told by the doctors she could go home in a few days, if her progress continued. It would appear she was making a miraculous recovery.

Eighteen months earlier, the hospital had been awash with Covid cases. Slowly but surely, it was getting back to normal. Even so, there was still a steady stream of long Covid sufferers, mostly among the elderly. When Jeremy turned up, Cecilia was sitting in a chair, a blanket across her legs. Her face lit up as Jeremy walked in the room. He thought she looked so much younger than the day before. Her skin seemed brighter, more the colour of someone on the mend. Her high cheek bones had pink in them, her hair was swept back and pinned in some way that extenuated her features. She looked composed, almost as if waiting to be asked to walk on the stage or, as in this case, to be interviewed. Her smile was welcoming.

"Jeremy."

She said it as if he was a member of her family. He walked up to her to take her hand. He wasn't sure of the etiquette in the circumstances.

"Why so formal?" she said, "Kiss me."

She offered her right cheek. He was confused. She noted his hesitancy.

"Why so shy? Surely you know me well enough to kiss me now?"

His thoughts were confused, as he had barely known her a short while, but he bent towards her and kissed both her cheeks. Both he and Cecilia had lowered their masks for ease of talking, although the policy of the hospital was still that they should be worn at all times.

For some reason, he was feeling nervous. He then took Cecilia's hand and kissed it. Straight away, it calmed him as it had the sweet smell of soap.

"Why, aren't you the gentleman! Sit Jeremy."

Again, he dutifully sat.

"How did you sleep?" he asked.

For some reason, he felt on edge. She sensed his nervousness.

"I slept like a baby. It was probably the best night's sleep I've had in months. I think, Jeremy, I might put it down to you visiting me."

He coloured up.

"Tell me, Jeremy, about your family."

The question surprised him slightly, because he was there to find out about her, but he told her the background to his family. After not too much detail, she said,

"Very cosmopolitan."

He smiled at her, but he was eager to move on.

"I want to ask you a more sensitive question."

"By all means, I'm all yours," she said, laying her hands open towards him in a grand gesture.

"Well, I've been thinking. Maybe I could do a larger piece, maybe for the nationals. I'm pretty certain there would be plenty of interest."

She smiled graciously and seemed to take her time to answer.

"I have much to tell, Jeremy, are you sure you have the time?"

His heart missed a beat, because he felt a well of excitement in his stomach. His thoughts were this could be the making of him. Cecilia felt young again. She knew she only had an audience of one, but this could be the biggest part she'd ever played.

The attractive nurse came into the room to check that Cecilia was ok. She passed Jeremy, then took Cecilia's temperature.

"How's our most beautiful patient this morning?"

Cecilia almost blushed.

"I see you also have the handsome young man here again

today."

Jeremy went uncontrollably red.

"He's a good-looking boy, isn't he nurse? By the way, Jeremy, this is Sofia. She's very kind and gentle."

"We met by the coffee machine down the hall. Mr. Bakshi was lost for words."

Jeremy smiled.

"I was lost in thought at the time, nurse."

"First names, if you please," said Cecilia. "I dare say he was thinking about me!"

As Cecilia said it, she giggled to herself, as if she was a little girl. Sofia smiled.

"I guess I'd best get on with my work, leave you two to talk about life."

As she left the ward, a peaceful calm fell over the room. It was as if Cecilia and Jeremy had come to a starting point. A place that's like virgin snow or flat calm water, waiting for someone to just leave a footprint or make ripples. Cecilia set sail.

"When I was small, we lived in a crumbling Victorian building, that was let out to many people. My mother always smelled of soap. The endless hours she spent doing washing for people made sure of that. There was a small yard that was forever hung with sheets waving in the breeze. She wore herself to the ground for money to keep us alive. As the years went by, I helped her. I longed to go to school, but my mother needed me."

"What about your father?"

"He was only around occasionally to take all my mother's money. He would then disappear again. He was a violent drunk. I wished him dead. There were plenty of times, when I was growing up, that he would leave my mother black and blue. One day, the police came around. I was about ten years old. They told my mother he had fallen in the river and drowned. My mother cried for days. I could never understand why. He gave her nothing and had taken everything. I did feel guilty for a while, because I thought my wish had come true."

Jeremy wrote every word she said. He tried to ask questions that were relevant, but, on the whole, he did the right thing and let Cecilia tell her life story.

"None of this is common knowledge. Nobody has written my biography. I'm not sure how much detail it requires."

She said it in a stern way, as if to signpost the way forward. Jeremy revelled in it. As the sun crept across the room, he realised this was no small thing she was telling him. This was Cecilia's life, although it was only just scratching the surface.

"I'll come back this evening. Would that be ok?"

Cecilia had a dreamy look on her face. He could see she was there, back in the past. He kissed her gently on each cheek. She offered up her hand. It would seem that Jeremy Bakshi was now her handsome biographer.

Jeremy stopped at the coffee machine, realising that two hours had shot by. He sat at a small table, sipping his coffee, checking his notes.

"Hi, Jeremy! How's your girlfriend?"

He knew it was Sofia. He smiled and asked her if she wanted coffee.

"Latte please, everything else in that machine is awful."

"Cappuccino is ok."

"Who do you work for then?" she asked.

"I'm self-employed, freelance, with contacts on the local rag."

"Are you doing a story for the local paper about Cecilia?"

"To tell you the truth, I think it's bigger than that. It's almost like she wants me to write her biography."

"You need to be sure, Jeremy, because she does seem very forgetful at times."

He noted Sofia's concerns.

"Cecilia has said to me she will be out in a few days. Is that true?" he asked.

"Yes, but she's not well, she could relapse at any time. We need the bed, because we have a backlog of patients for surgery, because of the virus."

"Why is the other bed in her room empty then?"

"A shortage of beds that work. That one is faulty. It's what they call a double whammy for the NHS."

The conversation turned.

Jeremy looked into Sofia's eyes, which was a beautiful thing to do. They were the perfect shape, almost like those of an angel. In some strange way, he felt like he already knew her. He could feel something that moved him inside, a warm, sensuous feeling that made him want to be part of her life. He felt confident that the feeling was mutual or why would she go out of her way to speak to him again? The movement of her head made a strand of dark hair fall across her face. He felt the urge to use his hand to move it to one side, but she did it for herself. He sensed that she knew there was something going on between them.

"Would you.....?"

In perfect unison, they said the same two words. They burst out laughing, both then saying,

"You first!"

Jeremy felt a rush of certainty.

"Would you like to go out for a drink sometime?"

"Oh," she said, "I wasn't expecting that. I was just going to ask you if you wanted another coffee."

Jeremy felt like a fool and was hesitant to speak for sounding even sillier, but she laughed.

"Yes, of course. I would love to go out for a drink sometime."

16.

Jeremy was feeling as if life had turned around, even though he had nothing to complain about. He had been thinking for some time that reporting for the local paper about humdrum things could be tedious. Now that he was talking to Cecilia, he thought he had something he could get his teeth into. Having a date planned with Sofia had raised his expectations even higher.

So, when his best friend called him to go out Friday night for a few drinks, he wasn't keen. He and Duman went out once a month, often being joined by Nigel. The three of them had known each other from school and had always kept in touch. Duman, a mechanic, worked for a large garage in the town. Like Jeremy, he was twenty-four, but unlike Jeremy, he was now on a good wage. So, he could afford to throw a bit of cash around. Nigel also had a good job, with a wage to match, in the police force.

The friendship the three shared had stood the test of time and they all usually enjoyed their nights out. Jeremy, at first, was reluctant, but, in the end, was happy to go. At least it would take his mind off the two new women in his life.

Three young men sat in a bar. A pint of shandy sat before each of them.

"So, Jeremy," said Duman. "How's the world of journalism?"

Jeremy had already informed Duman and Nigel that he was writing about Cecilia Walters. He thought it gave him an air of importance. Until they both messaged back, *I thought she was dead!*

Instead of answering, he decided to ask Nigel how police work was going on a particular case.

"Any more information on that big murder case you were working on, Nigel?"

Nigel looked blankly at Jeremy, who continued,

"You must remember! During the pandemic, five celebs who were all killed in strange circumstances."

"Oh, sorry. Too many cases going around in my head. That one is going nowhere at the moment."

Jeremy was familiar with it, because he had reported on it at the time. Nigel then filled in a few gaps on the case.

"The first death was Tracy Bowman. It was believed to be accidental. If she's included, it would make six dead. The fact that they are all high-profile social media personalities, we think links them. There are other things, but I think it might be best to say no more than that. At this moment in time, it's a cold case. Whoever did do it was certainly a professional. If it's ok with you, Jeremy, keep that information to yourself. Nothing is confirmed as yet."

Duman had gone to get some serious drinks in. He brought back three lagers, plus three shots.

"Have I missed anything?"

Jeremy and Nigel said "No!"

"How's the mechanic-ing, Duman?" asked Nigel.

Jeremy laughed. A wry smile came over Duman's face.

"You two have no idea what my job's about, do you?"

They both shook their heads.

"I can't remember," said Nigel, "the last time I looked at the engine of my car!"

"Me neither," said Jeremy, "my dad's taxi firm fixes my car."

"I rebuilt two engines this week. It was really interesting," said Duman.

The other two both pretended to yawn.

"Ok, ok," Duman said. "Point taken, let's get pissed."

Nigel went for more drinks.

"I was just thinking, Jez," said Duman, "was this actress good-looking?"

"In her day, she was beautiful. In some respects, she still is."

"Oh," he said, "not girlfriend material then?"

Jeremy laughed.

"My parents are both on at me constantly," said Duman, "to find a nice Turkish girl and settle down. The thing is, I've got my eye on the receptionist at the dealership where I work. She's beautiful, funny, but certainly not Turkish."

"I guess," said Jeremy, "I don't have that pressure. There's no way my dad can ask me to marry an Asian girl, when he married an English woman."

For a moment, Jeremy thought about Sofia, who he was pretty certain had Mediterranean blood running through her veins. Nigel was quietly drinking, listening, but not contributing to this part of the conversation.

"Well, Nigel, what you hiding?" asked Duman.

Nigel was unwilling to talk, which was a mistake, as far as the other two were concerned. Five minutes later, after several assaults as to where he might be satisfying his sexual desires, all he would say was,

"I am currently investigating a long-term relationship with a person who I cannot name."

Both Jeremy and Duman thought it was a hilarious answer. So, they bought him an extra pint of lager.

Saturday morning saw Jeremy waking from a fitful drunken sleep. All he remembered was being dropped off by one of his dad's taxis outside the house, then being sick in the kerb. It was midday before he went downstairs. He was then met by his dad's disapproving face.

"I know, Dad, I'll make sure everything is put right."

He wasn't certain if he'd done anything, but it often worked out better if he showed attrition before the dad storm hit. Dad said no more. However, his mother was less kind.

"I hope you clean that mess up in the kerb outside!"

"Yes mum, I will, it's in hand."

Maya came in at that moment.

"I hope it's not in your hand, you filthy animal!"

Jeremy sneered, half smiled, as she sat by him at the kitchen counter. As usual, his mum busied herself. His dad was checking his phone. Maya leaned forward, then ruffled Jeremy's jet-black hair, so it looked even more of a mess.

"How's the head, baby brother?"

"Better if you left me alone. Anyway, what are you doing here? Aren't you supposed to be overseeing your minions at the restaurant?"

"No, I'm here to see Dad, about an idea I have."

Jeremy suddenly realised he hadn't got any will to live, then dropped his head onto his crossed arms and groaned.

"Sleep little baby! Save your strength for the old woman in your life!"

Into his arms he mumbled, "There's more than one."

Maya jumped onto these nearly intelligible words.

"Hah! So, who's the other woman? Is she old too?"

Maya waited a second.

"I won't leave you in peace unless you deliver the goods!"

"Arghhh! Why did I open my big mouth?"

"Because if you didn't, I would find out anyway and punish you more!"

Jeremy turned his head, opened half an eye, and whispered, "Her name's Sofia, she's beautiful."

Maya reached over, smoothed over his hair.

"Rest little one, your secret's safe with me."

Maya and her father left the room to talk, followed by her stepmother. Jeremy then went back to bed.

He recovered enough to slouch around the house for the rest of the day. A few text messages came back and forth from Sofia, most of which were about Cecilia going home. Between them, there was the odd text that was like searching fingers, trying to find the sweet spot in their burgeoning relationship.

By the time the evening came, Jeremy was comatose, but quite hungry. He was surprised to find Maya had stayed and was eager to know what was going on. Being a Saturday night, neither Mum nor Dad were cooking. It was traditional that they had a takeaway. A relaxed atmosphere prevailed around the house. One of Dad's taxi drivers had been asked to collect it from the best Thai takeaway in the town. It wasn't till they were eating that Jeremy posed the question.

"So, what's happening? Why the big meeting?"

"There's nothing big about it," said Maya, it's just a proposal I was making to Dad."

"Ok, let's hear it then, unless it's a secret. It must be something significant, because at no time can I remember you having a whole Saturday night off from the restaurant."

"I asked Dad for a loan to start me up on my own. I have some money, but not enough to get me what I need."

Straight away, Jeremy raised his hand, then high fived Maya.

"Yeah, good move May!"

She immediately high fived him back. There were smiles on all their faces.

"I'm guessing Dad agreed."

Jeremy looked at his dad, who smiled.

"To be honest, there was no question," he said, "Maya produced a perfect business plan."

Maya had a satisfied look on her face, which said it all.

"So, what are you going to do, sell vacuum cleaners door to door?"

Maya whacked him in a friendly way across the shoulders.

"No, I'm starting a brothel on the other side of town!"

A look of disapproval came over their parents' faces, meanwhile Maya and Jeremy started laughing.

"Have you talked to Kazi about it?" asked Jeremy. "Perhaps he might like to invest in you. After all, he's making lots of money."

"No! I know he's our elder brother and wise in the way of business, but he's also a pain in the arse. He's too controlling and his beliefs are miles away from mine. You know what he's like. Whereas Dad just looked at my plan, thought about it, then said yes."

"Tell Jeremy what you're going to do," said their mum.

Maya told Jeremy about the old marketplace in the town, which had lain empty for years. A company had bought it with an idea to turn it into a specialised street market. The idea would include a few select restaurants, that would be in the centre of the improved building. The restaurants would sell food from all around the world, north, south, east, west.

"My food would be from the east, obviously."

As she told him, he could see the excitement on her face, which made Jeremy overjoyed for her. She then listed the different types of food that would be on her menu. Maya glazed over, lost in the dream of it.

"Have you packed in your job at the restaurant?" Jeremy asked.

"I'm giving my notice shortly. I want to be hands-on from the start. I'm willing to do anything, to get it going as soon as possible."

More high fives passed between them, even with their mum and dad. Jeremy added himself to her workforce if she needed it.

Jeremy went to bed in a calm and peaceful way. So different from the night before, when he'd been drunk as a lord. He lay in his bed. Sofia came into his mind. Knowing she was on a night shift, he sent her a text.

Thought of you before I closed my eyes xx

He did think he might be going too far, but he didn't care. As he dropped off to sleep, he hoped a mutual feeling between them might rise above any self-doubt.

The next morning, he promised himself that he would research Cecilia Walters. Like a proper journalist would do. He wasn't going to be wishy-washy about it, he wanted to deal in facts. To help him along the way, he promised himself to watch a couple of her films in the afternoon.

Kazi came around at lunchtime with his wife and five children. He was an importer and exporter of material from India, saris being his main imported item. He was a tall man with an imposing personality, with which he looked down on Maya and Jeremy. His problem with Maya was he wanted her to marry a nice Asian man, his best friend. As far as Jeremy was concerned, Kazi saw him as a half-blood. Over the years, Jeremy had got used to it and had risen above Kazi's beliefs.

Sidu, being the father of them all, had obviously softened his feelings on religion, whereas Kazi had very strong beliefs. His father chose to sit on the fence to keep control of everyone. The children ran around in the garden, that was plenty big enough, as the adults talked. It wasn't long before Maya's plans emerged, to which Kazi frowned.

"I've a good friend who would make you a good husband. He is in a lucrative job. You could settle down and have children."

"Not this again, Kazi," said Maya, "I'm not like you. I don't believe what you believe. I think women are something in their own right, not just baby machines."

Kazi's wife, Sarita, smiled broadly. Kazi saw her and looked cross.

"Look, you should follow Sarita! She knows her place!"

Sarita dipped her head in respect.

"Oh, my God, Kazi!" said Maya, "You're something out of the dark ages!"

"Stop it! Stop it now!" said Sidu, "Behave yourselves! This is a respectful family day! Hold your tongues!"

The TV was on in the living-room. Jeremy had sat down to watch a film. His mum was putting away the crockery from the dishwasher. His dad was catching up on paperwork. Jeremy had his feet up, happy that Kazi had left with his wife and children. Not that he didn't like children. He just liked the peace when they were not there.

He'd searched the internet for more Cecilia Walters films. He was happy. He had several films, as well as TV series, ready to consume for research purposes. The first was another Agatha Christie, which didn't impress him one bit but, as always,

Cecilia was first class. One thing was for sure, her beauty equalled her acting ability. Later he was joined by his mum, dad, and Maya who had just had a long hot bath. None of them minded the early version of Silent Witness they were watching. Of course, they were intrigued to see how Cecilia Walters had looked and performed, all those years ago. Two programmes went by, snacks and toilet breaks in between. At nine o'clock they were all crimed out, but also impressed at Cecilia's performances. Mum and dad went to bed. On the whole, they all saw it as a good day.

Maya sat idly on her phone, finding her way through her social media pages, while Jeremy sent texts back and forth to Sofia. Jeremy stopped and looked at Maya.

"When do you think you will have the food venue up and running?"

She pondered the question, her legs snuggled under a comfort blanket.

"Six weeks! I'll have to get my head down and work hard."

"Well, if you need any help here and there, you can count on me."

He had already said he would, but now he really meant it.

Maya reached across, wrapped her arms around Jeremy.

"Aww, thanks, Jez."

"Mind you, I'm not much good at DIY, being organised, or even that reliable," he laughed.

She smiled.

"It's wonderful that you offered, but I know that's not true! You know your way around a hammer. Your bedroom is tidier than mine and you've never let me down."

"Shit," said Jeremy, "there's me thinking I was just sounding helpful. Not sure I was volunteering to hold your hand!"

Maya stared at him, then proceeded to pounce on him and tickled him till he couldn't breathe.

"Ok, ok! I give in, I'm serious, I'll help."

Jeremy went to bed. He was enjoying having Maya back home. It was like being a little kid again.

Jeremy slipped in and out of sleep, his mind taken over by events. It seemed that in such a short time, his world was full of things to think about.

Next morning, he yawned his way to the kitchen, the house being silent as the grave. It would seem that everyone had upped and left him to his own devices. It was just past eight. He felt like he had missed the best part of the day.

He turned on the TV, watched the news with subtitles, then plugged in his smart speaker. For the next half-hour, he had a mixture of the latest pop music and old classics. While eating cereal and toast, he honed his dance moves on the kitchen floor. The music was so loud, he nearly had a heart attack when his mum suddenly appeared in the kitchen. He quickly closed down the speaker, then waved sheepishly to his mum.

"You and Maya seem so much happier than I can ever remember, there must be love in the air?"

"Er, yes Mum. It's because we love you and Dad so much."

She shook her head.

"There are things you're not telling me, my baby."

The endearment meant that she was after morsels of truth. He knew it was hard to resist his mum's searching questions. So, he turned up the music, moved over to her then sang along. He held her round the waist, then spun her around to the beat. Within a few minutes, the song finished. Jeremy left the room leaving his mum dizzy and none the wiser.

Jeremy went to the offices of the local newspaper to see the editor. He didn't really have a boss, but he did have to provide stories to make an income for himself. He wasn't alone, there were others like him, but he liked to think he had an edge over them. Especially now, because he thought he had an exclusive. His thoughts were to sell Cecilia's short story to his editor, then keep the bigger one for himself. The only problem being, this was all in his head. He couldn't be absolutely certain Cecilia Walters would continue to employ him as her biographer. He just had the feeling she might do.

17.

Jeremy sat in the office opposite his editor, John Scotland, a burly man with well-worn features and rugby player's ears. A character that you could imagine might have spent time in a Glasgow bar, a scrap yard, or a boxing ring. The truth was, he was brought up on a farm. Had a soft southwest accent and wouldn't hurt a fly. His weapon of choice was telling staff, or people like Jeremy, that he was giving them the moon. In truth, they usually ended up with some stale cheese and no job to speak of. Such was the way of the newspaper business.

"Jeremy, how long have you been working for us?"

"It's been about two and half years now."

 "I could have sworn it was a lot longer."

For some reason Jeremy was feeling nervous. Even though he knew John's large bulk was mostly harmless, he was sure his tongue was going to hurt him more.

"The thing is......"

Jeremy was only a young man, but he had been around long enough to know that those three words never preceded good news.

"The thing is all of our self-employed journalists are going to get less for their stories. It would seem that we need more advertising, because it pays more money than the news does. Until we can get more, someone has to suffer. So, I'm getting each one of you in to let you know."

Jeremy sat staring at John Scotland, as he prowled around the office. Jeremy imagined that he looked somewhat like a lion who had lost his mate, or maybe he had eaten his mate. Jeremy couldn't be absolutely certain. He felt this was far worse for John than for him. After all, there were other newspapers.

Trouble was they were in bigger cities.

Jeremy had survived on the small income that came in from covering stories for the newspaper. He had even had the odd story on local TV, but this was a bit of a shock to his system. Especially as he thought he had one of the best stories he had ever had within his grasp.

"I've got a great story at the moment," said Jeremy.

John planted his large bulk on his chair. Jeremy could have sworn he heard the chair say, *Please no!* Maybe it was just his imagination.

"Go on."

"It's about a famous actress who is suffering from the results of long Covid."

John stopped him, before he could add anymore.

"No, we don't want any more Covid stories, unless you can track down the bastard who started it all. We need new stories. Different stories. I'll pay for nothing that involves Covid. People are as fed up with that as they are with Boris fucking Johnson."

Jeremy felt deflated. Now he was only going to get a pittance for anything he submitted. The thing was in his hands. He probably had the best story ever.

He left the newspaper offices, looking for solace. He headed for a café in the town, where he knew he could find like-minded journalists. The café was a haunt for many who needed to pass the time of day and fill up on a fry-up. In the corner sat two other journalists that Jeremy worked with. He also considered them friends. They both looked unhappy.

"Gail! Tony!"

He raised his hand in a high five, they reciprocated.

"You've had the chat with big John," said Tony.

Jeremy nodded, then asked,

"What do you think?"

Tony sipped his coffee, as Gail spoke.

"Maybe it's time for retraining. This business has become so computerised. I'm waiting for the robot to come in the door and vacuum us away. I've got two kids who want to go to university, a husband who's happier with a pint in his hand, rather than mine. To top it all, I'm on reduced income as from today."

"You're lucky," said Tony, "my wife has gone, taken the kids, and life's shit in a bed sit."

Jeremy had nothing to complain about. He was living at home, knew his options were way better than either of theirs. He sympathised with them, as they all shared the hard world that they were trying to report on.

The café had the customary steamed-up windows, with a constant smell of something frying. Not long after, they all tucked into bacon sandwiches, which Jeremy paid for.

"Have either of you," he asked, "ever attempted to write a book?"

They both laughed.

"Several," said Gail, "One half-finished, which I abandoned, because my husband now sleeps in the spare room, where I was writing it. It's not for the faint hearted, or someone with hardly any time in the day."

Jeremy looked at Gail. She was world weary. She did look after herself and, in some ways, he found her attractive, but she needed some TLC. She had that hungry look on her face, a look that was common to journalists. One that said *talk to me, I need to know what you're thinking, I want your story.* Tony was the same. He did look like he was doing better. Being on his own seemed to suit him. It had given him the space he needed to concentrate on doing other things.

"I'm nearing the end of a book."

Jeremy and Gail looked at him in surprise.

"What's it about, Tone?" Jeremy asked.

Tony hesitated. It wasn't in his mind to share a plot with anyone, knowing a good idea could be stolen. Thinking maybe this was just paranoia, he gave them a gist of what it was about. "A detective who is finding it difficult to crack a case, discovers this young autistic man who saw the crime, but no-one believes him. The detective, who has all the old world values of an ageing policeman, becomes almost like a father figure to him. The crime then gets solved. On the back of that, the detective discovers, after working with the young man, that he is mind full of facts and figures. So, then, he secretly employs him to help solve other cases. To cut a long story short, it becomes a partnership that works.

As you can imagine this is seen as a breakthrough for people with a certain gift. Of course, there is resentment in the police force for using such a person, but results matter."

Jeremy and Gail looked at Tony, then they lifted their coffee cups up to him.

"You're a dark horse, Tone," said Gail, "you've said nothing about this before."

"I guess I just got my head down, now I'm on my own. I sent the first few chapters off to a few, sorry, a lot of publishers."

Jeremy and Gail looked dumbfounded.

"If it wasn't so fucking early, I'd say let's go for a drink,"
Said, Gail.

"I've got a story," said Jeremy. "It's not much at the moment, but I think there's something in it. Saying that, the big man wasn't interested."

Jeremy told them briefly about Cecilia Walters. They both knew of her and, to their credit, both Gail and Tony encouraged him to pursue the story. More importantly, neither of them thought she was dead. As he left the café, Jeremy had a text.

Hi Jeremy, how is your day going? I've just finished my shift. Do you fancy some lunch somewhere? Sofia xx

The two kisses placed after the text brightened his day.

Two hours later, Jeremy met Sofia at an Italian restaurant in town. They greeted each other outside. Jeremy kissed Sofia on each cheek, just before they sat down at a little table outside.

"I love watching people," she said, "it's so therapeutic, good for the heart rate."

"Is that a medical fact?" he asked.

She laughed and said, "I don't know, but I know it relaxes me."

"It must be, because yours is a stressful job," he said.

"No more than anyone else's. Don't you think yours is? I mean, trying to find stories to write about for the papers, must be very hard work and stressful."

They smiled at each other. A waitress took their order, then, not long after, came back with a couple of glasses of wine.

"Normally, I'd forgo wine until the evening," said Sofia, "but I need a drink. A man in his fifties died this morning. He'd been suffering with a long Covid condition. His heart just gave up."

"I'm sorry. It must be difficult when you lose people like that. It's strange, because I've been looking for stories concerning the Coronavirus, but my editor has said he doesn't want any more."

"All the more reason why you should pursue Cecilia Walters. She's far more interesting."

"Yes, but he doesn't want that either."

"You mean, he doesn't want a story about an amazing actress like Cecilia?"

Jeremy looked thoughtful.

"Maybe I didn't sell it very well to my boss."

Sofia smiled.

"I think I know why!"

"Why?"

"Because you can see a bigger picture, that you want to put your name to."

This comforted Jeremy. That was the way he felt about it.

"Have you been in touch with her yet?" she asked.

The question just hung there. It was obvious that he should have communicated with her, but for some reason, he'd thought she would have contacted him.

"I don't think for one second, Jeremy, that you will hear from Cecilia."

He then felt like a fool. His journalist natural instincts seemed to have come amiss.

"Shit, you're right! I just naturally assumed she would call me when she felt she was able to talk."

"Trouble is," said Sofia, "I'm not sure she will ever be well enough. Unless she makes a remarkable recovery."

He thanked her for her professional opinion about Cecilia. They settled into an everyday conversation and enjoyed their time together like old friends or even lovers. There was a reluctance in the air. It seemed as if neither of them wanted to go, even though both of them had things to do.

"When can I see you again for a proper date?" Jeremy asked.

"You mean this wasn't a proper date? There's me thinking we might get married next week!"

He laughed. She looked serious. It would seem that Jeremy hadn't quite got the feel for Sofia's sense of humour yet. They shared the joke. Jeremy wasn't certain about Sofia, but he could feel a heightened expectation rushing through his veins.

"Anytime I'm not on a night shift! How about Friday?"

They shared kisses as they parted. Both of them walked away, looking back over their shoulders, sharing a wave, as they disappeared into the lunchtime crowds.

18.

Jeremy acquired Cecilia's address, as well as her phone number. He drove to a once sophisticated part of town, that still had many ageing properties. Even so, it was still a nice place to live. Jeremy parked his car outside a 1920s Odeon style apartment house. It looked impressive. Most of the ornate features were intact and well maintained. A six-foot topiary hedge was wrapped around the house and garden, which was imposing. The two-storey property was divided into four apartments. Cecilia's was on the right-hand side as you looked at it, on the second floor. The main entrance to the four apartments was at the centre of the building, with a wonderful ornate door. Above it was a hazy-looking sun made from stained glass, with fields, hills and rivers weaving through it. He buzzed the bell by Cecilia's name. He did it several times before she answered.

"Hello, who is it?"

Jeremy immediately recognised Cecilia's voice.

"Hello, Cecilia, it's Jeremy."

A moment or two hung there, as Jeremy looked out over the garden. He wasn't a gardener, but he was sure someone loved to keep this place neat and tidy.

"Jeremy, my dear! Come up!"

As he set foot in the hall of the building, the light from the stained-glass window adorned the large reception area. He looked up at it; it was like a lost era had been awoken especially for him. His heart felt lifted. His mind went back to when he had visited the museum in the city as a child. The smell of polished wood and the past permeated his thoughts. The whole property was like walking back into the nineteen twenties. The tiles on the floor were a beautiful mosaic of the era. The lighting was pure Art Deco.

He made his way up the stairs, where prints by Klimt had been hung on the walls. Jeremy stood outside the door, then knocked. After a suitable pause, Cecilia opened the door. Even though she was not well, Cecilia looked divine. She was wearing a dressing-gown with many flowers embroidered upon it. On her head, she wore a multicoloured silk scarf, with a large feather sticking out of it, which mesmerised him, because it shimmered as she moved.

"I was wondering when you might appear, Jeremy. Welcome to my queendom. It's not much, but it's at the heart of what I am." She said it in a regal way, as she gestured to him to enter her abode.

"I'm sorry, I wasn't sure if I should just turn up or make an appointment."

"It's of no consequence. You are here now and I'm glad to see you."

This expectation gladdened Jeremy, because he wasn't sure how he was supposed to act in the circumstances. He stood in the hallway, which was like a small gallery. The walls were adorned by photographs. Cecilia was present in most of them, along with other actors and signatories. A few in particular caught his eye. He couldn't help it; he was drawn to them, like a butterfly to a flower.

"I see you have an artistic soul, Jeremy."

Four photographs in black and white stood out.

"These are amazing, they are so stark, but somehow have a warmth as well. Are they of somewhere local to here?"

"Yes they were taken just outside the city, in the country along the canal."

"More than anything," he said, "they seem lonely."

She smiled.

"Jeremy, come in! I think that you and I have a lot to talk about."

Her warm words comforted Jeremy, as his nerves settled. Cecilia guided him into the living room. He followed her through to a large open space, which immediately took Jeremy's breath. He stood, glued to the floor, as he took it all in. Nearly every fragment of wall had a piece of art or a photograph upon it. He was no connoisseur, but he knew when something was original and when it was not. He was immediately drawn to an oil painting in a small frame.

"Is this an original Lowry?"

"Why, yes, of course!"

It was a painting of a man walking, his head down, a cloth cap on his head, his hands thrust into his coat pockets. A warehouse was in the background. In the near distance, a small boy was playing with a dog.

"Amazing!" Jeremy said. "How did you come by it!"

She stood by him, looking at it, almost as if it was for the first time. She stared into it.

"I was in a play in Sunderland. In those days, I would spend all my free time looking at, and buying, art. I saw this in a little shop. It was so gloriously simple, but it told a big story. So, I bought it. To be honest, it wasn't very much money in today's terms, like the rest of the art in this room. Sometimes, I would buy a piece of art, not thinking about my own welfare. In those days, like now, it was important to look after your figure, so I ate very little."

He walked around the room. Just like the rest of the house the apartment was steeped in 1920s style. One after another, paintings, drawings, even pastels adorned the walls. There was something they all had in common; they were somewhat incomplete, or the artist had stopped before they were spoilt. This gave a great variety to the whole collection, but also gave an insight into the mind of Cecilia.

"Would you like something to drink?" she asked.

Jeremy nodded. He was so caught up in the ambience of the whole property, that he'd almost forgotten why he was there. She left the room via a glass-panelled illuminated door, which had flowers curving this way, then that way, in many colours. The door she left ajar, as she made some tea. He continued to look at the paintings. As he did so, he asked questions.

"How long have you lived here?"

"Since the late 1970s. I bought it on the back of a big film, one of the first I starred in."

Among the paintings and photographs, he could feel her history. It was almost like floating on a cloud of nostalgia.

"Does it worry you that you have all this valuable artwork around you?"

She brought the tea in. She didn't seem to have any airs or graces, unlike when he'd first met her at the hospital. She was, without doubt, more comfortable in her own surroundings.

"Why? Why should I worry?"

"Because it all must be worth a small, maybe even a large fortune."

She contemplated the question and knew it to be true.

"I suppose to me, they are worth what I paid for them, which, looking back, was not a lot at the time. They are my friends. I accumulated these because it's easier for me to talk to a piece of art, than to a person."

Jeremy felt saddened by these words, his curiosity deepened even more.

"Before we go any further, Jeremy, you know I am not well. Today is the best I've felt in months, but I know, from what the doctors have told me, that things could get much worse. So, I want to say a few things about my life. What's more, I want you to write them down."

He could feel a tingling sensation at the ends of his fingers. Like any writer worth his salt, this was music to his ears.

"First of all, there have to be ground rules. Only what I say can be used. Not too much fancy dancing with my words. If I feel unwell, leave me, don't pester me. I will get back to you. I do need to pace myself."

He had already found a place in his heart for Cecilia, even though she was nearly forty-five years older than him. He could even feel a physical attraction. It wouldn't be long before there was a mental attraction as well.

She poured the tea. Like everything else in the apartment, it was reminiscent of the era. The tea set mirrored it well, being one by Clarice Cliff. As he sat there, he felt as if he had been transported back in time. He took care not to act like a caveman; he was more used to a mug than the best China. She looked on, then smiled. Even though she had already started to tell him about her past life, he didn't want to take anything for granted. However, he knew if she trusted him with her life story, he was sure he would do a great job. So, for both of them, it was win, win. Cecilia then seemed to slip into an easy pose, as Jeremy got out his notebook and a new Dictaphone.

19.

"Jeremy, do you know of the theatrical masks?"

He thought about it for a moment.

"Yes, I do. Do they use something like that on the BAFTA award?"

She looked rueful.

"Yes, I'm aware of the BAFTAs. I was nominated several times. I have never won one."

She seemed tetchy as she said it.

"The masks or muses I'm referring to, go way back to the Greeks. The sad face represents tragedy, the name being Melpomene. The happy or comedy face was Thalia. They were the daughters of Zeus. So as not to get too bogged down in all the symbolism, this is where I start my story. Actors are constantly wearing masks, to show their ability to educate, explain but, mostly, to entertain."

He listened, then tried to digest what she had said. He said nothing. Like before, he thought it better to let her flow. She seemed to gather herself, as if she was trying to dig deeper and get something off her chest.

"Remember, then, not everything you hear or see is what it appears to be. Sometimes bigger things are going on behind the masks we wear. To laugh or cry, a mask can hide them both. That applies to us all."

Because his relationship with Cecilia was still in its infancy, he took in the words she had delivered, then felt excited to be in her illustrious presence.

"As I've already informed you, Jeremy," said Cecilia, "my childhood was confined to a back-to-back slum, the best that money could rent in the fifties. Two rooms with not enough room to swing a cat. That expression stuck with me as I got older. Why would anyone want to swing a cat in a room? I had no idea why."

She paused. Jeremy noted that she became very animated when something got under her skin, which in itself was not unusual but, in some ways, it became a performance piece all on its own. She continued.

"As I grew up, I understood words are like a painting. They are a flourish to the tongue to illuminate life. As I said before, my mother took in washing. It was everywhere. On a good day, the little yard we had would be like a sailing ship, white sheets flapping in the wind. It was so hard for my mother. She wanted things for me, but spare money was almost impossible to come by. She did her best to educate me, teaching me to read and write, just enough to get me by."

Jeremy stopped her.

"You have spoken about your father, but do you remember anything good about him?"

"The only positive thing that I can remember is that on the night I was born, my mother said he treated me like a princess. I am not sure exactly what she meant by that. I can only assume that he wasn't drunk, for once in his life. She told me I was no bigger than a couple of bags of sugar. The midwife told her to pray for me. Religion has never been a strong point in my life, but I think she had her prayers answered, at the time. As I've already said my father fell in a river and died. My mother got over it."

He could see the emotion in her eyes. She was near to tears. Stoically she continued.

"As I've already said, I started school late. Fortunately, even though I was behind, with the help of a wonderful teacher, Mrs Aberdare, I eventually caught up. My mother then suddenly died, just when things started to look better for us both. Her health had deteriorated over the years, because of all her hard work keeping us both alive. The washing in the end killed her. She developed pneumonia. In a matter of weeks, she was gone."

She stopped for a moment, as the emotions came to the surface. He wanted to say something, but she quickly pulled herself together.

"At thirteen, Mrs Aberdare, who I had become very close to, gave me private lessons at her home. I was in care with the local authority, so school was the centre of my being. I wanted to learn. I was hungry for knowledge. It seemed I had so much to catch up on."

She stopped again and looked into Jeremy's eyes.

"One thing is for certain. Whoever your parents are, eventually, you have to make your way. However, like them, you are at the mercy of the gods. The throw of a dice, or the turn of a card. For me, it was as humble as it gets, but I'm all the more proud of my background.

A wonderful thing then happened. Mr and Mrs Aberdare asked me if I wanted to live with them. I think, by this time, they saw me as the child they could never have, having been told they wouldn't be able to become parents.

As you can imagine, I said yes. I loved it. It changed my world. Not long after, they adopted me. I had my room with pretty wallpaper, a wardrobe, and a desk. The simple things were like treasures to me. What's more, I felt spoilt. The day I moved in, it was like a new page had been turned in my life. The amazing thing was that they encouraged me to join things, to broaden my horizons. It was a wonderful time. They encouraged me to join an amateur dramatics club, which was everything I'd ever wanted. I fell in love with books. I consumed them like the air I breathed. Years passed quickly. When I left school, I got an office job, typing. At that time, women found it very difficult to get good, rewarding employment. Even if they were very well-educated. Philomena Aberdare had worked hard to give me a good education, but not enough to go any further, so I left school when I was fifteen. The truth was my true love was acting. So, every moment I had, I spent pretending to be someone else. Whether it was in the mirror or just being with other people, my time was taken up learning to act. By the time I was eighteen, I was part of an amateur theatre group, my head full of literature. Actors were where my attention was. About this time, I struck up a friendship with a girl called Imogen. She was what people called a wild child. I was her sidekick. Somehow, we had a perfect friendship. I was the rock and she was blowing in the wind. I loved her, we were the best of friends. We went to concerts, we saw the Beatles, the Stones, anyone who was touring the country. Of course, our minds were on the theatre as well. We managed to get bit parts in plays, even pantomime, at the theatre in the city. Mostly, we worked backstage, painting sets, and moving them around. It was sheer unadulterated fun! Of course, Imogen and I wanted more."

She paused. She looked flushed and excited, the youthful exuberance in her words had scooped her up and then cradled her in her memories. She gazed into the distance, looking through him as if he wasn't there.

"It was a time of such great happiness, as well as tragedy."

"In what way was there tragedy?" he asked.

"There were auditions for parts in a new play coming to our theatre. We were asked if we would like to have a go. Not speaking parts, a maid, or a butler, that sort of thing. We had learnt from rumours, that the director of this play was a bit of a dirty old man. These were words they used in those days. Although we were young, we were wise to such things going on.

On the day of the audition, there were a few of us waiting. One by one, we were interviewed for a part. Imogen went in. After what seemed like a long time, she ran out crying, then left the theatre. I ran after her but couldn't catch her. Imogen was beautiful and she had curves in all the right places, so she was attractive in more ways than one. Straight away, rumours went around the theatre, but the whole thing was covered up. The director left before anything could be exposed. His deputy stepped in to continue the auditions. I was with Imogen for days after. She suddenly changed. She became quiet, introverted. Imogen had always been eccentric and wild but, inwardly, she was as innocent as the snow. After some time, she told me that he'd tried to rape her. What's more, this director had told her unless she had sex with him, she would never work in the theatre again. Her outward personality led him to assume she was easy prey. The man had his card marked. There was a long list of people he had tried to abuse."

Cecilia stopped. Her earlier beautiful memories had been blown away by those of Imogen. She sat taking small breaths, as Jeremy went to make some tea.

"The tragedy of life is not death but what we let die inside us while we live. Norman Cousins"

She quoted the words, as Jeremy stood in the kitchen making the tea. She continued, as he brought the tea in.

"From that day on, Imogen was never the same. Something died inside her. She retreated into her world. I did my best to try and take her out of herself, but she stonewalled me, refusing to even see me. These days she would have had help, but then she just stayed at home with her mum and dad, and then we lost touch.

"How did that make you feel?"

"I was devastated. She was my best friend, but I had to carry on, play the part, whatever it may be.

About a year later, her mother and father contacted me, to say Imogen had taken her own life. I can't even describe how it affected me. At her funeral, I promised myself that, one day, I would get revenge for Imogen."

Cecilia was exhausted. Jeremy knew it. The conversation slipped from the sad to the necessary, as Jeremy realised that Cecilia was not looking after herself.

"Do you like curry?" he asked.

"As a matter of fact, yes."

"I don't think you're eating properly. Next time I come, I'll bring some of my dad's. It's superb! You'll love it."
She smiled. He smiled. They both felt as if something had been done. So, he left her to rest, promising to come back the next day.

20.

It wasn't long before Jeremy was home. It was late afternoon. He was full of optimism, singing along to a C.D. player in his mum and dad's kitchen. In the middle of making a plain crisp sandwich, he heard a voice calling,

"Someone's in a good mood! Not sure about the song though!"

He was singing along to an ABBA song badly, the words completely mismatching the music. He was oblivious to her comments and continued to sing. Maya came in from the hall and stood in front of him, as his body swayed from side to side. He caught her eye, she stared at him, her hands on her hips. She laughed. He was unfazed by her being there, smiled at her, picked up his sandwich, and then started singing to it loudly. It was as if it was a microphone. He took a big bite out of it. Crisps fell onto the countertop. Swallowing quickly, he carried on singing. Maya went round to his side of the counter. She turned up the music and then joined in with him, singing joyously. She picked up the other half of the crisp sandwich and then they sang together in crisp harmony. A few ABBA moves were mocked as they sang. After the track ended, Maya realised it was a golden hits album that belonged to their mum. Another track followed. The music was so loud that they never heard their mum come in through the front door. She watched them in the throes of their routine, then decided to join in.

The three of them moved around the kitchen, singing and dancing to the music. When they stopped and the enjoyment of the moment settled down....

"What the..." said their mum, "there are bloody crisps everywhere!"

"Wasn't me," said Maya, "it was Jeremy."

A sibling standoff took place, as Maya turned and exited the room, laughing as she went.

Later on, they sat around the dining table talking about their day. Maya told them about working at the marketplace on the new restaurant idea. She was excited by it and wanted them to know how good it was. This was followed by Jeremy, who told them about Cecilia and the book he was going to write. As days go, it wasn't a bad one.

In his bedroom, Jeremy took to texting Sofia. His mind was consumed by how things had changed in just a short time. Because she was on a shift, he guessed she wouldn't answer until the next day. However, within minutes she texted back.

That's great news about Cecilia! Well done for going to see her. I'm sure she'll have lots to tell you about her life. You must fill me in with the juicy bits. xx

Jeremy felt uneasy. He wasn't sure he wanted to divulge anything to anyone about Cecilia. At least not until he had finished the book. He texted back to Sofia.

That would be telling, wouldn't it? Anyway, nothing of any consequence, as yet. XX

The morning came with a song from ABBA still residing in Jeremy's head from the day before. Over and over, he sang it. After trying to eradicate it from his thoughts while taking a pee, he made his way downstairs. As usual, his dad was out at work. He couldn't help thinking his dad worked more in retirement than he ever did before. These thoughts formed questions in his mind, almost like fine dust, to be wiped away, to make room for more important dust later on.

As he was eating his cereal, the music came back into his head. *Knowing me, knowing you, aha,* He felt irritated by the song, as it seemed to have permeated his whole being. For a second or two, he thought he must write a piece about songs that get stuck somewhere in the far reaches of the brain. Maya came into the room. She heard him singing the song, then started laughing.

"Oh, for fuck's sake," he said, "I can't get that tune out of my head!"

"I'm the same, only it's Dancing Queen! I can't tell you how many times I've tried not to sing that this morning!"

"Coffee?"

"Yes please, put it in my to-go cup."

Maya was dressed and ready to leave.

"What are you doing today?" Jeremy asked.

"Bank manager first with Dad to sort some money out, then back at the market."

She sidled up to him, putting her arm over his shoulder.

"I was wondering…?"

"I've got no money," he said, "I'm brassic, broke, zilch!"

"What I want from you is far more important to me."

"No, my time is taken up from now till next Christmas."

It wasn't. He had guessed what she wanted, but it was in his nature to tease her as she did him. She looked at him with her sad cat's eyes.

"OK, you know I promised to help anyway, just for a few hours later on. I need to keep Cecilia happy. She may be my only income for the next few months. That's if she has any money and the energy."

"I might be able to employ you soon," she interrupted, "when the market restaurant is up and running."

He looked at Maya with disbelief written all over his face.

"Can you honestly see me as a waiter, running around after annoying kids and pensioners all day?"

"I was hoping you'd wash the dishes and clean the floors."

The words hung there for a second, as she then started singing.

"*Knowing me, knowing you, aha.*"

She held onto the last note, as she quickly escaped the room. All she could hear was,

"You're a total arse, Maya!"

It was mid-morning. Jeremy was ready to go when his mum came in. She had been to his dad's offices to do a few invoices. She was strictly part-time now but, like Sidu, seemed to be spending more time working than being at home. Her life now revolved around the house, the garden, and playing her part in the extended family. Strictly speaking, Jeremy was her only child, but Maya had a big place in her heart. As far as Kazi was concerned, the jury was out. Up to now, they had never fallen out.

"How is Cecilia, Jeremy?" asked his mum.

Jeremy loved it when he and his mum had these moments. It was special. They talked about their feelings. She was aware that Jeremy had something or someone else on his mind, that he was keeping a secret.

"Cecilia's good. It's a slow process, because she has been so ill. Judging by yesterday's standard, I could tell she has one hell of a story to tell!"

"Anything else you want to talk about?" she asked.

"No, that's all I can think of."

She put her hand on his.

"You know you can always talk to me about anything."

For a moment, Jeremy felt that his mum was asking searching questions that he didn't want to answer.

"What are you asking, Mum?"

"Nothing, just interested to see if my only true son is emotionally entangled with someone of the opposite sex."

He didn't put up much of a fight.

"Alright, alright, I met a girl called Sofia. We had a meal together. She's a nurse, she was a big help in establishing my involvement with Cecilia."

He said it like it wanted to be said. In many ways, he was relieved, as it was always impossible to keep secrets from her. A warm hug followed. He felt like a child again, but he was happy with that. It made him feel good inside. He was in his mid-twenties, a man of the world in many ways, but there was nothing quite like an embrace from his mum.

21.

Jeremy made his way across town to where Cecilia lived. It was one o'clock by the time he arrived at her apartment. She had given him a pass key to get in the main house entrance. He knocked on the apartment door. It was a while before she answered.

"Welcome, Jeremy!"

She guided him into the living room. She was wearing a robe that was a patchwork of many colours, stunning to the eye. She turned, then looked into his eyes, taking his hands in hers.

"Let's take a journey to a far-off place! Explore different worlds! There will be gardens of burgeoning fantastic flowers! Beautiful valleys! Velvet green hills. We will stare at the stars! New skies! New suns! Galaxies!"

The moment was almost surreal. As he stared at her, he thought she looked otherworldly. At that moment, he thought, what was she on, had she been drinking or taking drugs? However, he knew this was her, the actor. The eccentric behaviour was in her blood.

"Ok, but can you tell me where you got this amazing gown from first?

She scooped the hem away from her feet.

"This old thing? It was a costume I wore in a fantasy film. It took months for the wardrobe department to embroider. It's original, but the film was a flop, although I like to think my part in it was a triumph."

She paraded along the room as if it were a fashion house. The moment had passed. Her wish to leave, to go to another celestial plain, was on hold.

"Let's say I had an understanding with the costume

department. The film had lost so much money, they sold off everything, for a song."

He could tell that Cecilia was feeling better. Maybe, it was the medication or the fact she was telling someone about her life. Whatever it was, it was fine by him.

"Before we start," he said, "I have something for you."

"A bearer of gifts! Where is your chariot, kind sir, that has them?"

Jeremy was happy to be her audience. After all, she was in her element. He passed her a plastic container.

"It's one of my dad's curries. I'm sure you'll love it!"

She held it, stared at it, then placed it to one side.

"Please thank him for me, I am truly grateful!"

There was an air of politeness in her words, but he could see she was expecting something a little more exciting.

Before they got down to talking about her life, there was a process for setting up the mood. It was tea. She liked to drink it, as did he; it seemed to settle the nerves. After which, she sat in her chair, then made herself comfortable.

"Where were we yesterday?"

"Imogen, your friend and the dirty director!"

"Yes, that was tragic in many ways. I'll never forget his name. Charles Farthing. His reputation went before him. He was feared by all, not just girls and women, but also boys and men. He had no preference. However, he did find a suitable end!"

She stopped. Jeremy was eager to know more.

"So, what happened to this Farthing guy and more importantly Imogen?"

"It's too much for me to go into at the moment. Let's move on! I will have more to say about that part of my life further down the road."

"Ok, where did you go after leaving your hometown?"

"I applied for backstage work at The Old Repertory Theatre in Birmingham, where I hoped I would hone my skills, learn more about acting and actors. As You Like It was the first production I remember. It was good for me, because I knew very little about Shakespeare. I was lucky, because I learned as I went along. Of course, then I fell in love with his work. I was a rookie, as the Americans would say. I was in my early twenties. All I can say is, that I was hungry and enthusiastic to know more, and it was the perfect place to do that. About this time was when I met a few of the now famous people in the theatrical world. Most of them were about to star in the celestial heaven that I wanted to be part of."

"Who were they?"

"Too many to mention here. Maybe another time."

She waved the thought away, as if there was an irritating fly in the room, then continued.

"The city was vibrant, in comparison to where I used to live. The theatre was amazing. The wonderful thing about it was everyone was so talented. All I hoped was that some of the talents would rub off on me. It wasn't long before I was able to do small parts on stage. They were never much, but it was a great learning curve. I was never formally trained. I auditioned for everything I could."

"What about your adoptive mum and dad? What did they think of you leaving home?"

"They encouraged and supported me, by sending money, so I could afford better lodgings. To be honest, after what happened to Imogen, I thought I would never feel happy again. However, it turned out to be a fabulous time to be alive."

Cecilia often seemed to glaze over, as she waxed lyrical about her life. Jeremy could see in her eyes that she held this time dearly next to her heart. He let her ponder her considerable past.

"It was about this time that I met Rupert Blaine."

"Rupert Blaine, the famous Shakespearean guy?" he asked.

"Yes, the very same!"

"Wow!"

Jeremy was aware of a few larger-than-life characters in the acting world. Rupert Blaine had starred in, as well as directed, many Hollywood blockbusters but, like Cecilia, in recent years, his star had faded somewhat. Still, the information peaked Jeremy's imagination, not that he wasn't already engrossed in Cecilia's life. Her eyes looked hazy, as she seemed to think of other things.

"I'm with the Japanese as far as taking tea is concerned!"

She strayed from her story.

"Japan is somewhere I would love to have gone to. The people, the country, the cherry trees!"

Jeremy's journey with Cecilia seemed all-encompassing.

"Maybe you'll go one day, when everything is back to normal," he said. She smiled.

"You're a good boy, a fine young man, but you know full well I'll never travel anywhere not while I'm plagued by these Covid symptoms. Anyway, I'm not a good traveller."

She sipped her tea slowly, then continued.

"I met Rupert when I first started working at The Old Rep. We just sort of hit it off. We were part of the company. It was like a meeting of minds. So much so, we generated towards each other, then we became an item. We were more or less the same age. He, however, had way more experience than I had, so he took me under his wing.

"I was staying in a little bedsit that wasn't the best. Also, it was quite a distance from the theatre. Rupert asked me if I would like to move in with him. It seemed a perfectly natural thing to do. He had these rooms at the top of a house, where there were lots of arty types residing. It was wonderful. It had a great atmosphere. We turned it into a sort of love nest. We used a small amount of money to decorate it, because it was so drab, uninspiring. After all, we were arty people too.

Before long we had papered, painted, and then put up posters in our small flat. Posters in the seventies were the poor man's works of art. I had this big poster of a daisy, which dominated one wall. One night, not long after we had re-decorated, Rupert sat next to me on the old sofa. We smoked some cannabis and drank some wine. I was a cannabis virgin, as well as a virgin, virgin."

She giggled to herself at the thought of it.

"The cannabis made me feel as if I was floating away above the clouds. Then it happened."

She stopped talking. He knew it was a seismic event that she was going to talk about. He waited patiently.

"Rupert slowly undressed me, although I was wearing little anyway. Up to this moment, we had only ever gone so far. It was as if we were both waiting for the time to be perfectly right. Don't get me wrong, I had had quite a few boyfriends who were eager to have sex with me. Sometimes the feelings were reciprocated, but until that moment, it had never seemed right. He was gentle, understanding, caring and loving. We just seemed to glide into the sexual moment, like ships gently nudging each other on a calm sea. For me, it was heavenly, a defining moment in my life. From that moment on, I thought why had I postponed this till now? All I remember, as the night ebbed away, was an album by Jose Feliciano. It was the one with California Dreaming on it, made famous by the Mamas and Papas. The whole thing was a beautiful dream. From that night on, Rupert nicknamed me Daisy after the poster we had made love under."

She looked into the distance. He could see she was living the moment all over again. It seemed an appropriate moment to stop. Maybe it was the stories, maybe the memories, but it was obvious to him that Cecilia looked so much better.

"Would you like some of the curry I brought you?"

She laughed at the suggestion.

"So, Jeremy, you are thinking I need something hot to continue talking about my sexual awakening?"

It had never occurred to him, but he saw the funny side of her statement, laughed with her, then with a reassuring sound in her voice, she continued,

"Yes, that would be nice!"

She had no microwave, so he found a saucepan and started to heat the curry. He asked if she had any rice. Twenty minutes later, they sat at her table in the living room, eating a delicious meal.

"My word!" she said, "This is beautiful! It reminds me of the marvellous Indian restaurants in Birmingham when I lived there. It was a time of discovery for the heart, the mind, the whole being."

Jeremy's face lit up. He was proud of his dad and his heritage.

"My dad's family had a restaurant back then, and some of them still do. When my dad came over from India, that's what he did. Trouble was, for him, he found it too claustrophobic. He told me he couldn't stand the heat of the kitchen. That's when he became a taxi driver for the company he now owns."

Two glasses of water sat on the table, and Cecilia raised hers.

"Good for him! Cheers!"

He picked up his glass.

"Cheers!"

Jeremy felt proud of his dad. Not that he wasn't already, but it made him think. It must have been a hard life back then.

After they had eaten, the afternoon slipped into a sort of apathy as both of them felt tired. Cecilia closed her eyes, then slipped off to sleep. Jeremy could feel his eyes going, so he sat up and made a few notes. Left to think, he decided to look at the art on Cecilia's walls. Before he did, he lay a colourful blanket across her. He noticed the door to Cecilia's bedroom was ajar, then nervously walked in. From the moment he was in there, he thought this is for research purposes only.

Curiosity is the centre of anyone's personality. Like the rest of the apartment, it was steeped in the nineteen twenties. Bedside lamps, wallpaper, hanging rails even the bed and wardrobes had that distinctive style. It somehow warmed his soul how perfectly kept it was. On one bedside table, there was a photograph of Cecilia and a man that must have been Rupert Blaine. On the other, there was a more recent one of them. On the walls hung beautifully framed watercolours. He could see the signature R. Blaine on a couple of them. Jeremy was no expert, but he thought they were quite accomplished. Above

Cecilia's bed were two more; they were nudes. He guessed they were of Cecilia. They were perfect. As he left the room, he felt awkward, almost like he had betrayed a confidence.

He went to the toilet, the only place that was not dedicated to the 1920s, then returned to the living room. Cecilia was still asleep. He decided to leave a note.

Dear Cecilia. I'll be back tomorrow. Love Jx

22.

On the way home, he had a text from Sofia asking how his day was. He decided to answer it later. There was another message from Maya, asking if he could come over when he was free.

I'm free now, see you soon. Xxxx

He made his way into town. The town centre always made him feel good. The marketplace in particular was receiving a well-deserved facelift. Like most towns and cities, it had been hit by a lack of investment. The continual obsession with shopping from home had made things even worse. The pandemic was the tin hat on the situation. Some people, however, by sheer endeavour, had weathered the storm. They were now seeing many people come back to spend money. Small coffee shops and pop-up street food stands were scattered throughout the big, open, central square. It was obvious to Jeremy that local and national governments should do more to help keep town centres thriving.

The thought was quickly chased away, as he entered the old open market. Scaffolding was everywhere, as the interior was being painted after a big refurbishment. The new owners of the building were responsible for that. The stall holders were now working flat out to equip their units for the opening day. Jeremy was amazed by the revamped Victorian building. It looked fabulous. Every stall was made of recycled materials and was entirely different from the next. Colourful awnings and flags hung in the air, creating a happy, relaxed feeling in the whole place. It was noisy, as the scaffolding was slowly being taken down. He could see Maya's stall. Like most of them, it was not quite finished. As he approached, he saw Maya busily cleaning down the brand-new stainless-steel work surfaces.

"Hi, Sis! Looks like you're ready to go to me!"

She looked at him with a look of disdain.

"The place opens in a week! I've got tons to do!"

"I thought you had loads of time?"

"The owners of the building foolishly brought the opening date forward and advertised it in the media. So everyone here is now panicking."

"What can I do?" he asked.

"First, get me and Chai a coffee each."

"Who's Chai?"

A woman of eastern origin came towards the stall, carrying cardboard boxes. She dropped them on the stainless-steel counter.

"That's the lot, May!"

Her face lit up, as she looked at Maya.

"Chai, this is my half-brother, Jeremy."

"Pleased to meet you!"

She smiled broadly, as she greeted Jeremy.

"Likewise," he said, smiling back at her. He liked her immediately. Chai moved toward Maya and then kissed her. The action surprised Jeremy, his mind rationalised it. He knew that Maya had had no interest in men, but this was the first time, as far as he knew, that she had shown any interest in anyone.

"I'll get the coffees," he said.

"I'm sorry, but can I have a chai latte?" Chai said. "Did you know, they named it after me?"

The funny moment was lost on Jeremy, as both Maya and Chai looked at him.

"Oh, yeah I get it!"

They all started to laugh. Moments later, he went off for the coffees. When he got back, Maya was on her own again.

"Sorry about that! I should have told you about Chai. Truth is, I haven't told anyone yet. I need to tell Mum and Dad. I'm pretty sure they have guessed that I'm a lesbian."

"To tell the truth, Maya, I'm pretty sure they know!"

"I suppose," said Maya, "up to this point in time, I hadn't found anyone to love. More importantly, anyone to love me back!"

Jeremy could tell by her demeanour that this was a big moment for Maya. He immediately hugged her.

"The only reason I've never come clean is because of Kazi. He's such an arsehole about the real world! If he wasn't my brother, I'd disown him!"

"How long have you and Chai been together?" Jeremy asked.

"About a year now. It was Chai who inspired me to do this. She started working at the restaurant last year. She told me to start my own business. She thought I was good enough to make a success. That's when the rumour came up about this place. The only problem we have is not living together anymore. We can't afford the rent on a flat until this takes off."

"Where's Chai living?"

"Like me, she's gone back home to live with her parents."

Jeremy hugged Maya which brought a few tears to their eyes.

Later that night, Jeremy was worn out, as were Maya and Chai, who went home. One thing Jeremy was not good at was physical activity. He never considered himself to be that way inclined, which was strange because he had a perfectly good body. He always edged on the side of being a bit of a nerd. The sofa was a better friend than a bike or sports equipment could ever be. The TV was on loud. Jeremy, Maya, and their dad were all fast asleep in front of it.

"Oh my God," said Florence, "I've heard of the four horsemen of the apocalypse, but you three could wake the dead."

The comments woke them all up, which persuaded Maya and Jeremy to go to bed. In his bedroom, Jeremy had several texts from Sofia, asking how his day had been. He told Sofia that Cecilia and Maya had dominated his day, he was exhausted. He continued to have a short conversation over text with her, which, in the end, sent him to sleep.

Ella and Nigel were on the sofa. Nigel had moved in with Ella.

It was a secret they were trying to keep from anyone at the police station, where relationships with colleagues in the same environment were frowned upon.

"I was talking to Jeremy, my journalist friend, the other day," said Nigel, "about the cold case we still have, from the pandemic."

Ella was half listening, as she was watching a soap on TV.

She didn't respond.

"Are you listening to me?"

She shot him a look.

"You know I love my soaps! Work is stressful! I need downtime."

She stared at his face. She knew she needed to pay attention. Their relationship was in its early stages. She didn't want to unsettle it by not being attentive. She paused the TV.

"Go on, what did Jeremy say?"

"So you *were* listening! There's me thinking I was the wallpaper."

She leaned over towards him, then kissed his lips.

"Never wallpaper, maybe a coffee table or a comfy chair."

She smiled and then they laughed.

"Well, what was this conversation about? Obviously, you gave him no information about it."

He gave her a disapproving look.

"Of course not! Jeremy was just curious to know if there was any movement on it, that's all. Anyway, I was thinking, is it ok if I bring it up tomorrow in our meeting?"

"Ok by me," she said, "as long as there are no costs involved, go ahead."

The next morning at the police station, Ella and Nigel arrived separately. Usually, every morning, they reviewed the cases that were on the table. Today, however, Nigel addressed Amber and Ethan, as Ella looked on.

"Ok guys, let's have a moment and look back at a cold case, the social media killings. Can we do some research to see if any more information has come to light, since the last time we looked at it? It seems to me enough time has gone by. Maybe something has turned up."

"It's strange you should say that, Nigel," Ethan said, "I was looking through our records the other day. That case had a flag on it. It turns out there has been some information sent to us from Spain."

A look of surprise came over Ella and Ambers's faces. Nigel's, for some reason, was expressionless. He then went over to Ethan's computer. Ethan started to read it out before Nigel had a chance to.

"It says here that the six names we sent to Spain have all been tied up with a bunch of petty criminals, who lived there as teenagers. There's a list of things they did, it looks to me like they were a gang of some sort."

Ethan's confidence had grown. He now seemed competent. Although, now and again, his attention levels waned. They all looked at the information that had been supplied.

"I think," said Ella, "that Nigel has made an excellent call on this case. Ethan, get onto the Spanish police to see if you can get more background on the six."

Ethan looked thoughtful, then he muttered to himself.

"The Celeb Six!"

"Pardon?" said Amber.

They all looked toward Ethan. He was staring into the distance. Amber sighed.

"What's up with you, Ethan?" asked Ella.

"It's ok, Ella," said Amber, "he does this sometimes, goes off into a world of his own."

Ethan repeated,

"The Celeb Six! Wouldn't that be a great name for a book or a film? A murder mystery set over several continents. Starring Brad Pitt, Charlize Theron and many more Hollywood stars. I can see it now, coming to your cinema soon."

He spread his hands, then stared. Ella, Nigel and Amber were almost speechless as they waited for Ethan to come back down to earth.

"Ethan! Ethan! Are you with us?" asked Ella.

Suddenly, Ethan realised he had been daydreaming. He looked at the others, then went bright red.

"Oh, sorry, was I talking aloud? Forgive me! I'm a bit of a film buff! Guilty secret!"

"It's ok, Ethan, no harm done," said Ella, "but, in honour of your moment just then, the case file shall have the name, The Celeb Six."

Ethan's face was a picture.

As mornings go, Jeremy's was much like all the others of late. He was trying to form a pattern that Cecilia was happy with. This did mean, till around lunchtime, he was kicking his heels. Other journalistic work had taken a back seat. Maya had cajoled him into working at the market again. He didn't mind; he thought it best to help her, rather than vegetate. As yet, he had not got enough material to do very much with Cecilia's biography. Before he went to the market, he met his journalist colleagues at the usual café in the town. Tony and Gail were already there. He high fived them, as he went to sit down at their table. They were drinking hot chocolate.

"Wow! Is this a celebration?"

"You could say that!" said Tony, "My publisher has given a green light for my book to be published."

"Are you sure we shouldn't be down the pub having a proper celebration, Tony?"

"No, can't stand the fuss."

"You do realise, Tone," said Jeremy, "you have to help push the publication. It won't sell itself!"

"The publishers have given me money, Jeremy. They think it'll be a best seller! There's even talk of someone picking up the rights to it!"

Jeremy and Gail were open-mouthed at the luck of it, but they both knew it was no easy task to get a book this far. They both congratulated him, then wished him the best.

"How are things with John Scotland and the Daily grind, sorry,

Record, Gail?"

Jeremy was curious because he had spent the whole week working with Cecilia. All other stories were on hold to him.

"I've done a few small pieces for it. Doesn't look like anything will change, Jeremy. How is your old lady friend, the actor? Are you going to write her bio?"

"I've started! That's why I've kept away from the newspaper. The truth is, I'm happy. No money, but it's exciting, engrossing at the same time!"

"You'd think differently if you had a mortgage and kids!"

Gail grimaced as she said it. The heavy words were delivered to Jeremy as a parting gift, as he decided he needed to leave.

"Aren't you staying, Jeremy? We were thinking of a big breakfast, black pudding and all the trimmings."

"Maybe next time! I've other things to do today."

As he left, he realised he had to make this thing work with Cecilia or he might have to re-train to be a bricklayer. The only problem with that was that he wasn't remotely practical in any way.

23.

He turned up at Cecilia's with a spring in his step. He was going out with Sofia later and was looking forward to it. He let himself in, then made his way up to Cecilia's apartment, knocked on the door and waited expectantly. It was longer than usual. An anxious feeling came over him, then he heard her voice.

"Come on in, dear boy!"

He let himself in. Cecilia was sitting in her easy chair, propped up, looking comfortable, as always impeccably attired. The tea set sat regally awaiting to be used.

"Shall I pour?" she asked. He nodded his head. It seemed to Jeremy that Cecilia looked even better today.

"Where were we yesterday?" she asked.

"You and Rupert had become an item."

She seemed eager to dive into the story.

"Oh yes, my dear Rupert! You know, I didn't know he was bisexual at that time. He was dashing and attractive to everyone. I thought I was so lucky he was with me. I suppose I was innocent in many ways, as there were quite a few gay people that hung around with us. It wasn't obvious to me at first, but a passing comment by one of our group said Rupert looked happier now he was sleeping with me, rather than flirting with men. It hit me hard. He was happier because our relationship had made him look heterosexual."

"Why would that be?" Jeremy asked.

"At that time and, even now, gay people didn't come out, as they call it, because of how it might affect their careers.

"Did you feel let down or used?" Jeremy asked.

"No, strangely! Because I knew he loved me. The problem was

not knowing and hearing from someone else. As Shakespeare said, *Love is blind.* It is and I was!"

"What did you do? Did you break up?"

"I don't know why, but it seemed to bring us closer together, somehow made us stronger. As time went by, he got better parts, and so did I. We played off each other, spending hours learning our lines together. Apart from the theatre, we both got parts on TV. We were living the perfect life. It didn't seem as if anything would spoil what we had."

"What happened then?" asked Jeremy.

"I became pregnant. At first, I thought my world was crashing in. I told Rupert and we were both shell-shocked. I had no idea what to do. Of course, a termination seemed obvious. Neither of us was cut out for the task of bringing up a child. It seemed like ages before I could work out what the right course was to take. Rupert went out one night, which he often did. I knew what he was doing. I had got used to his ways. For some reason, it gave us space. However, with me being pregnant, everything was different, so I decided to disappear before anyone noticed my condition. I went home to my parents, till it was over."

A tear came to her eye, as she said the words. Jeremy felt for her.

"Would you like to break for a while, Cecilia?"

She nodded and he looked at her closely. She seemed vulnerable, older than the person with whom he'd started talking, an hour ago. He went to the toilet, taking his time. Cecilia was in the kitchen when he came out. He stood at the kitchen door and looked at her.

"Would you like coffee for a change?" she asked.

"Er, yes."

The dreaded *er* slipped from his mouth.

It seemed to go by her, or she ignored it.

"That would be nice!" he said.

"I'll make it the way I like it!"

She boiled milk in a saucepan, then poured it onto the coffee in the cup, and then whisked it quickly. They sat back down together in the living-room. Jeremy held the hot coffee in his hands and sipped it.

"This is wonderful, so comforting."

She smiled, as he said it.

"Yes," she said, "you can keep that new fan dangle stuff that you buy from these modern coffee shops. This is the only way to have it. Also, it takes me back to when I used to make it in the seventies."

Cecilia looked lost in that era. The story of her pregnancy was shelved for the moment.

"What did you think of the paintings?"

He looked at her, puzzled. Her eyes strayed towards the bedroom.

"Oh!" he said, "those paintings!"

He had no idea she knew he'd been in her bedroom. He then felt embarrassed.

"Sorry, I was curious, and you were fast asleep."

She still had her hands wrapped around the coffee cup. She was enjoying every sip.

"My honest opinion," he said, "they are truly beautiful, especially the life drawings. Are they of you?"

A big smile appeared on her face.

"Although I do say so myself, Rupert caught me perfectly."

"There's no date on them. When was it?"

"It was the beginning of the eighties, nearly ten years after I became pregnant. We had moved in and out of each other's lives. I had completed a few big films, and so had Rupert. He was at The Royal Shakespeare theatre in Stratford. Out of the blue, he wrote to me. He had a friend who had a beautiful cottage on the south coast, which overlooked the sea. A photograph of it was attached. It looked idyllic. Of course, I jumped at the chance to spend some time there with Rupert.

He'd planned it months in advance, so we could avoid problems concerning our conflicting careers. It was early summer. We arrived a day apart. The cottage was so much more than any photograph could portray. It was as if our relationship was starting all over again, the only problem being Rupert seemed troubled. I expected intimacy but, after several bottles of wine, he shied away. It wasn't long before I found out what was on his mind. He told me he had read something about young men dying in America from some sort of virus. He had consulted a doctor, a close friend, who was also gay, who then informed Rupert that the disease could get out of hand. He warned him that he should be careful who he had sex with. As soon as he told me, he broke down.

I somehow felt privileged that he had wanted to share his concerns with me. I hadn't heard of AIDS until that moment but, after Rupert told me about it, I did feel vulnerable. It wasn't until the next day, when we'd had a chance to sleep on it, that we both felt more relaxed. We never slept in the same bed. The truth was, we were just happy to be together. So we just settled down to a week in wonderful isolation. At that time, neither of us was aware of what was about to follow."

"Was that where he painted those watercolours?"

"Yes! It was a wonderful location, the feeling, the all-encompassing perfect freedom, I had not realised how much our work had taken over our lives. It was like we were free."

A few moments of silence passed, as they both finished their milky coffee.

"*Sometimes good things fall apart so better things can fall together.* Marilyn Monroe. She was the mother of all things tragic."

Cecilia said it and caught the moment perfectly.

"It was a week before Rupert found out if he had been infected by AIDS."

Jeremy was on the edge of his seat.

"The doctor told him it was negative, and he was ok. We both had friends that had died of AIDS. It was devastating. I can't explain how it changed the way most people lived their lives."

As they sat there in the shadow of that memory, Jeremy became aware of her emotional swings, although he sat in wonder at her worldliness.

23.

There was a small Italian restaurant, not far from a multiplex cinema, where Jeremy and Sofia had decided to meet. The idea was to eat, then go to the cinema. They had already talked via text about how much they enjoyed watching movies. So, it seemed an obvious thing to do. Jeremy was early. He decided to go into the restaurant and then wait. It wasn't long before Sofia arrived. He'd sat almost opposite the door. He saw the vision of loveliness that was Sofia. She wasn't thin. She had curves in all the right places. He was stunned when she walked toward him, wearing a figure-hugging red dress, reaching just above the knee. A red and black shawl was scooped up over her shoulders, then hung down her back. Her dark hair was loose. It seemed to shine, as the lights of the restaurant reflected off it.

Jeremy was taken aback by how beautiful she was. He smiled, then she came over to him.

"I hope I'm not too overdressed."

Jeremy's mind tinkered with the words for a second, then realised he'd already started to take her dress off in his mind.

"No, you look divine."

Sofia looked at ease.

"I do have a coat in the car, just in case it rains."

The information for some reason eased Jeremy's mind. Maybe because she imparted to him that she was practical as well as beautiful. She touched his hand.

"By the way, you look dashing."

He was wearing a black suede jacket and grey trousers, with a white shirt and blue tie. It was conservative, but he felt comfortable. It went silent as they looked at the menu and the waiter took their order for drinks. They both smiled and then they laughed.

"Isn't it ridiculous," said Sofia, "how we do this to ourselves, dress up, and put our nerves on edge? It's almost like we have never met."

"Maybe that's part of the excitement," he added.

He looked at her as he said it. Her head was down slightly, studying the menu. He tried to analyse this amazing woman that had popped into his life, like a burgeoning flower into his empty landscape. She caught his eyes and there was a moment between them. His head seemed to take a spin, adrenalin mixed with expectation and he could feel his temperature rise. He did his best to control his feelings, as they both continued to consult the menu. They ordered, then they carried on talking about things that mattered little. The food came, which they both did battle with. The pasta in various forms was entertaining. A couple of glasses of wine later, they were like a couple who had known each other for a long time.

"Are you a big fan of Italian food, Sofia?" he asked, as he scooped up the sauce from his plate with a piece of garlic bread.

"I like all things Mediterranean!"

She looked as if something had come into her mind, then said it.

"My father was Spanish. He died before I was born. I never knew him!"

"I'm sorry, what about your mother?"

"She died, too, when I was about ten. She drowned!"

"I'm even more sorry! That must have been devastating!"

"It was, at the time! I've learned to live with it."

She looked down and ran her finger around the top of the wine glass, then seemed lost in thought.

"The strange thing was," she said, as she continued to play with the glass, "there has always been a question mark over it, whether it was an accident or someone else involved."

Jeremy was fascinated as to why, but before he had a chance to follow up with a question, she snapped out of her trance.

"This is no way to talk, is it Jeremy? I don't want to get maudlin about my past!"

He wanted to dig deeper, but she would have none of it.

"Let's have dessert!" she said, "the bigger the better!"

They smiled at each other, the mood lifting immediately.

"Where was your mother from?" he asked.

"She was from the Midlands, but she did like to move around the country and abroad."

Jeremy felt for Sofia. He had always lived at home and had a loving family around him. He couldn't think what it would be like not to have them there. He wanted to pursue her story, but Sofia was quick to turn the light on him.

"What about you?" she asked, "How about your mother and father?"

"My dad owns A2Z&BACK, the taxi company."

"I've used them often," she said. "Does this mean I'll get a discount from now on?"

Jeremy smiled.

"Not sure about that! I don't even get one. My mum works for my dad, although they are both supposed to be retired and taking a back seat. My dad came here from India, had an arranged marriage, had two kids, then his wife died of cancer. He married again sometime later to an English woman, my mum."

He said it as if it was dictation. She found it funny and laughed.

"What?" he asked. "That's about it in a nutshell!"

"Maybe, one day," she said, "you can give me the story of the tree it came from."

He laughed with her, then felt warm inside at the thought of spending more time with Sofia.

The potted history of their short lives drew lines between the dots, then they coloured in a few empty spaces. It eased their curiosity for the time being.

After enjoying their Italian meal and warm conversation, they walked to the multiplex. They found more space for popcorn and Coca-Cola. The film was loud, brash, violent, fun and satisfying.

A coffee bar was attached to the cinema complex. They agreed to finish the night by drinking hot chocolate with marshmallows on top. Later on, they were the only ones left and it was closing time. Like two lost souls that had found each other, now it was hard to let go. He wanted it to go on, but he couldn't take her back to his mum and dad's house. She had the same feelings, knowing her little bedsit wasn't the best place to go back to either.

Jeremy walked Sofia to her car. The rain had started to fall. She quickly got in after he'd opened the door for her.

"Get in!" she said.

He did, as the rain fell heavier.

"Wow!" he said, as the heavens opened. The rain seemed to batter the roof, then it turned to hail. They sat and watched it bounce off the bonnet. They were spellbound at the way the weather had suddenly changed. Outside, it seemed as if nature was making a play for their attention. The same could be said for their feelings inside the car, as the windows steamed up gently. They looked at each other, said nothing, then found a comfortable embrace as they kissed. The hail subsided, but they didn't. The kisses were intense as they got familiar with each other's touch. As quickly as it came, the rain abated. The sound of their kissing was sensuous, searching. Sofia broke off as if to slow the excitement to an easier pace. Jeremy also slowed, to see where it was going. She then took his left hand and brought his open palm up to her mouth. She pressed it against her face. He was fascinated and excited at the same time. He could feel her lips gently kissing the inside of his hand, while she looked into his eyes. Inside, Jeremy's body was doing summersaults, as sexual desire started to get out of control. Almost as quickly as the hail had come, it had gone. She removed his hand from her mouth and put it on her breast. He wasn't sure, but fairly certain that Sofia was aware of his adoration.

"I think we should wait for another day when we can both

enjoy this moment better."

As she said it, he knew she was right, but only in so much as he knew comfort would heighten the act of making love. At this moment, however, he would have been happy to be dangling off a cliff edge in a snowstorm. If only he could enter into the kingdom of heaven that was Sofia.

"I guess," he said, after a few moments of contemplation, "there's always another day."

In their minds, the frustration was there for them both. Words were difficult to find, to fill the space where sex should have been. They kissed gently as they parted, but they knew it was a kiss that meant: I'm waiting.

When Jeremy got home, he thought everyone was in bed, so he let himself in quietly, only to find Maya sitting on the big sofa, watching YouTube on her laptop. She never looked his way, as he got himself a glass of water. He sat down, put his feet up, and then looked over her shoulder.

"So, is this your porn when Chai's not around? Because if it is, you need help! What is that?"

She looked towards him, then sneered at his comment.

"It's cauliflower pepper fry, bozo!"

She then looked at him again.

"Wow! Well, look at you Mr. smarty pants! Who have you been chasing tonight? I'm pretty certain it's not Cecilia Walters!"

She waited for an answer that he was not willing to give.

"I know you were not out with Duman. A. Because you look too nice to go out boozing with him. B. Because if you had, you wouldn't be here, you'd have your head down the toilet."

"Oh, that's so cruel, you heartless creature!" he said. "But, oh so true," she added. The thought loosened his tongue.

"I went out with Sofia."

"Is she something special," she asked, "or is she something bog standard?"

The subject of toilets being brought up twice was intentional by Maya. She was having fun.

"Ok, no need to be so sharp! It's been a long day!"

"Does that mean you didn't get your way?"

"It's only our second date!"

"That means she should be pregnant by now!"

He threw a pillow at her head, which she neatly avoided.

"Is the Xbox still attached to the TV?" she asked.

"Should be! I haven't disconnected it."

"Do you fancy a fight or a battle? Like we used to!"

In both their minds, it seemed like a great idea, as they were both frustrated for more or less the same reason. An hour later, after many a fight in a virtual reality world, Maya surfaced as the victor, which she wouldn't let him forget for quite some time.

As Jeremy lay in his bed, dreaming about Sofia, he smiled.

"This was probably one of the best days of my life, so far," he told himself as he slipped off to sleep.

Maya continued to tease Jeremy the next morning, especially about the game she had won. Jeremy was taking it in good heart. After all, there was many a time when he had beaten her, fair and square.

"Are you with me this morning, bro?" Maya asked him with an American accent. She high-fived the air in front of him. He laughed, as he placed some bread in the toaster. He then lifted both his hands and she reciprocated. They did a boogie together, then separated. There was an animated few minutes, as they danced to the music on the radio. When the music stopped, he said, in a bad American accent,

"You're bad, sis!"

Later that morning, Jeremy found himself moving far too many boxes. He was continuing to help Maya and Chai organise the eatery. His painting skills were employed, but he was found wanting. However, Chai, who was far better at DIY, then took over, to Jeremy's great relief. Overall, he was enjoying the experience. It was detached from anything he'd ever done before. He realised that he needed to branch out more and do other things. It went through his mind that, if the writing hit the fan, he might just try some other occupation.

Around lunchtime, they stopped for something to eat. Some of the other eating places were testing their menus on the workers and other stall holders. From Turkey to the Americas, there was a wonderful array to sample. There was great camaraderie in the market hall, with everyone trying to help each other. It was all for the greater good. Maya and Chai were happy, they now knew they were good enough and, what's more, they were up for the challenge.

"Game on," said Maya.

24.

By the time Jeremy got to Cecilia's, he was high on the euphoria of Maya's and Chai's dreams, although he was tired from the night before. He let himself into Cecilia's house and, as he did, she was at the bottom of the stairs. He jumped in surprise to find her there. She looked at him, unmoved. She was holding letters that had been delivered.

"You should look after your nerves," she said, "Calm yourself or you'll have a heart attack!"

The words resonated because she was always calm and collected. It never occurred to him to ask how she managed to take so many things in her stride, without ever falling apart. After the usual taking of tea, which for him was always a calming experience, he pursued the question.

"Have you always been so laid-back, Cecilia?"

"A good question. That takes me back to the seventies. It was a time when music was God. Nearly everyone loved what they heard. Bands and artists of all descriptions had something to say. Some of it was a bit out there, but even some of the weirdest music has stood the test of time. Love and Peace were King and Queen. It was fabulous. I started to meditate then, to get through the ups and downs of life. It was the only way to deal with disappointment and the trials of life. In a way, it was my go-to place.

About that time, I met some Hare Krishna devotees on the streets of Birmingham. I took a leaflet, then went to a few meetings. I liked what they were saying. What's more, George Harrison was a follower. Of the four Beatles, he was my favourite!"

"My father's Hindu," said Jeremy, "he's talked to me about that.

He tried to teach me about eastern religion and its spiritual branches. To tell you the truth, I'm on the fence as far as religion is concerned. I feel the same about politics."

"It's the best place to be, Jeremy, if you're a journalist. Meditation, however, is a frame of mind you should try sometime.

As for Krishna, it is consciousness and, as you know, Jeremy, Hinduism is a religion. Hinduism is a territorial term, Hare Krishna is a philosophy to understand God. Hare Krishna is an eternal servant to the lord. Hindus worship Krishna but also worship others.

The main thing I found was that meditation gave me peace of mind. Especially when I was on a plane where all things passed."

She went quiet as if she was reflecting on that piece of peace that had passed.

Jeremy's dad had never pushed the Hindu faith onto him. His mum had no religious feelings whatsoever. His parents wanted him to find his path, and in some ways, that's why he had become a journalist.

Jeremy wanted to guide Cecilia back into her life as an actor.

"When did you come back into acting again? After your forced break?"

"It was complicated, very difficult to talk about here. It did take longer than I thought it would and left me with mental scars but, after a while, I started to act again."

"What happened then, that left you that way?"

She sat there but seemed reluctant to answer the question. He quickly moved on, so as to not let the story get bogged down.

"So, how was Rupert?"

She responded quickly, as if the pressure had been taken off.

"Rupert had moved on, although we often wrote to each other. He told me of a B&B just outside Birmingham, where he knew many actors got cheap lodgings while working at theatres in the city.

He also told me to visit his agent, which I did. It wasn't long before I had the odd part come my way. Although I say it myself, my experience, plus my short break from acting, gave me an added hunger for better things. Perhaps it gave me the edge over other actors at the time."

Jeremy was missing something, as Cecilia wanted to forge forward in the telling of her story. It seemed to him she had skipped past an important piece of her history. Mainly, what happened when she went back to her parents. When he went back to it, she waved her hand to one side as if it was of no consequence. Reluctantly, he left it and moved on.

"How do you feel now," he asked, "about those up-and-coming actresses who worked alongside you all those years ago? I suppose I'm thinking of the ones who have been honoured by the Queen."

The room went ghostly quiet. It was if someone had suddenly died. Cecilia looked angry, something he'd never seen in her before.

"My tongue will tell the anger of my heart, or else my heart, concealing it, will break. William Shakespeare.

Many things have encamped in my heart and my head over the years, but none hurts more than not receiving an accolade for one's life's work."

"Why do you think they passed you by?"

"I was not in the right place at the right time. Sometimes I don't think I fitted in with the luvvies that sit at the top table of the profession. I did however receive the odd award from the general public when certain TV productions were entered into a category. Usually, it was magazines and newspapers.

There was a time when I made it known that I didn't want any kind of recognition. I had very strong feelings about royalty. Earlier on in my career, I did tell you I was a communist. Perhaps that hung over my head for many years. However, I must say, I wasn't unhappy about that. I did realise, as time went by, that fighting the system is like trying to turn the tide. Nature wins in the end.

After the millennium, a part of my life imploded. Maybe that was the reality check that put awards and most things into perspective."

Jeremy was aware that, at that time, Cecilia's life had hit a brick wall. He had done some research but, up to this point, he was unable to find out what had happened to her to bring it about.

"What was it then? What had happened?"

She looked at him more coldly, so much so that he wondered if she was acting a part or if she was going to say nothing about it. He waited and waited. It was as if a master craftsman had come in and, within a few minutes, had built an impenetrable wall between them. Her stiff unmoving body sat there, her eyes looking into the distance.

The silences that the two of them had shared were now mounting up. This, up to now, was the longest. Cecilia was playing a game. She seemed to be enjoying it. It was a game of chess that neither of them acknowledged. The only problem was he knew she was always going to win.

"I've been thinking!" she said, without moving a muscle or even blinking an eye. He looked at her, as she carried on talking.

"I've been thinking. You must be out of pocket. You're doing this for me and yet you have no recompense. I must see to it that you are rewarded for your services!"

The complete about-face of the conversation was almost bewildering to him.

"I can't let you carry on until I put your finances right!"

He was silent, as he had no idea what to say. He'd just assumed he would have to carry on without any money until the book was at least half done. His thoughts were just to keep going, then see how it all stacked up, before maybe approaching a publisher, who then, he hoped, might give him an advance. After all, she was a famous actress. Cecilia got up and left the room. Within a few minutes, she came back, then gave him a cheque for two thousand pounds.

"That should help, for now. I know you live with your parents, but you need money to live on."

He held the cheque as if it was a medal for some great feat he had achieved. He wanted to be gracious and not undermine the wonderful gesture. In the back of his mind, he was so happy, because he could now give his mum some rent.

"You don't need to thank me; it has been remiss of me to expect you to come here nearly every day without payment. After all, this book will be about my life. I don't want you to think I'm not grateful."

As he held the cheque tightly, he felt a need to speak, if only just a few words to tell her how grateful he was. Cecilia then seemed impatient and wanted to continue the roller coaster that was her life. Up to this moment, she had gone backwards and forwards with great abandon. In some ways, Jeremy was slightly confused. However, he was pleased he had recorded the whole thing, or he would have no idea how her life would all fit together. Cecilia then ran with the story. It was her way of changing the subject.

"What were we talking about earlier? Oh yes! I contacted Rupert's agent, who asked me to go to see him as soon as possible. It was a formality. Within a few days, he signed me up. In less than a week, I was working again on a drama for TV, that would start shortly afterwards. The audition was a piece of cake. Meanwhile, another part had become available back at Birmingham Rep. I was asked to stand in for a role in a play that was up and running. A bad case of flu had taken hold of some of the cast, so it wasn't long before I was busy and acting again."

"Can you recall the drama that you were going to act in on TV?"

Up to now, her memory had been perfect. She got up and made her way to her bedroom, bringing back what he assumed to be her diary. She opened the book, which was A4 in size. He could see clearly it had age attached to it. The corners and sides were well worn. It seemed to Jeremy that nearly every page had pieces of paper sticking out of them.

"That book looks like a big book of memories," he said, "it appears to have more than just a bit of history!"

She held it carefully between her two hands and studied the gold braiding along its edges, then almost lovingly ran her hand along its spine.

"I think," she said, "that the spine of a book gives more support to the mind than any amount of psychokafuffle!"

The word that she made up on the spot seemed perfect for whatever she was about to say.

"This book is my mother, my father, my baby, my mentality. It's my go-to place for my most important memories, and this one tells me where the bodies are buried."

He looked at her closely and thought this was a strange thing to say. Immediately, Jeremy wanted to see it. She could see that in his eyes.

"No! This is just for me!"

She held it tightly to her chest, as if it was a baby.

"Do you have everything written down word for word?" he asked.

"No, not everything, but all the important things and I do have others as well!"

Jeremy then imagined a hidden library somewhere in the apartment.

"It was Upstairs-Downstairs," she said, "I played a maid. It didn't seem like much of a part at the time. but the programme became a hit with the public. After that, other things were offered to me. It became a very productive time for many of us actors. Like me, Rupert was busy, but we still kept in touch. We would meet whenever we could in our busy schedules.

Film and TV work could often be tedious, with endless hours of make-up, dressing up, and sitting around between takes. Although I did enjoy mixing with other actors, whenever I did, we would usually end up talking about scandals involving others. I suppose, like all professions, tittle-tattle is a fact of life."

This pricked up Jeremy's ears.

"Any scandals that could be told here?" he asked.

"They would all be old news now, probably not very

interesting."

Jeremy was doing his best to get into Cecilia's mindset.

"I know Rupert was a big part of your life, but did you partake in any other liaisons?"

A wry smile came across her face.

"Yes, I did, but not always intentionally. As you can imagine, working closely with someone of the opposite sex or even the same sex, brought about close encounters. This contact with another actor stimulated the mind as well as the body. For me, it was the kissing, which could be ghastly at times. Especially if the other actor smoked. I've never been a smoker, so my breath should always have been fine. There were times when I was playing opposite the right actor and I didn't want the kissing to stop."

"Did you have many affairs that way?"

"A few. The truth is, they didn't last long. You have to remember that you're dealing with so many egos battling for affection, as well as adulation. Something has to give. It was a game. As long as you realised it was just that, then no one got hurt. Maybe, here and there, vanity was bruised, but if you play the game, someone will lose. I took these things in my stride. Of course, I took precautions. History had reinforced that.

There was this beautiful actor. I say beautiful because he was. He was way better than handsome. Phillip Dickinson was his name. He was perfect, tall, dark and had great physique. He had a voice that just melted my insides. It was rich and smooth like chocolate. As you can imagine, playing opposite him in a sex scene made me very nervous. I've had my fair share of sex scenes over the years. He was one of my first. These things are carefully choreographed, everything has to be in the right position, lighting, cameras, body bits."

She spoke with a smile on her face, as if it was happening right there and then.

"We were lying together for what seemed like hours, but I couldn't get my lines right. So we had to re-take over and over again. The reason being that his penis was hard all the time, pushing against my leg. We were wearing the equivalent of flesh-coloured pants, to save our embarrassment. It was funny in many ways. Needless to say, we, or should I say I, got through it. At the end of the filming, Philip asked me if I wanted to go for a drink. As you can imagine, I jumped at the chance. If only just to talk to him more intimately, out of the sight of cameras and crew. Although he was a profoundly shallow man, I got so drunk that we went back to his hotel room and had sex."

She felt the need to pause. Jeremy thought maybe it was just to recall the moment a little better. She started to laugh, not a small laugh, but a big one. So much so, that Jeremy instinctively started to laugh with her. For a few minutes, she found it difficult to rescue her senses. Eventually, she wiped tears from her eyes. Her face, which was now quite red, cooled in the quiet that followed, then their eyes engaged.

"Look away, or I'll start again!"

He did. She gathered herself.

"It was the worst sex I've ever had. I may have had too much to drink, but I can remember his penis was minuscule. Bless him, he did his best to arouse me, but it was all a failure. I quickly sobered up, then I went to the bathroom, wishing I had just gone back to my hotel. I got dressed, then left!"

"Did you speak at all?"

"Yes, as I was going to leave, I saw a rubber tube on the bed, next to Philip. It looked like a weapon, about eight inches long and pink. As far as I could see, it was crudely made to simulate a penis. It was strange. I felt in two minds. Part of me was sad for him, the other part was laughing at him. He told me he wore it whenever he played a part that involved a sex scene. It was all so surreal. He was the whole package, I thought, apart from a certain part of the package that was not!"

Jeremy was amused.

"The cheek of it was," she added, "he asked me if I could keep it to myself, as he felt so embarrassed by it."

"Did you?"

She pondered the question for a moment, then smiled.

"Would *you*?"

Jeremy looked at her, then smiled.

"No!"

"Exactly! I'm sure in some ways it would have broken the trade description act!"

Again, they burst out laughing. This time, it took longer to regain control of themselves.

"How do you think you would cope in today's current climate, where women are calling out those who had abused them?"

"I think it's about time. Way back when I started, there was too much ignorance. It suited the heavily masculine side of the industry. Women were a bit like pawns in a chess game, almost dispensable. The other side of that was that it could be fun and lots of women gave what they got. I did, but not all women are like me. If I was used in any way, I would get revenge. It was simple if a married actor was using a situation to his advantage. I, for one, would blow the whistle on him. In a similar fashion, that goes for anyone who abuses. There are still those in the industry, who think they can treat people of any sex badly. In my opinion, they should be dealt with severely."

Jeremy was certain that Cecilia had plenty more skeletons in her cupboard, but he decided to change the subject.

"What did you do with what you earned? Did you buy yourself a little bolthole abroad?"

"No! I did buy this place in the mid-to-late eighties. As I've already told you, art has always been my guilty pleasure. Rupert told me to buy a property, rather than rent, because he had bought a small, terraced house in the suburbs. He suggested buying a house on the same street as him, but I was not wanting a garden or the maintenance that comes with such a property. So, I bought this place. The four apartments have full use of the garden, we have a gardener and someone who does the maintenance."

"Do you still have any friends in the industry?"

"I have a few, mainly from when I started up in my acting career. Some, like me, went on to become bigger stars. Others fell by the wayside, for whatever reason. I keep in contact with some of them. There are, however, some who are not here anymore."

She looked saddened by the statement.

"Do you want a break, Cecilia?"

"Maybe in a minute or two!"

He continued, knowing any time now she would give in for the day. He wanted to keep the questions easy but relevant.

"Are you into technology at all?"

She laughed at the thought of it.

"I don't possess a mobile phone! I'm old-fashioned that way. If my agent ever needed me, he would call me on a landline. Not having those things never affected my work. Rupert bought me a laptop years ago, telling me email is the way to communicate. It was not for me. He is what they call technically minded. There's little that he doesn't know about computers."

Time was getting on and Cecilia seemed ill at ease and tired, so Jeremy got up.

"Let's leave it for today," he said, "I can see you're tired, I'm tired too. Is there anything you need?"

"No, I'm ok, I have provisions. I have a man who drops things by. There's a corner shop that's become a Tesco. Fortunately, I can go there. They deliver."

The thought comforted Jeremy, as he had been worried about her welfare. He kissed her on each cheek.

"I'll see you Monday. If you ever need me, call. You have my number!"

She squeezed his arm. He pulled out the cheque she'd given him.

"Thank you," he mouthed silently.

They shared a warm smile, then he let himself out.

25.

Sunday morning, Jeremy was lying in his bed at peace with himself. He stared at the ceiling he'd been staring at for most of his life. His phone pinged; he'd just switched it on. There was a message from Sofia. All he'd received the day before was a text saying, *It was a wonderful night xxxx*

Now, as he lay there, a waterfall of words appeared on his phone. It was as if she was talking to him, lying next to him. Her words turned him on. *If I was there now, you could touch my body, feel my heart beating Xx.* One after another, all similar in meaning. He answered immediately. *If you were here, I would kiss you all over. Xx.* She responded immediately, then the sex text came thick and fast. So much so, that he knew that he was going to have to remedy his pent-up feelings by self-gratification. It was nothing like the real thing, so he had to make a plan.

He lazed the morning away, reading the Sunday papers. His dad bought them all. Like Jeremy, he was an avid news watcher and commentator. That's where Jeremy got his interest in journalism from. They would often argue about politics. His dad was a conservative with a small c, and Jeremy was a socialist, without an agenda. The clashes between father and son were short and sweet, both knowing full well neither of them would win. However, they both loved the battle. Jeremy had waded his way through the front pages, which were mostly about the recriminations of Covid. Boris Johnson and his government had managed to spend billions, but still too many people had died. The grandees of the Tory party had found his foppish games tiresome. Too many cutting newspaper headlines had sealed his fate. Britain was in a post-

Brexit-Boris-Covid-pandemic, and the government ministers were running around like rats in a storm drain.

Jeremy left the papers to try to relax. He got another text message from Sofia. She had managed to get the day off, by exchanging her hours with someone else. *Hi Jeremy, would you like to go for a walk somewhere?* He jumped at the chance, replying, *Where?*

It did mean he would have to make an excuse to miss Sunday lunch with his half-brother and his wife and their children. So sad, he thought, then smiled to himself. His mum and dad were not happy he was escaping. He told them he had a date with his new girlfriend. After that, they said no more.

Jeremy and Sofia met somewhere neither of them had been before, but both had heard it was a nice place for a long walk. It was a picturesque spot, just outside of town, *The Coffee Cup:* a mobile caravan, sat in a car park overlooking the river. A beautiful Victorian footbridge reached out to the other side. It was a wonderful setting, the weather matching the scene. They sipped their coffees, as they moved along the path. It wasn't long before they found a bench to sit on.

"I'm surprised," said Jeremy, "that there aren't more people here."

"I believe, at this time of day, it's more for runners, dog walkers. After lunch, it's more families and lovers."

"So, we should have come later then?"

"Is that what we are, Jeremy? I wasn't sure you wanted to put a name to our relationship!"

He realised, when he said it, that he may be overstepping the mark, as he wasn't sure what their relationship was as yet. Something about Sofia confused him. Maybe it was the journalist in him, which made him suspicious of all things. This was probably the reason why he was single up to this point in time.

"What's that phrase?" he said, "Let's carry on, see how it goes."

"I haven't heard that one before, have you got a book of quotes like that to suit the situation?" she asked.

"Yes!" he said, then he made a move to get an imaginary book out of his inside pocket. She smiled. He pretended to hold it in his hands, as he turned the pages. He stopped.

"Here's another one."

He pointed with his finger.

"Things not to say to your girlfriend, while reading from an invisible book of quotations."

He paused, and she went along with his game.

"Well, what does it say?"

"It says, why waste your time talking when you could be kissing."

He turned to her, then pulled her towards him and kissed her. His thoughts were lost in a haze of wonderful feelings, that were mixed up in colours, lights, and darks. A tingling sensation visited all of the nerve endings in his body, which somehow made him feel like he was hovering above the ground.

"Did you feel that?" he said, "I think the world just fell in love with the moon!"

"Does that mean that I am your moon?" she asked.

"Only if you never let go!" he said.

"Oh, I see. It's more about gravity than love, then?"

"Whatever it is, the moon has hung around the earth for millions of years, so what do you think?"

She pondered it for a moment, then, as she got up, said,

"I bet I could beat you to the tree!"

"Which tree?"

"The biggest one!"

A tall oak stood out among the willows on the bank. He stood up dreading the thought but, from somewhere, the desire was there to try.

"Ready, steady..." she said, then started to run.

"Cheat!" he shouted, then ran after her. He made a good fist of trying, but she still won. They were both breathless, hands on their knees, then they started to laugh. After they'd caught their breath, they continued to walk along the river, like any other might-be lovers would have done.

26.

Jeremy let himself into Cecilia's house on Monday morning. He made his way upstairs, then tapped on the door. There was no answer. She didn't come to let him in, so he used another key to let himself in. He called her name, then announced himself. He looked around the rooms, then he tapped on her bedroom door.

"Come in Jeremy! Don't dawdle!"

Immediately, he felt like he was at school and was about to be told off by the teacher. Cecilia was propped up in her bed, looking like a Queen who was calling in her courtiers. She was wearing a red velvet dressing-gown with a gold braid along its edges. Her hair was tied back away from her face. She beckoned him forward, looking over her reading glasses that were perched nimbly on her almost perfect nose.

"Look at this! Come here and have a look!"

She seemed irritated in some way. She was holding what looked like a book. It was large, A4 in size, quite thick with a plain, cream cover. Impatiently, she made him come to her side of the bed.

"See this, it's a script my agent sent to me!"

"I thought you were too poorly to take any parts!"

She looked at him as if he was something the cat had brought in, although she had an aversion to felines.

"Look at this? That's my part, Eleanor!"

She pushed the script in front of his face. He looked through the pages. He'd never seen a script before, so he found it difficult to understand what she was getting angry about.

"As far as I understand it, you play someone's grandmother!"

He was surmising, but he thought he'd best say something.

"Yes, exactly, and I'm fucking dead on the second page!"

She seemed to say it and play it, as if it was a part in itself. Her dramatic emphasis on the word 'fucking' was perfect. Jeremy could listen to Cecilia's highs and lows all day long because it was as if her life was a continual drama. He had had a thought that when she was feeling better, he'd take her out for a meal, mainly because he wanted to see her interact with other people in her natural surroundings.

"You're not getting this are you, Jeremy? You're not tuned into what I'm trying to say!"

She waited, then stared at him. The dramatic pause was intentional, but he was playing her game.

"So, Cecilia, you are annoyed that you've been offered a part that's not big enough, even though you know full well you can't do the part."

"That is ridiculous, I could play this part in my sleep, now or at any time. The insult is to think I've been offered such a minuscule piece of work. My agent knows full well I'm worth so much more than this!"

"Perhaps he's protecting you. He must know how ill you've been. Maybe he just wanted you to do a small part to get back to acting again. Did he contact you and find out how you were?"

"Of course, many times!"

"So, what did you say to him?"

"That I've had COVID and continue to have my ups and downs!"

"There you are then! He's trying to look after you!"

She looked flabbergasted.

"It's still a shitty little part!"

"Will you do it?"

"No, I'm not well enough!"

For some reason, neither he nor Cecilia was in the same place, even though they were now sitting opposite each other in the living room. Jeremy couldn't find it in his mind to ask the right questions.

"You seem a little off today, Jeremy. Let me make some tea."
She looked into his eyes.

"Have you found love, Jeremy? You seem to me like someone who might be in love. I would be disappointed if it wasn't me you were in love with!"

He smiled. He did love her. Since the day he'd met Cecilia, he had found it hard not to be in love with her.

"I see! It's the lovely Sofia. She's, my competition! I can see and feel it now!"

Cecilia was very perceptive, but he was dismissive.

"No, I'm not in love with anybody else but you, Cecilia!"

He reached his hand forward and placed it on hers.

"That's as maybe, but I can't stand in the way of the younger woman!"

She said it with humour in her voice and wrapped her hands around his.

"Are you seeing her?"

"We've been out together a few times. We are seeing each other tomorrow."

"The third date, in my day, was the turning point. Maybe more than just kisses are exchanged at such a time!"

"You mean you usually had sex on the third date?"

"The song said to love the one you're with. It didn't say to wait till the third date. Sex can be an involuntary thing and so can love. I usually went with the flow!"

The exchange was gentle, easy going. It was like two old friends exchanging thoughts about the weather over tea and cakes.

"I have it in my mind," continued Cecilia, "to write a few letters to old friends and maybe a strong one to my agent. So if you don't mind Jeremy, let's leave it for today. We can reconvene on Wednesday if you like."

She gave him a knowing look, smiling cheekily, then rose from her chair in her regal, red velvet dressing-gown. They walked together towards the front door, and she turned to him just as he was leaving.

"Well there's a rose in the fisted glove
And the eagle flies with the dove
And if you can't be with the one you love honey
Love the one you're with, Love the one you're with,
Love the one you're with, Love the one you're with.
Stephen Stills."

She quoted, half singing the last two lines. It was perfect.

"Don't forget, Jeremy, this has all been done before. Just listen to any love song. Love is about the lyrics. They are like the blood that run through your veins."

As usual, Cecilia's dramatic thespian delivery was worthy of a full house at The Royal Shakespeare theatre, but all she had was Jeremy. He, of course, soaked it up. He hugged her, then bowed to her, kissing her hand,

"My queen."

She nodded her head in approval.

"My prince."

This was their world, their stage.

"Isn't it true," said Cecilia, "that we are all players, if not in a fictitious story, then in our own? It's just that the scene is in a different place, with a different backdrop. There is more to life than any amount of imaginings and we are all taking part in what can never be foreseen!"

27.

Sofia had Jeremy's address. His mum and dad had left for work. Maya was at the marketplace. Jeremy knew that he had the house to himself for most of the day, so he had a spring in his step. He was excited. He just hoped he wasn't too excited. It wasn't long before Sofia turned up. She looked fantastic. Her tight jeans showed off her beautiful curves, a loose cream shirt was worn over a cream T-shirt. Jeremy thought she looked impeccable.

"Do you fancy a coffee?" he asked.

She smiled and nodded,

"If you like!"

She seemed to purr it, but maybe she didn't. Jeremy wasn't sure. His mind was already in a place that was making him very nervous. He went through the process of making coffee, as she looked around the living area.

"Oh my God! This place is lovely!"

She walked from the kitchen over to the sofas and looked out into the garden through the bi-fold doors.

"I bet it's wonderful living here!"

He agreed as she looked at the photographs on the wall.

"Is this your dad?"

He looked up from making the coffee.

"Yes, that's him!"

"He's the guy who was driving the taxi I came in!"

"What? You mean you came here in one of my dad's taxis? For fuck's sake!"

He stopped what he was doing. As he looked up, he caught Sofia's eyes. She started to laugh.

"Shit, you frightened the life out of me!"

She came around to the side of the kitchen where he was, then sidled up to him. Her perfume was intoxicating. He could feel his hands shaking. It seemed that the texts and expectation had built up his excitement too much. She cradled his chin in her hands, then ran her fingers over his jawline.

"I like this! It makes you look rugged, handsome, sexy!"

He hadn't shaved. He wasn't a vain person, but he also liked looking a little unkempt. She then ran her hand up through his hair and he responded by moving his hand around the back of her neck. He kissed her. It was gentle and soft as their tongues found each other. Jeremy thought he detected sweetness on her lips. Within seconds the room seemed to spin, almost as if he had had a few too many drinks. He felt almost overcome by the moment. His whole body seemed too hot. She responded by kissing harder. He did the same. Hands found things to undo. They helped each other undress. It was obvious to both of them it might be better to go somewhere more comfortable. So he grabbed her hand and led her through to the hall, then up the stairs to his bedroom. They both laughed, as they scampered up the stairs. The excitement was nearly unbearable, as they fumbled to relieve each other of the rest of their clothes. Sofia's mind was distracted momentarily

"Nice room!"

Posters of bands haphazardly adorned one wall. It was a large space, light and airy. She thought for a moment it was nearly as big as her bedsit. He was transfixed by the sight of Sofia's nipples pressing against the inside of her T-shirt. She became distracted, too, by Jeremy's obvious need to touch them. She removed her T-shirt as he danced to remove his jeans. She fell backwards onto his bed and pushed her jeans off. She lay there before him like a Greek goddess. Her body was everything that Jeremy had imagined and even more. He got onto the bed moving carefully next to her. She smiled at him. A moment hung there, as they shared the sexual tension. His fingers slowly moved over her, like he was playing a musical instrument, so gently you could almost hear the notes, which was her voice as she enjoyed his touch. He then moved his hands up to her beautiful, dark pigmented nipples. She closed her eyes and pushed her head back. For Jeremy, it was like Columbus, out searching for South America. He'd discovered land and was exploring the territory with abandon. He kissed her breasts, but he knew the excitement might be too much for him. As far as Sofia was concerned, she was enjoying every moment of his exploration. As he moved up to kiss her lips, he slid his hand down between her legs and ran his fingers through her dark pubic hair. These moments were accompanied by the drumming of Jeremy's wildly beating heart, something his mind had no control over. Especially when Sofia decided that she wanted to help. She pushed him onto his back. The moment took him by surprise. So much so, that he lay there as if a professional wrestler was asking him to submit. The truth was, he was so willing to do so. She took the lead and sat astride him, then grasped his wrists with her hands. She pinned him to the bed. Although he was happy enough, his ardour had subsided because of her domination. Fortunately, it was only seconds before he was ok again. She released her one hand and carefully guided him into position. He was lost in the feeling, as she sat above him, gently moving and moaning at the same time. He then joined in.

All of this was wonderful, amazing and mind-blowing, but he was uncertain if he could control his urges. He knew he had to divert his thoughts, or this moment would come to an end too quickly. He tried to think of things that would stop him from coming. He thought of his half-brother's kids, especially the youngest who was an absolute shit, then immediately thought of how inappropriate that was. For some strange reason, his mother's trifle came into his mind. The way she went through the process of making the jelly, letting it set, and then pouring on the custard. As soon as he got to the cream, he knew he might lose the ability to hold back.

So he gently pushed her off him and rolled her onto her side. She knew what he wanted, so he let him spoon her. This time he was in control, his thoughts fully taken up by entering her from behind. It was an amazing feeling. The power was now with him and he was in heaven. He then realised he needed to kiss her. She rolled onto her back, as he moved between her legs. On top of her, he paused to take in her stunning body and her beautiful face. They kissed, before he then pushed her hands back over her head onto the pillow. He kissed her again, a sensual aroma overtaking the moment. They both knew it, as a torrent of feelings overtook them and there it was. Jeremy had found the new world.

They lay together quietly soaking up the magical moment, all thoughts lost in the sheer joy of sharing each other's body. In both of their minds, they thought there was plenty of time to do it all over again, but they drifted off to sleep.

There was a scream that snapped Jeremy from his sexual slumbers. He jumped out of bed, completely naked, ran towards the bathroom, where he found Sofia coming out, wearing a towel.

"I was having a shower," shouted Sofia, "and an Asian girl came in and frightened the life out of me! I thought the house was empty, apart from us!"

As they stood there, Maya appeared, followed by Chai. There was a standoff of sorts, as Jeremy tried to cover his nakedness.

"Put some clothes on, Jeremy," said Maya, "I'll see you downstairs in ten minutes."

Maya was in the kitchen, making coffee.

"Would you like one, lover boy?"

She smiled as she said it.

"I'll have a latte," he said, then continued, "Why didn't you say something about wanting to use the house to be with Chai?"

"We never planned it," she said, "it just happened. A strange coincidence that we are here on the same day to entertain our lovers! Anyway, for that matter, why didn't you say something about being here with Sofia?"

"To be perfectly honest," replied Jeremy, "I thought no one was at home so why not? It's a sad situation that we had to do it so secretively."

"True, I'm not sure Mum and Dad would have welcomed the idea, do you? Especially me and Chai."

"I suppose," said Jeremy, "but, if we had asked, they may have understood."

"Yea, but where would the fun be in that?"

As Maya said it, a broad smile spread across both of their faces.

"I never heard you in the house," said Jeremy.

"We got here about 11.30," she said. "I'm guessing you were here a lot earlier."

He realised that he and Sofia must have dropped off to sleep.

"How come you're not at the market?" he asked.

"There were some safety issues yesterday that needed sorting out today, so nobody could access the building. How about you and Cecilia? Aren't you supposed to be at her beck and call?"

"I needed the day off to be with Sofia!"

"Must say, Jeremy, Sofia's a beautiful woman!"

She then grinned and cheekily added, "I wouldn't mind. That's if she wanted to stray!"

They both smiled and Jeremy took it as a compliment.

Refreshed from his day of love, Jeremy was ready to write his heart out and get to grips with Cecilia's story. He tapped on the front door of Cecilia's apartment, but there was no answer. He let himself in, then went through to the living room. Cecilia was not there, so he automatically looked into the kitchen. She was lying in a heap on the floor. He quickly checked to see if she was ok. She was alive, so he kept talking to her, even though she didn't respond. He knew how to resuscitate someone in these circumstances, but it seemed that she was coming around. After a while, he helped her up. She seemed so thin. Till now he'd never guessed how thin she was. She wore mostly oversized things that covered any sign of weight or lack of it. He helped her into the living-room to sit her down. She seemed to become impatient with him fussing over her.

"Don't go on so much! I'm ok! I just fainted!"

She said it in such a matter-of-fact way, that he felt sure it had happened before.

"You're not eating enough. Why are you letting yourself go like this!"

"I'm not letting myself go! This is normal!"

"Since when was it normal for someone to faint? I'll call a doctor!"

"No!" she said forcibly.

He looked at her.

"Right, you must eat and drink!"

Her argument had run out of steam, mostly because she was too tired. He insisted that she should lie down, so he took her to her bedroom, then helped her into her bed. She lay there, looking comfortable. He left the room, then fifteen minutes later, he came back with two boiled eggs, toast soldiers, orange juice and tea on a tray. He helped her sit up.

"Eat or I'll call a doctor!"

She feigned a smile, then dutifully ate the food. Not another word was said, as he sat there watching her.

"There! Are you happy now?"

She pushed the tray his way. There was colour in her cheeks, which eased his concern. They had an understanding that was somewhere between parent and child or husband and wife. Such things are hard to define. Either way, there was an unspoken love.

They sat there in the semi-gloom of the bedroom, as Cecilia slipped off to sleep. He was sat in a cushioned chair at the side of her bed. He relaxed, took in the room and felt at home. He got up to look more closely at the artworks that Rupert had painted. He stared at nudes of Cecilia and thought how beautiful they were. He looked again at the photographs of Cecilia and Rupert. There were others, too, but he had no idea who they were. He took a few photos of them with his mobile phone, then decided to leave Cecilia to sleep.

In the living-room, he enjoyed the silence. The Art Deco room made him feel like he was sitting in the past. He went through all his notes. His mind floated between his scribbling and Sofia. The excitement of the day before quickly consumed his thoughts. He couldn't be certain how long he'd been sitting there or if he had drifted off to sleep.

"Penny for them, or do I only need to make an educated guess?"

He was brought back to the room as Cecilia stood a few meters away from him. She looked like a different person. She was dressed. Her demeanour was much better, like that of someone who wanted to take on the world. She was wearing a long, black dress that, for once, didn't look oversized.

"My, you look beautiful, Cecilia!"

She changed the subject.

"How is Sofia?"

She asked the question with a playful glint in her eye. He coloured up and said nothing.

"I take it, by your silence, that it went well!"

They both smiled, then she acknowledged the way she was dressed, by curtsying to him.

"I thought I should make an effort for the man who saved my life!"

"I don't think I did that! Merely helped you back to bed!"

"You gave me the sustenance that helped me to carry on in this play that is my life's work!"

She said it with such pathos, then sat regally. The dress she was wearing was black with a red stripe of braid to the neck and arms.

"In some ways, Cecilia, you remind me of a queen on her throne."

She sat up straighter, as if to take on the part.

"I'm dressed a bit minimalist for that, Jeremy, don't you think? But why not?"

She seemed to assert herself and, within seconds, she looked around the room with the air of a sovereign.

"Where were we, kind sir....? It would seem that Sir Jeremy is at a loss for words. Maybe it's because he's astonished by my beauty, or is he just a stupid servant at my feet? Do I wait, or do I send him to the tower and have his head separated from his body?"

Jeremy went with the narrative.

"My queen, I am just lost in your beauty! It maketh my tongue turn in knots! Forgive me, I am a fool!"

He stood, then gave her an elaborate bow.

"I hope you don't think that I think you are a fool, for thinking I am beautiful. If that was the case, then your head would surely be off!"

It amused them both as they played the game, but some part of Jeremy felt that Cecilia revelled in it more than he did.

"Have you ever played Elizabeth 1?" he asked.

"Not quite, but nearly!"

The ambiguous answer would, he knew, be followed by a theatrical explanation, one he would welcome to add to her many stories.

"There was a famous film that I auditioned for the role of Elizabeth 1, but it was acquired by another actress. She, who will remain nameless, did a wonderful job."

She told him the name of the film. Jeremy seemed to recall it, but he thought better than to mention the name of the actor. Cecilia's eyes looked as if she had slipped into a dream, as she stared, then recaptured her thoughts.

"That's water under a very large bridge!"

"Did you have to turn work down?" he asked.

"Yes, it was a time of plenty. Most of us were competing for the same work. Helen Mirren, Judy Dench, Maggie Smith - parts were numerous. There was plenty of money around. You could never say that all the parts were great. However, a powerful performance would always lift the piece. I had a run in several crime dramas, including Agatha Christie and Silent Witness. They, like many other dramas, were bread and butter to all of us actors. Of course, choice parts came along, then were gobbled up by the elite of the acting world. I was up there with them for a time."

She paused.

"Even, dare I say it, in Doctor Who! The part was offered to me. I read the script. To be perfectly honest, I had no idea what the hell it was all about. Some people say that Shakespeare is hard to fathom, but for me, his work is like a children's book, in comparison to the twaddle I was given. To be perfectly fair to it, in latter years, I have watched and enjoyed it."

"So," he interrupted her, "at this time, it was all plain sailing?" He had it in his mind to move forward to try and find out where things started to slide.

"After the millennium, what was it that caused your career to come to a halt?"

He could see, she was thinking it through, then after a few minutes.

"As I said before, I'm not ready for that yet!"

He knew not to push it, so went down a parallel path.

"Did you keep seeing Rupert?"

"Of course! If we were ever near to each other or on tour, we would usually end up spending the night together."

Jeremy was curious to know about her other relationships, but for the moment she stuck to talking about Rupert.

"To be honest, Rupert and I had an open relationship. He was a gay person, albeit one with a bisexual state of mind. We seemed to be tied by our early years and our little tragedies. In this business, there is always the opportunity to meet someone you might find attractive and then develop an interesting liaison. Actors, in general, are so vain. Always shy, but so very vain."

It seemed, to Jeremy, this was the perfect quote.

"Cecilia, you have alluded to several things that, at the moment, you don't want to go into. Are they all part of the same thing, whatever that is?"

"It is and it isn't, they are and they are not. I'm sorry for being vague, or shall I say evasive, but I need to come to terms with talking about the deeper things in my life."

"You mean you want the story to unfold naturally!" he said.

"Yes, I think so. It's a question of it falling into place, but mainly at the right time."

Jeremy gave her a nod, as if he understood her thought pattern. Even so, he felt a little frustrated that he was being starved of the bones of her story.

Cecilia sat pensively, but a small smile crept across her face.

"It's strange, but I've only just come to realise that my life will be in book form! What a wonderful concept for an actor!"

"Maybe," said Jeremy, "it will be a bestseller and someone might play you in a film about you!"

These words made Cecilia stand up and pace the room. It was as if someone had informed her of some amazing news that she couldn't quite take in. She sat back down.

"Well Jeremy, it seems to me that, maybe, I should take this whole thing more seriously. Up to now, I have casually told you about my life and love. Perhaps now, the deeper things should be examined. Do you think you could leave me to think things through? I feel today has tired me greatly."

Jeremy was happy to shorten the day, Maya had asked him to help her later. Now he could take the opportunity to go back home, change and think of other things. Sofia and their relationship was at the forefront of his mind. He bid Cecilia a good day and asked her to promise she would eat and rest in that order. Like a guilty schoolgirl, she agreed.

28.

Jeremy had travelled to Cecilia's on the bus. In some ways, it was easier, more thought-provoking, than going by car. It also gave him a chance to think without having to negotiate the traffic. He sat among the masked and unmasked on the bus. Even though the pandemic was over, some saw it fit to not take chances. There was still confusion as to where the future lay on how to tackle its long-term effects.

As he skipped through his phone, looking at the newspaper headlines, he realised that the birds were coming home to roost on Boris Johnson and his beleaguered government.

Jeremy smiled to himself and was happy he was no longer part of the news-gathering world. He was now a writer and being paid to do it. He got off the bus and was surprised to see Gail waiting on the corner of the street. He stood behind her. Hundreds of people passed by in the busy confusion that all great cities have.

"If you've got fifty quid," Jeremy said, with hint of sinister in his voice, "I'll give you a great story."

Without moving and with barely a flinch of emotion in her voice, she answered,

"If I had fifty quid, I'd be in the pub getting pissed."

She turned to face him.

"I saw you getting off the bus, Jeremy!"

"I always said you were great at seeing what most people didn't," answered Jeremy. "You should be working for MI5."

"If I worked for MI5, I'd be as pissed off as I am now, and you would probably be dead."

He couldn't help thinking that Gail had a screw loose or

perhaps she was just undervalued. He knew she wasn't happy. It was eighteen months earlier that they'd ended up together at the newspaper's Christmas party. Gail was partially drunk, then unloaded her feelings about her marriage onto him. Jeremy was a good listener. So, they both got drunk.

One thing led to another. They then found themselves in a hotel. By the time they got to the room, they were overcome with laughter, just getting in the door, which was like trying to open a large safe. They fell on the bed, two drunken bodies giggling childishly. Feverish sex swiftly followed. There was no finesse, no sweet talk. It was an out-and-out lustful union. Looking at the ceiling of the hotel room twenty minutes later, they both felt satisfied, but regretful. Jeremy looked sideways at Gail's body. For someone ten years older than him, who had had two kids, she had a great figure. She then ran her hand slowly up his body to his face.

"You know this means nothing. I love my husband, my kids! I'm just frustrated with my life!"

She noticed, as she said it, that Jeremy had become aroused. He couldn't help it. She was good-looking, strong and knew what she wanted. He thought if it was wrong, it could be no worse for doing it twice. She quickly took charge and sat astride him. The first time it was fast, served the purpose. This time, it was slow, penetrative and seductive. At the end, it brought about a union that lasted for months.

They would meet up for a drink, then end up in an anonymous hotel. A night together was enough for both of them, then they would go back to their normal life. Jeremy didn't love her. He knew she didn't love him, but he felt somehow emotionally involved. The relationship ebbed, as time went by. It was finished well before Sofia was on the scene.

After a few moments of indecision in the street Jeremy asked if she would like a drink. The bar was almost empty. Lunchtime had passed.

"So, Gail, what's the problem? Are you ok?"

"Yes and no! Gerry found a receipt for a hotel that you and I stopped in six months ago."

Jeremy, who was taking a sip of his lager, spat some out onto his trousers.

"Bloody hell!" said Gail, "You're like one of my kids!"

She then laughed.

"It's ok, Jeremy, I polished over it! I managed to convince him that I was on my own reporting on a story."

This eased Jeremy's worries, as he took another gulp of his lager.

"That's not the problem! During our heated argument, there was lots of mudslinging. The upshot was that Gerry told me he had been seeing some little tart from the local supermarket and he was moving in with her."

Jeremy looked at her, dumfounded.

"Why didn't you tell him that you had been having an affair?"

"What, throw away my upper hand? No way! He's going to pay for this!"

Jeremy didn't think it was about money, because Gerry was out of work and had been for some time. Not wishing to become the focus for Gail's attention, now that Gerry was on his way, Jeremy started searching for a resolution.

"What about the kids?"

"I've talked to them. They seemed unmoved by it all. Gerry's input into the house emotionally, financially, has been minimal."

The conversation went quiet.

"Don't worry, Jeremy, I won't be calling on your emotional or physical support."

She smiled at him in a knowing way. He was trying to find the words to support her. In some part, he felt guilty. She then shifted the conversation slightly.

"You caught me at a funny moment," she said. "I'd been considering going to the supermarket, where this bitch works, then have it out with her. Seeing you made me realise I would be too much of a hypocrite to do that."

She placed her hand on his thigh.

"It made me realise, there's more of a life out there."

Jeremy felt the urge inside his body. Going by their past, it would be easy to slip into that feeling that they got from each other.

"I'm letting you go, Jeremy! I'll be fine."

He didn't know what to say. Up until that day, he had considered Gail a part of his history. He was now engrossed with two other women in his life and was all the happier for it. As they parted, they hugged, then kissed each other on the cheek. Gail seemed happy after seeing him, which made him feel good inside. Just as she was going to walk away, she turned and kissed him on the lips.

"All that being said, maybe there's always another day. You have my number."

He wasn't exactly sure why, but Jeremy felt as if he was walking taller, but something felt dangerous inside, as he made his way home.

After a shower and a change of clothes, Jeremy entered the kitchen. His mum had come home and was making hot chocolate.

"Would you like one, Jeremy?"

The smell took him back to Sundays when he was a kid, when they would all sit together and watch a movie. Popcorn with hot chocolate was the highlight. It always made him think of such happy times.

However, Jeremy had a feeling his mum was after something. He sipped the mug of memories, as the flavour slipped down his throat.

"So, how's the new girlfriend?"

"That makes it sound like I've had loads, Mum."

"Oh, I'm just thinking about the ones you never told me about!"

"Are you playing mind games with me?"

She laughed.

"No, but if I did, you'd lose."

Jeremy felt slightly uncomfortable. One thing was for certain.

His mum was a formidable woman. He didn't really want to go there, so he thought it would be best to just talk about Sofia.

"I think Sofia is different," he said, "she's fun and very pretty."

"That makes her sound like a pet."

"You know what I mean, Mum! Also, she's so good to be with."

"That's better! So, when do we get to meet her?"

Jeremy hadn't thought about this, what with Cecilia taking up his time and now Maya wanting some as well.

"Soon," he said nervously.

"How about on Sunday? The whole family could meet her."

His mind said *Hold the horses!* He was in no mood for Kazi and his tribe to go anywhere near her as yet.

"Leave it for the moment Mum! I'll talk to her first."

His mum gave him her sad, lonely face and she pretended to cry.

She often did this to Jeremy. It was her idea of fun. It always made him smile. He went around to her, hugged her and kissed her. She immediately smiled.

"Soon, Mum! Soon!"

29.

Jeremy made his way to the new market to help Maya and Chai. Up to now, Jeremy and Maya's parents had left Maya to get on with her venture, without interfering; something that Maya was very happy about. She knew that, like all parents, they would more than likely make it worse, not better, if they got involved.

Maya hugged Jeremy. It seemed to him that it was an emotional moment, as she held him for more than three seconds. He remembered someone telling him once that three seconds was key to how emotionally attached you were to that person. Ten seconds later, she was still hugging him.

"This means so much to me, thank you!"

As they let go of each other, he saw a tear in Maya's eye, then he realised he had never been party to any of her deep emotions. To him, Maya had always been the rock in the family. He then drew her towards him. They hugged again. Chai was lingering in the background.

"Oh my God, can I join in?"

She wrapped her arms around them. Jeremy and Maya were amused by it, then opened up the hug to include her. They stood there in an emotional throng, none of them exactly certain as to when to let go. When they did, Jeremy glimpsed up at the signboard above, then read it out loud.

"East of Maya. The best of Asian cuisine. Great name for the restaurant, Maya!"

"Yeah, I think so! Chai and I spent quite some time playing with the name. We're trying to think of a bigger picture. Today we're here in this small market area with twenty covers and takeaways, but soon I'd like a restaurant on the high street or, even better, on the river!"

Jeremy was happy with Maya's ambition and was pretty certain she would achieve what she wanted.

"Ok," said Maya, "there's work to do."

They then set about organising things for the big opening of Maya's restaurant, just a week away. Later, Maya hit the sofa, feeling exhausted. There were still lots to sort out. However, she was content she had everything in hand. She mindlessly switched the TV on, then scrolled through the text messages on her mobile phone.

Jeremy had gone to have a shower. Maya didn't know if her mum was in, but was certain her dad was at work. The interviewer was talking to some celeb about a book she had written. Maya looked at the TV, caught a few words of the conversation, then went back to her phone. Jeremy appeared clean and refreshed. He was wearing boxer shorts with an oversized T-shirt, on which a graphic of iron man was printed. Maya looked at him.

"My superhero!"

Jeremy smiled, looking down at the T shirt.

"If only," he said, then looked at the TV as he rubbed his hair dry with a towel. "Isn't that….?"

"Yeah, it is," said Maya. "The woman who laughs every time she speaks."

"Oh my God!" he said, "She gets on my nerves!"

"You, me and nearly everyone else," she agreed.

"How do these people get famous for doing fuck all?"

Jeremy had bile in his mouth, then the woman on the TV said,

"Yes, my book is about my journey and how show business has treated me!"

For the first time ever that he could remember, the words were not followed by her inane laughter.

"Why do these people become famous for doing sod all, then moan about how it has affected their mental health! To me it is as if they are blaming everyone else for their self-inflicted problems!"

Jeremy looked as if someone had poked him with a stick. He continued.

"It just annoys me! I've watched this programme before, It's a platform for buddies in the media! I don't know why they can't get the odd unknown writer on here who has had a life. In my opinion, it's just another form of nepotism!"

"My oh my, someone doesn't like vacuous, no-real-talent celebs!"

Maya laughed as she said it. Jeremy saw the funny side, then smiled. At that moment, their mum came in with a book in her hand.

"Oh, I'd like to watch this!"

Both Jeremy and Maya laughed, echoing the TV celeb's laugh. It surprised their mum.

"I've just bought her book," she said.

"Why?" asked Jeremy.

"I don't know. I just saw it in the supermarket, thought it might be a good read."

"What has she done Mum?" asked Jeremy.

As Maya paused the TV programme, Mum looked blankly at him. She was struggling to think of what she was famous for.

"Didn't she have a number one song?"

"No!"

"Wasn't she in that TV programme? You know, the one with all the other actors who got murdered. Dead People Don't Walk!"

"No! And it's Dead People Don't Talk!"

She then hesitated. As she was about to say something else, a chorus of "No!" came from both Jeremy and Maya, which confused Mum.

"So, you bought a book about a celeb," stated Jeremy, "but you have no idea what she's famous for."

"I just thought it would be a good read. What is she famous for, then?" mum asked.

They both said in unison,

"Laughing!"

They then mimicked her laugh again.

"I think the world is going fucking crazy," said Jeremy.

"There's no need for that sort of language in this house, Jeremy!"

Mum would often swear her socks off, but at that moment she felt got at, then Dad came in and Maya un-paused the TV programme. The woman TV celeb burst into one of her infamous laughs.

"Isn't that the woman.......?" Dad said.

Jeremy, Maya, and their mum said in unison,

"Yes, it is!"

"You know, I have no idea what she is famous for!"

As Dad stood there with the question on his lips, the others laughed.

Jeremy went to bed. He had a glow inside of him. He felt his world was full to the brim. It was like a cup of hot chocolate with marshmallows and sprinkles on top. He drifted off to sleep, as he texted Sofia hearts and kisses.

The next morning Jeremy arrived promptly at Cecilia's house. Up to then, he had never seen any of the other people in the building. On this particular morning, he met one as he let himself in. Jeremy opened the front door. He then found an umbrella tip pushed into his stomach.

"And who are you, young man?"

As Jeremy was still retrieving his key from the lock, he felt another prod, which took his breath. He managed to wheeze the words.

"I can't tell you if you continue to prod me in the stomach!"

An elderly man stood squarely in front of him, an old brown trilby hat tipped forward over his scowling face. He was wearing a black Macintosh that made him look sinister, although he was at least a foot shorter than Jeremy. Just before another prod was launched into him, Jeremy grabbed its end.

"Stop it!"

The man paused, then rested his umbrella on the floor.

"Well?" the man asked.

Jeremy was annoyed, feeling compelled to grab the old man's umbrella and break it over his knee. He restrained himself.

"I'm a friend of Cecilia, Cecilia Walters!" said Jeremy.

"Yes, I know Cecilia Walters!" the man said. "She lives in the building. So what do you want with her?"

For a moment, Jeremy wasn't sure if he'd stepped into an alternate reality, governed by a doorkeeper wearing a black Mackintosh and holding a deadly umbrella. Jeremy did his best to be polite, as the small man with a now more intense face, again asked,

"Who are you? And what do you want of Cecilia Walters?"

"I'm Jeremy Bakshi, I'm a very good friend of hers!"

"You're a friend of who? Who is hers?"

Jeremy became speechless, as the conversation went around in his head.

The old man then physically pushed Jeremy to one side, without saying another word. Jeremy was surprised at how strong he was for his height and age. As he walked down the path, the old man was muttering to himself. He then put up his umbrella, even though it was a perfectly fine day.

Jeremy continued to Cecilia's apartment and let himself in. He was never quite sure what to expect, as he entered, going by experience. The small mad doorkeeper was still on his mind. Cecilia was in her chair, sitting bolt upright looking alert and quite beautiful. She was wearing an Indian sari, which seemed to sparkle, as the light from the morning sun caught it.

"Good morning, master Jeremy!"

The greeting made him smile, because he knew that if Cecilia was in a good mood, they might move forward quickly on her memoir.

"Tea?"

She presupposed his answer, then began to pour as he sat down.

"May I say, Cecilia, you look quite wonderful today!

"Why, thank you, kind sir! To tell you the truth, I probably feel better than I have for a long time. Touch wood!"

She did the time-honoured thing, then pressed her finger onto her head, even though there was plenty of wood within touching distance.

"Your neighbour accosted me at the front door," said Jeremy.

"That's Mr Silverman. I believe he has lived here since the day he was born. Unfortunately, he has bouts of dementia. Somehow, he manages to see to himself, although his daughter does come to care for him several times a week. In the Second World War, his parents escaped from Germany. However, his grandparents were captured, then sent to a concentration camp. He seems to be fixated on that part of his family's history. Now he often thinks the Nazis are coming to take him away!"

Jeremy told Cecilia about his encounter with him.

"I'm surprised he remembered who I was!" Cecilia remarked. "Whenever I meet him, he always challenges me, asks me who I am, which is quite funny sometimes. I pretend to be someone else, anyone from Queen Elizabeth to Greta Garbo. Usually, any name satisfies him!"

They both smiled at the thought of it.

"I am well aware," said Cecilia, "that we are all candidates to some form of dementia when we get older!"

A solemn moment followed. Tea was consumed before they started. Cecilia's face then looked pained, as if she was feeling ill.

"Are you ok? You don't look well!"

"I feel I need to go back," she said, "to the beginning. Fuck! Fuck! Fuck!"

She didn't act it; it was from the heart. He could feel some inner primeval force from inside her, as she shouted out the words. She then put her head in her hands.

"There are things that I keep hidden! Things I try to forget! Things that I find so hard to talk about!"

He sat patiently.

"My sins are many! If I believed in God, l guess I would have been hell-bound a long time ago!"

He knew, by the way she was speaking, that it was something they had touched on before. She took a deep breath.

"As I've said before, I went back to my parents when I was pregnant. They were wonderful, so supportive. We talked about my choices. I was convinced, when I went home, that I would have to have an abortion, but they appealed to me that adoption would be a much better alternative. How could I say no, when they had adopted me! After all, they made me as happy as I could be. Anyway, I consented to their request to have my baby girl adopted. My parents even offered to look after her, but both of them had health problems. So, I decided to go through the correct channels."

She stopped, looking relieved, almost as if the greatest secrets of her world had been revealed.

"Are you ok, Cecilia?"

She nodded, then continued.

"For a long, long time, I told no one. Eventually, I told Rupert, who was supportive, not critical in any way."

The whole thing hung like a shroud over the room, and then her face changed.

"No," she then said, assertively, "I'm not going to be party to these emotions! I've done this so many times in the past, when I was feeling low. In those days, I would put it behind me, then move on. I would suffer inwardly, but my acting got me through. I want you to know, Jeremy, that there were precious few so-called experts to help support someone like me, or anyone, for that matter!"

She looked reflective and a little worn out, but she carried on.

"Looking back, there must have been someone, but I chose to leave it behind me. I suppose the truth was, I didn't want any help!

Many years later, I discovered that the girl grew up in a family that loved her. For whatever reason, she became a rebel. It wasn't long before she was in trouble at school. By the time she was a teenager, she had a catalogue of suspensions. She ran away several times. Eventually, she left school. Being a teenager, mixing with the wrong crowd, more trouble followed. Around that time, the social services contacted me, because Natalia, the name I'd given her, asked if she could see me!"

Jeremy's face was stark, as the surprise news was placed before him.

"When was this?"

"The dates, I'm not certain of. For that, I will have to consult my diary, but it was sometime after the millennium."

She smiled to herself.

"It was a strange time, because there was so much fuss about computers failing to work, as the year turned to two thousand. Even so, it seemed to me, as that year opened up and optimism grew, the years that followed, for me, got worse."

She stopped for a moment to reflect on the stressful time of her life. Her mind seemed to come back to the moment at hand.

"As I said, social services contacted me. They asked if I would like to meet Natalia. As you can imagine, my world was thrown into the air. I wanted to see her, but was well aware that she had many problems. Maybe I should have just left my past behind. However, I chose not to.

It was arranged. I was going to see her. I was so, so nervous, I could hardly sleep, but I felt I owed it to her. On the day we were supposed to meet, I had a phone call. She had gone, disappeared. I met her social worker, who brought me up to date with what had been happening. The list was endless. She had been taking drugs most of her teenage life. Of course, everything bad was linked to that!"

Cecilia took a breath, then sighed. Jeremy was still spellbound by this news. He was eager to know more. He patiently waited, but then thought better of it.

"Do you want to leave it, Cecilia? Take a break?"

Jeremy was now familiar with Cecilia's habits, so he went about making something to eat. The sun shone brightly through Cecilia's windows, then moved slowly across the room. A pleasant smell of food cooking filled the apartment.

The break, along with the food, gave her the energy to continue.

"I had been filming solidly for a week on a new production," she said, "I was half asleep sitting in this chair, then there was a knock on my door. There stood a thin, pale, young woman. She was dressed haphazardly, like a homeless person. Her face was drawn and worn out, older than her years. We looked at each other. I knew it was Natalia. I could see it in her eyes, even though she had dark, tired rings around them. It looked like alcohol and drugs had taken their toll. After fainting on my carpet, she woke up and I helped her to the sofa. We talked about things that I can't remember now, but after she'd had a few hot drinks and something to eat, she began to look better. I hardly knew anything about her, but somehow I knew everything about her. Can you work that out?"

"How did she know where you lived?"

"That was easy. She had my name. It's not as if it's hard to find me or anyone you want to these days. I may be old, but I know how it works. How she got in my building? I think I can put that down to one of my neighbours letting her in."

Jeremy listened attentively. This was like liquid gold to him.

"Eventually, she came to live here. I nursed her, and she started to look like a beautiful young woman. Healthy, even happy. It was an emotional time. We seemed to bond very quickly!"

"Did you tell her who her father was?"

"No! I didn't tell her that her father was Rupert Blaine. I thought it best to keep that from her until it was right to do so."

"So, how did the relationship continue?"

"I still had plenty of work, so I thought she could stay here to recuperate, which she did. She then told me she had found a job, working in a supermarket."

"How long did this take? Did you believe her?"

"It was about a month in total. No, I didn't believe her! I thought the only way we could move forward would be for me to try and trust her.

Being in demand gave me little time to spend with Natalia.

I guess I was never the maternal type. Even though we had become close, it wasn't in the conventional sense."

"What were the parts you were playing at the time? Were they mostly detective series?"

"Yes, I had become something of an established figure, as far as crime was concerned. It's amazing how much you can learn about the criminal mind when you research for that type of programme!"

"I'm guessing," said Jeremy, "that things started to go wrong for you and Natalia!"

"You could say she was trying to pull the wool over my eyes. She asked me to give her money, so she could rent a place of her own. I decided to help out, which became a regular thing. If it wasn't the rent, it was something else. Natalia became a convincing actor. I suppose nuts never fall far from the tree. I believed her because I wanted her to get better. When a few things disappeared from my apartment, then I realised she was stealing from me."

"That must have been heart-breaking, especially as you must have been getting on so well."

"What made it worse, late one night, Natalia came to my door with a man. He was quite well-dressed, although he looked sweaty. I could hear a strange accent, which confused me. He looked high on drugs. So was Natalia. She could hardly walk!

He said, *'So, you're the famous actress, Cecilia Walters! Nice to meet you.'*

He put out his hand, but I refused to shake it. I couldn't understand why she was with this man. She had never mentioned she was in a relationship. It was obvious that he was manipulating her. Of course, there was some emotional attachment that I couldn't fathom. I asked him what he wanted.

He said, *'I'm Matias, your daughter's boyfriend. I'm pretty sure, Ms Walters, you wouldn't want this in the newspapers!'*

He then showed me some photos of Natalia taking drugs!

We were now in my living room with Natalia lying on the

settee. I wasn't stupid. I know these things always end badly, when it comes to blackmail. He asked for money, or he would sell the story. He wanted £5,000 in cash, or he would give the media the photographs. After trying to think it through, I said I would get the money. The surly guy left my apartment. Natalia slept it off on my sofa.

The next morning, I cancelled some filming. I made up a story that I was feeling ill. I nursed my Natalia. It was strange. I had never looked after anyone other than Rupert. It somehow softened me, but only for a short time. I realised, then, the situation was becoming untenable.

I gave the money to Matias. I met him in the street in a public place. I gave him an envelope, then he gave me what I thought were the negatives."

"What was it, then, that he gave you?" Jeremy asked.

"Just the photographs. I know it was a stupid thing to do, but he was gone in the blink of an eye.

Natalia promised she wouldn't do it again. She moved back in here for a while. I should have guessed it would all go wrong, as more things disappeared from the flat!"

"What did she take?"

"Mainly jewellery from my bedroom, things that could be pawned for quick cash to keep this pimp Matias happy. I confronted Natalia, who denied everything. I told her to leave and she did. As she left, I decided to follow her. I had done all the TV work, I knew how not to be spotted. It wasn't long before she met him in the town, in a back street. It was difficult to see. She kissed him, then he manhandled her. He was angry at what she was saying to him. I knew then I had to do something to stop this from carrying on!"

Jeremy was riveted by the story and had little reason to ask questions, as Cecilia continued.

"It wasn't long before he was back for more money. Meanwhile, I had not seen Natalia since that day. Matias called me on the phone asking for more cash. This time he said he would give me the negatives. He wanted fifty thousand pounds. I said all

I had was thirty thousand. I thought foolishly that this would stop him.

The problem was when emotions get caught up in events, it's hard to see an outcome at all. I just hoped it would turn out right. It was arranged that we would meet in a well-lit place by the canal. There were many walkways for an easy escape if I needed to. It seemed that life was mirroring art. I felt as if I was in a film. The only thing was this hurt so much! It was strange, somehow. I thought I could protect my life and my newfound daughter.

When playing a part on TV or in a film, hopefully, you end up with a dramatic piece that excites, entertains. Real life, however, is far more dangerous, terrifying even. It was about nine in the evening. No one was around. It was misty, damp and spitting rain. I had a bag with the money in, which I kept held tightly to my chest. I approached a footbridge that crossed over the canal. I could see Natalia and Matias. I felt angry that she was there with him. Natalia's arms were wrapped around her stomach. She looked like she had not slept. I asked Natalia if she was ok and she nodded her head. I gave Matias the money.

I asked him for the negatives. He said nothing. He just gave me an evil grin. He started to walk away, laughing to himself. Suddenly, like a rush of wind, Natalia ran at Matias. She grabbed the bag, then pushed him into the canal. I watched as if it was in slow motion. He plummeted towards the water. His head hit the sidewall as he went. I could tell straight away that he would not survive, as blood poured from his head into the water. I stood like a stone monument in shock, but Natalia was gone."

"Wow! Oh my God!"

For the moment, that was all Jeremy could say, as he took the story in. He'd never thought for a second that Cecilia had this kind of history. Cecilia looked relieved as she sat back in her chair, having divulged what had happened.

"You're the only person who has heard that story, "she said.

While Jeremy's mind tried to take it in, Cecilia got up and went to the kitchen. She came back with a glass of water, then sat to wait for Jeremy to speak. He was at a loss for what to say. It was still going around in his head. After some time, Jeremy asked, "What happened next?"

"I waited for what seemed like ages, but it couldn't have been long. In the darkness of the water, the body of Matias lay face down. Ripples of water were still hitting the side of the canal, the streetlights catching them as they went. I was in a state of shock, on my own, not knowing what to do!"

"What did you do?"

"I snapped out of it. I knew no good would come of staying there. So, after a few minutes, I left. I was in a state for days. The police discovered the body. There was no evidence of me or anyone else being involved. Later, it became clear that Matias Perez was known to the police for selling drugs. He had a list of felonies in Spain, Ireland and Britain!"

"What of Natalia?"

"I heard nothing! She disappeared without a trace!"

"How did that make you feel?"

"In some ways, I was relieved. Now she had some money, maybe she would have a better life, without someone controlling her. That's all I've ever thought! Perhaps she is happy, out there somewhere!"

He needed to ask her.

"What about the negatives?"

"Yes," she said, "what about them? That was the question in my mind. I thought the police would come knocking on my door, but they didn't. It was obvious that Matias didn't have them. It did occur to me that Natalia had them. She'd then disappeared with them and the money. To tell you the truth, I don't think I'll ever know."

So many questions occupied Jeremy's head as he tried to keep his mind in order. Before he could ask any more, Cecilia added, "A couple of months later, I employed a private detective to try and find Natalia, but to no avail. The detective told me she may have left the country, but he couldn't be certain!"

"How did you cope with it?"

"I threw myself into work. I asked my agent for anything! Even though I knew I was already doing too much. I contacted Rupert and told him the truth about what happened to Natalia. He was amazingly supportive even when I told him what happened to Matias Perez.

The only problem was, after all that had happened, I'd burnt myself out. I think that's the popular phrase. I had just finished working on an arduous mini-series, then I ended up in hospital suffering from a mild heart attack and, what was worse, depression!"

"So, was this when everything changed for you?"

"It was. I had to take a break, re-think my career. I asked my agent to put a halt to my work. Fortunately, I had just finished the mini-series on TV, so I could relax. Of course, it didn't take long to start worrying about being without an income. I had always been one to spend as I earned, especially on art. With thirty thousand pounds of my savings gone, selling a piece of art would give me what I needed to get by, but I didn't want to do that. I bided my time and did my best to get better."

Jeremy was now party to a crime but, to be fair to all concerned, it seemed a justifiable end to Matias Perez. This, however, slipped into the back of his mind, as he took care not to tax Cecilia anymore. Even though she looked tired, she was in good spirits. It was as if she felt better for unburdening herself of that part of her torrid past. It was in his mind to ask her another question, before he left for the day.

"Have you ever considered counselling, Cecilia?"

She looked at him ruefully, then got up from her chair. She moved around the room like an ageing panther looking for somewhere to rest.

"The phenomenon hasn't passed me by," she said, "I did partake in the act of mental examination."

For some reason, it conjured up in his mind an uncomfortable clinical act, rather than something undertaken in a relaxing situation.

"When I took part in such consultations, the act of regressing was too uncomfortable for me. Being taken back to when I was a child was too dark. I was told by the psychologist that it was necessary to find the root of the problem. My argument was there was no root, it was the seed that was the problem."

Cecilia paused, then looked at Jeremy, waiting for his mind to lock into her thought pattern. It didn't take long.

"Oh, I see! You mean Natalia!" he said.

"Yes, exactly! The seed being my daughter. The problem with the shrink was she was fixated too far back. The truth was, it was when my daughter came back into my life, and then she was gone. That's what brought about my depression!"

He sat there, almost like an extension to a psychiatrist, trying to think it through. She could see what he was thinking, then said,

"All I can say is I did try to reach out. Unfortunately, it didn't work!"

"What have you learnt, then, Cecilia?"

Here, she seemed reluctant to say more. It was as if someone had called time on this consultation, but it wasn't him. She became a little impatient with him. She wanted him to leave it for the day. He could feel it. The conversation had opened up old wounds. A short time later, after the usual pleasantries, he left.

A crossroads seemed to lie in front of Jeremy, as he drank coffee back at home. At the forefront of his mind was a need to research Natalia. Where had she gone? Was she still alive? The death of Matias was also high on the list. One thing was for certain, this story alone was a sensation for Cecilia's biography.

"What have you got to smile about, Jez?"

Maya had just breezed into the kitchen. She also seemed happy.

"I suppose," said Jeremy, "that Cecilia's life is way more surprising than I ever could have imagined."

"Good to hear. You wouldn't want it to be full of platitudes."

"Far from it," he said, "it's more like a rollercoaster ride at the moment, with intrigue thrown in for good measure. However, I think sometimes she's playing games with me. My feelings are that she's making me work for it. Whether it's to make a better story or she's just being bloody-minded, either way, at times it's taxing my abilities!"

"Perhaps that's why she's doing it, to see if you're capable. So you'll make a better job of it!"

Jeremy seemed lost in the things that were filling up his head.

"Maybe you're right, she's a cunning sly fox. I suppose I must up my game to catch her! How about you, then? Why are you so happy?" he asked.

"Why shouldn't I be? I'm starting my own business. It's a fabulous venue. I'm in a warm and loving relationship. To top that, the sun is out."

Jeremy was well aware of Maya's hopes and dreams. For the last few weeks, he'd bent his back to help her achieve a small part of it.

"Who's coming to the opening?" asked Jeremy.

"A famous chef off the TV. A few minor celebs," she said.

"Who's the famous chef, then?"

"One who has a familiar face, but most people can't remember his name."

"I could ask Cecilia to come, if she feels well enough."

"As a matter of fact," said Maya, "that was something I was going to ask."

"To be honest with you, she seems so much stronger, but I'm not sure if she would be happy to mix with wannabe celebs. I'm not sure exactly why, but she seems to have an aversion to most people of that ilk. It's something that keeps reoccurring in her stories. She becomes somehow dark and preoccupied whenever one is mentioned. To me, she seems a little obsessed with those who become famous for being famous."

"I'm with Cecilia on that one," said Maya, "Please invite her, I would love to meet see what she was like. I'm sure Chai would too!"

"I'm not sure she will come. She might find the whole thing too much, but who knows? She is a force unto herself!"

30.

Ella, Nigel, Amber and Ethan had had an addition to the team, Bahni Sharma. She was a DC like Ethan. The pandemic had gone, crime was on the rise. Ella's small team needed her badly, to help with the increasing workload.

Ella was an enthusiastic boss, sharing many hours on the streets, investigating like the rest of her team. Bahni Sharma joined Ethan mainly to research crimes. Amber would now be free to help on other cases. Ethan was only a few months in front of Bahni when it came to experience, but he knew the team better. So, he quickly thought to take Bahni under his wing. Ethan became fascinated by Bahni. She was in her early twenties like him. She had wonderful deep cream-coloured skin, which looked like that of a China doll.

In his experience, which, up to this point in time, was limited, he thought she was the most beautiful woman he'd ever seen. His fascination had him looking at her more than he should have been. So much so that she became irritated by his attention. Alone in the team office, they continued their work, researching cases.

"What's the problem, Ethan? Is there something wrong?"

He shook his head. He then decided to go over to her and talk.

"I'm sorry, I just wanted to say, I think you are quite stunning, Bahni. The way you dress, your makeup or your lack of it!"

She moved her chair away from him, surprised at his continual interest in her.

"If you don't stop it right now, Ethan, I'll have to report you for sexual harassment."

He immediately put his hands up and then moved away.

"I'm so sorry. I don't mean like that; I'm not coming on to you!"

She looked at him quizzically. He then realised his terminology might be taken the wrong way.

"Oh shit! I'm sorry again! All I'm trying to say is, as a gay man, I find you very attractive in a non-consensual way!"

She relaxed, then laughed.

"Thank you," she said, "that is a lovely compliment!"

They both seemed to relax.

"If you don't mind me asking," said Ethan, "where does your family originate from?"

"Wolverhampton!"

He stared at her, and then she laughed.

"Very good," he said, "you're funny as well as beautiful!"

She then looked a little embarrassed at all the compliments.

"Originally, my mum and dad were from Bangladesh. They moved here over thirty years ago. I have four sisters and one younger brother. He gets spoilt."

A potted history followed, as they both felt easier in each other's company.

"So," he said, "what do you think of our team?"

She looked a little bewildered.

"I would say it's less a team and more a small group!"

He smiled, then agreed with her observation.

"Yes, I guess you're right! I get a little bored with all this computer work. I thought, when I joined the police, I'd be out there on the streets, running after criminals, catching them, cuffing them, then sending them daaahn…!"

She laughed at the way he emphasised the last word.

"Do you think you've been watching too many cop programmes, Ethan?"

He screwed up his face.

"Maybe, but there has to be more to it than this."

"You mean," she said, "if you were cornered by a twenty stone skinhead up a dark alley, you would be happy to cuff him and send him daaahn, Ethan?"

He looked at her with an element of doubt on his face.

"Probably not, but I think I could kick him in the testicles!"

She had a wry smile on her face.

"That's that sorted then," she said, "you could put your cuffs around his dangly bits!"

His face looked appalled at the thought of it, then she laughed. He walked back to his computer, then sat down.

"I'm happy on the computer," said Bahni. "Out there on the internet, there are billions of atomic particles mixed with electrical charges, which may come together to solve a crime. All we have to do is press the right buttons to find the answers. And the best thing about it is, that you don't get hurt. Of course, then, as you put it, Ethan, we can send them daaahn…!"

He gave her a reluctant smile as she settled to her computer. All that could be heard was a heavy sigh from Ethan.

31.

Duman was keen to have a night out on the town. So, he contacted Jeremy and Nigel, who were reluctant to go. Duman did the time-honoured thing and called them lightweight old men. Eventually, they decided they had little choice. Their plans usually entailed a quiet bar to have a drink, then catch up with each other's news. The usual handshakes and high fives followed, as they sat opposite each other.

"News?" said Duman.

Both Jeremy and Nigel looked at each other. Jeremy was keen to update them on Sofia and Cecilia. However, Duman wanted to find out more about Nigel's involvement with his boss. He was cagey, his answers far from enlightening. Two pints later, both Jeremy and Duman got it out of him.

"Is that not frowned upon, Nigel, you shagging the boss?" asked Jeremy.

Both Duman and Jeremy laughed. Nigel looked a bit agitated, because he knew talking about it would bring about amusement on their part.

"I suppose it's ok," said Duman, "because she can call you her toy boy!"

"Ok, that's enough! I knew this would happen if I said any more about it."

Duman went off to get lagers. Nigel leaned over to Jeremy, then spoke quietly, as if someone might be listening.

"Jeremy, can you ask any of your journalist friends, if they can remember anything about The Celeb Six?"

Jeremy looked at him, surprised that he was talking about the case again.

"Firstly," said Jeremy, "that's a great title! You should be a journalist, not a detective! Secondly, why are you still obsessed with this case?"

Nigel thought for a moment.

"It's not anything like an obsession. It just seems to me that all the answers are there. I just need to find them!"

Jeremy looked quizzically at him.

"Isn't that always the problem? Why are you stuck on this one?"

"I think it's because it was lockdown. We didn't have the people on the ground or even the ability to follow it up. The truth is, it's like the perfect crime and it bugs me that I can't unravel it!"

Duman had returned with their usual tipple, lagers and shots. They downed them quickly, then decided to move on. As they were walking along the street to another bar, Jeremy said,

"Nigel, if I were you, I'd move on from that case. It's messing with your head. Before you know it, it'll ruin your relationship!"

The alcohol was talking. Nigel seemed to be more relaxed, as the three friends sauntered along the road, linked together like brothers in arms.

Nigel knew getting legless would be frowned upon. After all, he was a police officer, but his friends had triggered something in his mind to let go at least for one night. The three of them found themselves trailing around a string of pubs, eventually ending up at an old-fashioned disco to party the night away.

A taxi picked them up to go home. Jeremy was first to get out. It was early in the morning. He somehow managed to get into the house and then find his bedroom without making too much noise. As he lay on his bed, he thought of Sofia. The ceiling was moving anti clockwise. For some reason, he thought he and his bed were moving in the opposite direction. He remembered nights in his youth when he had drunk too much, but this was at the top of the pile for an out-there experience. He needed to sleep, but his dreams were intertwined with alcohol, murders and disco music.

He awoke, not wishing to move, as his head would not let him.

His immediate thoughts were fragile. All he could think was to stay perfectly still till his senses came back.

From somewhere in his dreams, he heard banging on his door.

"Wake up sleepy head!" called Maya.

There was a long pause.

"Leave me alone, I'm dying in here!" he said quietly.

Maya opened the door.

"Coffee? You know, baby brother, you're making a habit of this!"

He moved his body with the utmost care, groaning as he did so.

"Oh, thank you, Lord," he said, as she passed him a couple of paracetamol. He swallowed them. He then sipped the coffee.

"It's nice that you think of me as God, but if I was, I'd probably smite you just for fun!" she said.

Her voice was bright and amused at his predicament.

"Anyway, I'm being kind to you for being such a tower of strength these last few months."

He groaned, and she felt his head.

"It's ok. It feels like your elephants have gone home to have some sleep. I'll tell you this, Jeremy, you got off easy. Dad told me one of his taxi drivers dropped off Duman and Nigel in town. He said the last he saw of them, they were dancing in the millennium fountain."

A smile came over Jeremy's face. Not long after Maya left the room, his elephants came back.

Sofia was preoccupied. Her split shifts had become a bit of a burden. Her small apartment hardly gave her space to relax. She had only been in her job since the virus struck and had had little time to settle. When each shift finished, she crashed, waking only to get something to eat, before going back to work. Things had eased down over the last six months. Jeremy had helped to bring back her sanity.

She had spent most of her childhood in southern Spain, then qualified as a nurse in an area where there were many ex-pats. Over the years, she had always wanted to work in Britain, but the opportunity had never offered itself.

She applied for a job just before Covid 19 spread across the globe. As soon as she landed, she felt immediately at home. She jumped at the chance to give the NHS a hundred per cent. At the time, they were screaming out for qualified staff.

Both her parents were now dead, so she wanted to find out more about her roots. Her stepmother told her what she could, but there was so much more she wanted to know about her mother's past.

She had had little time to adjust, but now she was coming to terms with things. It was in her mind that she would love to entertain Jeremy, but the thought of inviting him back to her poky little flat did not appeal to her. Especially now, after spending time at Jeremy's house.

Jeremy had recovered from his self-inflicted hangover and was feeling fine again. He had entered Cecilia's apartment. As he walked into the living-room, Cecilia barked at him.

"Look at this girl here, Jeremy! Sacha Mills, in this magazine! What do you see?"

Jeremy walked over to the table and peered over her shoulder at Sasha Mills. He knew who she was. There were several pages about the young woman in the magazine, photographed in various dresses and swimming costumes.

"Look at her make-up," said Cecilia, "She looks like someone's been practising on her face!"

To Jeremy, Sacha Mills's face was the same as you would see on any minor celeb of her age, especially the fake tan. Jeremy said nothing. He knew if he did, he would be wrong, so he waited for Cecilia to vent her feelings as he knew she would.

"What has she done, Jeremy? What has she done to deserve all this publicity?"

"She came second," he said, "in I Want to Be a Pop Star! She came third in Big Brother!"

Cecilia put up her hand to stop him.

"Yes I can read that, but what has she done?"

Jeremy was at a loss as to what to say. He knew what was griping Cecilia, but he didn't know how to pacify her annoyance.

"What's worse, it says she's been offered a part in a play in the West End! I mean, I ask you! What's the business come to?"

She threw the magazine to the floor, got up and walked over it.

"That's all that's good for!"

She went into the kitchen, then called him.

"Tea?"

"Yes please!"

It was as if a different person came out of the kitchen than had gone in. She was carrying a tray with a teapot and cups on it.

"Shall I be mother?"

"That would be nice."

She looked at him, deadly serious.

"If you've researched me properly, which I hope you have, you will know by now that I played the wife of a serial killer in a mini-series. For me, I thought it was implausible, even though it was based on the truth. I ask you, how does a wife who has been married to a man for nearly twenty years, not know he murdered ten women?"

Jeremy knew what Cecilia was talking about. It was the series she was working on when she became ill and it brought about her heart attack. He also knew it was the time she was nominated for a Bafta for her part in that series, although she didn't win it.

Jeremy had also read that a popular female actor, who happened to be a dame, had won the Bafta. It was as if someone had stolen an apple from under the nose of Cecilia, made even more difficult to swallow, because Cecilia had thought that that apple should have been hers. Jeremy had it in his mind to look more closely at the part she'd played in the mini-series.

Cecilia arose from the chair with a look of indignation on her face.

"What do you say to a walk, Jeremy? I haven't been for a walk for quite some time!"

He agreed. She then disappeared to her bedroom. When she came back, she was wearing a long dark coat with a hood. Jeremy thought if he gave her a wand, she would have looked good in Harry Potter or Lord of the Rings, which reminded him of something he'd read.

"Is it true that you auditioned for parts in Harry Potter and Lord of the Rings, Cecilia?"

It was an innocent off-the-cuff question that he thought would be easy to answer. She stopped dead still in the middle of the room, as if to make a dramatic pose, then said,

"One is full of magic, fairies and monsters, the other is full of monsters, fairies and magic. Those things are the stars, not the actors."

She eloquently disposed of the question. Who was he to disagree?

"Don't worry, Jeremy! I'm over Harry Potter and The Lord of the Rings. I'm not sure I would have had the stomach to prance about doing magic spells and look serious at the same time. I don't think it was for me! Anyway, my mind was away with a different kind of fairy at the time!"

She looked at him with a wry smile on her face. He felt relieved.

"Where shall we go?" he asked.

"There is a beautiful park within walking distance. We'll go there," she said.

Jeremy was not a man for outdoor things, although his outing with Sofia by the river had started to change his point of view. They walked down the street, then, shortly after that, into the park. The sun was partially hidden by clouds. Other than that, there was a chill in the air. Cecilia gloried in the moment, taking deep breaths, almost like a child on the day it was born.

"Smell that green, Jeremy. It's intoxicating!"

As usual, she did this with airs and graces befitting an actor of her stature. It seemed to Jeremy, as he watched and listened, that she was taller, bigger than the character he already knew. She was supreme in doing this. As she walked, her arms reached for the sky. She quoted Shakespeare dramatically.

People were walking past and looking, some even pointing. It would seem that, even now, Cecilia could pull an audience. Nobody came over, as she continued to enjoy the moment, then it came to Jeremy: it was as if she was a bit of street entertainment. His only fear was that someone might drop a coin or two at her feet, which would surely put the cat among the pigeons.

"Are you missing the limelight that being a famous actor brings, Cecilia?"

For some reason, she chose not to answer. Instead, she spoke of nature.

"Look at the trees! They have reached their optimum growth, as the summer is coming to its end. The breeze is caressing their beauty as the leaves dance in perfect rhythm!"

Her arms seemed to move in time, as autumn's burnished leaves were falling. The path meandered through multicoloured flower beds, then onwards down to a small lake with a red metal bridge straddled across it. Life was back to normal, and Cecilia seemed revitalised by it. Jeremy was amazed by how beautiful the park was, a park he had never known was there.

He noticed that Cecilia had slowed. It was obvious that, in her condition, she should be careful what she did. It wasn't long before they found a bench where Cecilia could catch her breath.

The environment was perfect. It was as if there was a new page to write on, as Cecilia stared into the distance.

"As for your question, Jeremy, no I do not miss the limelight. I don't miss the glare from the public eye! The constant criticism, or playing someone else! I have learnt that it hurts as much as it compliments my life!"

Jeremy's mind was lost in the view. He thought of Sofia, of how nice it would be to be sitting there with her, then, as if his mind had been read,

"How is your Sofia, Jeremy?"

Cecilia was perceptive.

"Sofia is good, although I haven't seen her for a week or so."

"Why is that, pray tell?"

"Many things. There seems to be a lot on my mind, then, of course, she's busy and we have nowhere really to be together!"

He then told Cecilia about the day when Sofia had come back to his house when his mum and dad were out, after which she laughed.

"That story reminds me of a comedy I was in, in the seventies. It was a very successful farce. It wasn't unlike a carry-on film. Very popular then, very un-PC now. It paid well and had a long run, but it wasn't for me."

He listened, hoping another interesting story had come into her mind.

"There were many up-and-coming actors in the production, which had a regular turnaround of new faces. The older, more experienced actors would get bored, so, to liven things up, they played pranks on the younger ones. Two, in particular, were both experienced in the ways of the world. Let's call them Fred and Cynthia for the sake of argument. At least once a week during the show, one of them would strip off and stand naked on the other side of a door that was part of the set. During a monologue on stage, the new young actor would hear a knock at the door. He or she would then go to the door, expecting to converse with whoever was there. Of course, they were then faced by the naked actor! You have to remember, Jeremy, no one in the audience could see the naked actor."

"Oh my God! That must have been shocking for the young actors!"

"It was! It could be very funny but, amazingly, while I was with the production, no actor corpsed!"

Cecilia re-focused on Jeremy and his dilemma, then placed her hand on his.

"Don't worry! I don't mind if you're in love with Sofia! There's room for others in our relationship!"

She smiled at him; an ironic smile that somehow rang true. He realised that he was indeed in love with more than one woman.

"Cecilia, would you do me a favour? Would you come to the opening of my sister Maya's restaurant?"

There was no hesitation on Cecilia's part.

"Yes! Why not?"

He explained that it was the opening ceremony of several street eateries in the marketplace.

"Don't worry! Of course, I will come!"

Maya was a bag of nerves, as she got ready for her big night. Jeremy decided to play pranks on her. In his mind, he thought he was helping to take her mind off it. Both his mum and dad had to intervene, as the house was overcome with the emotion of the event. When Maya broke down in tears, Jeremy apologised to her. During the fracas, Maya let slip her relationship with Chai to her Mum. She was very understanding and not surprised by the news.

"We best not say anything to Dad yet. Let me speak to him first."

Maya was relieved. The whole thing of starting a new business and keeping her sexuality secret had become too much for her.

"So I was helpful then?" asked Jeremy, as he looked at Maya in the kitchen just before leaving the house. Mum was drinking sherry, Jeremy and Maya were drinking lager. Their dad was outside, cleaning the car.

"Why's Dad cleaning the bloody car?" asked Maya.

"You know what he's like! He wants things to be just right!"

"That might be true, Mum, but he'll wear the paint away!"

They all smiled at the thought of his attention to detail.

"Anyway, he's nervous for you!" she added.

"Nervous that he might lose money, you mean!" Jeremy said, then regretted it. Strangely, Maya agreed.

"Yeah, that could be true!"

"I'm sorry," said Mum, "that you both feel that, but Dad has got all the faith in the world in you kids."

She said it as if she was talking to a couple of teenagers rather than adults.

Maya and Jeremy looked at each other, then immediately did their best to build bridges. They both got up and hugged Mum.

"Ok, ok, that's all very nice and welcome, but you might think about doing that to Dad once in a while."

They both looked crestfallen, just like a couple of teenagers.

What happened next returned the room to anarchy. Maya had only downed half her lager, so Jeremy drank the rest. Maya whacked him over the head with her hand, dislodging the glass, now empty.

"Sometimes you can be quite common, Jeremy! You should have asked if I had finished!"

Maya looked at Mum, then at the broken glass that lay on the kitchen floor. Tears came into her eyes.

"For God's sake, you two! Will you please stop it?"

There was a strange atmosphere. It was as if Jeremy and Maya were simulating a time when they were toddlers, a time they never shared.

The whole thing had become too much for Mum, Florence, who left them to sort out the broken glass and the argument. As she left, the two siblings made up and started laughing.

Sidu had finished the car. He came in and found Florence upset in the hall.

"What's wrong, love," he asked.

"Same old, same old. Those two are arguing again!"

"Right!" said Sidu, "I'll sort this!"

He went into the kitchen, followed by Florence.

"Dad!" they called, then walked over to him mobbing him with hugs and kisses.

He was surprised by the overwhelming attention, which he didn't fight off. In fact, he was revelling in it. Of course, all their Mum could do was smile.

32.

People had started to gather in the centre of town. Banners and bunting were everywhere. The marketplace was as pretty as a picture with fairy lights put up by the town council. A brass band had been employed to play in the middle of the square. They were playing a medley of popular hits. There was a party atmosphere, which, together with a warm night, put a smile on people's faces. Maya, Jeremy and the whole family met in the square. Kazi made a point of wrapping his arms around his sister Maya. He kissed her on the cheek before congratulating her on her business venture. It disarmed Maya; she was almost speechless. They were a small part of the story, as many other people joined in the celebrations at the opening of the venue.

The Lord Mayor was there to declare it open. Even so, none of the market restaurants were serving. It was decided that they should enjoy the opening and the free food laid on by the developer.

A hog roast was planned for later and fireworks would follow. Duman and his new girlfriend joined Jeremy and Sofia amid the crowds of people. It became a noisy affair, which passed off without a hitch. The fireworks were set off in the park for safety reasons, so everyone could see them.

As some slipped away, the square became quieter. A good many revellers hung back to take advantage of the hog roast. Jeremy sat at a table with Sofia, Maya and Chai, talking about the success of the opening of the venue. Mum and Dad met Sofia and Chai briefly, which brought about many smiles, then they went home. Kazi hung back as his family went back to their car. He then asked to speak to Maya on her own.

"I know," he said to Maya, "that you're making an effort here, and in some ways it's admirable, but I still think I could find you a good husband!"

"For God's sake, Kazi! Won't you ever let it go? I've told you so many times, I'm not interested. Anyway, I already love someone!"

He looked surprised.

"Do I know him? Please say he's Indian!"

She felt a rush of blood and said it.

"It's Chai, she is Asian. To be more specific, Chinese."

He was flabbergasted.

"This can't be true! You must be fooling yourself. I won't have this, Maya! You can't do this!"

"I've done it many times, Kazi, with Chai and other women!"

"I'll stop it Maya; I'm going to see Dad. Just wait and see!"

Chai could see and hear the heated discussion that was taking place between Maya and Kazi, then went over to see what she could do. As she got there, Kazi was leaving. Chai stood by Maya, who was shivering and shaking at what had just happened.

"You ok, Maya?"

"Yes, I'm fine, just fucking angry!"

It didn't take long for Maya's mood to lift. For the first time in years, she had stood up to her big brother. Now she knew she had to face her dad, but not tonight. Tonight, she was having fun!

Jeremy caught sight of a dark, looming figure, coming across the square. He knew it to be Cecilia, making an entrance. He hadn't thought she would come. However, he realised for Cecilia to appear now would have more impact, as all the dignitaries had gone home. There was still a small crowd of people congregating around the hog roast. Cecilia was wearing a purple velvet cape and hood. She approached the table where Jeremy was. He stood up as she got nearer. He bowed in front of her and kissed her hand. She looked like the star attraction, almost regal in her attire. She pulled down her hood. On her head, she had a sequinned bandana, which made her look like something from a mythical storybook.

She stood there, perfectly still, as Jeremy played the part of one of her courtiers. Photographs were taken. A few of the people there knew who she was and wanted the moment caught on their mobile phones. Jeremy then introduced her to Maya and Chai.

"How are you feeling now?" asked Sofia.

"I am still occasionally breathless, but I'm ok."

As she said it, she stuttered to take breaths.

"You sure know how to make an entrance, Cecilia," said Maya.

"Yes," said Cecilia, "it comes with a certain amount of experience."

As the knowledge of Cecilia Walters's presence filtered through the crowd, more people came to see. Jeremy was hoping this might happen. He had already made sure a photographer from his old newspaper was attending. Jeremy saw an opportunity for Maya and Chai, so got them to stand next to Cecilia for optimum publicity. Gail was also on hand to write the story for the newspaper.

Overall, Jeremy was feeling pleased with himself, as were Maya and Chai. The night air cooled, so they all retired to a local bar. Jeremy encouraged Gail to talk to Cecilia, but always made sure he could hear the questions. After all, he didn't want Gail stealing his thunder.

33.

The next day, across the front of the newspaper, was written, *The New Marketplace. Opened by the Lord Mayor.*
Many dignitaries attended, including the famous actor,
Cecilia Walters.
A photograph of Cecilia with Maya, Chai, Jeremy, and Sofia accompanied it. There were other photographs and interviews, but Cecilia's part in the headlines dominated the piece. It had all been very well-orchestrated.

Jeremy was half asleep. The night before had taken its toll. He heard a loud knock on his door. A feeling of déjà vu filtered through his head, as he was beginning to fear he was becoming an alcoholic. His eyes didn't want to open. Maya entered his room.
"Some coffee for you, to wake your mind up!"
She sat on the edge of his bed with a big smile on her face.
"I'm so happy today, Jez, I can't tell you! My heads in the clouds!"
"I'm pleased for you, May, now leave me to die!"
She didn't, then she showed him everything on her social media page. It was like someone had lit a fire under her. She was bubbling away with enthusiasm. He was finding it hard to concentrate, but he did his best to listen. His comments, though short, were positive.
"By the way," she said, as she was closing his bedroom door, "either stay in bed or go out later, as Kazi will be over for lunch with the kids!"
Jeremy collapsed in a useless post-alcoholic stupor and was all the happier for it. He just hoped he could sleep through the rest

of the day.

Messages accumulated on Jeremy's phone, as he managed to avoid the best part of the day. Kazi had brought the children around. Jeremy could hear them playing in the garden, their high-pitched screams ringing out, as well as an argument in the distance, as his mind drifted in and out of sleep. He was happy he'd escaped it all. Mum and Dad wouldn't be happy, but Jeremy could live with that. Sofia had texted him a few times asking how he was. She commented how nice she thought his parents were.

Jeremy's only recollection of the night before, was of Cecilia leaving the bar, with a certain amount of mysterious finesse. Past that point, he remembered little.

He lay on his bed and closed his eyes. The gnawing sensation in his head had started to subside. He was still feeling very delicate. For some unknown reason, he could hear ABBA music resounding in his head again, then he remembered the Karaoke bar.

Jeremy answered Sofia's third text, reluctantly.

Hi Sofia, I have a dim memory of last night, but it hurts too much to remember. Not sure if I did anything stupid. How about we meet later?

She answered almost immediately.

That would be nice. How about the first place we dated?

He agreed to meet her later on in the evening, then went back to sleep.

The house was quiet as Jeremy went downstairs. Even though his hangover had gone, Jeremy trod carefully. He found his mum on the sofa in the living room.

"Hello, my darling boy, what's it like to have the world at your feet?"

He moved towards the counter in the kitchen and made himself some tea. Mum then asked him,

"Are you feeling a bit worse for wear? I hear you had a good time last night!"

He wanted his mum to tell him what she'd heard but preferred to wait till he met Sofia. He thought one version would be enough for his fragile mind.

"Where's Dad? Don't tell me! At work! I thought owning the business meant you got minions to do the hard stuff!"

"Someone's off sick," she said, "Anyway, you know what he's like! He's only happy when he's out there driving!"

"Don't you get fed up with being on your own, Mum? I would if I were you!"

"No, not really! You're here and so is Maya a lot of the time as well!"

"Yes, but that will change when Maya moves in with Chai, and I move...."

The words came out without thinking and he stopped before giving away all his intentions. He quickly added, "but not for some time!"

Mum looked unfazed.

"Yes, I suppose you will, if you stay with Sofia. She's a lovely girl, sorry woman!"

In the space of not so many words, he and his mum had shipped everyone away for a life of partnerships. As far as he was concerned, his mum was moving a lot quicker than he was, which surprised him.

"Don't worry about me son, I've seen a lot! I've done a lot! I think I can cope! If there was no one here I'd find something to do."

These words rolled over him and soothed his anxiety. He sidled up beside her on the sofa and put his arm over her shoulder. She snuggled into him. He kissed her on the head and said, "There, there."

It was as if he was the parent. She smiled a smile that said it all. Not long after, he got ready to go to meet Sofia.

Sofia was sat outside the restaurant sipping a tall latte.

"Am I late?" Jeremy asked.

"No, I'm early, I got bored at the flat."

"I'm sorry, Sofia, I should have asked you over for Sunday lunch!"

"You mean you've had Sunday lunch? I can't believe that I thought you'd be sleeping it off!"

He laughed, "You got me! I was in no fit state to do anything. I'm not long up!"

"I can see that, your attire is something to be desired, let alone your hair!"

He immediately pulled out his phone and looked at his reflection. His dark hair was skew-whiff. He did his best to push it down, which amused Sofia.

He then noticed that his T-shirt, mostly hidden by his jacket, was inside out.

"Ok, I admit it, I'm a mess!"

They both laughed. He looked into her eyes, meaningfully. She was caught unawares, then felt something different inside, a tingling sensation. She realised there was a question in his eyes.

"Well?" he asked.

"You want to know the sort of fool you made of yourself in the karaoke bar!" she said.

She paused for a moment for dramatic effect.

"First of all! I must say you haven't got a bad voice, but Maya's is better. You, me, Maya, Chai, Duman and his girlfriend, Toya, were drinking lager with chasers, not long after Cecilia left in a taxi!"

"Hang on," he said, "Duman's girlfriend's name is Toya? He never told me, or if he did, I didn't take it in. Mind you, there was so much going on. I must have been transfixed by her red Afro! She's quite stunning. She reminds me of a pop star!"

"I see," said Sofia, "you can remember everything about her, but not her name?"

He looked sheepish. Sofia smiled.

"Yes," she said, "I agree she is stunning, and yes, she looks like a pop star. She's got a place on a TV talent show."

Jeremy looked guilty for not remembering.

"Anyway," Sofia said, "after a few more drinks, we were all fairly drunk, but you seemed to be merrier than most. Why you stripped down to your pants when you sang Islands in the Stream with Maya, I don't know!"

Jeremy's mouth dropped open in disbelief. It then occurred to him she was fooling with him, but she carried on talking.

"Toya was spectacular, tackling two Adele songs in a row. She has an almost operatic voice. We were all impressed!"

Jeremy couldn't place himself at all. There were big gaps he couldn't fill.

"The only thing I think I can remember is singing Dancing Queen!"

Sofia smiled.

"Yes, we sang that together. My voice is not that good. However, you lifted my performance. You being in your pants made it even more entertaining!"

He felt certain she was winding him up, then laughed at the ridiculous picture she was painting.

"I'm sorry! I don't believe you! You're pulling my leg!"

She then took out her phone. She showed him a video of him singing, removing his shirt, then his trousers. He buried his head in his hands, as he recalled parts of what happened.

"If it's any consolation, Jeremy, we all thought what a wonderful entertainer you were. She patted his back. Do you need a drink, something alcoholic?"

He put up his hands in surrender.

"No, don't talk to me about booze!"

He sipped his coffee slowly. He had never been a partygoer or someone to let himself go in any way, unless it was with his mates.

Sofia leant across and kissed him on the lips, which seemed to rescue his thoughts.

"When I lived in Spain," said Sofia, "it was common to see people stripping off in bars after drinking too much. It's fun, letting your hair down!"

He raised his head, then said,

"Ok, I guess it's no good worrying about it."

"Shall we eat?" she suggested, "You must be hungry now!"

He agreed. As the evening passed by, the ambience of the small restaurant seemed to wrap around them like a warm blanket. They shared a bottle of wine, of which he only had a few sips. Afterwards, they decided to find somewhere to stay in the town. A four-star hotel was close by. Neither of them had ever been there. One thing was certain, they wanted each other badly. The hotel foyer, the furnishings, the flowers impressed them both. It was an expensive place to stay.

No one was at the reception desk, as Jeremy reached to press the bell, then a young woman sprang out of nowhere as if she was a jack in the box.

"Yes sir, madam, good evening!"

Both Jeremy and Sofia took a step back.

"I'm sorry I surprised you; I was looking for paper for the printer."

She was dressed elegantly in a blue jacket with gold braid to the collar and a white ruffled shirt which seemed a little fussy.

"Hi, Mr. Tamagotchi, how are you?" she asked.

The words came out of her smiley, business-like mouth. Immediately, Jeremy was confused and flustered. A moment of shock occupied his whole body as he tried to place himself and the receptionist together. Panic set off an avalanche of blood that ran recklessly through his veins. He realised that there was something familiar about her. Words came to his head and he answered her question.

"I'm fine thank you, but I don't think I've met you before and that's not my name!"

His words were confident and assertive, which threw the receptionist. She then looked at him with Sofia and looked embarrassed.

"I'm sorry, I'm new to the job!" she said.

"Do you have a room for the night?" Jeremy asked.

The receptionist quickly got into her stride.

"Your name, sir?"

"Jeremy Bakshi!"

She then consulted her computer and asked him for his bank card details. She reached for a card key, then placed it on the counter. Her face and body then seemed to become those of a flight attendant, just before take-off. She directed them to the lifts.

"Have a nice stay, Mr. and Mrs. Ta.. Sir, Madam Bakshi…!"

She seemed to bite her tongue, then immediately looked down at her computer.

The lift opened. It seemed enormous. A small palm sat in the corner. Mirrors made it look even larger. Sofia's silence was about to break.

"So, it would seem you have a double life. Who is this person, Mr. Tamagotchi, that I've been dating?"

For some reason, in all the emotions that cascaded through Jeremy's thoughts, the word dating stood out. It was as if, up to now, this thing they had together wasn't serious. He thought he'd be cool, calm and sophisticated.

"Ok, I'm a spy. Tamagotchi is my operational name!"

Sofia burst out laughing.

"So, you don't think I've got the balls to be a spy, Sofia?"

He pulled himself up, so he could see himself in the mirrors standing taller. He then drew in his stomach and pushed his shoulders back. She looked at him and studied his pose.

"No, sorry!"

He let go of the pose. He was doing his best to keep it light, hoping they could laugh it off.

"What's the story then, James Bond?" she asked.

"If I told you that, my dear, I'm afraid I'd have to kill you!"

His James Bond accent was woefully bad. She wanted an honest answer. By this time, they were inside their hotel bedroom. The sexually charged feelings that they both had had dissipated. Sofia sat in one of the large chairs that were in the room.

Jeremy settled in the other chair. It seemed like there was an ocean between them, so he moved closer. She looked relaxed but said nothing. He decided to speak.

"I had an affair with a colleague, a married woman, not long ago. It happened when we were both drunk at an office party. Somehow the relationship just kept going. We used a hotel, just outside of town, a two-star functional place, a couple of times a month for about six months. I always paid in cash and I used Tamagotchi as a pseudonym. I realise now that the receptionist downstairs used to work there. It would seem she's gone up in the world."

He smiled at Sofia thinking it was a sufficient answer for her to understand.

"So, who's the woman you had the affair with?"

"No one of any importance!"

"She's important enough to have been intimate with many times, so what's her name?"

He didn't think it was relevant, but it looked like Sofia wouldn't be happy unless she had the name.

"Gail."

"You mean Gail, who interviewed Cecilia the other night?"

"Yes."

He didn't know why, but he felt guilty. There was a stand-off or more precisely a sit-off. She got up, said nothing, then went to the bathroom. He took off his jacket, then idly looked around. It seemed like most hotel rooms, anywhere, just slightly grander. In the moments that passed, he considered the time that had gone by since his affair with Gail. It seemed to him that his life had been turned around for the better since Sofia and Cecilia had come into his life.

The bathroom door opened behind him. He didn't move; he had no idea whether Sofia was leaving, staying, or even speaking to him. He could see, from where he was sitting, her reflection in the bedroom window, as it intermingled with the city lights outside. He felt her hands on his shoulders, moving rhythmically as she massaged his muscles. It made him moan with pleasure.

"Oh, my God! That feels so good!"

She said nothing, as she relaxed his tension. She then ran her hands through his hair. One thing he knew for certain, was that Sofia wasn't leaving. She then moved her hands down his body from behind. She kissed his neck gently nibbling at his skin, then she concentrated on one spot. A love bite would appear later that would be hard to hide. He didn't care. As he sat there, almost motionless, she undid his shirt, then ran her hands over his naked chest. She moved around him, climbed onto his lap. He took in her beautiful naked figure, as she proceeded to pull him forward off the chair down on top of her. She was waiting, as he struggled to remove his jeans, socks and underpants. While fighting with his clothes, he looked at her delectable body that was lying there. Like before, when they made love at his home, he sought to divert his excitement by thinking of other things, but this time he thought it a waste of time. So he concentrated on enjoying the moments. Although he was still only half undressed, they became one. Murmurs of pleasure from them both filled the room, but it wasn't for long, as they both realised there was no comfort on a hard floor.

They then continued on the bed. They gently took their time to re-engage. This, however, was followed by trying different positions, to get the most out of their need to explore each other's bodies. Some might say that this is a serious business, while others find it fun. Sofia and Jeremy realised that being together and doing what they were doing was the best fun they'd ever had. They laughed at the situation, but the serious bit was the all-encompassing climax, after which they collapsed into a sensual heap of contentment. As they lay in each other's arms, sleep then overtook their fevered lovemaking.

Before it was light, they came together in an even more heated connection. It was almost as if they knew it might be some time before this happened again. They awoke entwined, which aroused them both. However, time was getting on and they realised they would have to leave very shortly. In a rush, they showered, then dressed, almost like a couple who were familiar with each other's waking moments. They sublimely left the hotel room.

As they made their way to the lift, they both felt a euphoric feeling inside, one they didn't share in words but smiles. At first, they both felt they had left something behind, the lack of luggage being a strange feeling. In the lift, Sofia asked,

"Why Tamagotchi?"

"Spur of the moment thing! Just thought about the game I loved when I was a kid and said it!"

"Maybe Gail thought you were a bit of a nerd!"

Jeremy thought about it for a moment. His affair with Gail was just about sex. He was pretty sure no emotions got spent apart from lust. He didn't share that with Sofia. All he wanted to do was leave that world behind him. He then said,

"I guess I was, and I still am!"

"You're my nerd and so much more!"

She hugged his arm, then kissed him on the cheek. As they caught their reflection in the mirror, they smiled. Neither of them looked as tidy as they had done the night before. The reflection made an almost perfect picture of two people in love, the only problem being the words had not been said.

As they walked through the foyer, which was quite busy, the young receptionist was still on her shift. Another was dealing with a few other guests. The young receptionist looked up, as Jeremy dropped the key card on the counter. Looking straight into his eyes, she was about to automatically wish him a good day, but his knowing look put her off. He caught up with Sofia, who was waiting for him just inside the front doors. Sofia said aloud,

"Do you think we should come back next week for a shag, Mr Tamagotchi? It's such a lovely place to stay, and the beds are so bouncy!"

Everyone turned to look at them. Sofia waved, then said with an American accent.

"Y'all, have a nice day!"

She linked Jeremy's arm as they left the hotel. He was embarrassed beyond belief but saw the funny side of it as they walked away.

34.

Jeremy turned his phone on, as they made their way back to get their cars. He had several texts from Maya and his mum. Almost immediately, his mum called him.

"Oh, there you are Jeremy. Do you think you can come home? Only Kazi is giving Maya a lot of grief!"

"What! Why?"

"The usual! He wants her to marry this friend of his!"

"Why doesn't he drop this? He knows it's a lost and outdated cause! Where's Dad, Mum?"

"He's taken a friend to Manchester airport because his flight was cancelled in Birmingham!"

"OK, I'll be home in half an hour!"

He could tell by his mum's voice she was concerned about Maya. He explained what he knew to Sofia.

"Can I come along?" asked Sofia. "I've nothing else on today. I was hoping we could do something together, later!"

His thoughts hung there for a moment, thinking about the night before.

"If you don't mind shouting and an argument, I would love you to come!"

Half an hour later he and Sofia went into the house. His mum was trying to comfort Maya, but she was crying too much to be consoled. Kazi was pacing up and down, continuing to lecture Maya. She wasn't listening.

"For the sake of the family, you should marry!"

Maya thought that Kazi had taken on board her words about her sexuality but, for some reason, he was still obsessed with the idea she would marry a man, in particular, his friend.

"What's your problem, Kazi?" asked Jeremy. "Maya has told you she's not interested, over and over again. Don't you get it? She's in love with a woman! Why don't you let it go and accept that Maya is a lesbian?"

Kazi's face seemed to burn as he got angrier.

"She's not! She's confused! She needs a man in her life! Zamia is that man!"

Jeremy put his head in his hands. Mum got up and moved towards the kitchen.

"Does anyone need a drink, maybe a few moments of peace from this arguing?"

"Keep your nose out of my family's business, Florence! It's nothing to do with you!" Kazi said.

"Don't talk to me like that! If Dad was here, you wouldn't talk to me in that tone of voice! Have some respect!"

The smackdown shut Kazi up, but the words he'd said upset Florence, which would have consequences when Sidu got home.

Kazi was still agitated with the situation. It was as if he thought he could make Maya do his bidding. As far as he was concerned, men had the last word on what women did. Unfortunately, for him, his dad didn't think like him anymore. Kazi seemed to be taking advantage of Sidu not being there to enforce his agenda.

"Look, Kazi, this is a free country!" said Jeremy, "A country you were born into! Why are you keeping this up? Maya can make her own choices! She's not a teenager who can be manipulated by some religious ideology!"

The words of wisdom hung there like a breath of fresh air.

"The non-believer half-blood speaks," said Kazi. "You're a mishmash of races, Jeremy. So what do you know about ideology?"

"I know one important thing about what you're saying, Kazi. It's outdated! Most of all, wrong!"

Kazi realised he was getting nowhere, so he angrily barged past Jeremy, then left the house.

There was calm. Maya had stopped crying and Mum was making tea. The relief was tangible as she looked at Sofia and said,

"I'm sorry that you have come here today to witness this fiasco!"

"I'm sorry too!" added Jeremy.

Maya surfaced from her misery, then coffee and tea were served on the dining table. She was quiet, but happy. Kazi had gone.

"He's a bit of a pig!" said Sofia. "If he was my son, I'd disown him!"

This brought smiles to all their faces.

"He's my brother," said Maya, "Sometimes, I have no idea why he's such a bully.

"It's clearly his religious belief," said Jeremy, "coupled with his need to dumb everyone down. Give him time, Maya, he'll accept your way of life eventually!"

Jeremy patted Maya's hand as he said it.

"Whatever it is, it's not welcome in this house," said Mum, "So, Sofia, I wouldn't be surprised if it's put you off!"

"I like a good argument," said Sofia, "it's great therapy to start the week off!"

They laughed. The light relief was welcome, as Maya seemed to relax. They talked about what would be her and Chai's first night at East of Maya. As for Kazi, he wouldn't be welcome.

In the heat of the moment, Jeremy had forgotten he should be at Cecilia's. He left the room to call her, but she didn't answer. He wasn't overly worried, because she rarely did. He went back into the living-room and asked Sofia if she wanted to go to see Cecilia. She agreed.

As luck would have it, the old man, Mr. Silverman, was leaving the house, as they arrived at Cecilia's. This time, he was on the path just outside the front door. Jeremy and Sofia stopped opposite him. He stood there before them, like a diminutive knight, standing guard in front of his castle. His hunched, umbrella-in-hand figure somehow framed a comic moment.

"Who are you?" asked Mr. Silverman.

"I'm John Lennon and this is Yoko Ono!"

This surprised Sofia, who was confused by the answer that Jeremy gave.

"We're here to see Cecilia!"

"You mean Cecilia Walters!" he said, "I know her, Mr. Lennon, but I don't know you!"

"It doesn't matter, Mr. Silverman. Cecilia is expecting us!"

"She might be, but I'm not, so be on your way, or get off the path!"

They stepped to one side, as the small man pushed past them, then out of the gate. He immediately put up his umbrella. There were no clouds or rain in sight. As Jeremy let himself in, he explained that Mr. Silverman responds the same way to everyone he encounters.

"One day," Sofia said, "you will probably be the same, Jeremy. You shouldn't mock!"

"If I get to be as old as he is, I'd be happy to be that way. At least he seems healthy and happy in his madness."

Jeremy let himself and Sofia in. He heard Cecilia's voice from her bedroom. Sofia followed him closely, looking at the works of art as she went.

"Are you ok, Cecilia?" Jeremy asked, as he went into the room.

"I'm fine, I'm just fatigued after the endeavours of the other night. I think it was all the excitement!"

"I'm sorry about that," he said.

"Don't fuss, I'm fine. I'm as strong as a very old ox!"

Sofia peaked from behind Jeremy.

"I see you have brought me the competition for your heartstrings, Jeremy. How are you, Sofia? You're looking well, and if I may say, you look somehow different. If I wasn't mistaken, I'd say someone was in love!"

Both Jeremy and Sofia looked embarrassed. As usual, Cecilia

was making a big play for the centre stage, with a slightly bigger audience this time.

"Love can be found in the eyes, before it has made its journey to the heart!" she said.

There was an awkward silence. Sofia, not wishing to pause too long on the question, moved forward, then held Cecilia's hand. In doing so, she took her pulse.

"I see the caring part of your soul is always on duty, Sofia!"

"It's second nature to me, it's who I am!"

"It's a beautiful thing to have, to be someone who cares so much!" said Cecilia.

Sofia seemed embarrassed, as Cecilia looked deep into her green eyes and held her hand.

"You seem to be in fairly good health for someone who's had Covid 19," said Sofia.

They both smiled at each other. The moment, or whatever it was, hung there until Sofia broke it.

"Can I go and look at your paintings? They look divine!"

Cecilia nodded.

"Thank you, nurse!"

Then she let go of Sofia's hand. Jeremy who was standing to one side, wasn't quite sure about the interaction, but saw it as part of Cecilia's eccentricities. Sofia looked around the living room. Wall space was at a premium. Hardly a piece of wall could be seen. Paintings and photographs seemed to clutter the eyes, but it was still impressive. She dreamily spent time studying named and unnamed artwork, then went into the hallway, where mainly photographs were hung. Sofia found a few that were interesting. Her mind was as if it was on a cloud, as she moved from one old photograph to a more recent one. She couldn't help envying Cecilia's past and all her family and friend connections.

Suddenly one stood out. It was a black and white one, a group of young people outside what looked like a theatre. She stared closely at two people arm in arm among the throng of others. She could see Cecilia, who must have been in her early twenties, and guessed the man was Rupert Blaine. She stared into the photograph at the couple. Her thoughts made her feel dizzy. Impulsively, she took it off the wall. It said on the back: *Birmingham Rep. 1968. The gang.* She then looked again at the photograph, transfixed by Cecilia at such a young age. The more she studied it the dizzier and more confused she felt. Something familiar in Cecilia's features intrigued Sofia. She then put it back.

After about half an hour, Jeremy appeared from the bedroom. Sofia had sat in Cecilia's easy chair, in order to try and correlate the information that she had seen in the hallway. Sofia's thoughts were dancing. She had it in her mind to leave but thought better of it.

Jeremy looked at Sofia, who seemed miles away.

"Are you ok?" he asked.

She snapped out of her hazy, far-off thoughts.

"I'm alright! I just feel tired!"

"I'm not surprised, we didn't get much sleep last night!"

A warm, engaging smile passed between them.

"Cecilia has dropped off to sleep," said Jeremy, "Before she did, she said to go and enjoy the day!"

As they left, Sofia seemed quiet, hardly saying a word. Before they got to their cars, she asked if it would be ok if she went home.

"I think I need to catch up on my sleep, Jeremy!"

Jeremy understood how she felt. They shared a brief kiss, then went their separate ways. Even though Jeremy felt the same as Sofia, he had a space, deep inside, after she had gone.

35.

There was disappointment, as Jeremy told the family that Sofia wasn't coming to the marketplace for the real opening. His explanation that she was overtired because of shifts, fooled his mum and dad, but Maya looked at him with a wry smile on her face.

"You can't fool me," said Maya, "I know what you two have been up to!"

All Jeremy could do, was smile.

Maya and Chai's first night of being open went well. As it did for the whole venue. Jeremy and Mum helped backstage, clearing the tables, washing up. Maya was eternally grateful. At first, she'd been really nervous, as she thought her brother, Kazi, would turn up and spoil everything, but she was consoled by her dad who said he had spoken to him about his appalling behaviour. Unfortunately, they all knew that Kazi had not buried his beliefs for good.

The night ended with them celebrating back at home. To Maya's relief, Chai was invited back too. In the warm atmosphere of Mum and Dad's house, Maya felt complete. Later, Jeremy lay on his bed. He texted Sofia about the evening, hoping she would answer and share his feelings. Nothing came back. It didn't trouble him too much, because he knew she was on a later shift.

Sofia was in her little flat on her computer, staring at its ever-changing information. She was looking for answers to her questions. Her life, like Jeremy's, had changed for the better. The difference was, his was shared by a family with all its ups and downs, whereas hers had so many empty spaces. She saw Jeremy's texts, but did not answer, even though she really wanted to.

The next day, Jeremy was staring off into space. Cecilia, who was feeling much better after her rest, insisted on bringing in the tea. She sat in her chair and poured.

"I see we're not here today?"

The question hung there.

"I see a dragon at the window, breathing fire, and it's going to come in and eat you, Jeremy!"

His name she said in a louder voice. He snapped out of it.

"Sorry, I was elsewhere!"

"You mean you're not giving me a hundred per cent of your attention? Tut tut, dear boy, be off with you and get some sleep!"

Before he could speak, she went off on a little rant.

"Why, oh why, isn't a hundred per cent enough for modern society? When all's said and done, it is the correct way to phrase it. Why go further? Saying a hundred and ten per cent? Do these people who say such things just like listening to their own voices?"

The question and the rant left Jeremy dumbfounded. He had no idea what she was going on about.

"Ok, Jeremy! Tell me what's on your mind or go home and rest!"

"Nothing really, nothing that's worth talking about!"

"Since you got here, you've hardly said a word, so let's have it out, now!"

"Sofia!" he said, with a sigh in his voice.

"The course of true love never did run smooth!" she said, then was about to say more.

"Please, Cecilia, Shakespeare can stay out of this!"

Jeremy was annoyed. She was being playful and was trying to lighten the mood. Indeed, she was full of something more than normal. It was as if she was on a high. Jeremy being so into his thoughts had missed it completely. He then realised there was a smell of cannabis in the air, and something in her demeanour confirmed it.

"Where did you get the cannabis?" he asked.

"Ah, that would be telling!"

Rather than pursue the question, he said,

"Have you anymore?"

"Why, of course my dear boy! I shall get it!"

She moved quite gracefully from her seat to her bedroom. More of the smell of cannabis filled the living room. A few minutes later, she was back and had lit a joint. She took a long drag on it and passed it to Jeremy who did the same. He coughed profusely. After a short while, he stopped, as he took a few deep breaths.

"Cecilia, how can you smoke this stuff in your condition?"

"That's why I can, because of my condition! I've been so low! I needed something to try and get myself off the floor!"

Jeremy took in another lungful of the mind-changing drug, although it wasn't changing his mind. It was lightening the load that had affected his day.

"This will keep you on the floor, Cecilia! Anyway, you said you never smoked.

"To tell you the truth, Jeremy, I've never smoked tobacco. I did say I had indulged in cannabis. However, it's been years since I've had any. My source is very hush-hush!"

She put her finger to her lips, laughed, then Jeremy joined her in the conspiracy.

"Shhhhhhhh!" they said together, which amused them both.

"So, Jeremy, what troubles your heart, about the most beautiful and lovely Sofia?"

The words floated on the air out of Cecilia's mouth. Somehow, Jeremy seemed to be looking for them in the smoke that floated above them both.

"She's captivated me, imprisoned my heart and she's thrown away the key!"

"Oh, Jeremy, I think I could help you to become an actor! You have the words! All you need now is the training. I would just like to say Sofia is an unknown force, a breath of fresh air, unique in every way!"

After this glowing critique of Sofia from Cecilia, Jeremy felt lucky to be even in the same solar system, let alone to have shared the same bed with her. They passed the joint back and forth. He'd never seen Cecilia like this. It was somehow like peeping through a window, then seeing her in a different world.

"Secrets, Jeremy! I have secrets to tell! Maybe I will tell you, but not quite yet!"

"I think you have already told some secrets, Cecilia!"

"That's as may be!"

She leaned forward to be near his ear, then she looked around, as if someone just might be listening in.

"These are bigger secrets, secrets that will....."

She stopped abruptly, putting her finger up to her lips again, then, almost intentionally, she gracefully slid from the chair onto the floor. She started laughing, which in turn set off Jeremy. He then did his best to lift her, but not so gracefully. He tumbled to lie next to her, as their joint laughter petered out.

"There are watermarks on my ceiling!"

She seemed to become more lucid at the sight of the offending stains.

"They're not stains, they're clouds in the sky!" he said.

She looked again.

"If they are clouds, someone has stolen my ceiling!"

They laughed again at the ridiculous thoughts that they were exchanging. Jeremy lifted himself up to his knees, then stood with difficulty, at which point he offered his hand to Cecilia. She smiled, then took it.

"Why, kind sir, you are my rock! I will build a castle for us to live in until it is time to go!"

As she stood in the heather that surrounded them, their dream castle appeared. Its walls, drawbridge and moat could clearly be seen through the cannabis mist. Flags adorned its ramparts. It was as if they were in medieval England. He then kissed the lovely Lady Cecilia, and she kissed him back. In the moments that passed, it was as if they were in a world that embraced all the emotions that had bonded them. In his arms, Cecilia's eyes closed. He struggled but then managed to lift her. She was lighter than he'd anticipated. So, he carried her to the bedroom, then lay her on her bed. He did his best to cover her with a throw. She was fast asleep. He was stunned at what had just happened, although nothing really did. He called his dad's taxi company, then left a note.

My dearest Lady Cecilia. A wonderful time full of untold secrets and shared emotions. So unforgettable. Love Jeremy. Xxxx

He waited outside for the taxi. When it came, it was his dad driving it. As Jeremy got in, Dad said,

"So, this is where the famous Cecilia Walters lives?"

"Is there any time when you're not driving a taxi or working in the office, Dad? And yes, it is where Cecilia lives!"

"No need to be angry, son. I mean no harm!"

Jeremy realised the cannabis had worn off. All the things that had disappeared from his mind, had come back to interfere with his thoughts.

"Sorry, Dad, it's been a very strange few weeks, following an even stranger few months!"

As Dad drove, Jeremy looked at his phone. No texts whatsoever from Sofia. It was getting dark as they got home.

"Dad, what's the problem with Kazi?"

His dad contemplated the question, as he parked the taxi.

"It goes back to when his mother was ill. He was the oldest. I think he shouldered a lot of responsibility. I was doing my best looking after their mum. The long-term illness took its toll on us. I think Maya came out the best, which made it worse for Kazi!"

Jeremy realised he'd never asked questions about this before. He always supposed none of them wanted to talk about it.

"Kazi seemed to go into himself," said Dad, "He found what he needed in religion. I went the other way, questioning why any God would do this to my family. Maya seemed to float along doing well in all things. So, I thought why try to fix something that won't get fixed? The trouble is, we are all broken and looking for someone to put us back together. Your mum did that for me. Chai, it seems, late in the day, has fixed Maya, but Kazi remains broken."

"I would have thought," said Jeremy, "that being married and having five kids would have filled up his life with happiness."

His dad laughed.

"You think?"

They both laughed.

"Yes," said Jeremy, "I see what you mean! Sometimes his brood drives me crazy. They're well-behaved, but so many voices and so much hard work!"

"This is when we should have thoughts for Sarita," said Dad, "She is the perfect wife for Kazi, but we both know she's not happy either. Kazi should give her more room to speak!"

"Perhaps, Dad, it's time for someone to tell him how much of a fool he is."

"Maybe you're right, son!"

36.

Jeremy was loitering with intent outside a block of medical staff accommodation. It was about ten o'clock the next morning. The building was not too far from the hospital where Sofia worked. He'd tried several buttons on the entrance door, but no one responded. He sat on a wall, thinking how little he knew about Sofia. His journalistic skills and natural curiosity had let him down. As he was scrolling through his phone, someone opened the door to the building and came out. Jeremy quickly got up and slid inside. Sofia's bedsit was on the fourth floor. That much he knew. He took the stairs, not wanting to trust the lifts.

When he got to her door, he waited for a moment, then knocked. He knocked again before deciding to call her name. This brought someone out into the corridor from an adjacent room.

"Can you please be quiet? Some people are sleeping and need peace!"

He realised, in his fervour to find Sofia, that he wasn't really thinking straight. It did, however, make someone available, so he could ask questions.

"Sorry, but I'm looking for Sofia Moran!"

The young man was tall, thin and his skin was very pale. A white t-shirt and shorts made him look like a ghost. The words he spoke, although angry, sounded effeminate.

"If I knew anything about her, why would I say anything to you?"

"Because I'm her boyfriend," said Jeremy.

"All the more reason why I wouldn't tell you! You might be a perv, a troll, or a rapist."

"What the fuck! Do I look like a person that would do any of those things?"

The young man raised his eyebrows.

"Well, as a matter of fact, you do look a little strange!"

Jeremy chose not to rise to the young man's baiting.

"I'm worried because I've texted her. She's not answering her phone at all. She could be in danger!"

He looked at Jeremy and considered his obvious distress.

"The only thing I can tell you is I spoke to her two nights ago. She had a suitcase and was walking towards the lifts. There was something on her mind because she went straight past me. When we were working together in the wards, she would always make time to talk. We used to have such laughs!"

A smile came over his face as if he was with her at that moment.

"And?" Jeremy said impatiently.

"Ok!" said the young man, "I'm trying to help you here!"

Jeremy lowered his head and tried to cool down.

"Anyway," the young man said, "I managed to stop her just before she got in the lift. She said she was going back home, and that's all I know!"

He stood there, staring at Jeremy, as if the information was perfectly succinct. Jeremy turned, then walked away. The young man tutted loudly, then called after Jeremy.

"No thank yous! So rude!"

He then slammed his room door loudly. Jeremy was certain that the young man must have woken half the block.

Jeremy's mind was lost in thought, as he left the building, but he realised, for whatever reason, Sofia had left to go back to Spain. He also knew she was going in order to get away from something or somebody. His only worry was that *he* might be that somebody. He decided to call in a favour from his friend, Nigel, who might find out more than he could.

First, though, he had a prearranged appointment and he was late. The café was as steamy as ever, the cooking aromas drifting out of the door. It was hidden down a back street, frequented more by journalists, police and the emergency services than the general public.

Jeremy joined Gail and Tony. On the table, two brand-new smart novels sat completely out of place. They all high-fived each other.

"So, this is the beauty!"

Jeremy picked up the book, then brought it to his nose to smell. He thumbed a few pages.

"There's nothing quite like the feeling of a new book."

"Ok," said Gail, "get a room, Jeremy! Your erection is showing!" The comment was typical of Gail. It did bring about a laugh from both Jeremy and Tony. The truth was, she felt the same way about books.

"Tony, you've signed it with love and kisses! "Jeremy said.

"Alright Jeremy, he did the same with mine!"

Gail looked a little peeved at Jeremy's gushing. Tony was riding the wave of euphoria.

"This is magnificent! I'll treasure it always!"

Jeremy continued to be enthusiastic as he admired the front cover: a pebbled path was disappearing into a forest, a grey mist hung in the trees.

Dark Shadows Lane. A murder mystery by Tony Marshall in gold letters written across it, made it look impressive. It was the real deal. In fact, in just a few short weeks, it was nudging the top ten bestselling books.

"I've been told," said Tony, "it could get to number one!"

Both Gail and Jeremy were overjoyed for Tony.

"Big breakfasts all round! I'm paying!" said Tony, then asked, "How is the biography going, Jeremy?"

He had it in his thoughts to wax lyrical about what had happened so far, but his mind was hung up on the whereabouts of Sofia.

A waitress brought over their breakfasts.

Jeremy asked Gail how John Scotland had liked her article on the market opening and, in particular about Cecilia's part in it.

Gail's eyes lit up, as she broke the egg on her plate with the corner of a piece of toast, then ate it hungrily. Before she could answer, they both asked her if she had eaten.

"No, but the kids did. As usual, in the rush to get them out to school, I missed breakfast. As far as big boy Scotland is concerned, he did say, *good job, Gail!*"

Both Jeremy and Tony looked at each other.

"Shit!" said Tony, "I never got praise like that!"

Jeremy nodded his head in agreement.

"It seems sad that faint praise from someone like John Scotland makes us sit up, then feel good!"

"I'll take it every day of the week," said Gail. "Since you two have gone, my workload has gone up and so has my news space. Now, if I can shift the kids over to my worthless ex and his tart for the odd weekend, I might be able to concentrate on *my* sex life. As she said it, she winked at Jeremy, then asked him,

"What's wrong, Jeremy? Have you got girl trouble? How is Sofia?"

Gail glanced at him with mischief in her eyes.

"Who's Sofia?" asked Tony.

"She's a beautiful Spanish girl who seems to like Jeremy!"

Gail was having fun at Jeremy's expense.

"She's half British!" said Jeremy, "and she disappeared a few nights ago, gone without a trace."

"Oh Jeremy, has she dumped you, or have you bumped her off?"

Gail was having a great time prodding Jeremy where it hurt. To push it home, she made a good job of a Spanish accent then she fluttered her eyes at him. He did find that funny, as did Tony.

"Ok, ok, less of the ribbing, please. No, and I'm not going to cry either, so, Gail, shut it!"

He looked tense as Gail playfully pretended to zip her lips.

"Alright, let's be friends," said Tony, "Is there anything we can do, Jeremy?"

He then explained what had happened. He had an ulterior motive because they were all journalists. He thought many minds might find one person. The banter that had gone before calmed down, as they jointly thought it through.

He never told them about Sofia finding out about his affair with Gail. He wasn't sure it was relevant anyway. After much deliberation and a further cup of tea, they came to the conclusion that he needed to go to Spain. All in all, he felt as if he'd hit a brick wall, but talking to them had eased his anxiety. Jeremy's day had started busy. It wasn't going to stop. He was happy to be that way, what with Sofia's disappearance. He needed his mind to be occupied.

The next stop was at the marketplace where Maya and Chai were prepping for a lunchtime menu. He talked, as they busied themselves. He asked if they had any knowledge of Sofia's whereabouts. On hearing the question, Maya became aware that Jeremy was upset. She then comforted him, having no idea what might have happened to Sofia. While she did this, Chai listened to their conversation. Chai then stopped chopping vegetables, as she remembered something.

"One second!"

Jeremy and Maya looked towards her. She waved her knife in the air, as if she was trying to find the memory.

"When we were all in the Karaoke bar, I saw Sofia talking to Toya. They seemed to be in a deep conversation at the back of the bar. I don't know why, but they were engrossed in whatever they were talking about. Maybe Toya knows something?"

Jeremy got up and walked over to Chai, then leaned across the counter and kissed her on the lips.

"Thank you! That's a lead I can follow up on!"

She immediately laughed, then smiled and said,

"Nice kiss, Jeremy!"

"Now, now, you'll make me jealous!" said Maya.

Chai looked over at Maya.

"No one kisses like you, Maya!"

Jeremy left them to their love and prep.

37.

At Cecilia's, he let himself in. He could hear her singing along to Fly Me to the Moon on the radio. This was the first time that he had heard any media in her apartment. He stood perfectly still in the living room. It was truly amazing to hear her. The place felt warm, welcoming and happy. Cecilia came in, as always dressed eccentrically, this time in a flowing dressing gown he had never seen before. He was stunned by its beauty. It was covered in all the colours of the rainbow and captured the style of the nineteen twenties. She was unfazed by him being there.

"Tea?" she asked.

She had already made it, so she carried the pot to the table. The radio had been turned off.

"Someone seems happy today. May I also say that dressing gown is phenomenal?"

"Oh, I wore this in a big Agatha Christie series. I made it to the end and I was a suspect. The clothes, as always, were beautiful! I think it could be said that I acquired this without permission."

She smiled mischievously, then stood for a moment, creating a pose for him to look at. She held the embroidered lapels up to her face, then pursed her lips naturally. He applauded her. She did look elegant.

"To respond to your first point, yes, I feel happy. Why shouldn't I be?"

Jeremy had left her fast asleep, after they had shared some cannabis. He had kissed her, rather innocently, but he was aware that a lot of emotions had passed between them. All he could think of was how wonderful it was to see her so happy.

He had it in his mind to say nothing about the present situation regarding Sofia, knowing full well it would bring him down. So, he tried to pick up where they'd left off, but Cecilia would have none of it, because there was something else on her mind. She sat forward on her chair, her eyes staring, almost as if she was trying to see what happened in the past more clearly. As always, her diary was sitting beside her on the chair.

"Love!" she said.

Her hands were sitting slightly interlocked on her lap. It was almost as if she was holding that very emotion carefully for him to see.

"Love, it seems to me, is hard to find! When you find it, if you do, it is almost impossible to keep! Well, that's true in my case!"

As she said the words, Jeremy could feel the passion in her voice.

"There was a time when love was as far away as the moon. I thought things couldn't get any worse, after my daughter's disappearance, my downfall in the acting business and my heart attack. At that time, even Rupert, my best friend and confidant was a stranger to me!"

Her voice had been light and airy up to then, but with great aplomb, her voice lowered, seeming almost tortured. Jeremy was then pulled into her dramatic storytelling.

Cecilia's eyes then tightened, as if there was a mist descending over her whole being.

"I was walking along a canal, not so very far from here. It was autumn, one of those days where the light doesn't get any better than dull. That's exactly how I felt inside. My feelings were almost dragging along the muddy towpath. There wasn't a soul around. To be honest, if there was, I didn't see them. In the past, this walk was a friend to me, having spent hours just enjoying the peace, hearing and watching birds. Usually, it was a place for me to regenerate, then take stock. But on that day, the mist, the grey, was creating a heavy effect on my whole being. Narrowboats were dotted along the canal, tethered up to the bank. Some were occupied. You could tell that by the smoke that came from the fires down below. Oh, how I would have loved to have been down there, sitting in front of a warm fire, in that compact space, maybe drinking tea."

Her eyes and facial expressions were telling the story as much as her words. Jeremy was transfixed.

"Many a time in my life," she continued, "I'd longed to go onto a narrowboat, but, for whatever reason, I had never had the opportunity. So, in my mind, it was just a little dream, a comforting one.

An old, red-brick bridge straddled the canal. It was a pretty thing, with scars in the brickwork where the narrow-boat workers would walk with their horses. I went up onto the bridge, then looked towards the town. The lights from the town were twinkling brightly, reflecting off the water. I don't know why, but at that moment, I thought all I needed to do was just lean over the wall. In seconds my life would be over. I knew I couldn't swim. Some say canals aren't that deep, but I was sure I wouldn't have put up a fight. So that would have been it. The end!"

She sat there, almost as if it was a fact and she had committed suicide that day. Jeremy could feel the emotion in the air. He kept quiet. It was as if they were both waiting for a minute's silence to elapse. He broke it.

"What stopped you?"

"Faze! Faze stopped me!"

"Who or what was Faze?"

"He was a total stranger, standing there in front of me. I then heard his voice say, *Can I take your photograph?* I turned towards him. I was surprised. I thought I was all alone. We looked at each other. He moved his head to one side, as if he was waiting for an answer. His appearance made me smile. He was wearing a large, dark, well-worn leather hat with several feathers sticking up out of it. His coat was similar, made up of many pieces of leather, looking like patchwork. It appeared heavy on his back. Multicoloured trousers protruded down towards cowboy boots.

In some ways, I was shocked, because he wouldn't have looked unusual if he had had a rifle, maybe some beaver pelts wrapped around his waist. However, he did have an expensive camera clenched in his hands. He smiled. I just said, *why not?* He didn't say much. He just clicked away, asking me to move this way or that way. It seemed perfectly natural. I don't know why. The sky got lighter, the atmosphere seemed more convivial, then he stopped taking photographs. He offered me his hand. I shook it. We shared a smile.

'*Faze Tussock,*' he said.

I almost curtsied. It was as if he was my knight in shining armour. The only thing was, he was dressed in leather rather than chain mail. I studied his face which had a lived-in look to it. It was as leathery as his hat. He had a long scar on his left cheek, which stretched from below his eye down to his chin. In some ways, that made him look even more handsome. It seems ridiculous now when I look back, but I'm certain it was meant to be. He saved my life!"

Jeremy interrupted her.

"Do you believe in fate then?"

She hesitated.

"No, I don't think I do. Everything that happens to us is accidental, with a sprinkling of coincidence!"

The answer was ambiguous, especially after what she had said earlier. In her mind, however, it was perfectly succinct. There was no conclusion to draw from this. It was her way of colouring outside the lines, making it a slightly bigger picture. She poured more tea, which was still relatively hot, kept that way by a very ornate-looking tea cosy. She then continued.

"Faze hit me like a bolt from the blue. I had fallen in love with the moment, which had given me this man. For some reason, I can't explain why, it felt as if someone else had taken over my life!"

She stopped, then looked at Jeremy.

"You must know that feeling when you meet a total stranger. Somehow you connect, then something about it creates a fire inside!"

He thought for a moment about what she'd said. He knew exactly what she meant but said nothing.

"Faze guided me from the bridge back to the path. He asked if would like a drink or something to drive the cold out. It was a few miles to the nearest pub or place to eat. I also knew my own home was a good distance away. After a few minutes of walking, he said, '*Step on board.*' I then realised I'd passed this narrowboat earlier, with the smoke gently puffing out of the chimney. He kindly held my hand and guided me down to his kingdom!"

She took another sip of her tea to bring gravitas to the moment, then continued.

"I don't know if you've ever desired to go on board a narrowboat, Jeremy, but it lived up to all my expectations. It was cosy, warm, like a piece of heaven, almost like a womb!"

He watched Cecilia, as she waxed lyrical about her experience. Although his life had been fairly full up to now, he realised maybe it was the simple things that really mattered.

"Faze was uncomplicated, living a very simple life with the minimum of possessions. More importantly, he was happy. He said, '*Look around.*' So, I did, while he made us a hot drink. It didn't take too long to explore. I moved forward to the front of the boat, where there was a toilet and shower. As you can imagine, just enough room! Then a bedroom with a small double bed. At the front, there was a snug area where he developed his photographs. Many were hanging up to dry in the small area. From what I saw, I realised he was a very talented photographer.

I came back to him. He was putting two cups onto a table in the small living area that combined a fire and cooker. It was a perfect space for one, maybe two, who were close or in love. He had made a hot toddy with more than its fair share of whisky, which took me by surprise. It melted my insides to make me feel completely at home!"

"Tell me about Faze! What was he like?"

"He was in his mid to late thirties, much younger than me. He looked like he had lived a hard life. As he took off his hat and heavy coat, it was clear from his muscles that he must have worked out at some time or had a manual job. To me, he had sex appeal. Also, in so many ways, he was mysterious. If truth be told, he had the look of Heathcliff about him. Like him, Faze was a man with few words, at least at first. As the afternoon went on, we talked freely in the cosy surroundings. He told me he had spent most of his life working on the canals. Before that, when he was younger, he had lived in a commune with his mother."

Jeremy was curious about the man's name and how he came by it. Cecilia smiled.

"That was something I was curious about as well. He told me his mother had met a man who was a traveller. They had a brief relationship, resulting in Faze. His name came by accident. When his mother was asked what she would call the baby, she said,

'I don't know,'

The next question was about the father's name. She then said,

'I can't remember, I was high at the time. It was a phase I was going through.'

The name Phase stuck, the spelling changed for convenience. The sadness for Faze was that his mother died when he was a teenager. The commune broke up, so he hit the road. He had many jobs, as you can imagine, mostly labouring. He could do little else, having had no formal education. In his teens, he worked for a friend on the canal. It was long enough to be in one place for some time. By pure chance, a solicitor found him, when his name was recommended to do odd jobs in the local village. Faze discovered that his grandparents had died and left his mother a sum of money, which naturally came to him. So, the long and the short of it was he bought an old narrowboat to renovate, then never really looked back!"

She was obviously lost in the memory, as her eyes seemed fixed on nothing in particular, then she snapped out of it.

"Faze told me this, as we shared another hot toddy. I can still smell the coal fire and the overall intoxicating aromas that filled that small space. It had been the most wonderful afternoon, but I needed to go home.

He was a perfect gentleman, guided me off the boat, then walked me back to where there was streetlight. I'd sobered up by this time and was perfectly happy to walk home on my own. He bid me goodnight. I kissed him on the cheek. We didn't speak of seeing each other again. I just walked home, went straight to bed and slept like a baby!"

The story was another turn in her life that Jeremy wasn't expecting.

"You have to remember, in all of this, my life was at an all-time low. In some ways if it wasn't for Faze, I'm sure I would be dead now! I often look back at it as a turning point. He had given me a reason to wake in the morning. I saw the sun, a new day. Even the rain was a wonderful experience, once again.

A day or two later, I found myself being drawn back to the canal. He was there by his boat on a stool, cutting pieces of wood with a penknife. It was like watching something from the past, seeing him there. He called it whittling. I watched him turn scraps of wood into spoons, knives, all sorts of things. It was strange. We hardly spoke. He offered me some coffee, as it was fairly early in the morning. He gave me a stool to sit on.

The sun was shining. It felt like spring had arrived, even though it was still very early in the year. Eventually, we talked of things that were around us, the birds, trees, the countryside as a whole. It was magical, just being there with him. He had no interest in the world that I was part of. So I felt like I was stepping back in time. I grasped the life wholeheartedly.

After spending a few days going backwards and forwards to see him, we just gelled. He told me he was going for a trip further north, then asked me if I would like to go with him. Of course, I said yes! It seemed the right thing to do. I locked up my apartment, then made arrangements for all contact to be via my agent. Work had dried up anyway, so there was nothing to worry about!"

"So, what did that entail? How did you fit into Faze's way of life?"

"It was a joy to behold! I learned from him and he learned from me. We didn't talk of love, he wasn't that type of man, but it was there. We shared the wonder of travelling. I think you have to remember, most of my life was about moving around, whether it was with plays or on location. The only difference was the mode of transport, that's all. Up and down the canals we went exploring, moving slowly through the countryside, visiting places I had never been before, all the time meeting people of a like mind. The best times were when we moored up, then joined other canal people. We talked about their history as well as the history of the canal. It was enlightening and educational!"

Cecilia's face seemed to be that of a small child, which then grew serious, as she recounted other things.

"Faze had a past that was quite dark at times, which he related to me, usually after a drink or two. Long nights on a canal boat, especially in the winter, would often bring out stories that he had experienced. He'd survived his whole life hardly being able to read or write but was infinitely practical. It seemed natural to me to want to help him. Between enjoying the simple lifestyle, I taught him. He was a wonderful pupil. He picked it up fast. We both enjoyed the challenge. Him teaching me the ways of canal life, me giving him a chance to learn how to read and write better.

He had smoked all his life, but he never did in the boat. Usually, he would just go outside and sit at the stern. He would have his small wooden stool perched precariously against the tiller, where he would smoke into the night. He had this uncanny ability to blow smoke rings through smoke rings, which was quite magical. Sometimes I would join him, if he had something stronger to smoke, then we would stare at the stars and feel as if we ruled the universe!"

Cecilia reached forward and touched Jeremy's arm, then she looked hard into his big brown eyes. He almost felt unnerved. It was as if she was looking into his deepest thoughts for a memory.

"There is nothing," she said, "like the feeling of being snuggled up warm with someone you care for on a narrowboat. The feeling is of ultimate intimacy. All you really want to do is make love. Of course, that is another way of keeping warm, because when it's cold on a narrowboat, it's perishing cold. I have never known cold like it. So, you have to keep that cosy coal fire burning, as winter goes on outside, which, as you can imagine, is a wonder to see. A frozen canal, the snow falling, winter walks!"

She was talking and dreaming of such beautiful memories. Jeremy was sucked in, hook, line and sinker.

"And then came spring!"

The look of a child was in her eyes. It seemed strange, but Cecilia was rolling through the seasons with joy in her heart.

"There were mornings of wonderful celebration, as the birds sang about the new life in the world. Sharing these things made me feel so alive. I was born again, because of Faze. He had saved me! I was in my fifties, happy with a man in his late thirties, as we both enjoyed simple pleasures."

Jeremy was happy, because he knew this was surely one of the best things, she had shared with him.

"Our time was our own and we experienced each day on its merits. We moved from lock to lock, county to county. We rarely troubled the middle of any town or city. Local shops would suffice our needs, then we would move on. We did use the pubs along the way. I've always been able to see the enjoyment in drinking, as did Faze, although, it's the only time I was ever fearful of him. A few times he had too much to drink, lashed out and hurt me. However, the next day, he never remembered a thing."

Jeremy's mind slipped, as he thought of Sofia. Some might say the most wonderful part about loving someone is the making up. Love, the unexplainable force, steps in, then somehow unites lovers against adversity. Up to now, his love had not gone that far. In some respects, he welcomed the thought. To be in the presence of Sofia, the feeling of the making-up was paramount in his mind. The only thing he really wanted to know was whether it was his fault that she had disappeared.

"At the time, would you have left him?" Jeremy asked. "Especially, as he hurt you!"

"No, because I knew it wasn't him. There was something else, other things in his past that haunted him. Anyway, it only happened twice.

At one time, Faze was no stranger to drugs. He told me he'd sailed close to doing bad things, but always managed to evade the law. That was when he took up photography. It channelled his emotions into something creative."

"What were these darknesses he suffered from?" asked Jeremy.

"He never talked deeply about it, but sometimes when we had the odd joint, he would then tell me how his mother had died. According to him, she suffered badly. Doctors and the NHS let them both down! I know that's not a popular thing to say, but from what he told me, I would agree!"

The time seemed to zip by, as they both got caught up in the story of Faze. Jeremy felt the need to eat but didn't want to make anything.

"Cecilia, would you like me to buy you lunch?"

"Why, young man, that would be mighty fine!"

She said it with a near-perfect southern American drawl.

"Give me fifteen minutes to get ready!"

Half an hour later, Jeremy was sitting making notes, unperturbed by the time Cecilia had taken. She then appeared and looked like someone who might star in a musical. She was stunning, wearing a dark blue tailored suit, beautifully designed to fit her. On her head she had a trilby to match. Across her shoulders, she wore a white silk scarf.

"OMG! You look fabulous!"

"This was from one of my many parts in films. It must be nearly twenty-five years old by now!"

"It looks brand new!"

"Yes, I've always known how to look after my clothes."

The beauty of taking Cecilia to a restaurant was twofold for Jeremy. Firstly, it released them from their familiar surroundings, secondly, it gave him a chance to show off his one-time top actor.

He had picked a French restaurant on the edge of town, whose reviews were phenomenal. By pure chance, Jeremy knew the man who ran it, so he'd managed to get a table. It also helped that it was still early in the day. Cecilia revelled in it. Her days of premiers had always brought the dramatics out in her soul. Even though it was only a small restaurant, she acted the part. People looked around, as she walked into the restaurant, even though they had no idea who she was. As they sat down, he smiled at her, enjoying the moment.

"You know, Jeremy," she said, leaning forward, then speaking quietly, "When Faze and I went into a pub, no one took a second glance! I was all the happier for it!"

They looked at the menu and both felt the need to pick something special. She continued to talk of Faze.

"I never tired of waking up on the Gipsy's Kiss, no matter what the weather was."

"The Gipsy's Kiss, that's an interesting name," said Jeremy, "isn't that cockney rhyming slang for...?"

Before he had a chance to carry on, Cecilia intervened. "Yes, Faze named It! He knew it would make people think, *gipsy's kiss, take a piss!*"

She laughed. As she said it quite loudly, the other people in the restaurant looked around, but Cecilia was unmoved. She caught Jeremy's eye, then they laughed together before she carried on. A second glass of wine helped her remember more. "Sex with Faze was a beautiful experience. Obviously the confined space pushed us together many times a day. I guess in those situations you can understand how rabbits feel!"

She laughed again, as she thought of it. Jeremy dutifully recorded everything she said, then smiled at her facial expressions. They skipped through the first course, which was tasty but small. There was more to the main course. As it arrived, Cecilia said,

"Oh, this is to die for!"

Jeremy was never one to understand the glorification of food but, with the main course, he had become a worshipper.

"I want to say here," said Cecilia, as she leaned forward conspiratorially, "Faze was well-blessed!"

She was on her fourth glass of wine. She was cheerful, but not drunk.

"He was a man of experience, tender, understanding, very loving. How could anyone resist him? I couldn't, for sure!"

She laughed again out loud. Jeremy had had two glasses of wine. He felt like a lightweight in comparison to Cecilia, but he laughed with her, as she recalled the God that Faze was.

She looked reflective, almost as if they were together again.

"The summer came," she said, "In what seemed like a short time we had managed many miles on the canals. I will tell you now, Jeremy, it is not a life for the faint-hearted. I was fitter then than at any time in my life. Going through locks is a tiring business. Also, the facilities were woeful in certain areas of the country, but that was part of the experience.

One beautiful day in the middle of July, we found ourselves down south at a river and canal festival. Many river and canal people had convened there, as well as the general public.

We found it difficult to find a mooring place, because of the number of boats. Not everyone was happy at the large number of people and boats that had descended on the area. So, there was a village committee that had put signs up everywhere with rules and regulations.

We had to moor somewhere. Faze found a spot that normally was ok, but this committee had put signs out to prevent it. Faze knew all the regulations for the canals, having been on them most of his life, so he tied up the boat. Within half an hour, a man in a blue jacket descended on us and told us to move on. As you can imagine, Faze was imposing, so you wouldn't want to mess with him. He quickly pointed out that the man had no right to prevent narrowboats from mooring there, but he was unhappy and tried to provoke Faze, who remained calm as a cucumber."

Jeremy could see clearly in her eyes, as she spoke, that Faze was indeed a man who had many attributes.

"He was sent away with a flea in his ears. We, however, had a wonderful day at the festival, but when we came back, we found several notes pinned to the door of the boat. All they said was, move!

I know it was bloody-minded, but it seemed like fun at the time. Let's just say that we treated all and sundry to the delights of our flesh. We threw off our clothes for the rest of the day and when the night came, we made love several times. We left the doors and windows open for all to hear. I will tell you one thing now, Jeremy, we didn't spare the horses."

She laughed like a child at the thought of it.

"The next morning, the police were there. Knocking on the door of the boat. The blue jacket man, who'd told us to move on was looking pleased with himself, flanked by two police officers.

I can't remember now exactly what they said. It was something like flagrant indecency, breach of the peace or something. Actually, the police were good about it. It was just this jumped-up jobsworth that was aggravating things. We agreed to move, or they would arrest us for causing a nuisance!"

She started to giggle. Jeremy joined in, which brought about more fitful laughter that neither of them could control. A few other diners looked across at them and stared. After a while, they stopped. She gestured to Jeremy to come closer to her, so she could talk quieter.

"Later, the man in the blue jacket came back with a few of his committee. I think they were trying to show their power over us. We appeared on the deck of the Gipsy's Kiss again, both as naked as the day we were born. Of course, we showed no embarrassment. They swore at us, then said they would get the police again. We took the higher ground, said nothing, then eventually we moved off. It was a wonderfully freeing feeling, as the Gypsy's Kiss chugged away from the little village full of stuck-up, tight-lipped, middle-class arseholes!"

Celia's words slurred slightly as the last words left her lips.

The dessert came. It was colourful, neat and consumed in two mouthfuls. Although it was beautiful, there was not enough of it to fill either of them. However, they both agreed the whole meal was phenomenal. The bill came. It was way more than he thought it would be. He thought it to be the best investment he had ever made.

It could be said that Cecilia had glided into the restaurant like a galleon, but there was no doubt about the fact that she was exiting like a wreck. Not far behind, followed Jeremy, her little dinghy, that was nearly sinking. Jeremy made a call for one of his dad's taxis. The driver was known to him, so he helped them both get back home with a minimum of fuss.

A couple of hours later, Jeremy woke up on the sofa at Cecilia's apartment, with a terrible headache. He was not a wine drinker. He knew this and was annoyed with himself for being sucked into the ambience of the moment. He went to the kitchen to get some water, drinking copiously to try and rid himself of his headache. A few minutes later, he knocked on Cecilia's bedroom door. No answer. He looked around the door, saw Cecilia, still in her blue suit, lying sprawled across her bed. Jeremy went in, removed her shoes, tried to make her comfortable, then threw a cover over her. He left her sleeping soundly.

38.

When Jeremy got home, it was early evening. His mum and dad were home. Maya was also there.

"Ah, the man of the moment!" said his dad.

"In what way?" asked Jeremy.

By now, he had sobered up. Even so, his head hurt.

"In the way you might find a couple of people, a little the worse for wear, in the middle of the day!"

"Oh, I see! You have a report from your team of detective drivers!"

"At least you had good honest company!"

His dad said it in such a way that it seemed a little patronising. Jeremy was feeling fraught and wasn't willing to get into an argument over it.

"Jeremy," said Mum, "nobody is getting at you. We're just a little bit concerned about how you're feeling regarding Sofia!"

He seemed to capitulate, then moved over to sit on a chair, although he still felt annoyed that they'd been talking about him behind his back.

"I must say I feel highly honoured, Dad! You taking time off to be here!"

"No need to be sarcastic! We are all concerned about the things that have been affecting you, Jeremy!"

He then felt like a wounded animal.

"You haven't taken time off for me as well, have you, Maya?"

"I was in the vicinity. Why are you getting so tetchy?" she asked.

"Oh, for God's sake! Leave me alone!"

Jeremy stormed off to his room. His headache had got worse. He lay on his bed, then remembered when he'd been lying on it with Sofia, not that long ago. The passionate thoughts somehow seemed to relax him. He let his body go, then went fast asleep.

The next morning, in his head, he calculated where he was, regarding Cecilia's biography. A comforting feeling overtook his thoughts, as he realised the material, in parts, was exceptional.

As usual, outside events were pressing, although Jeremy welcomed them. Tony had a book-signing. He'd asked Jeremy and Gail to be there for moral support. Jeremy wasn't certain why, as Tony's book was already a best-seller. The distraction, however, was welcome. They met in the café as usual.

"Someone's cheerful today," said Tony to Gail, as they all ordered a big breakfast. "Did you have sex last night?"

It seemed a reasonable question. She smiled as she sipped her tea.

Jeremy felt relieved. He didn't know why, but Gail's sexual activity somewhere else made him feel freer to think of Sofia.

"Spill the beans, Gail! Come on!" said Tony.

"Let's just say I met someone on a blind date. We are meeting again tonight!"

"Does that mean you consummated the relationship?" asked Tony.

"What do think I am, desperate or something?"

The words sat there for a few moments, as the silence got longer.

"Ok, ok. No, I didn't, but maybe tonight!"

They were amused by the banter, then Tony asked Jeremy a question.

"Any news on Sofia?"

Jeremy tried not to dull the moment.

"Not as yet, no!"

"How about your contacts in the police?"

"Zilch!"

They all became silent, as the food arrived. The practice of eating gave space for deep thought, that's if you're a barrister, a builder or a young man in love looking for someone he has lost.

Later, at Tony's book signing, the store was heaving. His story had caught the public's imagination. So much so, there was early talk of commissioning it for a film. Celebrity status was now beckoning him. Both Gail and Jeremy knew Tony deserved it. Jeremy stayed for a while, then decided to go over to Cecilia's. He was feeling more at ease, having decided to concentrate on what he could deal with; that was to draft the book. In some ways, he was hungry to try and move on.

Cecilia picked up where she'd left off the previous day, without a word about their meal at the restaurant. The fact that they were both very, very drunk was papered over.

"Christmas was wonderful on the canal. The dark nights made the Christmas lights so appealing. I had never experienced such friendliness in any other part of my life, in comparison to the canal community.

Faze had many friends around the Black Country and Birmingham. It was where he had worked all his life. He was a jack of all trades. Strangely, even though he wasn't good at reading or writing, there were many narrow boats that we went past that he had sign written. It was one of the many wonderful things about the man that fascinated me.

We ended up in Gas Street Basin in Birmingham for Christmas. It was wonderful. The people, the atmosphere, we even had snow, and the canal froze over! The community was tight and friendly. There was many a night we would spend going from boat to boat to celebrate. Of course, if anything went wrong, there was always someone on hand to solve it, whatever it was. I loved it, it was a marvellous time. I even managed to get Faze to go to the theatre with me. It wasn't easy. He would rather strip an engine down on a freezing cold day than do anything like that. He caved in after I convinced him it would be a wonderful experience. I know he did it for me! There was no interest in it for him!"

"What did you take him to see?"

"It was The Beggar's Opera! It was a colourful piece, so entertaining. Let's say it left a big impression on both of us. It reminded me of how marvellous the theatre was. It helped to put me back in touch with my roots, while lighting a spark in Faze, although it would never mean the same to him.

This was when I knew I had found my soulmate. What makes us different is what brings us together! In my life, most of my relationships had been far too brief and transitory! Now I had something that I could build my life around."

"Did you see anyone you knew from the acting world when you went to the theatre?"

"Funnily enough, no! I knew of some of the actors in the production, but none I had ever met!"

"Did you want that life back?"

She paused, then thought about it.

"To be honest, yes! I had spent my life treading the boards, as they say. It's in the blood and hard not to miss the excitement of it!"

Even though that thought hung there for a moment, she moved on.

"As time went by, we settled into a world away from what I was used to. I was in a relationship that had its ups and downs, but the ups were at such a higher level, the downs were forgettable."

"Can I ask you, did you ever find out about the scar on his face?"

"Yes, I asked him early in our relationship. He told me he remembered little about it. He did say that he drank too much and did drugs. The combination almost killed him. That was when he first got work on the canals. He told me a man called Caleb Smith found him on a bench between locks in the Black Country. Caleb told Faze he found him with a broken bottle stuck in his cheek. Faze remembered nothing about it.

Caleb was an old man, who was quite famous in the area as a working boatman. Up until the day he died, he was working his boats along the canal network. He was also known for his helpfulness and kindness to others, because of his upbringing by his violent, drunken father.

Caleb saved Faze's life. Apart from finding him, then taking him to hospital, he helped Faze redirect his life.

At the time, Caleb was also a member of Alcoholics Anonymous, so he became Faze's sponsor. Over the years, Faze did lapse, especially when Caleb died!"

"As time went by, did you feel this is it, my life is now that of a person who lives on a narrowboat?"

"To be honest, yes! Why wouldn't I? We welcomed my second new year on the canal, watching fireworks in the middle of Birmingham. A few days later, the new year made me feel like I had been on the canal all my life. After staying in the basin for nearly six weeks, we moved, then went north. Faze was sociable, but he did like the solitude of the endless miles of canals. Of course, around every corner, there was a vista to behold.

Before long, a festival of colour adorned the countryside as we travelled. Daffodils were a fanfare for the spring that was to come. It was simple, never easy, but satisfying, then sleep at the end of the day was always a joy!"

She stopped talking. Jeremy could almost see the spring-like colours in her eyes.

"Even though I had embraced the life, I still went back to my home to see if it was ok, to sort the post out, just make sure nothing was amiss.

We both found things to do. Faze already had his photography. I encouraged him to enter the photographs into an exhibition about the canals, where he won fans who also bought his work. At that time, we talked about buying a bigger boat. I suggested selling my apartment! With the proceeds, we could have had one custom-made. This to Faze was something he'd never even thought of. He told me he was happy with the Gypsy's Kiss. I couldn't move him on this point. He was as obstinate as a pig in mud. I understood in his mind that the narrowboat was part of his history, especially because of the link between him and his mother.

We came to a happy compromise by reworking the inside of the boat, making it more comfortable for the two of us. By the time Faze had done most of the work, it was like a palace on water, while still holding onto its old-world charm.

Another year came to an end too quickly, so we found our way back to Birmingham. As before, it was wonderful to be in a big conurbation, especially as I knew the city so well. I met new people, who became my friends. If Faze didn't want to go to the theatre or a lively spot in town, I had someone who would take his place. It was a perfect life, so perfect I never thought for a second anything could change it!"

"So, what happened?" asked Jeremy.

One frosty morning in January, Faze woke up, stretched, then got out of bed. It was very cold, so he moved through the boat then stoked the fire. I heard him making tea. This was a wonderful time of day, as we drank it in bed together.

'It's perfect out today, I think I'll go and take some photographs!' he said.

I thought nothing of it. He often took advantage of the early morning light.

The canal wasn't frozen, but there was a fine coat of frost everywhere. Sometimes, we would venture out together, wrap up warm, then find a deserted footpath where Faze would click away to his heart's content. For some reason, this one particular morning, I didn't go. I do remember putting more coal on the fire, so it would be nice and warm for him when he got back.

As always, we kissed as he left. I stood at the stern of the boat, then watched him walk down the towpath. The last thing I remembered saying to him was to get some milk. A mist drifted over the canal, as the sun cut through the buildings and trees, creating mystical shadows. I turned to go back into the boat and a robin was sitting on some firewood that we had on top of the boat. I was captivated by him, as he seemed to be singing for me. He was less than a meter away. It was truly beautiful. He was clearly trying to tell me something. I know you probably think I'm crazy, but that's how it felt!"

About an hour later, one of the other boat owners knocked on the window. Something had happened. I could hear sirens in the distance. I joined others who were congregating on the towpath, then we heard the sirens get closer. We made our way up the slope, with a few others curious to know what was happening. Out on the street, many people were tending to someone. Inside I already knew. It was instinctive. It was Faze. Somebody told me he had been hit by a car. Whoever was driving had gone without stopping!"

Cecilia stopped. Tears fell like raindrops into her hands. Jeremy moved over to comfort her.

"It's ok," she said, "it's just that it's been years since I've thought deeply about it, never mind talked about it!"

He did the obvious thing and made tea. It was the go-to thing to ease all things, then she said,

"Would you like something stronger? There's a vintage bottle of brandy in the sideboard, for special occasions!"

He opened the art nouveau sideboard, then pulled it out.

Within minutes, they sat opposite each other, brandy in hand. Cecilia downed hers in one go.

"That's better!"

Jeremy sipped his more conservatively.

"How did you manage to cope with the shock?" he asked.

"I think, from that point, everything went cloudy. Even now, I find it hard to think of it. I do remember everyone who lived by us giving me support! As far as people on the canals were concerned, Faze would be missed. People from far and wide came to his funeral."

"Did anyone in the media pick up on your link to Faze?"

"Funnily enough, no! I think the local paper had a fairly large piece about him being killed by a hit-and-run driver. There was information about the funeral, where it was taking place, but my part in the relationship was barely mentioned!"

"How did that make you feel?"

"To be perfectly honest, it meant very little to me. I don't remember what was going on at the time. However, I do recall the funeral. I know he didn't like black. So, I knew he would like one like his mothers, which he told me was very colourful.

Faze's coffin was borne down the canal on top of the Gipsy's Kiss to a cemetery not far away. Hundreds and hundreds of people lined the canal. It was truly amazing. For weeks, I stayed on the boat in a sort of daze, not knowing what to think or do. A few people tried to help, but I was devastated.

A month later, I left the boat where it was, not knowing if I would ever go back. My apartment became an escape from the pain. I rattled around in it for months, then I received some correspondence. The letter was from a solicitor who asked me to seek an appointment about Faze's will. I wasn't expecting anything because we had only been together a few years. The only thing I thought Faze possessed was the Gypsy's Kiss.

Anyway, to cut a long story short, I found out he had no living relatives. He had left me well over fifty-three thousand pounds, plus the Gypsy's Kiss. You can imagine my surprise, when I found out that he had done that. After all, we had only known each other a short time. I was staggered. It took some time to take it in. The one thing it did do was make me value my life, especially after what Faze and I had experienced together!"

Jeremy had sat listening to all of Cecilia's life so far. So much so, he felt as if he was part of her family.

Emotionally, he couldn't help feeling it was a wonder to behold. As usual, after these stories that Cecilia revealed about her life, she became either full of the joys of spring or a dark foreboding shadow. Jeremy was never sure how it would pan out. Suddenly, out of the blue, Cecilia asked him,

"So, what of Sofia? How is she? You've said little about her. I do hope our little love affair has not got in the way."

She said it with her tongue planted firmly in her cheek, although, in some ways, she was not so old that she didn't derive pleasure from Jeremy's attention.

"She's gone missing!"

Immediately, she sat forward in her chair.

"What do you mean, gone missing?"

"To tell you the truth, she has disappeared. I think intentionally. Something or someone has frightened her. She's covered her tracks and gone!"

"Where do you think she may have disappeared to?"

"Spain! From what I can gather, there's somewhere over there she'd rather be than here. Trouble is, I think it's my fault!"

"What have you done, Jeremy, to think that?"

He dropped his head into his hands.

"To tell the truth, I've no idea!"

"Why didn't you tell me earlier, letting me drone on about my life while you're suffering?"

She got up, then sat by him, resting her hand on his shoulder to comfort him. This act was somewhat of a strange thing for Cecilia to do. She was not normally a person to comfort or be comforted. In fact, the feelings she'd had over the past few months were almost alien, but, in her heart, she was warming again to the emotions that had got buried by the past.

He told her what had happened, and what he had done to try and find her.

"Go and see this girl, Toya! Find out what she knows!"

"But," he said. "We need to continue with the book. We need to move forward, get it done!"

"It'll sit for a while. Go! Go now!"

An hour later, on the other side of town. Jeremy met Duman for a coffee. Duman was in his work overalls. They sat outside a coffee bar. After hugging each other, Duman asked,

"How you feeling, Jez?"

Duman laughed then slapped Jeremy on the back.

"When we were at the karaoke bar, Jez, you were way out of it! Way past pissed! And as for taking your clothes off, that was on another planet!"

Jeremy had waves of remembering, but still couldn't fill in

all the gaps. He was sure that wasn't the reason Sofia had disappeared.

"Can I speak to Toya? Where is she?"

"What? You are not happy with having one good-looking chick, you want mine too!"

"No, no it's not like that, I just need to ask her some questions about Sofia!"

"What sort of questions, bro!"

"Like where the fuck has Sofia gone?"

Duman looked at Jeremy as if he was asking the strangest question ever.

"If you don't mind me asking, why would Toya know?"

"Because Chai told me she saw Sofia talking to Toya for a long time, so she might know something!"

"I'm sorry, Jez, I didn't realise. I'll call her right away. She might not answer, because she's doing an audition."

There was no answer, so Duman left a message, then gave Jeremy her phone number.

39.

On the way home, Jeremy received a text message back from Nigel, whom he had contacted to ask if he could find anything out about Sofia's whereabouts. He confirmed that Sofia had gone to Spain recently; she had landed in Malaga. Other than that, he had no further information. Even though it was sparse, it was better than nothing. It did come to his mind, however, that Sofia was very good at covering her tracks.

Not long after, he had a phone call from Toya. They arranged to meet in town. Jeremy didn't go for the uptown life, he far preferred a pub or a bar. As he went into the discotheque club, he found Toya and a group of wannabe singers with whom she had auditioned.

A heavy bass was on the track that was playing in the discotheque. A group of fifteen or so people were all in high spirits. Jeremy immediately questioned whether it was a good idea to meet there, but Toya informed him that it was his only chance, because of her work schedule.

Toya's fellow contestants were a sight to see, as they were all fresh in from the audition with varying arrays of stage clothes. Jeremy thought more South American carnival than a night out at the disco. He approached the joyous throng. High fives went around as Toya had to shout to introduce him to a few of her competitors. He knew she had what was needed to succeed in show business. It did help that she had a powerful personality and a wonderful voice. She guided him to somewhere quieter to talk. She wasted no time and told him what she knew about Sofia.

"While you were having fun on the karaoke, me and Sof talked about life," explained Toya, "We already knew each other after growing up in Spain. We weren't close, but I think we were friends. She used to come to my parents' bar with her mum and her friend. It was very similar to the karaoke bar the other night, but there the weather was almost perfect!"

He looked at her and concentrated on her lips, because the music was so loud.

"In my parents' bar, the customers were more likely to strip off completely, rather than just to their undies!"

She laughed and gave him an affectionate smile.

"Yeah, yeah, I get it!" he said.

"Sometimes, Sof and I sang together when we were kids! It was fun!"

Jeremy took in the new information. His mind was a bit hazy as he digested the news, then he chastised himself for not having asked Sofia more about herself.

"That's it really, Jeremy, we just passed the time talking about Spain and how nice it was to grow up in the sun."

"Where exactly?" asked Jeremy.

"Nerja, it's about 50k from Malaga."

He kissed her on her cheek, then hugged her very hard. She laughed loudly, her exuberant personality ever-present.

"She thinks an awful lot of you," Toya added, "she was talking about you all the time, couldn't keep her eyes off you!"

"Just one more question, have you any idea about Sofia's history?"

"There were rumours!"

"What sort of rumours?"

"Some people said her mum may have been involved in drugs when she was younger. As far as Sofia was concerned, she was involved with a gang when she was a teenager. Theft, even some drugs. They were a bit of a wild bunch. I'm not certain of all the details, but they all got caught up in a robbery that went wrong. I heard no more about her; it was almost like she had vanished off the face of the earth. However, later on, someone told me she was ok and had changed her surname!"

He looked at her, surprised at that part of her statement.

"Why did she change her name?"

"I'm not certain, but I think she did it so she could put some distance between her and the gang!"

"What was her name before, can you remember?"

"Yes, of course!"

She paused for a second, then said,

"Neele, Sofia Neele!"

Jeremy was getting a better picture of Sofia's life, but it didn't tell him why she had gone back to Spain, without saying a word.

He now thought he had enough information to book a flight to Malaga.

In Britain, the sun was shining. It was one of the hottest days of the year. When Jeremy got to Spain, it was pouring with rain. Malaga looked like any other town in bad weather - dismal, but for someone who had never been there before, it was exciting.

He climbed into a taxi, then asked the driver to take him to Nerja along the coast. The Albanian tried to engage Jeremy in general holiday chatter, but Jeremy's mind wasn't up to it. His first port of call was Toya's parents' bar on the edge of Nerja. One thing he did notice was how pretty the little town was.

The bar-restaurant was among a row of other businesses looking out to sea, which, at that moment, was being battered by what looked like a tropical storm. The name above the bar said *Tom y Mia*. He exited the taxi and ran for cover. A large awning was stretched out over the front of the restaurant, keeping the chairs and tables dry. He took cover just inside the doors of the restaurant and watched the deluge outside.

A young man was behind the bar, lazily cleaning glasses, humming an unrecognisable tune to himself.

"Buenos dias, señor," he said.

Jeremy answered by saying the same. He felt self-conscious as he said it but, for some reason, relieved.

"The storm," said the bartender, "is global warming. In a few years' time, the sea will be above our heads."

He looked at Jeremy seriously, then smiled.

"In half an hour, the sun will be out! It will be un día hermoso, a beautiful day!"

Jeremy took his word for it but wasn't sure if he was seriously thinking that the sea would rise that quickly in a few years.

"What would you like, señor?"

Jeremy was hungry. He noticed that English breakfast was on the menu, so he asked for it.

"In or out?" the bartender asked.

Jeremy was thinking that outside would be too wet, but then looked and the sun was shining. He opened the door and went out. Miraculously the clouds had disappeared. The sun was really hot. He then felt sticky, as steam rose from the drying pavement. The bartender had followed him out and was proceeding with a certain skill to remove the water from the awning. A cascade fell to the ground, then started to dry almost immediately.

Jeremy took a seat. Within a short time, people were moving along the road into shops, some taking to the beach. He took a seat under the awning and waited for his breakfast.

The view was perfect. An azure-coloured sea lay in front of him. The storm, now gone, had brought about an overwhelming feeling of calm. Perhaps all he needed was a holiday. He felt overdressed, as tourists walked by, more comfortably attired than he was. He then realised he had not thought any of this through, having only got one change of clothes. In his shoulder bag he had another pair of trousers, pants and socks. The trousers were similar to the ones he was wearing. He slipped off his long sleeve shirt, revealing a t-shirt which made him feel less clammy.

He realised, once he had eaten, that he needed to find a shop that sold something cooler to wear. While on the plane, he had researched Nerja. It wasn't like most Spanish places dotted along the coast. It could be said it was far more select, but still catered for all tastes.

After some time, his breakfast came, delivered by a short, well-built man with a red face. He smiled broadly, as he placed it on the table. It looked to all intents and purposes, like an English breakfast, but strange for some reason. The man's broad smile was followed by,

"Enjoy señor!"

The waiter was wearing a T-shirt and shorts with flip-flops that were overly loose. They flapped loudly as he walked away.

"Excuse me, are you Toya's father?"

The man stopped in his tracks. It was as if someone had just shot him. He turned slowly.

"Who wants to know?"

Jeremy guessed that Toya's dad wasn't the brains behind the business, but then he thought who needs brains to cook bacon and eggs? This made him think of his own culinary skills, which were zero compared to his sister Maya. He quickly answered the question.

"I'm a friend of Toya's! She asked me to say hi!"

Immediately, her dad took a seat opposite Jeremy.

"You know my baby girl?"

It was as if Jeremy had touched a caring button in her father's mind.

"I'm Jeremy! Jeremy Bakshi! I met Toya recently. She's a lovely girl and has got a brilliant voice!"

"I'm Tommy!" he said.

He put out his hand to warmly shake that of Jeremy, who was just about to put a piece of bacon into his mouth. Jeremy had noticed Tommy's accent.

"So, you're a Londoner! You found a new life in this lovely place!"

"Essex, to be more precise!"

Jeremy carried on eating, realising how hungry he was. As they talked, locals walked by, then passed the time of day with Tommy.

"You seem well-liked!"

"Oh my God, I love it here, although the business is non-stop during the summer!"

They seemed to drift away from talking about Toya, so Jeremy mentioned her again.

"Toya looks like she may get through this audition. It could be big time for her."

Tommy's eyes lit up again. Toya was obviously the light of his life.

"My girl, yes, she's a star! You know, when she sang here, this place was fit to bust, they were great times!"

"So, she learnt by singing in the bar?"

"Yes, then as she got into her teens, somebody said she should audition for one of these shows in Britain. It took some time, but she's there now. We are one hundred and ten per cent behind her!"

At that moment, Jeremy thought about Cecilia and her dislike of the phrase. Tommy looked down, as he spoke of Toya. Jeremy could see that he missed her badly and was so proud of his daughter that he just wanted to talk about her. Jeremy let him carry on.

After a while, Jeremy asked questions about Sofia and if he remembered her. Naturally, Tommy was curious as to why he wanted to know about Sofia, so Jeremy told him the story. Before Tommy could speak any more, Mia, Tommy's wife, came out. She had an ample figure. She had shape where Tommy had girth. She seemed to impose herself on them. Tommy looked uncomfortable but continued to speak of Toya and Sofia. Mia grasped the conversation, then dominated it, as Tommy was almost ordered to attend to the cooking. Mia was Spanish. Her voice was assertive, but attractive; she was obviously the boss.

"Sofia, she is the step-daughter of a friend who lives in Frigiliana. From what I know, she was in England till a day or two ago. So, you in love with her. Yes?"

"Yes!" he said, without thinking, realising it to be perfectly true. Mia took a pen from her pocket, wrote a phone number and address on it. Then, this handsome figure of a woman leaned over, kissed him on each cheek, saying,

"Sofia is so beautiful, nearly as beautiful as my Toya!"

She left him to finish his breakfast. It was in his mind to book somewhere to stop the night but, instead, he opted to sit and enjoy the moment with his latte. He followed that with a lager, then another, all the time taking in the holiday atmosphere. He wasn't one for foreign travel, often thinking to himself that to be a true journalist, he must have that inner wanderlust. As he sat there, he began to think that feeling might be rising in his blood.

Before he knew it, a couple of hours had gone by. He asked Tommy if he could order a taxi for him. He gladly did. Just before he left, Tommy said to him,

"If you need somewhere to stop the night, we have a few rooms we let to people we know!"

Glad of that safety net, Jeremy then said goodbye.

The taxi ride was at times a bit bumpy because of construction work just outside of Nerja. His overindulgence in lager was affecting his system. Even so, he enjoyed the experience, as the beautiful countryside passed by quickly. He saw Frigiliana on the hillside coming into view. Taken aback by how stunning it looked, he got out of the taxi without paying. He quickly apologised, by saying to the driver,

"This must be a wonderful place to live!"

The taxi driver who spoke perfect English, answered,

"No idea, señor! I live in a one-bedroom rat-infested apartment in a seedy part of Malaga and have an idiot for a neighbour!"

A second later, the taxi disappeared in a cloud of dust, back to Nerja. He looked around, then realised he needed a hat. A bar, along with a few shops, sat in his eye-line. He decided to investigate. It seemed to him everything was sleepily basking in the intense sunshine.

Jeremy entered one of the establishments that had a rack of hats and sunglasses sitting outside. He wasn't a man for hot weather; he was happy in the rain. Clouds were part of his mindset. If asked, he would say the best stories happen on a damp and cold day. However, as the day went on, he was finding a kind of peace, maybe even resolution in the heat.

He then tried to engage in a conversation with the shopkeeper. After her larger-than-life smile and her assistant laughing out loud, he decided to retire to a changing room to try on some shorts. He kept the shorts on, then purchased them, as well as some sandals and a hat. He didn't look like a sun worshipper, but he was fifty per cent cooler. The shopkeeper then pointed him in the direction of the address he was looking for. The sun was almost directly above his head, which now had the protection of a nice, broad-rimmed, raffia hat.

He slid on his new sunglasses. For the first time since he'd arrived, his eyes didn't feel continually screwed up. Ahead of him lay a sun-baked street, with, on each side, rows of pretty, white-painted houses, stretching off up the hill.

He walked slowly up the stone steps, admiring the flowers that adorned all the properties. It was as if there was a competition to have the most colourful plant sitting outside their front doors.

The narrow streets looked as if they had never seen a car, it was so peaceful. All that could be heard were children's voices and crickets in the near distance. He was aware of one flower that he knew and loved. Bougainvillaeas were latched onto nearly all the houses. The flowers looked so delicate, like coloured tissue paper swaying in the breeze.

It was obvious that the locals were taking a siesta. What else would you do in such heat? As he walked, he contemplated how it was possible to live in such small properties. Eventually, he arrived at the address. He knocked on the door. A woman answered. She was well-dressed and quite business-looking. Not really what he was expecting.

"Hi, I'm Jeremy Bakshi. Does Sofia Moran live here?"

She looked him up and down, suspiciously. She then called out in Spanish.

"Anita, alguien para ti!"

Without taking her eyes off Jeremy, she waited. Anita came to the door.

"Who is it?" she asked.

Anita was wiping her hands on a tea towel and looked a bit stressed. She then looked at Jeremy.

"What do you want?"

Anita was a diminutive figure, smaller than the Spanish woman. She had long hair, plaited many times with coloured material tied into it. Jeremy thought she looked like an ageing hippy. He noted she had a mild Liverpool accent, as she asked the Spanish woman to go inside. The woman got the message and left them to talk.

"I'm looking for Sofia, Sofia Moran. My name is Jeremy Bakshi!"

Anita looked puzzled, as if she wasn't certain what to say. Jeremy then decided to tell her why he was there. Anita seemed to soften. She became less tense and worried-looking.

"You best come in!"

He did so, she looked up and down the street almost as if someone might be watching. Jeremy went inside. His eyes watered as he got used to the light or the lack of it. Anita led him through to another room, which was much larger and, like everything else inside, so white. Jeremy quickly concluded that Frigiliana was a place white paint was made for. He also felt certain he'd stepped into Dr Who's tardis, because inside seemed so much larger than the outside would lead you to believe. He followed Anita through the living room then into a large kitchen, all of which looked modern yet in keeping with the decor.

"I can't believe the space in here!" said Jeremy, "it's phenomenal!"

"Yes! Most of the houses up here are like this," said the woman in perfect English. "However, two original properties were made into this one."

"This is Constanza, my friend," said Anita, "she's an estate agent!"

Straight away, Jeremy could see it. Constanza was indeed an estate agent. She fitted the bill perfectly. She must have heard

Jeremy talking about Sofia to Anita on the doorstep, because she seemed to soften to his presence. Anita made coffee which they all took onto a balcony overlooking the countryside. As he sat there, Jeremy took in the vista that he saw before him. The house looked down across fields that were mostly green but, here and there, a field had been planted with a crop that gave it the look of a patchwork quilt. The odd, white-washed house broke up the scene then it went onward towards Nerja and the Mediterranean Sea. It was quite breathtaking. Jeremy was lost in its beauty and how stunning it was. Anita then spoke of her life there with Sofia and her mother.

"This is Sofia's house," said Anita, "I am her stepmother. I met her mum nearly thirty-odd years ago in Nerja. It was a chance meeting in a bar. I was backpacking across Europe. We hit it off immediately. She was kind enough to put me up here, having only just bought this place. I got a summer job, then we became an item. Tia was pregnant with Sofia at the time. In many ways it was fortuitous, because, not long after, it was difficult for her to work. So, in the autumn, I stayed, found a permanent job. I learned Spanish, then before long, Sofia was born!"

Anita stopped to take a sip of coffee. At this moment, Constanza said she was leaving, as she had an appointment to keep near Malaga. Anita stood, then they kissed.

"See you later, Connie."

Constanza kissed Anita on the lips, then they hugged and exchanged an affectionate "Te amo."

Constanza then left. Anita seemed to relax. Jeremy was surprised how easy Anita was finding it to talk to a complete stranger about her life, but at the same time relieved.

"So, what of Sofia's dad? What happened to him?"

"Tia would never talk of him. I know little about their relationship. Sofia knows even less!"

Jeremy was hungry for knowledge about Sofia, so he decided to let Anita deliver the story, as she saw fit.

"You could say that Sofia brought us together. When the winter came it was quiet here with few tourists to speak of.

Tia had had a hard life from what she had told me. Drugs had almost killed her, but whenever I pushed her on the details she would just go quiet!"

She stopped and looked reflective as if she could see it all in her mind's eye.

"Of course," she continued, "when you're joyfully happy you see no wrong in anything. The years seemed to fly by. We opened a small shop to sell things that we had made. It was great in the summer months. In the winter, we just survived on those earnings. Sofia was growing up fast. It was an idyllic time although things were going on in the background.

About a year after, things changed when Tia went back to Britain. She told me she had to sort some things out. I looked after Sofia. She was no trouble. Every six months or so, Tia went back there for about four to five days. Whenever it happened, she became very tense and argumentative. When she returned, she was a different person. Truth was, she would never speak of what she was doing. I guess it didn't do any harm, but it annoyed me when she wouldn't communicate."

Anita paused, as if she was somehow about to climb a hill, then gathered her breath.

"About a week after Sofia's tenth birthday, Tia was found dead on the beach at Nerja. We were told that she had drowned!"

She stopped and looked at Jeremy, searching his face, as if he could answer the question in her eyes.

"Tia was an excellent swimmer, so how could she drown? The sea had been relatively calm. They said she must have had difficulty. The post-mortem report said it was accidental, but what of the bruises they found on her shoulder? I knew she was very fit. Every other day, she would swim in the sea. She was like a mermaid!"

Anita looked confused, deep worry lines appearing on her face. She was still looking for answers after all this time.

"As for Sofia," Anita continued, "it was difficult to know how she really felt, but together we weathered the devastation of losing Tia! A day goes by, then another, we laughed, we cried, we reminisced. We laid flowers on the seashore, then sang in her memory. I'll never forget! It's like she's here now, looking out across the sunlit fields with me!"

She stopped, tears in her eyes.

"Sorry, you don't want to hear this, but it's strange. It's been a long time since I've spoken of it. You must be a good listener, Jeremy."

"It has been said!"

He smiled and rested his hand on her knee. After settling herself, she offered him an alcoholic drink, which he welcomed, especially the ice. She continued.

"I can stay here as long as I live. That was the terms of Tia's will. Unless things change for me. Over the last six months, they have. I met Constanza who has become a good friend. She has a place in Malaga and has asked me to move in with her. I suppose I should do it. I think I need to move on. Like Sofia has. She has told me she wants to sell this place."

There was sadness on Anita's face. They both took a sip of their cold drinks. Jeremy changed the subject.

"Did she talk about me?"

"Apart from talking about selling, she said little. She's like her mother, she keeps her feelings close to her chest. Even so, I know her well enough to see something is troubling her!"

Jeremy felt concerned because he thought if he could only speak to her, maybe he could help.

"So, this place will be sold," said Anita, "and I'll receive a quarter of whatever we get."

"How does that make you feel?"

"Happy! I have many wonderful memories. I love Sofia as if she was my daughter and I know she loves me!"

Jeremy couldn't be certain, but he thought Anita might have been just as happy to stay there for the rest of her life.

"I'm sorry. I can't help you any more than I have, Jeremy. Just give her time to sort it out, whatever it is!"

"I have talked to Toya," said Jeremy, "back in Britain, about Sofia."

"You must be talking about Toya from the bar in Nerja."

"Yes, I am!" he said.

"Sofia did mention her," she said, "She told me she was in a talent show over there!"

"Anyway," he said, "Toya told me that Sofia changed her surname from Neele to Moran when she was a teenager."

Anita thought about the question, then she lowered her voice to a whisper, almost as if someone might be listening. The Spanish sun created a shadow under the parasol, big enough to hide a conspiracy, if there was one. For a moment, he felt like he was going to hear a terrible secret.

"For several years after, both me and Sofia tried to enjoy our lives, but then she got mixed up with some other kids at school. Sofia was the youngest of the group. They got into shoplifting and stuff like that. As time went by, it became obvious it was more organised. She had started smoking cannabis, supplied by someone who was fencing the stolen goods they had stolen.

I think most kids do this stuff. They get over it, then move on. The only problem was, this unknown person was controlling them. Someone who had money. Eventually, this big job came up. They raided a jewellers in Malaga. It went wrong, they all ended up on top of the building. In their attempt to get away from the police, she fell. She was left for dead. She was taken to hospital. It was touch and go for a while."

"What happened to the other kids?"

"They went to ground, the police couldn't find them. It was believed whoever wanted the goods helped them to evade the law."

"What happened to Sofia?"

"She was in hospital for months!"

The police had nothing on her, unless the others could be found. As time went by, the case just went away. That's when we changed her surname to mine.

"Wow, she had a colourful past!"

As he said it, Anita sat back. For some reason, she looked

relieved.

"Have you any idea who this person is, who had this influence over them?"

She shook her head. Jeremy wasn't a hundred per cent certain, but he felt Anita knew so much more than she was saying.

"She's very lucky," she said, "to have someone like you who cares about her as much as I do!"

He felt flattered and deflated all in one go.

"Just before I go," he asked, "do you have any ideas as to where or what her next move might be?"

"No! Sorry. She's like her mother! Elusive and hard to pin down!"

He hugged then kissed her and thought how lovely she was. He then noticed her looking up and down the street, as if she was looking for someone. He had a feeling that Anita was fearful of something. What it was he had no idea. He went down the hill past all the pretty buildings and beautiful flowers. As before, the question ever-present in his mind, was, where was Sofia?

40.

As Jeremy made his way through the arrivals hall at the airport back in Britain, he caught sight of Maya waiting. She had a piece of card held up with *Welcome Home Jez* written on it. As he got to her, he started to laugh.

"So, what's with the welcoming committee? I've only been away a few days!"

"I just thought you might need some moral support and I guessed you might want to talk. I also have a surprise, but that can wait!"

Jeremy looked quizzical, as he heard the intrigue in her voice.

A few minutes later, they found a coffee bar, then Jeremy told her what had happened.

"So, what's next, little brother?"

"I'm not sure! How can I find her, if she doesn't want to be found?"

"My feeling on that is we all want to be found!" she said.

He gave her answer some thought. He knew she was right, but he also felt that Sofia was doing more than just hiding.

"Come and see my surprise!"

She guided him to the short-stay car park, where a brand-new van was parked. On the side was sign-written *East of Maya. The best of Indian and Asian cuisine.*

"That looks magnificent, Maya!" he said.

As well as the lettering, there was an Indian elephant in full regalia framing it perfectly. He walked around it taking in the colourful, but tasteful, sign work.

"Are you sure about the elephant?" he asked, "You might upset the animal liberation lobby!"

"Oh, for God's sake!" she said, "You're such a tart, Jez!"

He started to laugh, as he enjoyed teasing her.

"It looks amazing, May, it's perfectly you, just what you need!"

She threw her arms around him.

"Yes it is, I'm so happy!"

Her excitement was tangible, as she hugged him hard, then they did a little dance around the car park in celebration. It was lovely for Jeremy because it took his mind off Sofia.

Later on that evening, he sat with his mum and dad after they had extracted what they could from the very tired Jeremy. He went to bed early. As he lay there, contemplating the last few days, he decided to get on with living his life.

The next day, Cecilia listened avidly as Jeremy told her about his brief visit to Malaga. He valued her opinion on what had happened. She sat in silence for a while, then said,

"I think, Jeremy, Sofia is a beautiful woman with a very strong mind. There's no doubt about it, something is troubling her badly. I'm sure if she thought you could help her, she would have asked you."

He looked at her and tried to assimilate what she had just said. His blank look annoyed her a little.

"Look, it's simple, Jeremy! All I can say is don't give up on her. If you do, she will see you as a feather in the wind or, even worse, a damp rag!"

Jeremy got what she was saying, but he felt tired of trying.

"Have you got jet lag?" she asked.

He laughed at the jet lag jibe, then lightened up.

"Sorry Cecilia, it's just that my mind has been so full, I'm finding it hard to concentrate!"

"What you need is a good story!"

He sat forward on his chair, seemingly eager to distract his thoughts.

"Emilia Gaston!"

She said it as if he should know who she was, then she paused. He looked unmoved, so she started her story.

"I met Emilia as a young woman. We both had small parts in productions at Birmingham old rep. Emilia was the same age as me and we worked together in the early years but, for me, she never had the fire inside to be an actor. Something was missing that gives every actor that certain pizazz. However, she did have an aura about her, that people were drawn to.

She came from a very well-off background. I believe her parents were loaded. Emilia had a very clipped posh accent, which got in the way of her acting. As you know, an actor has to be able to use his or her voice as an extension of the part they are playing.

As time went by, it became obvious that she was hopeless at doing this. Her one outstanding attribute was her ability to get close to people, then listen to them. I found it wonderful having someone to hear my intimate details and, most of all, to understand.

She continued to act for several years, small parts that seemed to satisfy her. Nothing of any consequence that would move her higher up the acting ladder. Before long, she turned tables by getting a job doing small reviews on new plays. She would talk to actors and then find out bits of tittle-tattle. This information, though small, found its way into magazines and newspapers.

The time she'd spent working as an actor, being backstage gave her the experience to talk about the actors and the parts they played. Somehow, she wooed her peers, then got a lowdown on their lives, and their loves. Of course, she gained enemies, those that didn't like her reviews. On the whole, she told the truth and as you know, Jeremy, the truth hurts!"

Once again, Jeremy was sucked into the world Cecilia was a part of.

"Over the years, Emilia's reputation went before her. She had become a well-respected critic and biographer. Having become revered by some impresario, dignitaries courted her. Deserved or not, she became an icon. To me and most of the actors I knew, she was kind, but most of all, helpful.

As she got older, she became grumpy about certain plays. One, in particular, she had no time for. It was a popular murder mystery that had a long, long run in the west end. Many actors had played in it, some good, some great, some distinctly average.

In one particular version of the play that she went to see, there were four actors in the lead roles that she found decidedly bad. So she ripped their performances to pieces in a review the next day. All the actors knew she wouldn't be kind. In fact, there were bets among them to see who got the worst criticism. Unfortunately, Emilia critiqued each one unfavourably!

Obviously, the actors were very unhappy. They were unable to forget the way she hung them out to dry. No matter how they tried, they could not beat her in a war of words that followed. She used her column as she saw fit, to back up her feelings.

Twelve months went by, then, just by chance, the same four actors appeared in a different play together. Emilia happened to be in the same theatre at the time, for a meal with friends. She was not there to see the play. Later that evening, after the play had finished, the four actors ended up in the bar next to the restaurant.

The play had been a critical success and they were enjoying a drink, while a few fans were asking for autographs. A frosty feeling spread through the bar when the four actors became aware of Emilia sitting in the restaurant area. However, the four got together, then took a celebratory drink over to Emilia. The room seemed to lighten, as it looked as if oil had been poured onto the water that was a bad feeling between them. She gladly drank with them. It seemed that bygones were bygones. Unfortunately, not long after, Emilia collapsed to the floor. The emergency services were called. All that could be ascertained was she couldn't breathe. She was taken from the theatre to the hospital, where she died on arrival!"

Jeremy was captivated with the story.

"So, did the actors have something to do with Emilia's death?"

"Wait and see!" she said, "It wasn't long before we heard

rumours that the four actors had spiked her drink with something that brought about her demise. Naturally, all four were then shrouded in intrigue. Let's say there was no love lost. The actors didn't lose any sleep over it. However, in the week that followed, they were interrogated, which stressed them out, especially as the play was a critical success. To top that, the play was cancelled, out of respect for Emilia!"

Jeremy was on the edge of his seat, waiting for the coup de grâce. Cecilia was aware of it, so she teased him by saying,

"Shall we stop for tea?"

He looked at her sternly.

"Ok," he said, "if you like."

Playing her at the same game, made her smile.

"Alright, I'll continue. The tension had brought the four actors, the acting profession, the newspapers, and a lot of the media to assume the actors might be arrested for Emilia's death. But, by the end of the week, a police inspector stood before a throng of people to deliver the truth.

'Emilia Gaston died from natural causes, derived from having acute appendicitis!'

Obviously, everyone was expecting a different announcement. The whole investigation wasn't helped by a series of strikes in small parts of the NHS which hindered the findings!"

Jeremy looked at her with questions on his lips. She seemed to get there before he said anything.

"The four actors acquired celebrity status, becoming front page news. They were now bigger stars in their own starry sky. Each one of them gained notoriety. As a result of which, they were offered some of the best parts on TV and in the theatre. None of them looked back and they all became very well off from the experience."

Jeremy looked happy.

"Good story, I must google it!"

"Why? Don't you believe me?"

"I do, but I always need to corroborate the story for the book, it's my job!"

She smiled.

"Tea!"

As days go, it wasn't bad. He felt he was making headway with Cecilia's life story. To his knowledge, he had at least two-thirds of a book already, maybe more.

41.

Jeremy, Maya and Chai received an invite to a show. Toya had earned a place on the talent show 200Seconds, where each act had just that amount of time to prove they were good enough to become famous. The new talent show was about to be broadcast on national TV. Jeremy was sat eating in the kitchen when Maya came in.

"Look, Jez, an invite to Toya's show!"

Her face was beaming. She was bouncing around like a rabbit in spring.

"What do you mean, her show? She has 200 seconds, then she will disappear into obscurity!"

"Woah, who shot the optimist?"

He dropped his head low over his bowl of cereal.

"Sorry," he said into his muesli, "I slept badly."

Maya scuffed up his hair playfully, which made him smile.

"You know it's not out of the question that Sofia might be there. After all, Toya is a friend of hers!"

The outside chance that Sofia could be there brightened Jeremy's thought pattern more than just a little bit.

Jeremy's time of reporting the news was a thing of the past. As he sat opposite Cecilia, a time of contemplation came into his mind.

"Cecilia, we've been reviewing your life for a while now, although it feels like I've known you a lifetime!"

"That sounds like a compliment. If it is, then I'm glad of it. The journey has been made so much better, because of you, Jeremy. Listen to us! We sound like old farts recanting our thoughts together. Sorry, one old fart and one handsome young man!"

"No way in the world are you an old fart!" he said.

They looked at each other and laughed.

Their morning ceremony of tea before anything had always set the tone for the day. An overall feeling of peace surrounded them, as they talked about events. The subject of Sofia was never far from the conversation, even though there was little to add to the situation.

"I think, Jeremy, that love is a forever mystery that infiltrates the system, plays havoc with the emotions, leaving the heart and mind in constant turmoil. Of course, it is also the most wonderful feeling in the world!"

His love affair with Cecilia was on a different level. Up to this moment in time, he had not been able to define it. As for Sofia, she had thrown his whole world, as well as his well-being, into a spin. He sought to push that thought to one side, maybe find a new way forward. The only way to do that, was to concentrate on Cecilia and persevere with her memoir. On this particular day, she seemed more business-like, even eager to get on with it. On her lap, her ever present diary.

"Charles Farthing!"

She opened it carefully, trying not to lose any of the loose pieces of paper. A photograph dropped to the floor. Jeremy quickly retrieved it. He held it, then studied the black and white photograph. Two young girls were standing outside a theatre. A poster was attached to the wall. It said *The Rolling Stones* then *TONIGHT* painted across it. The two girls had their arms over each other's shoulders and their cheeks pushed up together, as they looked at the camera.

"Wow," he said, "you were both stunning!"

He gave her the photograph. She looked at it.

"Why, thank you, young man!"

She then looked again.

"Isn't it strange how you can be there, almost like it was a second ago?"

Her eyes became misty, as tears gathered in the corners. He offered her a tissue, which she took.

"Thank you. I miss her so much. Imogen was the ultimate friend! We knew how each other thought, it was as if we were twins. When Charles Farthing did what he did, he stole my best friend, my sister, my heart!

Let me take you back to Charles Farthing, the sometime impresario and abuser. I never knew why, but it seemed to me that the establishment helped cover the tracks of people like him. The problem being, he wielded so much power, he could influence people on high, to cover up his misdemeanours. It was fear, I suspect, more than anything that helped him get away with it!

Charles was a big man in many ways, not just his personality. His figure had also grown over the years, after eating too much rich food, drinking too much wine! As you can imagine, he had very few friends in the acting world. Even those on the production side only tolerated him because of his power in the industry.

After Imogen died, I knew one day I would get my revenge. It was all a question of time. Until then, I had to carry on doing my job. Fortunately, Rupert had my back because he felt the same about the bastard, as I did.

Years passed. Both Rupert and I showed we were actors with promise. So, we were being offered great parts on TV and in film, but we were not household names as yet. An opportunity arose to give Charles Farthing his just desserts. Rupert had somehow got to know about illicit parties that Charles organised for the benefit of his perverted friends.

Rupert told me there were drugs, young men, young girls, bondage and abuse. The thought of it made me feel sick. He also told me big money exchanged hands at the time, with politicians, even police officers involved. It wasn't surprising that this corruption was rife. To tell you the truth, it amazed me how Rupert got to know about these things. All he ever said was, he knew someone on the inside.

Rupert got in touch with me. I had just finished a movie where I had a small part, but it was key to the story, so I stood to get my name higher up in the credits. I did die early on in the piece, but it was a good death. Some even said it was the best lifelike death in any movie at the time. Here I would like to say, in my mind, a movie is a film. It's taken many years for me to accept the American way of talking about going to see a movie, rather than a film.

Anyway, I digress.

He came to see me to ask me a favour. The favour he wanted was for me to visit Charles Farthing at his offices. Not something for the faint-hearted, but Rupert thought I could pull it off. The truth was, he knew I would willingly do it, if it meant getting back at Charles.

I made an appointment to see him at his offices. They were in the theatre district in London. As you can imagine, it was among a lot of Victorian buildings. He had offices on the third floor. I walked into the reception area, where a woman in her fifties was sitting, taking calls behind a tall, imposing desk. I still remember her. She was a cross between a bulldog and a brick wall. She was an unpleasant woman. Somehow, she seemed the perfect person to work for such an unpleasant man.

I waited in the small reception area for a few minutes, then Charles called me into his office, which was enormous. A big desk sat in the middle of an expensive oriental carpet. The walls had photos of Charles with many actors, actresses, dignitaries even politicians. It looked like he had his dirty fingers everywhere. That was the problem, he couldn't keep them to himself. At first, he beckoned me forward as his ample figure leaned against his desk. He said,

'Cecilia, welcome my dear! Long time no see!'

The truth was, I'd made it my life's work to avoid the lecherous fat man. This wasn't just *my* aim, there were hundreds like me. It was said if you go in to see him, you may not come out with everything intact, especially if you were young and inexperienced. The room had an air of cigar smoke, which in itself wasn't that bad. He called me towards him. Fortunately,

I knew him for what he was. So, I had diversionary tactics. He lifted his ample arms, drawing me close to him, then his sweaty hamster cheeks came closer. He tried to plant his lips on mine. I could smell cigar smoke on his breath. I did my best to avoid his kiss by offering my cheek, but it seemed hard to avoid them. My knee, however, was in the perfect position and I accidentally on purpose forced it into his groin. Both his hands went down to care for his genitals. It had been rumoured by those in the know, that he had no penis to talk of. Who they were, I had no idea and, frankly, I didn't want to know. However, there he was in all his glory, holding his groin. I felt a little victory deep inside. I made all the right noises to make it appear that it was indeed an accident. He retired to his chair at the back of the desk, still wincing from the pain. He then laughed heartily, before saying,

'It would seem, Cecilia, you indeed are a feisty young thing! What can I do to help a beautiful young woman like you?'

I made up some story about looking for better parts, mainly that l wanted to move up the acting ladder. I thought it was all rubbish, but he went for it. I guess he thought I was still innocent enough to be abused in some way. His eyes came out on stalks. It was as if I was gifting my body to him. I could almost smell his dirty mind thinking of ways to seduce me.

He then told me about these parties he had, which he called shindigs, where like-minded people in the profession would meet and have fun.

A knowing look came over his fat face, a smirk that made me want to throw up. He then asked me to come to his party and get help to climb the ladder of fame!

I knew what he meant. I then gave him my best acting smile, to convince him I was happy.

He then stared at me and narrowed his eyes, in which there was a touch of menace, then said,

'You must keep it to yourself. After all, this is a once-in-a-lifetime opportunity. It's our little secret!'

I have to say, Jeremy, I will always remember his words. At that moment, I couldn't hate anyone more than I hated that man, as a broad Cheshire cat smile spread across his face.

He wanted to walk me out, but I leaned across his desk and shook his sweaty hand.

He told me he would call to let me know the date of the party.

I left. Five minutes later, in a back street, I threw up. When I got home, I showered myself until my skin was red raw!"

Cecilia kept referring to her diary. Jeremy asked her,

"Do you have this written down word for word?"

"Why, of course! I would have been a fool not to. After all, we are talking about a fucking criminal here!"

He noted in her voice an anger he had not heard before.

Cecilia's stories were always compelling, but this one sounded particularly sinister. She seemed eager to continue, so dived headlong into the next part.

"I told Rupert what had happened. We had to be patient. About a week later, I received a phone call, not from Charles, but someone else with a terribly stiff upper-class accent. I guessed it must have been a private secretary or a manservant.

He gave me an address, which I knew to be in a leafy suburb of London. Rupert had found out it was an old gentleman's club, which was now a private residence. It was about the size of a large hotel.

It was a cold, dark, autumn evening when I turned up by taxi. I was dressed exquisitely in leather boots, a tight black skirt and a white blouse with a black jacket. I looked very business-like, but I was aiming for sexy. I could feel it. I think it was the suspenders and black stockings.

The imposing Edwardian building looked a bit foreboding in the darkness. My guess was the place must have acres of garden, because no other properties were nearby. The front was dimly lit, only the front doors showing signs of life. I saw a few people arrive before me. By the time I got to the door, they had already gone in. The door opened. A well-dressed man stood there, looking like a cross between a waiter and a security guard. It was light and welcoming inside. From what I could see, the furnishings were very much like those of a posh hotel. I was identified from a list, then let in.

You have to remember, Jeremy, when I did things like this, I acted the part. I took on the persona of someone else. In my mind, I was a tough undercover detective on a case to break a drugs ring. I needed to approach it in that way, or the whole thing would have frightened the life out of me. I had slicked back my hair, which was short anyway, so in some ways, I looked masculine. I thought, at the time, it would make me less recognisable. Rupert had researched the building. He was like that and still is. He was the one who did the brain work. It was always in his mind to get under the skin of anything. These days it would be easier but, back then, there was no internet to access such information. So, he did it the hard way and applied for the plans at the council offices, by playing the part of an estate agent.

He had already told me of a fire exit, where I could let him in later, but first I had to find Charles. This wasn't easy, because the security guards guided me to a large room where revellers were drinking. The room was dimly lit. I remember a grand piano with people on it in various sexual positions. This was happening throughout the room, on chairs, tables, the floor, in fact it didn't seem there was any space where someone wasn't inside someone else. I was so shocked; it was in my mind to turn around and leave.

I couldn't see Charles among the cavorting throng, but there were other people I did recognise from the industry, mostly men. As far as actors were concerned, there was no one I knew. It didn't take long before a couple of the clientele came my way, two half-dressed men pushed up against me. One of them said, *'I say, what have we got here?'*

'Fresh meat, I think!' said the other, *'Would you like a drink, sweetie?'*

'No,' I said, *'I'm sweet enough, dear!'*

They both laughed.

'Gin and tonic,' I said, *'lots of ice!'*

One of them dutifully went off to get me a drink, the other irritatingly rubbed his groin up against my leg. A bit like a fucking cocker spaniel. I so wanted to just smack his face, but I played the part and stroked his balding head. I asked if he knew Charles.

'Oh,' he said, 'you're one of Charles's poodles, are you?'

He then immediately moved away.

The other man brought me my gin and tonic but somehow had found someone else to play with. It seemed to me that mentioning Charles suddenly made me untouchable, which was fine by me. All I can remember was the sound of new romantic music playing loudly along with the smell of alcohol, perfume and sex, all of which was a heady mix.

Jeremy, it was a time when groups like Spandau Ballet and Culture Club were everywhere in the media and nearly everyone was sporting rose-red cheeks and mascara. It was bizarre! The more I looked around, the more the pile of bodies resembled that of a sweating snake pit.

I was suddenly joined by another man, who looked too overdressed to be in the room. He asked,

'Are you Cecilia?'

'Yes!' I answered.

He leaned closer towards me. He smelt strongly of Brut, a popular men's aftershave at the time. The thought and smell of it these days makes me feel ill!

'Follow me!' he said.

I followed him out of the room, taking in air as I stood in the hallway. I nearly fainted. The man in front of me walked on, so I tried to keep up. It wasn't long before another room came into sight. I have to say now, I'm sure most of the rooms we passed were being used for orgies, because I could hear the sound of music and moaning inside.

Room number 69 is where we stopped. The man seemed efficient. Obviously, Charles had security that was paid well to be discrete.

He opened the door. I stepped in. This was a smaller room,

although the music was similar and just as loud. I suppose it had to be, to cover the sound of sex. Fewer people were in there, but there was still plenty of sex on the menu. I caught sight of Charles at the end of the room. It was strange, as if he was a king on his throne, the throne being a leather chesterfield sofa. A young man was stroking his fat face and thinning hair. Another man sat opposite on another sofa; a coffee table placed between them. It was awash with drinks and white stuff which, at the time, I was innocent of. I quickly learned it was cocaine.

Charles looked as if he was completely relaxed, his ample arms stretched across the back of the sofa. His white shirt was open, revealing a vest. His trousers were off. The young man, who had been stroking his head, now had his hand inside Charles's boxer shorts. Charles looked as if he was in heaven. I made my way over to where he was sitting, taking care not to tread on any copulating bodies. This, however, was hard to do, because I found that many hands were trying to pull me down to join in what was going on. I managed to fight them off!

Charles opened his eyes, saw me, then pushed the young man away. He gestured for me to sit down. I sat opposite him, although he was keen for me to sit next to him. I pretended that I couldn't hear. The man who was sitting next to me was also half-naked. He leaned down towards the table, then did a line of cocaine. His head and body seemed to straighten, then he passed out and fell on the floor. Charles laughed like a child, as he saw the man drop. He shouted across to me.

'That's Dickie! He's my right-hand man! He's also hopeless at keeping up!'

I guessed he was the man who had rung me. At that moment, a thought came to my mind that might just get Charles all on his own. I leaned across to him and asked,

'Do you like what you see, Charles?'

I have to say now, Jeremy, that, back then, my figure was blessed in the right places. Charles had an eyeful of my ample cleavage. This is where my acting ability pulled me through. I pushed my breasts nearer to his face. I could feel his breath on them.

I told him I had a man friend in the building, who was willing to have a threesome. I didn't mention Rupert's name.

Things moved so quickly. He beckoned his security man to allow me to leave the room to go and get Rupert. Of course, the security man did not know that Rupert was outside. So, I asked him where there was somewhere to freshen up.

I was directed to the toilets which were situated on the ground floor. Rupert had told me that's where the emergency exits were. I opened the door, Rupert was sitting on a small wall, twiddling his thumbs. He said,

'You've taken your time!'

'What do think I'm doing? I replied, 'Having fun? It's like Sodom and Gomorra up there!'

'Sorry, I'm so fucking cold!' said Rupert.

He came in the door, I shut it behind him.

'What the hell are you wearing?' I asked, 'you look like an extra from a Pink Panther movie!'

Rupert stood there in a grey raincoat, sporting a trilby hat and a goatee.

'Take all that stuff off!' I said.

He then took off the raincoat and hat. Underneath he looked quite sexy in black leather trousers with a shirt open to the waist. Our banter continued.

'What's the goatee all about?'

'To keep my anonymity!'

'For God's sake, you're an actor. Just pretend to be someone else!'

We were like many other actors, totally obsessed about the part we were playing.

'I'm keeping the goatee on, I like it! I must say, Cecilia, you look rather fetching!'

I then told Rupert about the sex party that was going on upstairs and that I had changed the plan. Five minutes later, we found the security man who took us to the room Charles was in. Not long after, we were in the same room as Charles.

He was lying on a king-size bed. The security guard was then dismissed.

'Well, I must say, Cecilia,' said Charles, 'this is a bit of a surprise. I never thought you would go for this sort of thing. I just thought you were a prick tease. Who's your friend?'

I looked at Rupert. For some reason we had never thought that he would need another name.

'This is Rudolph!' I said.

Rupert shot me a look as if to say he didn't like the name I had given him. At this point, I don't think either of us had thought we would get as far as we had.

'Well, Rudy!' Charles looked at Rupert, 'I must say I like a man with facial hair. I hope you don't mind me calling you Rudy. I think we are all friends here!'

'Can we have a few drinks first?' I asked.

'Why not,' said Charles, 'let's get rat-arsed!'

Charles, who was already pissed, laughed heartily at the thought of it. This was the hardest bit, Jeremy. I climbed onto the bed, as Rupert made drinks.

'What would you like, Charles?' asked Rupert, who was standing by a table with lots of alcohol on it.

'Vodka and orange! I like your voice, Rudy, have you been classically trained?'

The question hung there. For some reason it seemed as if Rupert had got stage fright.

'Yes,' I said, 'he's trying to get into the business!'

'Well, Rudy,' said Charles, 'you perform well with me and Cecilia tonight, then the world will be your oyster!'

I started to do a sort of striptease to keep Charles's attention on me. I was doing a pretty good job because he was transfixed by my body. My thoughts were to do anything, so as not to be too close to him or have him touch me. Thankfully, Rupert picked up his game and brought over the drinks. Charles greedily drank his down without thinking, while watching me strip. Rupert, who was very much in the background, found that Charles had a hold of his hand. Rupert gulped down his drink, then he was pulled onto the bed. It was obvious that if Charles wanted anything, he wanted Rupert more than me. His hands were all over him. At that moment, Rupert looked paralysed by it. Charles had Rupert up against him. He then ran his hand up to Rupert's face and touched his goatee. It came off in his hand. *'What the fuck is this?'* he said in a loud voice. *'Is this some sort of shitty joke?'*

He looked at Rupert.

'I think I know you! You're an actor! Your name, it's not Rudolph, it's…!'

Charles's hand went to his throat.

'What the hell?' he screeched, *'I feel strange. The room's spinning. What are you doing to me?'*

I sat back at the edge of the bed. Rupert had managed to do the same. Charles had panic and fear written all over his face. We looked at each other, then knew this was retribution for what he had done.

'This is for all the people you abused, you bastard!' Rupert said.

He then added a short list of names, which reinforced the reason for doing what we had done. The names seemed to disappear into the darkened room. All the time, Charles was watching, trying to say words that couldn't be said. I don't know why I did it, because I knew he was dying, but I wanted to really hurt him. I punched him as hard as I could in the face.

'That's for Imogen. You pervert!'

Blood immediately poured from his nose. A few seconds later, he slumped forward, then groaned. Rupert took his pulse. He was dead!"

The story had blown the wind completely from Cecilia's body. She leaned forward, then rested her head in her hands.

Jeremy was shocked at what he had heard, even though he had sympathy for what she and Rupert had done. The room was as silent as a grave, as Cecilia sat in contemplation. Jeremy slowly took it in. After a while, he asked,

"Do you think that Charles should have been tried and sent to prison for his crimes, rather than be murdered?" Jeremy was feeling almost guilty for asking.

She raised her head, then looked at him. Her eyes were full of pure emotion, but her thoughts were perfectly clear.

"Nearly everyone has a secret about something they have done. It would be hard to find a human being who has got to a certain age that is perfectly free from all guilt. Of course, not everyone is like Charles. Murderers, rapists, in the most part, end up where they belong, in prison. Charles, however, had eluded everything and yet the greater part of society had thought him to be the cornerstone of the entertainment industry!"

Jeremy knew, in some ways, she was absolutely right, but felt it was a form of vigilantism. He felt uncomfortable that he was again party to a crime, even though he did feel that Charles Farthing got what he deserved.

"What was the outcome?" he asked.

"Strangely, it was reported the next day that impresario Charles Farthing had died of a heart attack in his sleep. No mention of a drug and sex party. It was a cover up. Too many famous people were involved, the police included!"

"Oh, my God," he said, "you do realise if you publish this, so much shit will hit the fan!"

"Yes, that's why I'm telling you! The whole thing was a conspiracy. The only problem, is even now they would deny it!"

Jeremy realised the more he got to know about Cecilia, the more explosive her story was. She smiled, gloriously happy to have it off her chest.

"You know that phrase," she said, "the more unlikely the story, the truer it will be!"

"Can I ask," said Jeremy, "what Rupert gave Charles in his drink to kill him?"

"Let's just say that Rupert came by it illegally. He knew people who would supply things like that for the right price. He told me the drug was untraceable and would bring about a slow, painful death!"

In the end, it didn't matter if it was traceable or not. It had had the desired effect. Not for the first time, Jeremy's mind was blown away.

"Shall we have a break?" he asked.

"Google Charles Farthing," she said, "you know you want to. I believe in the years after his death, the news of his misdemeanours caught up with his name. Like so many others in a position of power, he got away with it when he was alive. If you have a name in the acting world and you were touched by that man, then it will hurt when his name is brought up. He is not missed!"

She left him to sit and think. She busied herself in the kitchen, cheerfully humming, even a few words of a song breaking through. After a while, she came back in with sandwiches for them both. She sat down, then took a bite. Jeremy was mulling the story over, as he ate his.

"If Charles Farthing was found to have died of a heart attack, it would be impossible to prove that you and Rupert had killed him!"

Cecilia had a very pleased-with-herself smile on her face.

"Yes!" she said, "you are absolutely right. Almost a perfect crime, wouldn't you say?"

Jeremy had thought it over and over again, so it must be true. Why would Cecilia make it up? One thing was for certain, it would be front-page news!

42.

Jeremy left Cecilia in a good mood. It seemed to him that the more that was uncovered about her life, the more she felt better. The cathartic feeling wasn't lost on him. He was enjoying the journey as well, even though Sofia was a constant in his thoughts.

Later on, Jeremy was outside the old music hall theatre in the town, which, over the last few years, had been modernised sympathetically. It was the go-to place for all big productions in the town. He was meeting Maya and Chai to see Toya perform. It wasn't his type of thing. He felt slightly embarrassed to be there.

In his time as a reporter, he had written articles about young wannabe pop stars being taken advantage of. He could never quite work out what motivated people to do it in the first place. His jaundiced view wasn't shared by anyone else there. Maya and Chai were dressed exuberantly. If he didn't know the truth, he would have sworn they might be doing a double act later. Their smiles made him happy. They were dressed in brightly coloured clothes, with tassels and ribbons in their hair. He felt decidedly underdressed. In the queue to get in, Jeremy was constantly on his phone. Nigel had texted him to say Sofia had come back into the country. Everyone was buzzing around him. He seemed to be the only one who wasn't in tune with what was going on. Unfortunately, Jeremy's mind was full of Sofia as usual. A man at the door said,

"Mate, mate, ticket, ticket please!"

"Oh, sorry!" answered Jeremy.

The man scanned his ticket, then let him through. Jeremy felt very uncomfortable, then Maya and Chai joined him.

"Jeremy," said Maya, "I'll tell you what, see this as a job! Let's say you're writing a critique on talent shows for the Guardian, then you can justify being here!"

Before he could say anything, Chai asked,

"Are you sure you're not old before your time? Let go a little! Loosen up!"

She pulled him over to one side, so they were in no one's way. She moved around behind him, placed her hands on his shoulders, then worked them down his back. No one gave them a second glance. Weirdly, he could feel his body relaxing through his clothes.

"Imagine, Jeremy, if that was on your bare skin!" said Chai.

He couldn't help feeling like a dog having its tummy rubbed. The euphoria was overtaking his reservations.

"Ok, ok," he said, "I'm going to enjoy myself!"

Both Maya and Chai had a look of self-satisfaction on their faces, as they moved off to find their seats.

Jeremy leaned into Maya and whispered,

"Would it be possible for me to pay Chai to do that again?"

Maya laughed aloud.

"Chai, you have a fan of your magic fingers!"

Chai turned, smiled broadly, then said,

"Enjoy the night, Jeremy, have fun!"

It had relaxed him. He went with the flow and all the inhibitions of late were pushed out of his mind. On each side of the stage, screens had been erected, so everyone could see more of the acts. As it was being recorded for the TV show, the maximum impact was required.

After about an hour, Toya was the next act on stage. The expectation grew for the three of them. When she came on, they went crazy. Even Jeremy felt himself being scooped up in the party atmosphere. He was up on his feet, then clapping his hands like mad, singing along to the old classic song Toya was singing. After she had finished, gaining the most applause of the night, it became just a question of buzzing her through.

It was then that Jeremy saw her. Sofia was on one of the big side screens, a brief glimpse of her was shown in the audience. She was applauding Toya. Jeremy saw her, then pointed at the screen. Maya looked, but the camera moved away, as the applause subsided. Neither Maya nor Chai saw anything, but Jeremy was already vacating his seat to try and find her.

It wasn't an easy task to try and traverse the seats, then get around people to get to the aisle. He quickly made his way up to the circle. So many people made it difficult to navigate. Eventually, he got to where he thought she'd be. Then he looked towards an empty seat as people were sitting down again. She had gone!

Jeremy left the theatre to see if he could find her outside, but he had no luck. He went back in, ending up in the bar, on the off chance she might have gone there. That's where Maya and Chai found him after the show, drowning his sorrows.

"I guess you never found her," said Maya.

He asked them again,

"Did you see her on the screen?"

"No, we told you we didn't!"

"Ask Toya! She might know something," said Chai, "She'll be joining us shortly."

They left the theatre and went to an intimate bar, not far away, where they waited for Toya. Toya was alone. They all congratulated her on her move up to the finals of 200seconds. It didn't take long for Jeremy to quiz her.

"I left a ticket at the box office for Sofia," said Toya, "I asked her to come."

"When?" asked Jeremy.

"At the karaoke bar, weeks ago. I didn't think she would!"

"I think I saw her," said Jeremy, "but then she was gone!"

For a few moments, the joy of Toya's show slipped from the conversation.

"I saw your mum and dad in Spain, Toya," said Jeremy. "They were extremely helpful. I went to Sofia's house in Frigiliana. I met her stepmother!"

"Yes, I know! My mum told me!"

"I'm sorry, Toya, I don't want to rain on your parade, but is there anything else you can tell me that might help me find her?"

Toya looked blankly at Jeremy.

"No, I'm sorry, Jeremy, there isn't."

Just before he decided to leave, he said,

"I would just like to say thank you, Toya! You were brilliant tonight. The best in the show by a mile!"

Toya beamed, as they all raised a glass to her.

43.

Sofia had walked away from the theatre. Her collar was turned up to the cold night air. She hailed a taxi, then gave the driver an address. Fifteen minutes later, she arrived at her destination. After paying the taxi driver, she disappeared into the shadowy streets. There were heavy skies above. Rain looked certain.

Sofia felt that her life had become sinister and she wasn't quite certain who to trust. All she wanted to do was keep a low profile until she found out what she needed to know.

Sofia approached the house, which had a living room light on that made it look warm and inviting. She made her way quietly around to the back of the house, found a garden chair to sit on, then patiently waited. It had just started to rain. Fortunately for her, there was cover, because the garden parasol had been left up.

The moment gave her time to reflect on her life and, more importantly, her Mum's and Anita's. Her thoughts drifted, as she listened to the patter of rain on the parasol. Ironically, it made her think of hot sunny days, being on a beach with her Mum and Anita. It was a wonderful time, almost like paradise. However, she did recall her Mum being agitated occasionally, which spilled out onto all of them.

It was when her Mum went back to England. The event raised tension. Anita would always question why. Sofia was never party to any of the answers, being so young, but she was aware of the feelings that surrounded each trip.

For Sofia, it was an exciting event when her Mum came home, because she would bring back sweets or toys, as well as British food they couldn't get in Spain. Sofia believed that was why her mum went back to Britain.

As time went by, she realised that wasn't true. Sofia's thoughts were so locked in the past, she didn't notice movement in the darkness around her feet. She stifled a scream with her hand. She kept absolutely still, more from fear than intent. The tail of a cat was moving backwards and forwards around her feet, the cat purring loudly. Inside, Sofia's feelings were now doing the screaming. She had never been a lover of cats. She also believed she was allergic to them. As the panic spread through her body, someone must have looked out of an upstairs window. It was brief, a streak of light being created in the dark garden. After a minute or so, it went dark again.

At least the cat had disappeared. Sofia was feeling uncomfortable, the whole thing having made her nervous. She reflected about the night, Toya's performance having been phenomenal. For Sofia, it was a pleasant feeling, seeing someone she'd known as a child singing in a little bar, then grown up and doing so well. It was hard to put herself through this, but she didn't want to lose touch with what she was.

Seeing Jeremy in the audience had brought about a climax of emotions, which, at the moment, she was trying to keep in check. She was on a mission to find out all the facts about her family history, so she needed a clear head and no emotional ties. When in Spain as a teenager, she had honed her skills. She would often look back, remembering her ex-pat and Spanish so-called friends. One of them was a French girl, who was the ringleader. She was cruel and unforgiving, which kept them all in order. There was also some person controlling them, known to them as Grand Jefa, who orchestrated the crimes. Being so young back then, she never questioned who the puppet master was. She just did the job, questioned nothing. She was the perfect package, having been groomed like the rest of the gang. It would have continued, but they got overconfident when they pulled off a big crime. Sofia was a casualty, the scapegoat who nearly died.

She became aware that the upstairs light was off and had been off for some time. She decided to move. A small side window looked about right. There were no security lights, which eased her nerves. An old sash window gave little resistance to the small crowbar she pulled out of her shoulder bag. As she was climbing in through the window, she couldn't help remembering her life as a teenage criminal. So far, everything was going her way. She just prayed now that the property wasn't alarmed. It wasn't.

Once inside, it was just a question of finding a computer, or anything that would help her search. A light attached to her head helped show her the way. Looking around the kitchen, then the living area, she found nothing. She did see an awful lot of books and art, but no computer.

She stopped and admired the art on the walls, then she noticed a door below the stairs. Opening it, her muscles felt so taut, that she let out a few words of frustration.

"Don't squeak, please!"

The door did, but not enough to make her feel it could be heard upstairs.

"Yes!" she said quietly.

A set of stairs led down to a cellar. She slowly went down. It was surprisingly spacious, full of books, but there, on a small table, was a laptop. An easy chair looked inviting. She sat down, then opened the laptop.

"Bingo," she said, under her breath.

She then proceeded to try and access the computer. Passwords are a bane for everyone, so she looked around the desk for any clues, but no luck.

Up to this moment, it had gone perfectly, even though, inside, her stomach was turning over and over. However, her need to find out about her past kept her mind focused.

She got up and looked around the room. She caught sight of a few photographs that looked familiar. One interested her. It was similar to the one in Cecilia's apartment with Cecilia and Rupert standing together in front of a theatre. She picked it up, studied it, then turned it over. At the bottom, in small letters, was written: The Rep C&R 1973. She put the photograph back, then tried that as the password. It didn't work. She then went for the obvious and typed Cecilia's name in, it worked. Amazingly, it worked. This impressed her. The thought made her feel it was meant to be. The time was ticking by. She felt under pressure. As a teenager in Spain, she remembered one thing, not to hang about, but she knew she needed to try and keep calm.

A muffled noise came from upstairs, stopping her from continuing the search for a moment. She waited. It was a tense feeling inside that made her feel sick. She stuck to the task, working quickly through a few files. There were too many. There was a folder with Spain on it. She opened it quickly. Hundreds of photographs glared at her. Scrolling through them, none of them triggered any feelings at all. Among them, however, she found a few that stirred her memories, although they did make her feel confused and fearful.

They were of her as a child in Spain, none she had ever seen before. All taken from a distance. She quickly copied the whole folder onto her memory stick. It was time to leave before she got caught. As she closed the computer, she said to herself, *Rupert, you must review your security. It's pretty awful.*

She made sure everything was as it was before, then quietly climbed the cellar stairs. The light on her head helped her find the way back to the kitchen. As she got closer to the window, she felt something move by her feet again. This time, however, she was aware it was the cat. It brushed by her legs. She kicked out at the space that the cat had occupied seconds earlier, her frustration quite audible.

"You little shit, did you follow me through the window?"

The cat had disappeared into the darkness, then she realised she had left the window open. She climbed out, closed the window behind her, feeling happy that she had more information, although it wasn't the complete story. It just might give her more insight into her life.

44.

The quandary that Jeremy had was trying to rationalise why Sofia had suddenly disappeared from the theatre. The problem for him was, how to come to terms with the fact that she wanted to avoid him at all costs. This, of course, threw his whole being into a feeling of self-doubt.

Maya breezed into the kitchen. Her life was on an all-time high: her business was taking off, her relationship was blossoming, her big brother, for the moment, was off her case. Her disposition was hard to ignore, even though Jeremy wanted to. Wallowing in his darkness was what he wanted and he was doing an exceptional job of it. Maya moved around to him, as he sat eating his breakfast.

"Well, baby brother, what's on the agenda today?"

Her face was adjacent to his, as she sat on the next stool. He lifted his head with a spoonful of muesli about to go into his mouth. She grinned, then placed her finger on the end of his spoon, then let go which caused the muesli to spatter all over his face.

"For fuck's sake, May! You total arse!"

The muesli dribbled off the countertop onto his boxer shorts. He stood up as it continued to the floor. At that moment, Mum came in carrying a load of washing.

"Oh, Jeremy what a mess you've made!"

He stood there like a five-year-old, having no idea how to sort himself out. Maya was laughing so much that she was almost wetting herself.

"Right!" he said, "Revenge!"

He picked up his half-full bowl of muesli then threw the contents in the direction of Maya, who ducked out of the way of the oncoming breakfast cereal. Unfortunately, for Jeremy, Mum was right behind her. The muesli was now over Mum's chest, the rest dripping down onto her basket of clean washing.

"I guess," said Maya, "I best get to work! Can't hang about here, having fun like you two!"

Maya left the room. Both Mum and Jeremy were left speechless.

At Cecilia's house, Jeremy let himself in, then climbed the stairs without thinking. He took each step in his stride. When he reached the top, Mr Silverman was barring the way. As usual, he looked a little overdressed. It was a warm day.

"Who are you and what do you want?"

Jeremy hadn't got any patience for this.

"Joseph Stalin! I've come to liberate Berlin!"

Jeremy said it in a confident voice. Mr Silverman looked shocked.

"You should be dead, like Hitler. At least he committed suicide!"

The conversation slipped into an alternate universe and neither of them was perturbed by it. Jeremy grasped at his reality, not wanting to be sucked into the old man's condition.

"Mr Silverman, I'm here to see Cecilia Walters."

"Cecilia Walters?"

As Mr Silverman said it, he looked lost in a sea of fuddled memories that was his dementia, then his eyes focused on Jeremy.

"Who are you and what do you want?"

Jeremy wasn't absolutely sure, but he thought Mr Silverman really needed to be in care. The standoff was disturbed by a knocking on the front door. Mr Silverman waved his umbrella vigorously. He looked terrified, then shouted.

"Hide, for God's sake! Find somewhere quickly! They're here!"

He then turned towards his flat and shuffled away. Jeremy responded to another knock on the front door and wearily made his way down to find a postal worker.

"Mr Silverman?"

"No, but if that's for him, I'll take it!"

It wasn't big but too big to get in the letterbox.

"Thanks, guv, have a good day!"

The postal worker sauntered off down the path, whistling to himself. For a moment, Jeremy wished for a simpler life. He then made his way up the stairs, shaking the small parcel as he went. Something rattled inside. His mind couldn't help thinking what the hell it was. More importantly, would Mr Silverman have any idea when he opened it? He walked towards his door. Jeremy went to knock but thought better of it. He then placed it on the floor outside.

Inside Cecilia's apartment, it became obvious that Cecilia wasn't home. Since the start of his visits, he had never known her not to be in. He had a good feeling inside that she was venturing out on her own. Immediately, he went into autopilot by making tea, then sat in the chair opposite where Cecilia normally sat. In the silence of the room, his mind became vacant, which was strange, because, of late, his head had been so full of stuff, it had clogged up his thought processes.

After a while, his eyes grew heavy and he dropped off to sleep. Somewhere in a dream, he saw Sofia running along a beach throwing her clothes off. He could see her clearly. He was shouting her name, but no sound came out of his mouth. She seemed happy, laughing as she ran. He couldn't hear it, but he knew she was. He looked down to see his feet sinking into the sand, then panicked because he couldn't escape. The worst thing was, Sofia had gone.

He awoke abruptly. The dream seemed so tangible. Seeng Sofia so happy made him feel good inside. As he analysed the dream, he raised his hand to his mouth to find he had dribbled onto his chin. The room seemed cold, so he stood up, then moved around. He again looked at Cecilia's many pieces of art. He felt strangely relaxed, so he went into the hall to look at her photographs. Most of them were pretty random, going back over her career, at awards ceremonies, or outside a venue. He could clearly see these were happy times. However, he had only seen glimpses of her happiness over the last few months, which was when she had touched on memories that triggered it.

He then heard loud voices from outside on the stairs. He went to see what it was. As he opened the door, he could hear Mr Silverman, as usual, bantering with someone. It was Cecilia having an animated conversation with him.

"Mr Silverman," she said, "I live here. I'm Cecilia Walters, your neighbour for over forty years. Shall I call your daughter? You seem a little stressed out to me!"

"Stressed! My dear lady, you know nothing about stress!"

He then seemed to get agitated.

"Our world is being taken away! Go get your children and leave the country, before they come for us all!"

Cecilia knew that Mr Silverman was getting worse. Too often, he had laid siege to someone with his thoughts and feelings about the war. She could see in his eyes that he was lost to gaps in his memory. After calming him down, she escorted him back to his flat. She then called Mr Silverman's daughter.

"It would seem," said Cecilia to Jeremy later, "that Mr Silverman has been found a place in a home not too far away."

"Thank God for that!" said Jeremy, "He has become a bit of a nightmare!"

Cecilia looked at Jeremy thoughtfully, then said,

"*I became insane, with long intervals of horrible sanity.* Edgar Allan Poe."

The words captured the moment, then Cecilia added,

"I would suggest that all of us sit astride a wall that is sanity. Some of us will fall the wrong side. That's when it becomes so hard to climb back up!"

Jeremy thought when she said this that she was in some part

alluding to herself. This he knew because her story had now informed him she was sometimes teetering on the edge.

"Tea," she said, "I am without doubt in need of sustenance!"

Jeremy was eager to know where Cecilia had been, but he waited till she had a chance to settle, which took some time, because she had to change into something more comfortable.

When she re-appeared, she was as sophisticated as ever, wearing bright-coloured Arabian trousers with a shawl wrapped over her shoulders. As usual, she was entering stage left for her performance. The perception he had wasn't lost on Cecilia, who seemed to emphasise every move in front of him. He was beginning to think her eccentricity was turning into a madness of its own, the only problem being he was part of it.

"How are we, kind prince? You look well, although I feel you have not found your princess as yet!"

Her part in the drama saw her take her seat, almost as if she had just walked on set. Her arms were stretched out wide as if he should be showering her with gifts. He was used to her now. This was no different from every other time he saw her.

He mocked an extravagant bow, then kissed a ring on her finger. It amused her greatly. She smiled, then laughed.

"You lovely boy! Oh, how you humour these bones in fancy dress!"

He felt alarmed by her description.

"You are the most beautiful, talented actor, up there with the greats, my lady!"

The game that they played pleased them both. As far as Jeremy was concerned, it was amateur dramatics. For Cecilia, it was a stage. Applause was always appreciated.

"I've been to town to see my solicitor," she said.

"Why? Is everything ok?"

Jeremy felt a kick inside, almost as if something was about to change.

"No, just updating my will. I've been meaning to do it for months, years even, but the bloody pandemic saw fit to stop me!"

He was curious but couldn't think of how to phrase a question without being too nosy. She looked at him almost as if she was expecting it.

"I'm gifting a lot of my artwork to charity and a museum. What's in storage mostly."

"In storage? You mean you have more in storage?"

"Why, of course, Jeremy. I think you forget I made an awful lot of money from my films. I've never had a husband to divorce. I've hardly saved a bean. Everything I've made is wrapped up in art. It has so pleased me over the years."

"But if it's in storage, how can you appreciate it?"

"That's easy! Where I have it stored, it's hung, so every now and again I go and look at them. It's an uplifting experience! I'll take you someday soon!"

The way she said it, he thought she was in no hurry to die as yet, which in lots of ways made him feel better.

"Where are we then? How is the story of my life proceeding?"

The sudden change surprised him. He thought the subject of art was going to continue. So, he asked more about her collection.

"Overall, what sort of art pleases you most?"

She looked around the room.

"Nothing ostentatious. As far as art is concerned, sometimes small speaks in volumes. Anything too showy doesn't appeal to me at all!"

"Did you ever take advice from an expert?"

"God no! Why on earth would I take advice from someone who talks art? That would be like a dictator coming to dinner! Every time I've heard a so-called expert talk about a particular piece of art, I never see what they see. It's almost as if they are evacuating their bowels. I'm sorry, but so-called experts or critics of art have to justify their existence. Generally, they talk shit! For me, if my eyes see and my heart feels, then I will fall in love with anything, that's the way I am!"

Jeremy saw immediately the love for art in Cecilia's eyes.

"I suppose the art I have collected is a substitute for the love

I've lost or never had. In the early days of my acting career, when I was looking for pieces of art, it gave me a feeling of being needed. For example, the Lowry, the one you like so much. It looked sorry for itself. I don't think the man who owned the shop had any idea what it was. I knew who it was by, but I had no idea how much it was really worth. It was sometime later that another actor saw it, then said to me,

'One day that little painting will be worth a small fortune!'

The act of hanging it on the wall was as if I had a loved one in the room with me. I must tell you that many of my other paintings have shared all my innermost emotions. If that's not love, what is?"

He looked at her and understood her feelings. He found it difficult not to.

"Sod it, I'm not making tea," she said, "As you know, I only drink alcohol on special occasions. The only trouble being, how special an occasion has to be. Well, let's put it like this, I could have died with Covid, then someone else would be drinking it. So, would you like to partake?"

Jeremy thought for a moment.

"Why the hell not, you only live once!"

As she got the brandy out of the sideboard, a door next to it opened on its own.

"Is that a record player, Cecilia?"

"Why, yes!"

"We've never talked about what music you like," he said, "Where are you records?"

She then went to a cupboard that was built into the wall and opened it.

"There you are, have a look!"

He stood in front of a large selection of albums, all differing in musical taste.

"Why don't you play them anymore?"

"I do every now and again."

"Can I play something?"

She nodded. He picked an album, then placed it on her record player. She gave him a brandy. Several drinks later, they were both relaxed, listening to the music. Cecilia looked chilled. So much so, she talked without prompts from Jeremy. He pushed his head back into a cushion, taking in the warm comfortable feeling the alcohol had given him.

"I don't know why, but Rupert has always had a big piece of my heart," she said, "I've always found it hard to say no to him. He's the one director who I've let have the better of me. I know it was because he was my first love, the father of our child. Although there has always been something about him that frightens me, a darkness that I've never been able to put my finger on!"

Jeremy looked at her as she drew a picture in the air with her finger, that of a dragon, or mythical beast. She caught his eye.

"Do you see him as some sort of monster, Cecilia?"

She laughed out loud.

"No! Of course not! Are you a monster, Jeremy?"

He laughed.

"I don't think so!"

"If you were," she said, "what sort of monster would you be?"

She said it with a smile on her face. He laughed again, as his mind searched for an appropriate beast.

"Godzilla!"

"Ha! Cold-blooded! I have you down to be a warm-blooded one. I see you as a big brown bear!"

He was more than amused by her thoughts.

"I see! That means I would be warm and cuddly, but it also means I could eat you!"

He raised his hands in the air, as if they were claws, then made a growling noise. The act made her laugh, as she took another sip of her brandy.

"To tell you the truth Jeremy, if I was thirty years younger, I think we might be in the throes of a bear hug or two!"

The compliment brought a smile to both their faces. It would seem that as far as Jeremy was concerned, he was still a lightweight in comparison to Cecilia. She finished off another glass of brandy. As he took another sip, he looked up at the ceiling. The whole room appeared to be flexible, as if he was sitting in jelly.

It was dark when Jeremy woke. He heard some movement in the kitchen. Cecilia looked around the door.
"Tea?"
Jeremy took in the question, then replied,
"Yes!"
"How do you feel?" she asked him, as she brought in the tea.
He looked at his hands, then ran them through his hair. He sat up rolling his head around on his shoulders, almost as if to make sure it was still attached.
"I feel fine! I feel like I've had the perfect sleep!"
"Yes, Faze swore by that brandy. It's not normally a drink that you drink a lot of, but if you do, it has surprising effects."
Regardless of that, he drank his tea greedily.
"It does dehydrate you terribly. Like any alcohol, you have to treat it with respect!"
When she said these words, he replied,
"Cecilia, I don't think for one second, that the brandy we drank received any respect from either of us!"
He had a second cup of tea, then went to the toilet. As he stood there, he looked at his reflection in the mirror. He felt remarkably together, a feeling of all-encompassing confidence coming over him. He noticed the time on his watch: it was six o'clock in the evening. It was the first time in months he'd slept properly and hadn't thought about Sofia. Neither he nor Cecilia said anything about her. It was as if they couldn't find the words. After all, what could they say about the situation?
He came back into the living room, then she continued to talk.
"I've come to the part in my life where I accept what life throws at me. There was a time in my forties when my career was soaring. I couldn't put a foot or a word wrong!"
Jeremy relaxed into his easy chair and listened.
"I was in demand. Every which way I turned, there was work

coming up for me. I accepted a part in a TV whodunnit. I was only in it for half of the series. I had a friend, a writer, who said she thought of me for the piece. To be fair, it was fun being short and sweet. What's more, it was lucrative. For me, what was better than all of that was getting to know another actor. A young man called Jimmie Atherton. Usually, when you start a new production, you have a read-through, where you meet the other actors. It's a few hours of familiarising yourself with the script. The main players in the series are there, plus the new ones. That's where I met Jimmie. He was good-looking, charming and had a twinkle in his eye. He came across as overconfident but, as time went by, I got to like him more than I thought I would.

This particular programme was about a detective who investigates the death of a young man on a motorcycle, who crashes into a car. It appears to be an accident but ends up being murder. I was the motorcyclist's sister, then, as it went on, I became the romantic link to the detective. As you can imagine, by what I've said so far, Jimmie and I became close. He was ten years younger than me. Of course, I looked younger than most 40-year-old women. The thing was, we were falling in love, although, at the time, it felt like a fling. It was the first time I had ever ridden a motorbike, pillion of course.

It was wonderful, exciting, dangerous and fun. I found that Jimmie had woken me up from my sleepwalking into life. We became a couple, even though we were both so busy. We found time for our relationship, which often meant him riding to meet me in places far and wide. The thing was, I became besotted by him. It was helped by the wonderful summer. We walked, we biked, and we loved. Oh, how we loved!

Looking back, I know that Faze gave me the love I'd never had, but I also know that Jimmie gave me the thrill that love can be! I think the love I've had has been in layers, like comfort blankets. As I got older, they got thicker, each time I experienced it."

She stopped, looking almost as if she had been riding on

Jimmie's bike as she spoke, a smile and the look of satisfaction plainly written across her face. Jeremy didn't want to stop her, but he was curious.

"Do you think you'll ever fall in love again?"

"I thought that's what this was, you and me, us! I know there's a small difference in our ages, but isn't this the real deal, Jeremy?"

She looked into his eyes. His thoughts were of love. The love he had for her was immeasurable. Of course, he knew, deep inside, she was teasing him, but still, his mind got caught up in her magical storytelling. She laughed at his expression.

"Don't worry, Jeremy! We don't need to get married. We can just live together for now!"

He realised his face was a mask of confusion, then he laughed, their smiles engaged in a mutual understanding. She continued.

"As far as Jimmie and I were concerned, we were on a journey of expectation, excitement and, what's more, mutual respect. We were both experienced actors. I was at the top of my profession; Jimmie was not far behind. He had already played parts in several TV programmes, though his experience in the theatre was limited. He'd told me it was something he wanted to address.

A talent scout picked him out from an amateur production, when he was a teenager, then he got a part in a children's television series. From then on, he rarely looked back. These things were the landscape that our relationship was painted onto. Meanwhile, we revelled in our time together, our lovemaking was out of this world. He took me where I'd never been before. These days they talk of women finding their sexual plateau. The climax is the ultimate place to be. Jimmie took me there and I never wanted to come down. So, you can imagine how I felt at that time! I was in heaven with an Angel. Isn't it amazing how love and sex soften the edges of everything?"

Jeremy could feel the pull of love. Sofia's absence clawed at him, as Cecilia talked of Jimmie. Cecilia could see on Jeremy's face that he wasn't quite with her.

"Maybe," she said, "because of this late hour and our overindulgent behaviour this morning, we should leave the rest of the story for another day!"

"No!" he said, "I would like to know how the story ends."

"I must say, my prince, you are a glutton for punishment. By this time, it was autumn. As the nights closed in, we shared a few in the Lake District. I was on tour with a play that was critically loved. However, the public was not impressed. I forget the name of it, but the money was good. Fortunately, it was a short run. The Lake District is beautiful if you have the weather and we did. For two days, I was warmed to my core, sitting behind Jimmie on his motorcycle, worshipping the colours of the trees, the movement of the sun on the lakes and the wildlife all around us. And then at night with Jimmie inside me!"

She looked at Jeremy, to see if she could find a little bit of embarrassment on his face. He didn't stir! She felt pleased that he was so used to her, that he was almost un-shockable.

"Jimmie was also in a play, one that had rave reviews, where he shared the lead with a beautiful leading actor. Because I was riding on a sea of love, I somehow missed the signs as he phoned me, then told me that he couldn't see me for a few weeks, because he was too busy.

In this business, it doesn't take long for someone to drop the doubt into your head. One of the minor actors I was working with, a sharp-tongued gay guy, who also knew Jimmie, commented on how well he was getting along with his leading lady. I put two and two together, then quickly realised I was being replaced by a younger model. At the time, it broke my heart, but now, looking back, I can see I was just a fling for him. However, for me, I could have given up so much to be with Jimmie. It was all the more difficult, because the play I was in flopped. Even so, I was given good reviews for the part I played. I had no time to wallow in my misery, because I had a part in a film, soon after the play finished."

"Did you have it out with him?"

She thought about the question.

"We arranged to meet. He had no idea I knew about him and his leading lady. It was as if nothing had happened. In Jimmie's mind, he clearly thought nothing had. I know it was hearsay from another mischievous over-talkative actor, but I'd never known him to lie. I did not dance around my words.

'Am I going to be one of your trophies to brag about?' I asked, *'What turned you on? Was it her ability to dance across the stage into your arms, then into your bed or did she hold you tighter than me on your motorbike?'*

I had more to say, which was far more cutting, but he dropped his head to his hands and appeared to cry.

Even though he was clearly upset about what had happened, I knew it was pointless. He was a great actor. I felt that I had been a conquest! I left him there, in the pub. It hurt, but I was old enough to know when something was over!"

They both looked at the clock. It was past midnight.

"You can stay if you want to. The spare room is rarely used, there's a duvet in the wardrobe!"

There was no argument from Jeremy. They were both worn out. She asked him if he would like a nightcap. He answered,

"Yes! Do you have something warm and milky?"

She looked at him quizzically, then answered,

"Yes, milk!"

They both laughed.

"I'll tell you what," she said, "I will have the same, but there will be brandy in mine!"

They sat opposite each other, like an old married couple, thinking about what the day had given them.

45.

Sofia was sitting with coffee in hand, staring at the information highway in front of her. A laptop lay open, almost like it was yawning. She yawned back, feeling tired of the search, and from the night before. What she had was bits and pieces of a life that she had never known, still too incomplete to make sense of. Her nomadic life of the last month or so was taking its toll. Living in hotels was not only tiring but also expensive. She had accumulated enough money over the years to get by on, but now, having this lifestyle, it was starting to have an effect on her bank balance. The sale of her house in Spain was key to her survival. At least that was now in the pipeline. So she was fairly certain the house should sell quickly, now the pandemic was over. Messages from Jeremy kept appearing on her phone. She couldn't help feeling the tug in her heart. She didn't respond, mainly because she couldn't handle the emotion involved.

The coffee shop was almost empty, apart from a woman serving and a young man trawling through his phone as he sipped his coffee. Sofia paused for a moment, as she realised how modern technology had stolen everyone away from what they were really looking for.

She closed her searches, then thought back to when she was in Rupert's house stealing the file which had given her hundreds of photographs. She made her way through them. As she did so, she looked outside at the ever-darkening skies. The woman behind the counter looked across at Sofia and asked if she required another drink. Sofia's mind had become consumed by the photographs. She snapped out of it and said,

"Yes, that would be great! Thank you!"

Before her was placed a large hot chocolate, on top of which were many marshmallow pieces.

"There you are. It's a freebie. It's so quiet. It doesn't help that it's such an awful day."

Her voice was mundane, seemingly bored of being there.

"What are you?" the woman asked Sofia, "A writer?"

The direct question threw Sofia, although she was well aware the woman was just curious and wanted to talk. "I'm a nurse, revising for an exam!"

The answer was all she could think of.

"You won't learn much looking at holiday photos, if you don't mind me saying!"

The mild sarcasm stirred Sofia. She then looked at the photos off Rupert's computer on the screen.

"Yes, I suppose you're right!"

As the woman walked away from the table, she called across to the young man in the corner of the coffee shop.

"Would you like a cup of hot chocolate, on the house?"

The young man just nodded his head, then continued to look at his phone. The intervention somehow sharpened Sofia's need to find any link between the photos and her own life. So she pulled up a few relevant photographs on the screen, especially the ones of her when she was a child. However, these confused her, as they had been taken from a distance. By whom, she could only surmise. If it was Rupert, then why?

After a while, the young man went out of the coffee shop into the driving rain, then an old couple came in. Somehow, it lifted the mood of the woman behind the counter, which made Sofia smile, as she heard her chatting with the old couple about the weather.

In the moments that passed, a slither of hope appeared, as Sofia pulled up a photograph of what looked like a birthday party. There were children playing in a swimming pool. She couldn't be sure if she was one of those children. It wasn't perfectly clear. A couple was sat talking to a woman, who Sofia knew to be her mother, on the other side of the pool. She tried desperately to recall the event, but nothing would come into her head. After a few minutes, she sent the pool party photograph to Anita in Spain.

Hi Anita. Do you know who took these photos? I found them on Rupert Blaine's computer. Who's the couple talking to mum? Love Sx

Later on, at the hotel where she was staying, Sofia got an answer back from Anita, asking,

Can we talk on zoom?

A short while later, they connected. The usual pleasantries were exchanged, but Sofia was keen to find out more about the mysterious couple.

"I do have a hazy vision of them," said Anita, "It was your birthday party. I remember lots of kids. You were very happy! I was too! I also recall Tia being down about something. It was strange but, looking at the photograph now seems to bring back an awful lot of bad memories that followed."

Sofia knew what Anita was about to say.

"Not long after your birthday, Tia was killed!"

Sofia thought of her mother and tears came to her eyes. Anita could see Sofia was upset and shared her emotions.

They were both silent. It was as if they had agreed at some point not to talk about it anymore. However, the picture that they were now looking at, brought it all back.

In Sofia's mind, it turned over and over. Time never really heals, it just draws a veil over bad memories. Sometime down the road in life, these things are solved, or they become the problem that stops you from moving on. In Sofia's case, she knew that her mother's death was the one thing that stopped her from feeling free.

With a heavy sound in her voice, Sofia asked,

"What else can you remember, Anita?"

Sofia knew that Anita was holding something back.

"The two people in the photograph were from England. If I recall correctly, they had lived in Spain most of their lives. Tia had some sort of relationship with them that I was unsure of.

All I know is, they turned up at the party, uninvited. As soon as they did, Tia's mood turned dark. They didn't stop long!"

It was obvious Anita knew more than she was telling, but at least now her tongue was loosening.

"As you know, I never thought Tia's death was an accident. I always insisted she was too strong a swimmer to drown in calm seas!"

She hesitated, as if she was about to say something for the first time.

"In the past, Tia was tied into drug dealing. I don't know how or why, but somebody had some sort of hold over her. Looking back, I feel that she was trying to escape it, I'm pretty sure somebody had her murdered! One thing Tia was good at was keeping things to herself. We often had arguments about it!"

In the silence that followed, both Anita and Sofia were crying. What Anita had said had not surprised Sofia. The revelation wasn't new to her. She had suspected it for some time.

"Where did these people live, Anita?"

Anita hesitated. It was as if she was reluctant to say any more, but Sofia wanted to know.

"North of Malaga on the way to Santander, a place called Burgos. I gave their names and address to the police when your mum died. I told them I thought they were something to do with her death.

After weeks of hearing nothing, I enquired if they had investigated the couple. The police said they'd interviewed them and were satisfied they were nothing to do with Tia's death. My feelings are the police were corrupt in some way. After all, there is a lot of money in drugs, as you know!"

These words hit home. Sofia did know. Her own involvement as a teenager proved it. The emotion that surrounded their conversation left them both feeling drained, but Sofia had not finished.

"So, what were their names, Anita?"

"Perez. I'm not certain, but I think they were husband and wife."

"And what about the pictures of me, the ones that have been taken from a distance? It's like some sort of stalker had taken them!"

Anita looked at her blankly.

"So you've no idea who, or why they were taken?

"No!"

Anita was unmoved, although her eyes were still full of tears. Sofia wasn't a hundred per cent certain, but she thought Anita was lying.

"Right!" said Sofia. "I'm going to visit these people!"

"No, leave it Sofia! Move on! Find Jeremy and have a life!"

With the sound of Anita's warning in her ears, Sofia decided to go and find the mysterious couple in the photograph. A few days later, she flew to Bilbao.

46.

The flight and journey were unremarkable. After hiring a car, Sofia made her way south on the AP-68 out of Bilbao. The countryside was beautiful, after the suburban sprawl and the industrial fringes of the city. She turned off at Saño Auzoa, then kept going out on the A-625. When Sofia was younger, nothing would shake her, but at this point in time, her nerves had started to show. For that reason, she was fearful of what she might find.

The road was like many the world over. When you get deeper into the countryside, the isolation grows. Eventually, she stopped at the side of the road, where a small sign said Casa en Los Arboles. She looked down the track from the sign: it certainly was in the trees.

She had no plan at first. She thought she would just drive up and knock on the door, but she wasn't certain what to say. So she sat in the car and tried to think of a better plan. She decided to drive further down the road and parked.

It was hot outside, the air conditioning was on full. She thought how quickly she had become unacclimatised to Spain, after living in Britain. It didn't help that a mini heatwave was in full swing. She then decided to open the windows to let the heat in. The trip, though uneventful, had followed a traumatising time. She reclined her seat, then listened to the leaves on the trees, moving slowly in the warm breeze. Birds were singing in the distance, while cicadas were just feet away. She closed her eyes.

Sofia woke with a start, as she heard a vehicle coming. She was parked fifty metres down the road past the entrance to

Casa en los Arboles. In her rear-view mirror, a large four-wheel drive truck was pulling out of the track. It stopped, then, after a minute or two, turned to go towards Bilbao. She definitely saw two people in the truck. She was also pretty certain they couldn't see her, because she was lying down. She was hit by a rush of blood as she turned the car around, then drove down to the track. She drove slowly because the track was in poor condition. Her immediate thought was that the state of the road would definitely keep anyone away.

After about five minutes, feeling really shook up, she got out of the car, stood, then straightened her back. She stretched her arms up above her head, closed her eyes, then thought about how good it was to be back in Spain. In the middle of the pine trees, there was a large property. It was old but had been well looked after. There were many outbuildings. Dogs were barking from somewhere nearby. She waited, then took in the lie of the land. The thought of being attacked by dogs kept her near the car. A story was in her head, that she was lost and looking for a hotel. She had the sense to have memorised a property that was not far away.

The driveway had a circular flowerbed in the middle, which was well-looked-after and very pretty. For some reason, it eased her fears. The property itself, she thought was impressive.

After what seemed like an age, she made her way up towards the house. Small windows with shutters sat on each side of the double front Spanish-style front doors. The whole property had a rustic feel to it. She knocked on the door several times, waited, but nothing. It was quiet; even the dogs had shut up. At this point, she was certain whoever had gone out would be coming back soon. So, time was precious. She knocked again, then felt confident no one was inside.

She turned to go and look around the back but then thought to try the front door. It opened, with just a minor squeal on the hinges. She slipped inside. It was almost palatial. The hall had a grandfather clock and a large mahogany sideboard, which looked like a family heirloom. She looked in the rooms on the ground floor, then came to a large living-room with a kitchen leading off it. Sofia was aware that these people might be back at any moment and her heart started to beat faster. So much so, she could almost hear it above the grandfather clock. She stopped and tried to sum up who lived there. One thing was pretty certain, it didn't seem as if they were murderers.

The feminine touches made her feel at home. She was uncertain as to what to look for, but it became obvious when she looked closer into the room. Across one wall, there were many photographs. She studied them. They were pleasant to look at and eased her mind. Many were black and white, families, grandparents, parents. However, hardly any children. Then she saw the couple from her birthday photograph. She studied them, thought they looked like nice people. One photograph caught her eye, then another, which was of her mother.

The cold realisation, mixed with seeing her mother in early pregnancy, made Sofia's mind go into a spin.

She was there to uncover these people as being some sort of drug cartel, but now it looked like her mother was part of the family. Of course, she couldn't be certain. After all, a couple of photographs on their own meant very little. She quickly used her mobile phone to record what she saw, then made her way back to the front door.

She was relieved when she got in the car. Even more so when she pulled out of the bumpy drive back towards Bilbao. On the way, she saw the four-wheel truck go by. She gave an audible sigh.

She found a little hotel near the main road, booked in, then crashed from nervous exhaustion. Later, she sat on her bed. Even though the hotel was small, it was very comfortable and had fully functioning air conditioning. She relaxed, then sent the photographs to Anita in Frigiliana. It wasn't long before Anita called her on her mobile phone.

"You've been busy," said Anita, "I'm guessing you had your

heart in your mouth when you acquired these!"

"You could say that. Strangely, it was easier than I thought. What do you think Anita?"

"Well, you've learnt where Tia lived before she came to Frigiliana. All she ever said to me was she came to Spain after a bad relationship in Britain. The only thing she ever said about your father, was that he was Spanish. I'm not sure if that is true or not!"

Sofia was sat cross-legged, wearing very little.

"Are you hot up there in the north?" asked Anita.

"Yes! I don't know why but this heatwave seems unnatural. What's it like down there in Frigiliana?"

"Same as usual. The sea breezes help. It must be hotter up there because you're in the countryside!"

The weather report eased the tension but didn't stop the confusion they both felt.

"I have theories, suspicions if you like," said Sofia, "Most of it makes sense now, but as far as Mr. and Mrs. Perez are concerned, I'm at a loss. At first, I thought they were the people behind all the drugs, that ended up in and around Malaga and they had some sort of hold over Tia. The only problem with that is these photos, which make her look like she was part of the family!"

"As I've said before," said Anita, "all I remember is your mum being upset when she went back to Britain. I know it wasn't frequent, but when it came to the time, her mood would darken until she came back to Frigiliana!"

"Do you think, Anita, that every time she did it, she visited the Perez place?"

"Yes, you may be right! She always went via Santander ferry."

"Is it possible that she brought back drugs?"

"I can't be certain, but who knows! It would explain her mood swings!"

The last words lay a cloud over them both, then Anita added,

"What I will say is, whenever we talked of hard drugs, your mum was always against them. Saying that, we did like the odd joint now and again! So, what's the plan, Sofia?"

"I'm not sure, Anita. I think I will sleep on it. If I'm able to sleep, that is."

Sofia then decided to call it a day and went to bed.

The next morning, bright and early, Sofia found herself on the main road outside Casa en Los Arboles. She was nervous, but still drove down to the house. The four-wheel truck was parked on the drive. As before, she got out of the car feeling a little bit worse for wear, because of the track. She heard the dogs howling in the distance. She grasped the nettle, then walked confidently up to the large double-front door. She knocked and a small elderly woman opened the door.

"Buenos Dias! Soy Sofia Moran!" Sofia said.

The woman stared at Sofia, as if she was looking at a ghost. A large smile then shot across her face.

"Come in! Come in! We've been wanting to see you again for such a long time, Sofia!" she said in perfect English, looking so happy. She immediately moved forward and warmly hugged Sofia, who was uncertain how to react. She was then welcomed into the house and followed the lady into the kitchen, where a man was sat, drinking coffee. He looked up at his wife, who said,

"It's Sofia! Natalia's daughter!"

The man sat still, then, suddenly, an expression of joy filled his face. He got up off the stool, but then looked a little lost as to what to do next. It was obvious that none of them knew what to say or do. Sofia spoke first.

"I've no idea why I'm here, apart from to find out about my mother!"

Sofia could tell by their demeanour, that both of these people wanted to welcome her into their home.

"Would you like coffee?" asked the man.

"Yes, that would be lovely!"

The man continued to talk as they made themselves comfortable around a kitchen table.

"It's a long, odd sort of story, one that has its ups and downs, being both happy and sad. By the way, I'm Samuel Perez, this is Elizabeth, my wife!"

They both smiled, as did Sofia. A strange grasp of hands went across the table. A peculiar emotion seemed to rest in the room, as he carried on.

"We have lived here for over forty years," he said, "We are both in our seventies. My parents were Spanish, this was our home, and I grew up here. When I was a young man, I went to Britain to work. I was happy there. I enjoyed life. I met Elizabeth and we fell in love, then we married."

They smiled at each other and held hands. "Unfortunately, we could not have children. We tried. Oh, how we tried! In the end, we gave up, but someone suggested we should adopt. We went through the channels, filled in forms. We were assessed, then waited. It was a long time. No babies were offered to us, but an agency approached us who had several children on their books. The only problem was they came from broken homes and were between three and ten years old.

We gave it an awful lot of thought, then decided to try. We had both set our hearts on a boy. The agency had a boy called Mathew, who was around seven years old, that might suit us. As we went through the process, we were told there was a girl of the same age. They told us the boy and girl were almost like brother and sister. We decided to take Mathew. Our thoughts were if they both had problems, it would be impossible to cope with two. Eventually, we adopted Mathew.

Not long after, my parents here in Spain became ill. So, after much soul-searching, we moved here from Britain. My parents both died within the year. Rather than selling up, we decided to stay. It was hard at first, but we soon got to love it. The only problem was Mathew was an unhappy child. He resented being here.

Even so, he learned the language at school and decided to call himself Matias. He was disruptive, got into trouble, never fitted in. As he grew up, we constantly had the police here. He started using drugs in his teens at school. The rows we had were constant. We gave up when he reached sixteen, then he disappeared. We tried to find him, but he had gone without trace. After a while, we informed the authorities in Britain, in case he turned up there. That was that!"

He and his wife sighed. The man was as grey-haired as his wife was, the years had weathered them both. Sofia could see that, no matter what, their love had weathered better. They all reached across the table to hold hands again. Sofia was warming to them, as the story continued.

"One summer night, we heard the dogs barking outside. They are great security out here!"

Sofia thought that might be the case, but why leave your front door open? She decided not to say anything about that.

"I went to see who it was. It was Matias and a young girl. He introduced her as Natalia. We then realised he had found the companion he'd had when he was in care. Fate, it seemed, had brought them back together. Matias never said a word as to where he had been for nearly ten years. We were just happy that he seemed happy.

While they were here, we knew he was the boss. It wasn't long before they started arguing, mainly because he was so angry all the time. We also noticed they were both smoking cannabis. Then, after two weeks, they got up one morning and left. It was such a shame, because there were moments when Matias was sleeping, that we became close to Natalia. She was the child we should have adopted, not Matias. Natalia had made the wrong decision, as we had, having anything to do with him. We never saw Matias again. As you can imagine, we were not sorry!"

Sofia was captivated by the story, as certain things started to become clear. She also knew that there was more to come. The wizened-looking Samuel, with his much-lined tanned face, then asked Sofia if she would like to eat something. Sofia felt relaxed, content even, as Elizabeth got up and then laid out the table. Eggs were a big part of what they ate, with bread, tomatoes and mushrooms. It turned into a small feast. Coffee rounded it off. It was a wonderful feeling. In a short time she felt at home.

There was a promise that when they had finished talking, they would take Sofia on a sightseeing trip around their property, which had nearly fifty acres of forest.

Sofia waited for Samuel to speak again, but this time Elizabeth continued the story.

"As Matias's mother, I felt guilt, that somehow we had let him down, almost as if it was our fault. I couldn't forgive him, though, for the way he treated us. When he left here with Natalia, I felt he had ripped our hearts out again!"

Samuel took over, as the emotion hit Elizabeth.

"Our lives were back. We continued looking after this place. As you can imagine, it's not easy, but we love it. We have a few local people that work for us. We see them as friends. Our community is one where we all work together. We exchange, we diversify. It's the only way. If we didn't, we wouldn't survive!"

He said the words as if they were the cornerstone to their lives.

"One day, a taxi turned up. We were having breakfast, much like today. I answered the front door. There was Natalia, looking tired and drawn. She was in the early stages of pregnancy. We made her welcome, then what followed was months of sublime pleasure, as Natalia prepared to become a mother and then stopped being an addict. For us, it was a joyous time. We knew it was for her as well. Of course, we also knew it wouldn't last forever. This is not a life for young people, unless you're born to it, or love it. I think because of what had happened to her in her life, she became hardened.

So, before long, she started to look for a more vibrant future. She was fit, well-fed, and longing to move on. One late night, she told us she had got a job, just outside Malaga, working as a waitress. She knew someone who desperately needed help. They didn't mind the fact she was pregnant. Before she left, she seemed uneasy and nervous!

She had something important to tell us, that she'd been wanting to speak of, but didn't know how to!

All sorts of things shoot through your mind, when somebody says a thing like that. Fortunately, she didn't drag it out! She said,

'I killed Matias! I pushed him into a canal! He drowned! I didn't mean to, it was a spur-of-the-moment thing. He'd pushed me too far! He had dragged my mother into our dark world!'

We were shocked obviously, but somehow we were also relieved. He was a troubled person. We knew he would one day be a victim of his own crimes. Natalia cried so much, it was as if the floodgates had opened. We knew she cared for him, but we both felt she was crying because of what he had done to us as well!"

Sofia knew nothing of this. It was all a revelation, one that left her head swimming.

"All I would like to say to you, Sofia, is that your mother would be so proud of you. From where we stand, it looks like she gave birth to a beautiful person!"

As the words went into her thoughts, she realised that many things had been explained. Now she felt more at ease, but one thing still troubled her.

"Thank you so much! It's so kind of both of you. As you know, my mum died too young, under mysterious circumstances. Part of this quest is to find out what happened to her!"

They both acknowledged it, then they seemed reticent, as if they knew what the next question would be.

"Do you think my mum was murdered?"

"Yes!" they both said in unison.

The positivity was shocking. Many questions formed in her head. Samuel spoke first.

"I'm afraid to say, that it was down to Matias. He left a trail of debt behind him, all to the wrong people, those that participate in organised crime and drugs. Of course, they don't believe a debt dies, so they go after the nearest and dearest, mainly us and Natalia!"

The beautiful day outside was being gobbled up by the story, which was engrossing. Sofia became aware that both Samuel and Elizabeth seemed uneasy.

"Would you like a bit of fresh air," asked Elizabeth, "before it becomes too hot? We have chores to do, maybe you could help us?"

A welcome breeze hit them all, as they walked into the yard that led to the barns. Three large dogs were in separate pens. The hounds, as Samuel called them, were let out and immediately ran around crazily, delighted with their wonderful freedom.

"Don't worry, Sofia," said Samuel, "they are all as soft as putty!" Then they started licking Sofia's legs and smelling her feet. They didn't jump up at all. At the slightest gesture from Samuel, they stopped in their tracks.

Sofia had hardly had anything to do with animals during her life but felt immediately at home in the wonderful environment. They fed the chickens, as well as the many goats, then they took her on a short trip in a four-by-four out into the woods. It was a five-minute drive through tall pine trees. The bouncing vehicle and cool breeze rushing through her hair left her feeling invigorated. They reached a large clearing with many beehives.

"We have enough bees here," said Elizabeth, "to produce over 200 kilograms of honey, so, as you can imagine, nearly a full-time occupation!"

The more Sofia was in Samuel and Elizabeth's company, the more she got to like them. Samuel put on his protective gear, as he looked through the hives. Elizabeth and Sofia watched from a safe distance.

"Do you have someone in your life, Sofia?"

The question surprised her, although it was an obvious question to ask. She hesitated, because she knew how attached she was to Jeremy, but she realised she had not treated him well at all.

"I guess so!"

The ambiguous answer, without qualification, raised Elizabeth's eyebrows.

"You have or you haven't?"

Like Samuel, she had lines of age across her face, along with the same sort of weathered tan. Sofia looked at her as if it was for the first time and thought how beautiful she was. She had seen the photos of the younger Elizabeth on their living-room wall, when she was fresh-faced, young and innocent looking. Now she was older, looking more attractive for having an air of worldliness. How could Sofia not answer the question properly?

"Yes I have! His name is Jeremy. I think we feel the same way about each other. Unfortunately, all this stuff just came up, then got in the way. I had to find out about who I am and what happened to my mother. That's why I'm here!"

Elizabeth, who was standing next to Sofia, turned, then hugged her. For a second, Sofia wanted to pull away. The emotion was too hard to manage, but the scent of Elizabeth's beautiful soap-smelling skin, mixed with that of the beautiful day melted the ice in her heart.

A few hours later, after a simple lunch, another story came to light. This time, Elizabeth felt the need to fill in the spaces.

"We always felt guilty that we never communicated more with you and your mother. I sent the odd letter, which she answered, but we failed to come and see you. I think all our lives have been taken up with trying to get by."

Sofia reached forward and touched Elizabeth's hands. A moment of understanding passed between them. Elizabeth then seemed to gather herself as she wiped a tear from her eyes.

"The people, sorry, the mob who Matias owed money to eventually found us. Three men turned up on our doorstep. All of them looked intimidating, but one was very well-dressed. He was the boss, medium height, in his fifties, with greying hair and a ridiculous Mexican moustache. He looked affluent. He was how you imagine these people to be, smartly suited, well groomed, out of place here. He stood on our decking outside, then more or less barged his way into the house. He was charming and friendly at first, then gave us an ultimatum. Either we paid him what Matias owed him or we'd suffer the consequences. He said it was fifty thousand euros. I think you can guess the scenario. We have all seen something like it on television or in films. You just don't think it will happen to you!"

She paused for a second and looked over at Samuel, who was dozing in an easy chair, his eyes flickering every now and again, as she told the story. She continued.

"The man also said he knew where Natalia was living. If we didn't get the money, they would go after her. At first, we tried our utmost to get the money, but this was years ago, we were working hard to put this place right, as well as earn a living, so we failed.

It wasn't long before they were back. This time, it was just his oversized minders, who hardly said anything. We told them we couldn't get the money together, then they left. We were confused as to what might happen. Half an hour later, we could see smoke drifting through the trees. We quickly realised that they must have set fire to the forest. We made our way down the track to where the edge of our property begins. It was ablaze. There was little we could do. Fortunately, there was a natural break between the trees, it was early in the year and the ground was damp, but the fire spread quickly through several acres."

"Did you tell the police?" asked Sofia.

"No, the thugs said if we did, we would regret it. We also heard rumours that the police were taking bribes at the time!"

"How about neighbours? Could they have helped?"

"The relationships we have built up now were not in place then! The man and his minders came back, this time with a solution, one that was very difficult to swallow. It included your mother. He told us they would provide us with a van that they had adapted. All we had to do was go backwards and forwards to Britain, with second-hand furniture, via

Santander. He told us it would be easy. Just act naturally. We tried to ascertain when the debt would be paid. He never answered.

We had Natalia's phone number and address of the house she had bought in Frigiliana. She had told us that she had money from an investment. Nothing to do with Matias. Of course, we believed her. How she was paying the mortgage, we had no idea. At the time, we only had each other to sort this sorry affair out. We met halfway between here and Malaga at a little tavern. You were there, but you were very young at the time. You ran around the place while we talked. You were so happy. We were complete strangers to you, but you weren't shy at all. You were a piece of sunshine in what was a dark meeting for us all.

We talked of breaking the law and couldn't see any way around it. It was also obvious that it must be drugs that they wanted us to smuggle."

"Who was the man that asked you to do this?" asked Sofia, "did he have a name?"

Elizabeth was thinking it through, as Samuel snored gently in his easy chair. It gave the room a feeling of contentment, even though the story was harrowing in many ways.

"His minders called him Grand Jefa. In English, that translates as Big Boss, as you know. I do remember, however, when he spoke English, it was near as damn it perfect!"

"Do you think he might have lived in Britain?"

"I'd say there was a good chance, but who knows? It was Samuel and Natalia who went back to Britain. I had to stay here to look after the livestock. They had to go to many different places over there. Samuel told me these people were very well-organised!"

"How about here? Where did you drop the stuff?" asked Sofia.

"It seemed more haphazard here in Spain. Samuel and Natalia were told, after leaving Santander, to drop the van off in a wood, or some deserted back road. From wherever it was, I would get a phone call, then go and pick them up. It was never the same place twice!"

"It must have been nerve-racking. If you'd have been caught, you would have spent years in prison!"

"Yes, it was awful! Sometimes, we thought we must have the gods on our side. However, I'm certain the police had had their palms greased to help it run smoothly!

As the years went by, we slipped into it like it was a proper business. The strange thing was, we picked up some nice pieces of furniture along the way.

We tried not to think of the lives that were being ruined by the drugs. Then, something happened on a trip back from Britain. A young man tried to get friendly with Natalia. Not unusual I know! She was a beautiful woman. His questions spooked her! She thought he was an undercover policeman. The thing was, she had to do the trip on her own, because Samuel had been ill. Fortunately, she wasn't followed off the ferry, but it put the fear in her mind. She decided to tell the men who picked up the van that she wanted a meeting with Grand Jefa.

It wasn't long before a minion turned up to see us with another couple of heavies. He was happy to give us his name, announcing it like a threat. He said, in Spanish,

'I am Pacos. Don't forget my name! I am always going to be here.'

He then put his finger to Samuel's head, looked at us menacingly and said, *'In your minds!'*

He shouted at us, threatened us. It was terrifying. Fortunately, Natalia had left and gone home by this time. However, we told him we must have paid the debt off by now. He was a nasty piece of work, none of the softly, softly approach like his boss. We told him, in no uncertain terms, that we had to stop, and that Natalia was certain the police were onto us. He said to Samuel and me that the debt would be paid when he said so, not before!"

"So I'm guessing," said Sofia, "that you went to see my mother in Frigiliana to tell her the bad news and it was my birthday!"

Elizabeth looked at Sofia.

"How do you know that?"

"Because I have a photograph of the two of you at my birthday party and no others of you at all."

Elizabeth smiled.

"Yes, it was lovely to see you on your birthday! You all seemed so happy. We felt awful for bringing bad news. Especially as it was the only time, we ever visited you at your home. We didn't want to spoil your party, but we had to see Natalia about what this thug had told us. We knew it would leave your mother feeling down. She said she would come to see us as soon as possible, but we all knew there was nothing we could do. That was the last time we saw her!"

Time had flown by. The afternoon light was dimming, shadows from the sun's rays had crossed the room, as the story was told. Evening was beckoning. Although the story was hard to tell at times, the feeling that surrounded them was tangible and warm.

"You must stay, Sofia, you can have the room your mother had when she stopped here!"

Sofia was tired. She was happy to stay. Elizabeth showed her the room. It was airy, beautifully decorated. There were frills and pastel colours. As Sofia settled, she could feel her mother's presence. It was a weird feeling. She wasn't into any religion or spiritual things, but she could feel something.

The next morning, Sofia woke to a cockerel giving his all, as the dawn broke. It was slightly cooler than the day before, which she welcomed. She sat on the edge of the bed and looked out of the window at the pine trees gently moving in the breeze. Even though she still had questions, she felt strangely at peace being there. Downstairs, she could hear Elizabeth singing along to the radio. As she came into the kitchen, Elizabeth looked at her.

"I hope you slept well. Sorry about Boris and my awful singing, if we woke you!"

"Who's Boris? And no, your voice is beautiful!"

"Now I know you're lying! Samuel says my voice is bordering on painful. It's just that when an old British hit comes on, I can't help myself. Oh, and Boris is our cockerel. Sit, eat! Samuel will be in shortly. He's feeding the chickens and the noisy Boris!"

The table was laid beautifully with a variety of cereals, as well as savoury pancakes that Elizabeth had just made. Sofia poured herself a coffee, cupped both hands around it, took a sip and sighed inwardly. The peace inside her body made her realise that years had gone by without stopping to appreciate the simple things. It wasn't long before she thought of Jeremy. His intervention in her life had changed everything, but the gathering of information about her past had hit her like a brick wall.

Not long after breakfast, Sofia asked,

"What happened after my mum was killed?"

Samuel and Elizabeth looked at each other, unsure as to who was going to speak. Samuel picked up the reigns.

"Let's rewind a little bit. We didn't see your mother after we left the party, but a few days later she phoned us. It was strange. It was shrouded in half-said things."

"What do you mean?" asked Sofia.

'I can't say much over the phone,' your mother said, *'but I have a lead! I'm following it up! I have an idea and I'm going to carry it out, no matter what!'*

That was more or less it! We had no idea what she was talking about. We didn't have the opportunity to persuade her not to be reckless. She put the phone down. A couple of days later, she left a message on the answer machine, because we were outside working. It's still on the machine after all these years."

He switched it on.

"I've done it! I've done what I wanted to do! I'm pretty sure no one saw me. I'm hoping this'll put a stop to all this aggravation. Love to you both. Fingers crossed!"

"As you can hear," said Samuel, "it's not clear what she did. We just tried to join the dots. At the time, there was no way we could! Not long after that, we had a visit from Gran Jefa, plus his minders, which was stranger still. He said,

'I've been told you think you have paid me back, and you want to

end our friendship!'
It was creepy, but still threatening. We just listened, as he went into a tirade, storming across our living-room floor, saying, *'Someone has crossed me, someone has carried out an act of hostility against me and my organisation. I want to know who it is, so I can apply pain to whoever has done it!'*
He stopped, then looked at us both. Obviously, we had no idea what he was talking about, thank God. However, we were aware that Natalia had done something. His anger got nothing from us. All we added to the story was that Natalia was absolutely certain the police were onto his operation. We tried to lay it on thick, so he could see that there was no point in continuing to go back and forth to Britain anymore. His frustration showed on his face. We thought that was it! We had outlived our usefulness, we were going to die! He stormed from the house, as his goons left the place in a mess. It was terrifying. We knew he would go after Natalia. We called her immediately, then left a message on her phone. A week later, we found out she was dead."
Sofia asked,
"So, what made you think my mother was murdered?"
"One of Gran Jefa's minders turned up out of the blue. We were expecting the worst, but he was sorry about everything. He was genuinely remorseful. He then told us that he was not there in an official capacity, but he had left Gran Jefa's organisation and wanted to tell us about Natalia. He sat there at the table, then told us what he thought had happened. He said that Pacos had been mown down by a hit-and-run driver, which had left him on a life-support machine. Unfortunately, he recovered consciousness and gave a description of Natalia to Gran Jefa. Not long after, Pacos died, then Grand Jefa had Natalia murdered."
The revelation sat there, as Sofia took it in.
"Pacos was the nephew of Grand Jefa, the minder told us. As you can imagine, Sofia, all this time we were living in absolute fear for our lives. The only good thing that came out of it was

the minder gave us the impression that Grand Jefa wouldn't carry out any other kind of retribution. The minder then gave us an envelope with an address inside."

Samuel asked Elizabeth to get the envelope, which she gave to Sofia. Samuel then said,

"If anything, ever happens to us, take it to the police!"

"Why haven't you ever done that, or don't you trust the Spanish police?" asked Sofia.

They both nodded.

"We felt at the time," said Elizabeth, "we should let sleeping dogs lie. We could prove nothing. If we did involve the police, would it mean that Grand Jefa would come after us again? Time has gone by, we are still alive, I guess the minder was right!"

Sofia opened the envelope. In there was a piece of paper with an address on it, that was all.

"It's not far from here," said Samuel, "maybe an hour or so drive."

Sofia was confused as to how it would help anything. However, her mind was more at peace with itself for knowing more about her mother.

47.

There was snow in the air. The English countryside had the look of winter about it, even though it was early spring. Large snowflakes started to fall, creating shadows as they passed streetlights to the ground. Cecilia was wearing her long coat with a hood, which shielded her from the worst of the weather. She made her way up a well-looked-after road onto a private estate, making sure to stay in the shadows. Many trees along the way made this easy to do. As yet, the snow was not deep. The weather forecast had made it clear that it would not be around for long.

Cecilia reached her destination, which was a mansion surrounded by a wall and electric gates. She dropped her hood, then, out of her pocket, she took a baseball cap, which she placed on her head. Underneath her coat, she was wearing a delivery driver's uniform, from which she pulled out a small parcel. Then, she pressed the call button on the gate. A man spoke.

"Hello, who is that?"

"Delivery!" Cecilia answered.

"Let me see."

Cecilia held up a small parcel to the CCTV camera.

"Please leave it in the post-box!"

"I need a signature."

"Ok, come on up!"

The large ornate gate was unlocked. Cecilia did up her coat, then made her way to the house. Exterior lights enhanced the mansion's structure which was modern in design. The snow that was still falling made it appear even more impressive. Cecilia was cold, as she stood outside, looking in. Panoramic windows let the light shine out across landscaped gardens. The grounds were completely private.

She arrived at the front door, then rang the bell. The door opened a few seconds later. The man was in his seventies. He looked completely relaxed in a baggy cardigan, T-shirt and trainer bottoms. He was bald, apart from wisps of grey to the sides of his head. For his age, he looked in good shape. He stared at Cecilia.

"I hope you don't mind me saying, but aren't you a little old to be doing this sort of job?"

There was a smile on his face, as he said it.

"I hope you don't mind me saying, but isn't that a bit ageist, Mr. Garcia?"

He laughed.

"Oh my God," he said, "everybody has issues these days!"

Snow was blowing in through the door.

"Come in a second, I'll get my spectacles!"

She slipped into the house, where she shook the snow off her cap and coat onto the floor. It melted instantly. The underfloor heating was perfect. He came back wearing his glasses. She had a few moments to take in the impressive, large, modern hallway.

"This is truly amazing Mr Garcia!"

"Yes, it is!"

Cecilia presented him with the parcel. He then signed the machine she had in her hand.

"Thank you!" she said.

He stared into her eyes.

"Don't I know you? I have a great memory for faces!"

"Who may that be, Mr Garcia?"

Then a look of recognition came over his face.

"You're the spitting image of that Agatha Christie actress, Cecilia! Cecilia..."

He paused, then said, "Walters!"

The change on his face was then one of expectation.

"No!" she said, "but lots of people have said that!"

"It's uncanny!" he said, "You should join an agency as a celebrity look-alike!"

"I've had people say that as well!" she said.

For some reason, Mr Garcia was entranced by the idea of such a thing.

"It seems to me," he added, "it would be a hell of a lot easier than doing the job you're doing at the moment. Bloody English weather!"

"Where are you from then, Mr. Garcia? I detect an accent!"

"Spain, but I've lived here for many years now!"

"If you don't mind me asking, what do you do for a living?"

"No, I don't mind. Imports, exports!"

Cecilia knew exactly what he did. He had done well out of drugs, trafficking, extortion. The list was endless.

"Do you think I could use your lavatory, Mr Garcia?"

"Of course, go ahead! Down the hall on the left."

She took her time. It was a warm and pleasant environment. The very large hall area had nice pieces of art, mixed with tasteful furniture. She couldn't help being impressed by everything. When she came back, Mr Garcia was waiting. Cecilia stopped at a large, imposing painting on the wall, then looked at it.

"Do you like art?" he asked.

"I love Joaquin Sorolla! His landscapes are stunning," she said.

"For a delivery driver, you're very knowledgeable."

He looked at her from the side, as she looked at his painting. He had a question on his lips.

"By the way, what is your name?"

She turned to look at him.

"Cecilia Walters!"

He was stunned at her answer.

"But you....?"

"I know, Mr Garcia. You see, if I told everyone who thought I looked like Cecilia Walters, that I was Cecilia Walters, I wouldn't get my job done, would I?"

He could see her reasoning, but now more questions followed.

Mr Garcia was a big fan of her work and he told her so, then offered her a warming drink.

"Will you get into trouble if you stop for a break? Don't you have a tight schedule?"

"You were my last call, so, as of this moment, I have finished work!"

He showed her into the living area, which was more than impressive. He gave her what she asked for, whisky and water. She took a sip, then she cradled it in her hands. As it hit her stomach, she could feel it warming her blood. Mr Garcia sat opposite her with a broad smile across his face. He was overjoyed that someone had called on him. The fact that it was Cecilia Walters had sent his heart racing.

"Tell me if it's a coincidence," he said, "but I watched an Agatha Christie drama this afternoon. Unfortunately, you were not in it!"

"I suspect," she replied, "that you may be able to access many on TV all day, every day, Mr Garcia!"

"Call me Juan! After all, we could be friends. I am such a great fan of your work. Why is it that you now work as a delivery driver? You are such a great actor!"

"Why, thank you, Juan!"

Cecilia was now acting her way to a conclusion to this meeting, but needed, for the moment, to not have to show her intentions.

"As you may know, when actors have no work, it is called resting. These words cover so many reasons why we are not working, including waiting for a part, a break in filming, being too old. The list is endless!"

"Are you saying you're too old, Cecilia?"

"Not at all! How can anyone be too old to act? Acting is about being someone else. So age doesn't matter. The reason I mention it is because some are ageists in my profession!"

She started to feel a little impatient because she was feeling old and grumpy. She also felt she had a temperature.

"Do you live all alone, Juan?"

"No, my wife, Evita, is at her mother's, who contracted Covid 19 and has been suffering from illness ever since!"

Cecilia's body was starting to ache. She decided to get to the point.

"How's your memory, Juan?"

The harsh tone to her voice made Juan Garcia feel strangely cold.

"I'm not sure of your meaning. Why do you ask?"

He looked guarded, as if someone had asked him an unanswerable question. In his life, he had been a man with a violent and troublesome past. He didn't see Cecilia Walters as someone who could do him harm. But for some reason, he felt nervous.

"I have it on good authority," she said, "that you are the person in charge of an underworld gang that runs drugs in and out of Britain. Some might say, you are an outright villain, Juan Garcia!"

The words rolled off Cecilia's tongue. She was cool, calm and collected. There was no dancing around the accusations. She didn't feel she had time to drag it out. Juan Garcia laughed.

"I see it now! This is a prank!"

He laughed even more.

"This is good, very clever. Evita's away at her mother's and you think let's play a little trick on Juan. I get it guys. Do you have a camera somewhere recording this?"

He stared at Cecilia, as if she was wearing a hidden camera.

"Is it you, Morales?"

Cecilia looked confused.

"I think you'll find, Mr Garcia, this is not a prank!"

"C'mon, guys! Stop messing with me. Ok, it must be Dom, my brother!"

Cecilia was stone-faced.

"None of the above," she said, "but how about Tracy Bowman, Carne Woodthorpe?"

She then named the others she had disposed of.

"What the hell's going on here. This is not funny anymore!

Explain yourself or you won't be leaving here alive!"

For the first time, Cecilia's cool was breaking. She was feeling hot, too hot.

For a moment or two, her role was suddenly like words from some American movie. She felt a little dizzy. She tried not to lose track. She was in no mood to be criticised for her performance. She then composed herself.

"I have names, dates, phone numbers, addresses, which I acquired from these people before I got rid of them."

She was making it up, but she felt it might be enough to keep him away from her.

"The information will be given to the police if any harm comes to me."

Immediately, Juan backed off. He then sat down opposite her, staring at his hands. His immediate response was perfect because she was feeling faint.

"As you know," she said, "these people are no more, but they led me to you. Grand Jefa, the Big Boss!"

A wry smile came over his face.

"There's more to this organisation than me, Cecilia Walters, but I'd like to know what the fuck is going on? Why you, of all people, have come after me like this?"

"I'm afraid it's a long story, that I don't think I can give you, but I'll give an edited version."

At this moment, Cecilia didn't even want to do that, because she felt ill but, somehow, the great actor that she was summoned up the power.

"Matias Perez was one of your mules that moved your drugs in and out of Britain years ago. He was a despicable piece of work who ruined a girl's life. He got what he had coming to him. The girl was the one who ended his life. You and your heavies pursued her until, eventually, you had her murdered!"

Juan was listening intently, looking relaxed on his sofa. "Go forward a few more years. You had recruited teenagers near Malaga to steal for you, then extend your kingdom. They were your way of procuring people to move drugs into Britain, in years to come. However, one slipped the net!"

"Oh, this is a sad story," he said, "but what the fuck has it got to do with anything?"

"The girl who pushed Matias Perez into the canal, was Natalia Neele. She was my daughter!"

A look of recognition came over Juan's face. Cecilia continued.

"Sofia was one of those teenagers. Natalia was her mother. Sofia was left for dead. So, as you can see, Juan Garcia, as far as I'm concerned, you have a lot to answer for!"

She finished her drink. He was unmoved by what she had told him. He then spoke.

"They say you should never meet your heroes or the ones you hold in high esteem. It would seem they are right, whoever they are. To be honest, Cecilia, I don't give a shit about any of that, and I wish now I had never met you. I did not get where I am by caring about people, unless they are members of my family. Pacos, my nephew, visited your daughter and her friends in Spain, as I did. As far as I'm concerned, he was trying to retrieve what was ours. I then discovered that your daughter had run him down. He died in hospital. So, in my mind, we're even!"

The words that rolled off Juan's tongue sounded so Hollywood, she almost expected Al Pacino or Robert de Nero to suddenly appear.

"Juan, you are guilty of taking the lives of innocent people. I am here to speak and act for them!"

He moved towards her, then stared into her eyes. She could feel the menace inside his body. She stood her ground. Since the first time she'd started this quest to find and eradicate Juan Garcia and his followers, she felt truly in fear. However, even though her blood was running hot, she did her best to face him down.

"I'll give you 5 minutes," he said, "then I'll send someone after you. Fortunately, I don't want all your blood in my home. Also, out of respect, I will leave it to someone else to kill you!"

It was only a second, but she felt a sharp pain in her thigh.

"They will not be as kind as me and this will slow you down!"
She could see a small knife in his hand that looked like a letter opener, with blood on the end of it. The wound wasn't deep, but immediately she felt weak. Somehow or other, she knew she had to summon up the strength to get out of there. From somewhere she could feel adrenalin charging through her veins, her need to survive was the only thing on her mind. Now she knew he had a weakness. He needed other people to finish off his work. She held her leg with one hand, then looked at him and said,

"Be careful with your words. They may take flight, or they may fall, but whatever you say there will be an end to it all!"

He looked perplexed by her riddle, because that was what it seemed to be. She collected her coat, walked slowly towards the front door. Her coat was now cosy and warm, which made her feel better, as she slid it on. In the hallway, she looked back at Juan Garcia, then put her finger up to her lips. It took a few seconds to exit the house. The freezing air hit her hard. She wasn't certain why she felt so bad, but she could take an educated guess. The way she was feeling, she was almost certain Covid was still in her blood. She then walked as quickly as she could down the drive towards the gate. Once through, she carried on to the cover of the trees.

The snow had stopped, but it was frosty underfoot. A loud explosion was heard behind her. She looked back briefly, as plumes of smoke and flames reached up to the darkness above, the clouds having made way for a starry sky. All the trees that surrounded the area were covered with snow. It looked so festive as they sparkled, almost as if they were covered with fairy lights, as the reflection from the flames got higher. She walked on, limping more than before, tired to her bones. A thrill of excitement rushed through her body, as she felt she was onstage again. She could hear the sound of crackling timber behind her, it was so similar to that of an audience wanting an encore. She stopped, turned, then majestically took a bow. Her head was spinning, and her leg was hurting. A few minutes later, a car picked her up, which then disappeared into the night.

"How do you feel?" Rupert asked.

She settled into the warm car seat.

"Better, but the bastard stabbed me in the leg, and I think I have a fever. Apart from that, I'm bleeding on your car seat."

He glanced towards her. She looked shattered. She, like him, was glad it was over.

"The explosion was perfect, Rupert!"

"Yes," he said, "you're right. To be honest, it was much easier than I thought it would be, to get in. Although I did look the part as a telecoms engineer. It's surprising how easy it is to get to places when you mention problems regarding the internet. However, the explosive took some getting, but, as I've said before, everything is available on the dark net. As soon as you left, I knew Garcia would call his heavies. The telephone triggered the bomb."

She looked towards him.

"What if he had called while I was there?"

"Cecilia, would you have let that happen? Anyway, you gave him the riddle, as you said you would, didn't you?"

She half smiled, then thought about it for a second. She wasn't absolutely certain she would have done anything, because of the way she was feeling.

"Cecilia, you have always thought on your feet. As an actor, you're trained to react to the words you are given. If it goes wrong, then you quickly re-think it and move on. Is your leg ok? Do you need to go to the hospital?"

"No, I need my bed. Juan Garcia was an absolute shit!"

"Yes, he was! Now he is no more!" he said.

"What of his wife and his brother?" she asked.

"I think, "said Rupert, "that the death of Juan Garcia will put an end to their organisation!"

Her mind went back to Jeremy asking about her belief in fate. Maybe this was indeed accidental with a sprinkling of coincidence, but, under the circumstances, she was lucky to be alive.

48.

The snow was melting, the day was bright and clear. The air had an acrid smell to it, as plumes of smoke twirled up to the sky above. The emergency services were packing away their equipment. Ella and Nigel looked on.

"So, what do we know, Ella?" asked Nigel.

Ella seemed to be miles away and not listening to him properly.

"I think we should move in together," she said, "we can't keep it a secret forever. If we don't resolve the situation, our jobs might be on the line!"

"I was talking about Juan Garcia, Ella, not us!"

"I know! I know! I'm sorry!"

They touched hands, then felt connected.

"Ok, back to Garcia!" she said, as she got a grip.

However, Nigel's mind was now on their relationship.

"Ella, don't worry, I'll sort it. Like I said before, when it comes down to sherbet lemons, I want this one to last forever!"

Later that day, back at the station, Ella and Nigel faced their team.

"Right, you guys," said Ella, "here's what we have. The charred remains of Juan Garcia were found among the rubble of his burnt-out house. At one time, as you can see from the photos, it was a beautiful place."

Several photographs of the property were pinned on the board, before and after the fire. Nigel then added,

"From what we have been told by SOCO and the fire service, they are ninety-nine per cent certain it was a small bomb that did the damage. It just enough to puncture a gas line."

Ethan was quick to jump in.

"Murder then!"

"Stick of rock to Ethan!" said Amber.

The sarcasm left Ethan a little crestfallen.

"Ok, ok, no fighting!" said Ella, "Let's work together. This is not a competition!"

"If it was, Amber would come last!"

Ethan said it under his breath. Ella stared at both of them, then put her finger to her mouth.

"Can I say something?" asked Bahni. They all looked at her. "If I'm not mistaken, Juan Garcia was on FiF, and he was friends with all the people in The Celeb Six case." They all looked at each other, bewildered as to why this had not been picked up before.

"We still have to remember," said Nigel, "that FiF is a social media site. There are so many people on there, who make friends with total strangers. It's the nature of the beast!"

"I think," said Ella, "that's what we have here. Our Mr. Garcia is the beast! He has a history as long as your arm in underworld crime and yet he's only ever served time for tax evasion. That was over thirty years ago. Since then, he's managed to evade the law! We have to find his wife, Evita, who was not with him when the house blew up. We are certain she is an intrinsic part of his organisation!"

Ella held up a file in her hand.

"This is not a file, it's a book. This man must have friends in high places and a lot of money to buy his way out of trouble!"

"He hasn't now," said Ethan, "he's a crisp."

They all laughed.

"Yes, you're right Ethan! There will be many who will be happy he is, I'm sure. Right! Bahni, Ethan, you have got the job, look into this file. Find something that's concrete, so we can move forward and put this case to sleep permanently!"

She dumped the heavy file on the desk.

49.

Jeremy was as keen as ever to go to see Cecilia. He was about to leave the house, when an envelope dropped at his feet through the letterbox. He looked inside. A note said,

Dear Jeremy. I think I have Covid symptoms. It's best if you don't come around for a while. Cxx.

Over a week later, Jeremy was at Cecilia's. He knocked on the main door to her apartment, but, as usual, no response. He had got used to this process. In many ways, it gave him comfort. When he realised Cecilia wasn't in the living room, he automatically went into the bedroom. She was in bed.

"Cecilia, are you ok?"

He was concerned about her. She groaned a response, which wasn't at all clear. He decided to sit on her bed, then touched her hand.

"Oh, sweet prince! I am depleted! My body is still beset by fever! Please feel my brow!"

For a moment, he thought *what will I do when the book is finished and I no longer have a reason to visit Cecilia?* His heart immediately sank. He then felt her forehead with the back of his hand.

"You seem fine to me. Have you done the Covid tests?"

"Of course I have. Would I have let you come, if I wasn't clear?"

"I know," he said, "but hardly anyone bothers with tests since the figures of infection have gone down!"

He smiled at her and thought she just needed some attention. She gave him a withering look.

"Get me the thermometer! What do you think you are? A doctor?"

She said it sharply, but now that he knew her ways, her words were like water off a duck's back. He went to get it from her bathroom. She took it from him, then sat up.

"Did you have a late night or a few drinks?" he asked.

She looked at him with a scowl on her face. She took her own temperature, which was normal.

"This must be faulty! I feel much worse than what this is saying!"

Jeremy took his own, then showed her.

"It's fine, look!"

She looked, then shook her head.

"I'd say, if I didn't know better," said Jeremy, "that someone had a night on the tiles!"

She got even more tetchy, then told him to leave the room. She appeared half an hour later, washed and dressed and looking nearly as good as ever, although he noticed she was limping.

"Are you ok, Cecilia? Have you had a fall?"

"It's nothing! The bloody Covid is a curse, I tell you!"

She was then her brusque self again.

"I was thinking," said Jeremy, "now the book is more or less finished, is there anything you might like to add? Maybe a few anecdotes?"

A look of surprise was on her face.

"I hope that my life hasn't come down to fucking anecdotes, Jeremy! If it has, shoot me now!"

She feigned being shot. He smiled. It seemed to him that Cecilia was back, although he was aware that something else was afoot.

"Am I right or am I wrong?" he asked, "but to me, you seem as if you are lifted, your mood lighter. Even earlier, when you were not feeling well, there seemed a brightness to your eyes. So, what is it that has done this?"

The words glided through Cecilia's mind, as if they were on a cloud.

"Yes! I applaud you, Jeremy! You have grown beyond belief! You are indeed someone who can read me well!"

He felt pleased with himself, but she had not answered his

question. Both of them were quiet, but Jeremy was waiting for an answer.

"Oh, I see," she said, "you want me to tell you why I am so changed!"

The silence came back. It lingered there in that comfortable place that sat between them.

"No, not today!" she continued, "it's not the time, maybe not the place. Let it sit, let the dust settle, let the flames die, let time do its thing!"

Jeremy looked at her, confused, but she sat there stoically. Then he knew there was nothing more to be said.

"Tea?" she asked.

He decided to ask her something that he had wanted to know for some time.

"Tell me, when did you first get Covid?"

For some reason, she looked reticent. It was as if he was having to work twice as hard to get information out of her. She answered.

"It was back in lockdown some time ago now. I was playing a part, an important part, then it hit me. I knew what it was, but I just wanted to complete the piece. Once I had, I could let Covid take me!"

"So, you knew you had it and thought you were going to die?"

"Yes, but I was happy to go. I had done my best work, it was from the heart. I felt I was not only a great actor but a good mother!"

Jeremy looked confused.

"How was it that both things came together? What was the part you were playing?"

She seemed to find it difficult to continue. He sat back, then poured himself more tea, leaving her to think on.

"It's difficult," she said, "because it's where real life and acting collide. The whole truth, Jeremy, is that it's a different story from the one I've been telling you. It's one where I am playing the part of someone else, in a different scenario. It has a real outcome that affects real life. At this time, I would say to you that it may certainly change your whole view of me and my life, probably for the worst.

As to the moment when I contracted the virus, I'm not hundred per cent certain. All I know is I was doing a rendition of Gene Kelly's Singing in the Rain. The only difference being I played the part in a real street, in real rain, and my audience was a fox!"

Jeremy found it almost impossible to put it all together in his mind. What she had said was almost like a Chinese puzzle. If this was a revelation, at that moment, he was at a bit of a loss. She continued.

"If I tell you, it will put the cat amongst the pigeons. Maybe even turn our whole world upside down. It would be warts and all. Is that what you want Jeremy?"

The journalist in him was champing at the bit but, deep inside, there was a part that just wanted this to be a great biography of a famous actress. He wasn't sure how many more warts he wanted.

Sofia flashed into his thoughts. Being with her was up there with the idea of the book. He was buying that future, he wanted to share that with her. At that moment, he wasn't certain how much more he could cope with. The time then seemed to just ebb away, as Cecilia got tired very quickly. He left her in better spirits, but nagging in his mind now was a secret that he didn't pursue.

50.

Jeremy received a text, one that surprised him.

Hi Jeremy. Can we meet? xxxx

It was from Sofia, the first one in ages. When he saw the four kisses, his heart skipped a beat. He held onto the kisses, as if they were a piece of sunshine on a cloudy day.

Where? When? xxxx.

He kept it short and to the point, thinking he had to play the game. He put four kisses, then took away two. For some reason, he thought it was a childish thing to do, so he put them back.

A few hours later he was sitting outside the Italian restaurant, where they had had their first date. This was his idea; he was hoping that the gesture would reassure Sofia. He was early, she was late. In fact, at one point he thought she wouldn't turn up. Then, he saw her coming towards him, as beautiful as ever. He could feel his heart beating faster. So much so, he had to swallow to take a breath. She smiled, looking beautiful in a cream-coloured summer dress. Her dark hair was tied back, her shoulders bare. She looked as if she had been running.

"I'm sorry I'm late! It was the taxi driver! The guy got lost!"

"Wow, it wasn't one of my dad's was it? If it was, he might get the sack!"

"No, it wasn't, but he was new to the job!"

The immediate conversation seemed to break the ice, which they were both grateful for.

"Wine?" he asked.

"Yes, and water!"

He ordered them, as well as a second lager for himself. There was a brief silence as they both thought of what to say.

"How.....?" both said simultaneously, then smiled.

"I was going to say, how's the family?" asked Sofia.

"Fine, Dad's still working, Mum's still helping him. Maya is thinking of expanding her empire. Kazi is still a pain in the arse!"

She laughed, which eased the tension.

"How are you?" he asked.

"I'm sorry," she said, "I should have told you what was going on. Unfortunately, it's still not clear."

The confusing answer didn't help.

"Why didn't you just put it past me? I am a good listener. I'm sure I would have understood, whatever it was!"

They continued to swim in a kind of jelly that is misunderstanding.

"I think," she explained, "I needed to sort it out myself, because what was going on between us was too claustrophobic for me to cope with!"

The words bruised Jeremy. It was like she was saying he was not party to her thought process. Indeed, he had not been.

"Does that mean that we are not in a relationship anymore?"

As he said it, he thought it was a stupid thing to say, as she hadn't spoken to him or contacted him for so long. He just held onto the hope, deep inside, that they were still together. The wine, water and another lager were brought by the waitress. Sofia drank the water, which she followed with a large sip of wine. After she placed the glass down, she moved her hand over and placed it on his. This act forced an electrical charge through his body.

"This is not about us. It's about my past life. Where I come from, what I am!"

It was a bigger picture she was painting. So he listened.

"I've been trying to find out what happened to my mother, but you know that, having followed me to Spain!"

She looked at him, then he could see in her eyes that there was hope.

"By the way, Anita sends her love! I think she was taken with you, Jeremy!"

The comment made him feel good inside.

"She told me to tell you that she feels happier now. She has moved in with Constanza. I think she wants to make new memories with someone else."

Her hand was only briefly on his, so he felt naked without it there. The emotion was left with him. Perhaps she just wasn't certain how she felt about their relationship anymore.

"I want a meeting," she said, "with Cecilia and Rupert!"

The question threw him. He was confused as to why. He thought for a moment or two. Not for the first time, he felt adrift of what was going on. Maybe it was his emotional ties to her that had blurred his vision.

"Ok," he said with a question in his voice, "may I ask why?"

"No, not at the moment. Anyway, you will be there, so you will find out!"

The statement was unequivocal. They both took sips of their drinks. Jeremy felt a distance between them. She stared at him with her piercing green eyes, which snapped him out of his indecision.

"Yes!" he said, "I'll see what I can do!"

He had no doubt about Cecilia, who would be happy to see Sofia. The problem was he had no idea if Rupert would be there. Jeremy had never met him. Even though Cecilia talked about him all the time.

The impasse between them both was the silence that neither of them could break.

Sofia took her glass of wine, then downed it in one. Jeremy had hardly touched his second lager, he was without doubt confused.

"I'll go," she said, "I need to be somewhere!"

He thought for a second, *you're here Sofia, with me, someone who loves you.* The words went around in his head. He knew, however, that to say them would not help at this moment in time.

"I'll let you know when I've talked to Cecilia!"

He wanted to continue the conversation, but she seemed to

want to leave quickly. He got up as she went to go, then leaned to kiss her on her cheek. He saw tears in her eyes.

"Are you ok?" he asked.

"Yes, I'm fine! I've got hay fever!"

A brief cheek to cheek kiss was exchanged, then she walked away.

Jeremy sat back down, then tried to think through what had just happened. He knew he was missing something. He had a sneaky suspicion that he had lost his way. He picked up his phone and googled: lost my way.

Losing your way on a journey is unfortunate. But, losing your reason for the journey, is a fate more cruel. H.G. Wells.

Being a journalist, he had been guilty of stealing things and shoehorning words into his work. He looked at the quote, then realised he hadn't lost the reason for the journey.

Jeremy went home. The house was empty. It was the ideal place for him to sound out his thoughts. Unfortunately, he didn't hear anything that was making any sense. He then heard someone come in the front door, as he poured some coffee. Maya strolled in looking smart.

"I say! Someone looks stylish for a chef at lunchtime!"

She stood there, then did a sort of swirl, then curtsied.

"What you up to, Maya?"

"I'd love a cup of coffee, Jez. Hot, dark, and sweet, like me!" she said.

He smiled at her exuberance.

"Nice one, Maya. To tell you the truth, I agree, even though you are my sister."

Jeremy felt better being able to banter with his big sister. She made him feel grounded. Even more so, at this moment in time, because he felt like he was walking through mud.

"I've got an appointment with the bank manager," Maya said. "I have a plan that I want to share with her!"

"Wow, don't tell me! You're going into partnership with Jamie Oliver!"

She looked at him wide-eyed, as if he had said something near the truth. He placed his coffee down hard on the counter, then did a celebratory dance in front of her.

"Stop it! Of course not, you silly sod!" she said.

"I know," he said, "I just wanted to rise to whatever you might say!"

They both laughed at the silliness.

"Well, go on! Tell me about it!"

She proceeded to tell him about her idea: to franchise her restaurant name and her style of Asian food.

"What do Mum and Dad think?"

"Don't know, I haven't asked them. Chai and I have worked so hard these last months. I know there's money in it, but it needs to be bigger!"

"You don't need Dad or the bank, you need Dragons' Den. Silence hit the kitchen after he said it.

"You know something, Jeremy, you're a dick!"

He saw the funny side of it. So did she.

"All I've got to say is, Maya. I'm out!"

They both laughed at the ridiculousness of it.

"Truth is, Maya, if I had the money, you could have it!"

She came around to him, then they hugged.

"Talking of dragons, how's Cecilia?"

He was amused by her comment.

"More importantly, have you heard from Sofia?"

"Yes, we met today!"

"Hold the horses, you let me go on about my crazy ideas and you had a meeting with the elusive Sofia!"

He then told her what had transpired.

"I understand you feel deflated by it all, Jez, but you have to remember this is someone who is troubled by a past she didn't know she had. It also sounds like she's still looking for answers. So if I were you, l would cut her some slack!"

He nodded.

"I know you're right, I just needed someone else to say it!"

51.

The next day Jeremy arrived at Cecilia's. He knocked on her apartment door, then went to open it with his key. He was surprised when Cecilia was standing there.

"Good morning, Jeremy, are we feeling full of life today? Are you ready to take on the world of Britain's leading thespian?"

He could tell by her voice she was in a good mood! They made their way into the living-room. Strangely, she was underdressed, almost bland, if that could ever be said about Cecilia. Even so, she looked cool and sophisticated. Usually, she had something on her head or tied into her hair, but today she was wearing an Alice band to hold it back. The band itself looked to be pure gold.

"Do you have news from the publisher for me?" she asked.

Her voice was perky, almost sing-song-like, then she turned to face him in the living-room.

He didn't answer the question, but said,

"I met Sofia yesterday."

Cecilia had a look of surprise in her face and immediately asked,

"Is she ok?"

"She's fine, as far as I can make out!"

He didn't really think that, but for now, it would do.

"She wants a meeting with you," he paused for a second, then said, "and Rupert!"

"Oh! I see!"

Unfortunately, he didn't see! He had suspicions, that was all.

"In that case, I think that we should leave it for today!" she said.

Her mood instantly changed. Her face had the same expression as that which was on Sofia's. As they stood opposite each other,

Jeremy realised there would be no tea today or anything to do with the book. Cecilia's mind was deep in thought.

"I'll let myself out then. Oh, by the way, the publisher did say something! He wants to see us as soon as possible!"

She hardly acknowledged him as he left. He was fairly certain that what he had suspected might be true, but for now, he knew he had to wait until the meeting to find out everything.

Jeremy awoke to a day that was neither one thing nor the other, his mind straddled by so many emotions. The weather appeared to be just the same. He looked out of his bedroom window. The sky had voluminous clouds that were stretched out, dark, foreboding. A brisk breeze lashed rain against the glass. Not long after, the sun shone through the breaks in the cloud, creating an array of wonderful colours in the room. For some unknown reason, this gave him hope.

He slid on his dressing-gown, went to the toilet, had a pee, then went downstairs. It had been nearly two days. He had heard nothing from Sofia or Cecilia. He was feeling strange, like the whole thing had been a dream. Perhaps this was someone else's life, some other person's body. At the bottom of the stairs, there was a full-length mirror. It was perfect for checking if you looked ok before leaving the house. He stared at himself.

"Look at you! Your hair's too long, your beard's too long, your face is too long!"

He grimaced at himself, then smiled. He pulled faces and made noises to accompany each face. It amused him greatly, then he nearly jumped out of his skin, as the front door opened.

"Holy shit!" he said.

Maya stepped in, followed by Chai.

"Oh, bloody hell, Jeremy!"

They looked at him, with his dressing-gown hanging open, half-naked.

"Er, I'm doing my exercise!" he said.

He then waved his arms up and down in an attempt to back up the statement. He struggled to find words to follow, although there was no need. Maya and Chai seemed to have their minds on other things. He pulled his dressing-gown together, then brushed his hand over his untidy hair.

"What's up, sis?"

She said nothing, as she walked past him into the kitchen.

"The bank said No!" Chai whispered, as she went by him.

"Shit!" he said.

He followed them both into the house. Jeremy did the right thing: made coffee. He had seen Maya worse than this, but it still upset him that she was feeling bad. After ten minutes of nothing being said, the coffee had been drunk. He asked if they wanted anything to eat. They both shook their heads. He was starving but thought better of making toast.

"Ok," he said, "let's look at this from a positive angle."

Chai looked at him in expectation, but Maya did not lift her head.

"You know what you want, you need a plan!"

The words hung there on the end of his tongue, then there was nothing. Chai looked disappointed.

"We know this, Jeremy. All we need is an institution to believe in us!"

"What did the bank manager say?"

Chai was about to speak, then Maya lifted her head.

"Come back in nine months with some accounts, then we'll see!"

Jeremy wanted to carefully pick his words.

"Well, I suppose I can see that. You have to be fair. At least she didn't say don't come back at all!"

He knew that Maya was sensible, but he knew she had found the perfect location for her dream to take off. For him, this was a welcome distraction, because his mind had been consumed with Cecilia and Sofia for the last few days. After a while of talking about it, she came around. She thanked Jeremy for being helpful, although he did spoil it by saying,

"Have you thought about asking Kazi? He must be worth a fortune!"

Her face was red with anger.

"Are you kidding me, Jeremy? If I was lost, naked and hungry I wouldn't ask him for a penny!"

She vented feelings which made the veins stand up on her head. He had said the wrong thing. She forgave him because she knew he was just thinking of ways to help her, no matter how futile!

Earlier, Jeremy had sent a text to Sofia confirming that he had asked for a meeting. After Maya and Chai had left the house, he received a text back from her: *Thanks so much xxx*

The few words made him feel down, then he wished someone was there for him. His mother came through the door, carrying some shopping, so he helped her empty the car and put things away.

He was feeling lost, because he had an empty space to fill. The book was more or less finished. A draft had been sent to the publisher. He was confident that Cecilia would get a good deal from them. After all, he was writing about a top actor. What's more, there was a lot of tasty material in it.

"This is so nice," said Mum, as they sat opposite each other, cup of tea in hand. "It's been ages since we've done this, what with you writing, me and Dad working more than ever. We don't get time!"

"The book is finished. It's been sent to a publisher. I'm a man of leisure now!"

"Oh, my God! Congratulations on your first book! Well done!"

She got up went around to him, then they hugged warmly.

"But I sense that you're not happy!" she said.

"I'm more than happy with the book. Cecilia is perfect! She is the ultimate actor, so wonderfully eccentric, warm and funny. I am overjoyed with the result!"

"So, why are you consumed with other things? Is it Sofia?"

He was quiet. He wanted to tell his mum everything, but he wasn't sure how to do that. He told her the story so far.

"I think, Jeremy, you may have another book on your hands.

One about you and your life writing about a celebrity!"

"Cecilia wouldn't like that, anyone saying she was a celebrity. She sees them all as being cheap imitations of someone with real talent!"

Mum took a sip of her drink, then said,

"I think I'm with her there. It seems to me that, these days, there are so many people out there that are famous for being famous and that's all!"

The next day, Jeremy received a phone call. It was Cecilia.

"How are you, sweet Prince?"

Her comforting tones buoyed his heart.

"I'm fine, my Queen. All the better for hearing your wonderful voice!"

She laughed. She was just as happy to hear him.

"I have a date for the meeting. I'm sorry I've taken this long, but Rupert was out of town!"

The call was short and sweet, which didn't surprise Jeremy. He immediately texted Sofia with the details. She replied.

I'll look forward to it! Maybe some light might be shed on all of this! Thanks so much. Love Sofia xxxx

Unlike the earlier message, this one made his day.

His thoughts were clear. A mantra came into his head. If you're positive with other people, positive things will happen to you. Shortly after that, a completely different feeling came over him, then he asked himself, *When did I get to be so needy?*

52.

It was all about the day, but not about the weather which was continuing to be changeable. Jeremy turned up at Cecilia's feeling damp. He'd had the sense to take an umbrella which he left on the stand at the bottom of the stairs. He noticed Mr Silverman's umbrella was still there. The old man came into his mind. Jeremy couldn't help wondering if he was still obsessing about the war in his new home. He then felt sad about the way the mind eventually loses its direction.

He knocked before he entered Cecilia's apartment. He took his time. For some reason, he wanted to take everything in, as if it was the last time. He noticed the smell of josh sticks: it was Nag Champa, Agarbatti, which immediately relaxed him. The familiar smell would forever remind him of Cecilia.

The table was set out with the usual teapot, cups and saucers. The art nouveau set seemed to gleam, as a faint sun cut through the windows. A slow-motion feeling took over his thoughts, as he came into the room. He heard Cecilia's voice before seeing her.

"My Prince!"

"My Queen!"

He wasn't sure if what she was wearing was the same as what he had seen before, but it was bright, happy, multicoloured and hippie-like. He told her so. She kissed him warmly on his cheeks, then hugged him like never before.

"Well, what have you for me about the publisher?"

This part of the meeting was for them alone, the other one was scheduled for later.

"The publisher is good to go. If it all goes well and you're happy with the deal. It will be just a question of dotting the i's and crossing the t's."

She was happy.

"Would you like a drink?" she asked.

"You mean an alcoholic one?"

As he said it, he looked at the tea service set out.

"Of course," she said, "the tea is for later!"

She went to her sideboard, then reached in.

"I have had to buy more of the special brandy. It was the devil's own job finding it!"

There was a triumphant smile that went between them, as they raised their glasses.

"As you know, Cecilia, the publisher pricked up his ears when I first mentioned your name, then, after he'd read a few chapters, he was sold. There is no doubt in his mind, the book will sell!"

She was happy, he was happy. He could be happier, but he thought he'd just take small steps for the day.

"One thing, you have to decide on the title of the book!"

"I have been thinking about it," she said, then hesitated, as if she was trying to see it in her mind's eye. "How about, *Some Dame! A biography of Cecilia Walters. By Jeremy Bakshi.*"

Jeremy, who was sitting at the table, thought for a moment.

"You don't like it!"

She looked a little bit disappointed.

"Yes I do! It's perfect and so very apt!"

The fact that she had been overlooked, as far as being offered a title by the establishment had always grated her. However, Jeremy knew that if she had been offered one, she would have turned it down out of principle. Such was the mind of someone with so much talent. Of course, he also knew she was bloody-minded and stubborn.

"Cheers!" they said, then clinked glasses.

"Signed, sealed, soon to be delivered!" he said.

They both took a large sip of their brandy. He then asked,

"A question for you, Cecilia. Why did you not try to crack the USA?"

She looked as if someone had prodded her with a stick, then took a few moments to speak.

"At the height of my fame, as you know, I had been in many big productions. Movies with other famous actors. So you may imagine that would have been my next step!"

She looked thoughtful, as she summoned up her feelings on the subject.

"The truth was, Jeremy, I can't stand flying! It terrifies me. The very thought of getting on a plane makes me want to be sick!"

"How about by ship? Longer, I know, but at least you're not in the air!"

She looked pale, as he said it.

"When I did a big Agatha Christie film in the middle east, I took a short trip in a hovercraft across the north sea, then a long road journey to Egypt. Never again. It was not for me!"

A knock came on the door. Jeremy went to open it. Sofia stood there, looking almost perfect in every way, although her hair looked a little ruffled by the weather outside. She slipped off her coat, which was damp from the rain, then he hung it in the hall. He kissed her on each cheek. He couldn't help being overcome by her appearance and her aroma, which was intoxicating in every way. She seemed preoccupied, then only half-heartedly kissed him back. Jeremy steeled himself, his mind was still on the bigger picture. As he followed her in, Cecilia was already exchanging kisses with Sofia.

Almost immediately, he heard the door again. He felt nervous, as he knew this would be the legend that was Rupert Blaine. Jeremy opened the door. There stood a man who was only slightly taller than Jeremy. For some reason, he seemed much taller. Maybe it was the trilby hat, the dark overcoat and the scarf that completed his commanding appearance. As Rupert took off his hat, he then launched his hand forward and shook Jeremy's vigorously.

"Am I addressing Mr Jeremy Bakshi?"

His voice was rich and almost clinically perfect. Like Cecilia, you could instantly tell he was an actor.

"Er, yes, I'm he!"

Jeremy's response was almost like that of a child meeting his teacher for the first time.

"As you probably know, I'm Rupert Blaine. Can I come in?"

Jeremy was momentarily welded to the floor, but, within seconds, he took Rupert's things and hung them in the hall. He followed Rupert in, like you may imagine a puppy would follow its master. Cecilia introduced him to Sofia. The charming man that he was leaned into her, kissed her hand then her cheeks.

"Why! Aren't you a beautiful young lady!"

Sofia blushed. She, too, was impressed by the man.

"Tea?" asked Cecilia.

They all moved towards the table, then sat down.

"Shall I be mother?" she said, then proceeded to pour.

A small number of biscuits were piled artistically on a plate in the middle. Jeremy looked at Rupert and Cecilia. They had an air of acting royalty that had no crown. It was their demeanour that radiated respect. He wasn't sure if they were aware of it, but it was there. Rupert pushed his chair to one side, so he could cross his legs comfortably. A moment or two was taken, as cups were guided to take sips of tea, but there was a tense feeling in the air.

Jeremy felt more relaxed. He had decided to record the proceedings for curiosity's sake, if nothing else. He switched his dictaphone on in his pocket.

"I have to say, Sofia, you are quite an accomplished thief!" said Rupert, "although you should pay attention to detail. I do not own a cat!"

Sofia's face was that of someone who had been caught shoplifting. The statement threw Jeremy, not to mention Cecilia.

"However, I must congratulate you on finding the password for my computer. To be honest, I hardly store anything of consequence on my electrical items, for fear of snoopers!"

They all looked at Sofia.

"Ok, you got me, but how did you know it was me?"

"You pulled a folder of Spain, which was mainly photographs. You're the only one I know, apart from Cecilia, who would be interested in them. I also knew you were curious about your past."

"So, how did you get the photos?" asked Sofia.

Rupert waited, then said,

"Cecilia had asked me if I could find Natalia, your mother, when she went missing many years ago after Matias had died in the canal. The use of a private detective had turned up nothing. Time went by. Both Cecilia and I carried on with our lives. Then the name Tia Neele appeared in the Spanish news saying she had died in a swimming accident. Agatha Christie used the name Neele when she disappeared. Cecilia put two and two together, then guessed it was Natalia. It was a small almost insignificant news item in a newspaper, but Cecilia noticed it.

"So you think that my mother changed her name so one day she could be found by Cecilia?"

"Yes, I do!"

"But you haven't answered how you got the photos," she said.

"After Cecilia found out about your mother's death, I went to look for you in Spain. After some investigation, I found Anita. She was obviously still coming to terms with Natalia's death, but between the two of us we made a plan, which Cecilia agreed with.

You seemed happy, even though your mother had died. I talked to Anita about what Cecilia and I could do to help. Apart from the obvious things, we agreed that to pull you away from the life you knew, would only turn your life upside down even more. That's when I took those photographs of you.

Of course, in hindsight, we should have been better grandparents and told you. Although, at the time, both Cecilia and I were wrapped up in our careers."

His words were measured, calm, perfectly calculated. Sofia was shocked that Anita had kept all this a secret. Rupert continued.

"I know now that you will have bad feelings for Anita, but she was sworn to secrecy. Of course, we also knew you could have been in danger. The years went past, then you got mixed up with those young criminals, who worked for Juan Garcia, which culminated in you being left for dead by that band of hooligans! After that, Anita changed your name to hers, hoping it would give you another chance!"

Jeremy had realised his suspicions were correct.

"Talking of Juan Garcia," he said, "did you see in the news that he was found dead at his mansion?"

The room went silent. It was almost as if someone had said *'Let's play a game of hold your breath.'* Jeremy looked at Cecilia and Rupert who were stony-faced, while Sofia looked confused.

"Let me take you back to the 1970s. We were young actors, on the edge of burgeoning careers. We met, we fell in love, we had a relationship. It created a baby. We had no idea what to do, but for better or worse, we decided on a termination. Unknown to me, Cecilia didn't have one. For me, I was working hard to drive my career forward. Cecilia went back to her mother and father to stay for a while. It was there that she changed her mind, had our daughter, Natalia, then decided, with the support of her mother and father, to have her adopted!"

Up to now, Cecilia's face had shown no emotions, but the gravitas of being faced by her past took its toll. She stood up from the table to go to the bathroom. The space that was left behind was tangible. None of the other three wanted to fill it. At this moment, Jeremy looked at Sofia, realising that the woman of his dreams was only a few feet away. He smiled at her. She smiled back at him, almost apologetically. He was trying to find something in her expression that might say that she still loved him. Cecilia came back in, looking more herself.

"I'm sorry!" she said, then sat back down and continued to speak.

"I think life can be cruel. I made decisions that cast our child into a life I did not know of. Eventually, it came back to haunt me, then I tried to rectify it. I didn't do a very good job of that either. However, in the end, I did what I had to do!"

Rupert reached out to her. They exchanged a smile. After she'd gathered herself, Cecilia spoke again.

"I had no idea what had happened to Natalia. I concentrated on my work as an actress. I became famous, as did Rupert, but we were no longer in a relationship. One day, Sofia, your mother turned up with a young man called Matias Perez. He was, for want of a better word, a petty criminal, who was hell-bent on trying to destroy everyone around him!"

"I know," said Sofia, "I found out about him on my visit to Spain, where I met his parents, Elizabeth and Samuel Perez."

Both Rupert and Cecilia sat forward on their chairs, as Sofia said their names, then continued,

"I am rather good at finding out things, you're right, Rupert, and yet so many questions are unanswered."

Sofia then told them about what Elizabeth and Samuel went through when Natalia was with them. Cecilia and Rupert had no idea about this part of Natalia's life. All they were aware of was what Anita had told them. As they all let the information sink in, Sofia looked into Cecilia's eyes.

"How are you dealing with your cancer?"

A wry smile came over Cecilia's face, as both Rupert and Jeremy looked shocked at the announcement. She replied,

"One day at a time, that's what they say. I suppose it's quite true, because that's all any of us have got!"

Both Rupert and Jeremy wanted to speak, but Sofia carried on.

"I guessed what you had, Cecilia, when I was looking after you in hospital. I knew it wasn't Covid and I overheard the doctor speaking to you."

Cecilia addressed Rupert and Jeremy before they could speak.

"Rupert, you know if I had told you, you would have tried to stop me doing what I did. As for you, Jeremy, if I had told you, the book would have been full of sentimentality!"

Jeremy felt hurt that she had not told him, because he thought he was objective enough to cope with the emotions involved.

"Let's not go down this road," said Cecilia, "it is what it is. I have not kept it a secret this long to have you two become my carers."

Her strong, positive statement shut them up.

"Before you ask how much time have I got, let's say just enough. By the way, don't ask me the name of the cancer and where it is, because I choose not to acknowledge it. In that way, as far as I am concerned, it does not exist!"

There were many emotions in the room and even though Jeremy was a part of it, he also knew this was not about him.

Cecilia got up, moved over to Sofia, and wrapped her arms around her, as did Rupert. Jeremy observed this moment with tears in his eyes, as the emotions overwhelmed the room.

Jeremy was certain other questions should be answered, but felt he needed to leave them to their reunion. So, he made excuses to leave. They wanted him to stay, but he insisted and decided to go. He avoided any more emotional interaction, then went into the hallway. Cecilia followed him.

"My Prince, wait!"

He turned. She put her hands on his shoulders. For some reason, he felt like a child, just about to go to school. She looked into his eyes.

"Jeremy, you're not only my prince but also my saviour. If it wasn't for you, I doubt that I would have survived to this point. You gave me the will to look into my heart and find the things I had forgotten. Of course, you also helped bring Sofia to us."

"Cecilia, I think Sofia found you by herself. As for me, just listening wasn't hard to do. The thanks are all mine! It's been a privilege!"

She reached down to where there was a small parcel leaning against a wall. It was wrapped up in brown paper.

"This is for you, for being here for me!"

"It's ok! You do not need to give me anything! You're already paying me to write the book!"

"Let's call this a gift of love then! Open it when you get home!"

She held him, then kissed him.

"Don't forget, my Prince, a Princess always has to be fought for!"

He smiled, thanked her again, then left.

53.

Ethan and Bahni had been left to continue their search on the internet to find out more about The Celeb Six. Solid evidence was needed, so they concentrated on the task in hand. Both of them had had time on the streets, following up on cases. However, they did prefer to work together on investigations in the office. Ethan was somewhere else in his mind. He often found it difficult to keep his thoughts on the job in hand.

"You know, Bahni, I wanted to go into space!"

Bahni couldn't help laughing to herself, as she was searching on her computer.

"To do what exactly?"

He stared at the ceiling above his head. Bahni then turned and said to him,

"Are you seeing little green men now, Ethan?"

He tutted at her, then continued to look above.

"I think it was Toy Story! You know, Buzz Lightyear to infinity and beyond!"

He stood up, clenched his fist and pushed one arm above his head. He looked like a policeman who was trying to stop the traffic, but not Buzz Lightyear.

"What do you think, Bahni? Do I look like him?"

She looked at him and giggled. Something struck a chord in her mind. She was also transported back to being a kid again.

"I always wanted to be Woody!"

She had a dreamy look on her face.

"Don't you mean Jessie?" he quizzed.

"I see, I see. You're trying to pigeonhole me into a girlie role model. You should be ashamed of yourself, Ethan. And you being gay. You should know better!"

Ethan was horrified at what he had said. He started to garble an apology. Bahni laughed at him. She then stood up, pretended to draw an imaginary gun from a holster, and said, "Bang! Bang!" He struck Buzz Lightyear's pose again, then pretended that the bullet had hit him in the chest. Ethan went full amateur dramatics.

"Oh, no, Woody! Why did you do that, I thought you liked me!" He then fell to the floor. Bahni moved towards him and leaned over him.

"Buzz! Buzz! I do like you; I made a mistake; I thought you were someone else I'm sorry!"

Ethan opened one eye as he lay on the floor.

"How could I be someone else? Have you seen the costume? You could hardly mistake Buzz Lightyear!"

The surreal moment was broken, as they heard a voice.

"Hello, hello! What's all this then?"

Amber Catz stood in the door, looking at them. Ethan looked at Bahni, trying to find something to cover their silliness.

"We were practising CPR!" said Bahni.

Realising that sounded very strange, she then added.

"Ethan was showing me how to defend myself, then we thought CPR might be needed!"

For some reason, the hole got bigger. They looked like a pair of guilty school kids, as they took their seats once more.

"Right, I want you to write fifty lines saying, I must not act like a juvenile when the boss is not here!"

They pulled faces at Amber, then saw the funny side.

"Ok, miss," Ethan said under his breath, "how do you spell fat arse!"

Bahni couldn't help it. She burst out laughing, as did Ethan.

"Ok, Ethan, I heard that. For fuck's sake, get on with your work and don't forget to respect an officer in future."

Amber smiled to herself, as she left the room. She couldn't help having sympathy for them. After all, she had spent hundreds of boring hours researching stuff on computers.

The dust had settled, as Ethan and Bahni got back to their

research. Nigel came in and started to work on a different case.

"Nigel," said Bahni, "would you please have a look at this?"

Nigel went over. Ethan stretched his neck to try and see what was going on.

"That's interesting. Well done, Bahni, that's a very good find!" He patted her on the shoulder, then went back to his chair. Ethan's eyes caught Bahni's. She licked the end of her finger, put it in the air then drew it down, as if to say one to me. She smiled cheekily at Ethan. He mouthed to her,

"What is it?"

"Later!" she mouthed back.

He looked annoyed but went back to his computer.

54.

Jeremy was making his way home from Cecilia's. His mind was not in a great place. Having been part of something quite wonderful, he now felt lost. The quandary he faced was with his feelings, which he knew he had to keep or dismiss. But before he could do that, he received a text message from Nigel Faron.

'Hi, Jeremy. Would it be possible to meet ASAP?

It sounded urgent, so he called Nigel. They decided to meet in a coffee shop. Nigel was already there, looking at his mobile phone, when Jeremy arrived. They hugged.

"Well, this is good!" said Jeremy.

They looked at each other, as they both ordered a coffee.

"What's in the parcel?" asked Nigel.

"It's a thank-you gift from Cecilia, because we've finished the book!"

"Congratulations! Well done, Jeremy! By the way, how is Cecilia?"

"That's an interesting question Nigel, because I've just found out she has cancer!"

"Wow, that's a shock! Is it treatable?"

"I'm not a hundred per cent certain, as she won't say, but I'm guessing that it's terminal."

Nigel went silent as he tried to find the right words.

Jeremy didn't want to go into any more details, as his mind wasn't quite up to it.

"So, what's up Nigel? How is the world of crime-fighting?"

Nigel smiled.

"So, so," he said, "always problems. We are in the middle of one case and an old case is still on my back. As usual, we don't have enough staff to cover it. Blah blah blah!"

He took another sip of his coffee and looked a little tentatively at Jeremy.

"I'll tell you where I am," said Nigel, with a very official tone to his voice.

Jeremy suddenly felt nervous, as if he might be arrested for something he hadn't done.

"Certain things have been discovered recently by my staff that concern Cecilia and Sofia, regarding The Celeb Six case and, what's more, Juan Garcia!"

The combination stunned Jeremy. Nigel continued.

"Juan Garcia had, over the years, been entwined in these people's lives and somehow six people died in quick succession, then, recently, Juan Garcia himself. In the last few days, some information has been unearthed that may involve Cecilia in Juan Garcia's death."

Jeremy listened to Nigel's information and didn't feel surprised. Inside, he knew there was something about Cecilia's life that he felt she was keeping from him.

"To cut a long story short," said Nigel, "it would seem that Cecilia had a motive to kill Juan Garcia because she thought he was responsible for the death of her daughter, Natalia. Also more information has come to light that Sofia is Cecilia's granddaughter and was involved with The Celeb Six when she was a teenager, these things I guess you already know. I'm fairly certain that Cecilia was out for revenge. The problem is, there's a lot of things that point to this, but proving it may be very difficult. However, because of what you have told me about Cecilia's health, I'm not sure anyone would benefit from pursuing the case."

"I'm aware that Sofia is Cecilia's granddaughter," said Jeremy, "but don't you think it's a bit far-fetched to believe that someone like Cecilia is capable of such a criminal act?"

As he said it, he wasn't certain he believed it.

"Look, Jeremy, I have no axe to grind here. All I have now is my curiosity. The case may be impossible to solve. We have suspicions, but we need solid evidence."

Jeremy also had suspicions, but, like Nigel, he had no proof. Nigel appeared to be more at ease with Jeremy's silence.

"Anyway, Jeremy, I have more to add. There is what you might call a loose cannon that is Evita Garcia, Juan's wife. She has gone missing. We believe she was looking after her mother when Juan Garcia got blown up. Officers went to her mother's house to talk to Evita, but they were told she had gone and nobody knew where!"

Jeremy looked a little non-plussed, as Nigel told him this.

"You see, the thing is, Jeremy, Evita was the brains behind the business. She pulled all the strings. She wore the trousers! There's no saying what she might do. She might want revenge. My bet is that Cecilia, Sofia and anyone tied to them might be her targets!"

Jeremy was shocked at this statement. He immediately looked suspiciously around the coffee bar. The stony silence that followed had them both staring into their coffees. Not long after, they both left the coffee shop and embraced each other in the street.

"The other thing," said Nigel, "is Ella and me are going to get married. I was wondering if you would be my best man."

For a second or two, Jeremy stared at Nigel in disbelief.

"Wow, Nigel! That is brilliant news! I'm so happy for you, and yes, I would love to be!"

In the wreck of his own relationship, Jeremy saw Nigel as someone who had got it right. There were smiles on both their faces.

"Good luck with the book, Jeremy. Maybe you could get me a signed copy?"

"Yes, by all means! Thanks, Nigel, for...."

His voice tailed off, as he reconnected with his thoughts.

"It's ok, Jeremy. Neither of us are happy with the way this case has panned out. All I can say is be careful and keep safe!"

55.

Maya was at home when Jeremy walked into the house. She was in a sombre mood, which matched Jeremy's. She looked at him, as he came into the kitchen. They greeted each other in a lacklustre way.

"You look as bad as I feel!" said Maya.

"You could say that!" he answered.

"I just have!"

A small smile came over their faces.

"What's in the parcel?"

"You know Maya, I have no idea! Cecilia gave it me today, as a thank you for finishing the book!"

"Well, open it, then! Or shall I?" she asked.

He let her open it.

"Wow! Jeremy, this is amazing! It can't be original, can it?"

Jeremy was dumb-struck. Maya was holding Cecilia's LS Lowry painting.

"This is one of Cecilia's favourite paintings!" he said.

"Looks like someone thinks an awful lot of you, Jeremy. What's more, this thing must be worth a small fortune. I remember watching the Antiques Roadshow not long ago. There was this guy on there who had one of Lowry's paintings. He thought it might be worth a few thousand, then the expert said he would expect it to sell in excess of eighty thousand pounds!"

Maya's words were like stars in his head, as he realised what a wonderful compliment it was from Cecilia. He then stared at Maya.

"Can I talk to you about something. You must promise me, you'll tell no one!"

"Yes, of course, my sweet brother. Can I post it later on social media?"

He gave her a withering look, then told her everything he knew about Cecilia, Sofia, Rupert and, more importantly, about what Nigel had told him. The whole story was unravelled.

"So, what's the problem?" she asked, "You have a green light, Jeremy. From what I can gather, the police have nothing on anyone. Don't tell me you have some feelings of guilt for something that no one really wants to prove or even can!"

"But you're forgetting," he said.

"I'm forgetting what?"

"Evita Garcia!"

She started to sing.

"Don't cry for me Argentina, the truth is I've buggered off to Spain!"

She sang it with pathos in her voice and he couldn't help laughing.

"Do you think?"

"Yes, of course. She's gone into hiding. I bet she thought the police would put her in prison, then throw away the key!"

Jeremy's mind eased slightly, but, still, he felt nervous.

Maya picked up her phone. Jeremy looked at her, suspiciously.

"Don't worry, I'm Googling the Lowry!"

He made coffee. His mood had lightened a little, but he was so tired.

"Holy shit, look at this!"

She showed him her phone, then she picked up the little painting.

"This thing is worth at least fifty thousand pounds, but could be much more!"

As he took it in, Jeremy felt like he was floating on a cloud of disbelief. Their parents came in from work, so they shared the news about the painting. It was a joyous evening. They all retired to bed happy. Jeremy couldn't sleep. Something was nagging at him. He got up and decided to write a letter. The next morning, he woke early, then knocked on Maya's door.

"Maya, join me downstairs in ten minutes!"

He heard her tired voice,

"Ok, keep your hair on!"

He was excited, as Maya, still half asleep, joined him in the kitchen.

"I've made an appointment for you with your bank manager, later today!" he said.

"What the hell for? I never want to see her again! She's a twat!"

"You will, I promise you!"

He placed a letter in front of her. She read it, then read it again.

"You can't do this, Jeremy! It's your gift!"

"I know, but I'm sharing it with you. I want you to use the painting as collateral, so you can go forward with your ideas on the restaurant!"

"Are you absolutely sure?"

"Of course, I am!"

She threw her arms around him, her eyes full of tears.

"You're the best brother in the world. You do know this makes us partners in crime?"

"Please don't mention crime this early in the morning!"

She winked at him, then ruffled his hair.

"Don't worry, Jez, it will all come out in the wash!"

In some ways, that's what worried him more than anything. As a writer, he realised he had got comfortable in the world of just one story. Whereas, as a journalist, he was immersed in many. He decided to step back for the moment and give himself space. For a short time, he needed to think.

He found comfort with his friend Duman, who was now on his own again, after Toya had gone on tour, following her win in the talent show.

The first Friday of the month saw them both revelling in their joint lost loves. It wasn't a pretty affair, as far as nights out were concerned. They both got absolutely wasted, but it eased Jeremy's inner pain.

He also got back to meeting Gail and Tony at the café. The usual high fives passed around.

"This place never changes, does it?" asked Jeremy.

"No," said Gail, "it's like your body needs that naughty something that keeps bringing you back!"

"Saying that," added Tony, "is it big breakfasts all round?"

Ten minutes later, three big breakfasts were placed on the table.

"Well, Jeremy, when is it? The book signing?" asked Tony.

Jeremy was busy dissecting his egg with fried bread and tomato sauce as he answered,

"Next Saturday at the bookstore in town!"

Tony looked at Gail, then said,

"Look at us, Gail! Published authors!"

She looked at them, both demolishing their breakfasts.

"Wankers more like!"

They all laughed.

"It's your turn, Gail," said Tony, "you must have a good tale to tell!"

Gail immediately looked at Jeremy. He then went a bit pale, but she winked at him.

"Yea, I did think about writing about some washed-up woman who slept with a colleague. She becomes a glamour queen on TV, then ditches her job in the local newspaper. The problem was I thought it was a bit far-fetched!"

Tony looked thoughtful.

"Hang on! What's wrong with that? If you throw in a few murders, a jealous husband and maybe a drunken detective, then you might have something."

Gail and Jeremy looked at Tony.

"Sorry," said Tony, "my second book has a few plot problems! I'm looking for ways around it!"

They finished eating in silence.

56.

The day of Cecilia's book launch came. It was thought that many people would be gathering at the main bookstore in town. Jeremy had called Cecilia. She had insisted on a meeting before the book signing, in a bar adjacent to where it was being launched. He guessed it might be her nerves, although if anyone was nervous it was him. He had managed to keep his distance from Cecilia, Sofia and Rupert. In some ways, he was disappointed that Sofia had not called him, but he was pretty certain now that their relationship had been just a flash in the pan.

He was waiting in the bar, dressed for the occasion in a nice suit. His nerves were coupled with the knowledge that Evita Garcia was on the loose. It seemed to him that Maya's pep talk was wearing a bit thin. He was now feeling paranoid. He looked around the bar, to see if there were any shifty types in. The elderly couple in the corner didn't bother him, neither did the woman sitting on a stool, talking to the barman. However, the man who came in just after him and was staring at his phone was making him feel hot and very nervous.

Cecilia walked through the doors. She had had her hair cut in a pageboy style. In many ways, she seemed younger, dressed stylish and sophisticated. He did think her skin was a little pale, but that might be the lights in the bar. Jeremy went to the door to greet her. She smiled at him and said,

"My Prince, you are so handsome!"

"My Queen! You look glorious!"

He stood back, then kissed her hand. They smiled at each other, then he took her to a table. He could feel by holding her arm, that she was still quite thin. Immediately, he felt guilty for having been absent from her life for the last month or so.

A waiter brought a whisky and water for her and a lager for Jeremy.

"You know my tastes, my Prince!"

"Cheers!"

They clinked glasses.

"By the way," she said, "thank you for the champagne and the card you sent me. You didn't have to. The painting I gave you was for putting up with me for months on end!"

"You know, as well as I do," he said, "that painting is worth a small fortune!"

"No! It's only worth the love that it is wrapped up in, nothing more!"

"Then it's priceless!" he said.

They smiled at each other.

"Where's Rupert?" he asked.

"Parking his car."

"Why didn't you come by taxi? I told you to call my Dad's company!"

"No, no, Rupert insisted. He's hardly left my side since the last time you came!"

He looked pained, then said,

"I'm sorry, it's just that…."

She put her hand up to his mouth.

"You have no need to apologise to me for anything, Jeremy. In fact, it is I who should be apologising to you. As I told you before, I had other things I should have informed you of. I did try, but, for some reason, the words never came out. Therefore I need to clear the air!"

He then stopped her.

"I know."

"You know what?"

"I know about the six people who have died as well as Juan Garcia!"

He said it quietly, although no one was close enough to hear.

She looked visibly relieved.

"But how did you find out?"

"I have a good friend in the police force, a DS Nigel Faron, who told me about two people that they know of that maybe involved with these deaths."

Cecilia's face had a look of resignation upon it.

"Two people, you say," she said, "there is no one else involved. I take on all responsibility for their deaths. I am quite relieved and I am ready to face the consequences!"

"Well, he mentioned you and Sofia. However, as far as Nigel is concerned, there is nothing for you to face or Sofia. Apparently, they have no evidence to prove who carried them out."

"How is that possible?"

"I guess that the pandemic interfered with the police and their investigation of The Celeb Six. I was told by Nigel a professional carried out the killings. So, you're not only an amazing actor, you're also an excellent murderer."

He couldn't help smiling at her, even though, deep down he knew it was all wrong.

"Nigel did say he thought that all these people probably deserved what happened to them, in particular Juan Garcia!"

He lifted his glass to Cecilia. He hadn't got the heart to speak to her about Evita Garcia. What would be the point? His paranoia had eased during this time, as the man with the phone had now been joined by a very attractive blonde.

"To you, my Queen!"

Rupert then joined them. They watched a large crowd start to surround the bookshop. For some reason, he didn't ask about Sofia, because he thought she would be there later.

"Are you up to this?" asked Jeremy.

"Of course," said Cecilia, "it'll be just like going to a premiere. I have done that plenty of times in my life!"

As they got up, Rupert took her arm, then Jeremy took the other. They walked across the street.

When they got there, a man, representing the publishers, took Cecilia and Rupert into the back of the shop. Ten minutes later, they reappeared. As Cecilia came out, everyone in the shop applauded. She was then shown to a seat at the back of a pile of her books. Hundreds of people stood, patiently smiling, as they waited to have their books signed. Cecilia's demeanour seemed to have changed. She was on an adrenalin high. After all, this was her stage. These were her loving fans. She looked younger, vibrant, full of their love for her. Rupert leaned in towards Jeremy.

"We had a joint in the toilets," he said, "it's a bit like first-night nerves!"

Jeremy had hardly spoken to Rupert, since he'd first met him, but thought he would be an amazing person to write a book about.

With all the people waiting there, Cecilia picked up the first book, wrote in it, then turned to Jeremy.

"This is for you, my Prince!"

He went down on one knee, then kissed her hand. Everyone spontaneously cheered. He took the book, then opened it. It said,

To My Darling Prince, now go find your Princess! Xxxx.

There was a folded slip of paper that she also gave to him. Tears came to his eyes, as he knew the finality of the moment.

"It's ok," she said, then kissed his forehead, "it's not my time quite yet. The note is from Sofia. Go!"

Cecilia beamed. She was in her element. Now she belonged to her fans.

Jeremy got up, made his way through the crowds of people, then left the bookshop, with a maelstrom of voices still ringing in his ears and a sense of pride running through his body. He hit the air outside. A sense of relief ran through his veins. He opened the book, then pulled out the piece of paper. There was an address on it written by Sofia, and four kisses. The address wasn't far away.

The heavy rain from earlier in the day had moved on. The streets were wet, but now the hot sun had warmed the footpath, causing warm vapour to rise. The city and its people were all around him. His mind was consumed. He walked with purpose, a nervous excitement filling his body. It wasn't long before he felt like he was being followed. Maybe it was just his mind playing tricks. He dodged down an alleyway, then ended up on a quieter street. Needless to say, he kept looking behind him. When he felt safe, he made his way to his destination.

A sign on a wall said Gas Street Basin. He turned into the opening. It was like a doorway into another world. He walked down the cobbled path. At the end, laid out before him, was the canal. Many narrowboats were moored, none of them alike. All of them were painted in different colours and styles. Some had plants on top, buckets, pipes, even piles of wood. Short washing lines were strung across the odd one, with washing lazily moving in the warm breeze. He couldn't believe that this place existed, even though Cecilia had told him about it. It was like a hidden kingdom away from the hubbub of the big city. Tall shadows from the modern buildings loomed nearby but, still, the background was of an industrial era. Unsure of which way to go, he followed the path under a low bridge at the side of the canal.

After a few minutes, he found more narrowboats moored up. He could feel himself relaxing, because he could hear birds singing, even though there was still traffic noise in the background. He took a breath, looked at the sky and felt at peace.

He then saw one boat at the end of the row. As he got closer, he saw the name Gypsy's Kiss on the side. The ornate lettering was white on a red background with a black shadow. The whole thing looked pristine. At that moment, he saw Sofia pop up out of the doors at the stern. She smiled a big smile, which made him smile back. It was like everything was back to normal, whatever normal was. He got on board the Gypsy's Kiss, then stood next to Sofia. It was the first time in ages he felt as if he had her attention. His feelings inside raced. She kissed him, then hugged him. She stopped, then bent down to start the motor. The turn of a key gave way to a spluttering of smoke which filled the air. His body was full of excitement by just being next to her. She went to step off the boat. For a moment, he felt a pang inside, as if she was leaving him again. He reached out for her, caught her arm. She turned, smiled at him, then kissed him again. She then got off and released the boat from its moorings.

"I guess you're wondering," she said, "if I know what I'm doing! I bet you never saw me as a sailor girl!"

She laughed after she said it. He couldn't help feeling that someone had set her soul free. It was in his thoughts to ask the question, but he had other things on his mind. She continued.

"Cecilia gave me the name of a man she knew who then taught me how to work a boat like this. He was a bit of a flirt! I think he fancied me!"

Her words seemed to stir some jealousy in his head. She then looked at him and laughed.

"He was in his eighties!"

Jeremy tried to take it all in. Up to now, though, he was lost for words. However, Sofia seemed to be enjoying the moment. So much so, he kept quiet. The boat moved off slowly, then picked up the pace. The close proximity of Sofia kept Jeremy's mind captivated. They stood together looking forward as a wave of water came off the boat then hit each bank. She reached for his hand, then put it with hers on the tiller. She looked him in the eye. He could feel tears welling up in his. Their emotions gathered, almost like waves off the boat. She kissed him again. This time longer, deeper. The boat veered towards the bank, as they stopped kissing.

"Oops!" she said, "the man who taught me never showed me how to steer and kiss at the same time!"

She laughed, just like when they'd first met. He couldn't help it; he joined in and they laughed together.

"I'm sorry for the way I treated you," she said, "but I had to do the things I did, or I would never have found out who I was!"

"It's ok! I totally understand. If it was me, I would probably have done the same thing!"

He knew he wouldn't have, but that was another story. There

was an air of contentment to the moment, which was framed by the sound of the chugging engine. It seemed so perfect. It was like this was what they did every day of the week. They were sucked into the feeling of freedom, even though they were still surrounded by the heartland of the big city.

"By the way, Jeremy, Cecilia gifted the Gypsy's Kiss to both of us!"

As she said it, she let go of the tiller. For a second or two, Jeremy struggled to keep the boat straight. Sofia started laughing, as his face contorted in panic.

"Relax, go with it, don't fight it!"

The few words helped, as he got the boat under control. For Jeremy, there was a lot to take in. Obviously, he was overjoyed that he had a half share in the Gypsy's Kiss. After all, he felt he had lived through the story of it with Cecilia. At this point, the bigger story of how Cecilia and Rupert had killed seven people filled his head. He did his best to bury them in the back of his mind. And, for different reasons, Evita Garcia.

"So, what are your plans?" he asked.

"Oh, I thought maybe stop at a nice pub. We can have a celebratory meal, then who knows? Have you ever been in a boat like this? It's very cosy!"

She looked at him with her love-me eyes, and his body and mind were lost in them. She laughed again, then tickled him, which made them both laugh in unison. They relaxed in each other's company, then watched the scenery go by. As yet, they were still between locks and the industrial landscape that surrounded them, but in many ways, it was calming. She suddenly looked more seriously at him, then said,

"Cecilia gave me an envelope and a small parcel to give to you!" She went below to get it. When she came back up, she relieved him of the tiller.

"Go and have a look at the inside. It's quite beautiful! Apparently Cecilia has had this in a warehouse for years since Faze died!"

He went down below, then, there it was, just the way Cecilia had described it. It was small, it was quaint, it was perfect. The sun shone through the windows, and he felt an overwhelming feeling of life taking over his body. He opened the envelope.

My Prince. If you are reading this, then I know that you have found the beautiful Sofia. I cannot tell you what joy that brings to my heart, that we are all now united and that you are with her. Of course, the future is something else. If I've learnt anything, it is that you can only live one day at a time. So fill it with as much love as you can. Anyway, I digress. You may find the small parcel interesting!

He opened it. It was one of her journals. He briefly looked through it. He quickly realised it was a detailed account of how she and Rupert went about the killings. He went back to the letter.

PS. What you do with the information is up to you, but it might be wise to let Sofia read it. After all, it might lay to rest some ghosts. Of course, it could always be the plot of another book. All I'll ask of you is to wait until Rupert and I are gone. It's also possible that you may both find it just as well to burn it! That, Jeremy, I will leave up to you.

Now, my Prince, sow the seeds of love. The kingdom of happiness will be in the waves that you both create. Much love, Cecilia!

He went back up to Sofia, then stood next to her by the tiller.

"Is it possible that we can stop the boat, Sofia? I think you'd best read this!"

She didn't question him. As soon as she was able, she brought the boat to the side of the canal. After securing it to the bank, they both went below. He then gave her the journal to read.

"Tea?" he asked.

"No! Coffee, please, black no sugar."

He familiarised himself with the surroundings, as she made herself comfortable.

Sometime later, after being consumed by what she was reading, he heard,

"Mmm.....!"

Her face looked puzzled, but not upset in any way. He felt

impatient to know her thoughts. Before he could say anything, she spoke.

"I knew when these people came up in the news, that someone was obviously killing them off. For what reason I didn't know. However, I did know what they were capable of. I had no idea who was doing it. I am amazed, shocked and relieved! These people that Cecilia and Rupert disposed of, were one of the reasons I've found it so hard to deal with what's been going on now and in the past!"

There were tears in her eyes. She slumped forward, her head cradled in her hands. Jeremy sat by her, then pulled her towards him. She rested her head on his shoulder. A period of silence settled between them, as they both dealt with the information. Jeremy had something else that he thought it best to add, purely because of the imminent danger involved.

"There is another thing I have to mention, a person who has been missed in all of this."

"Who?" asked Sofia.

"Evita Garcia!"

Sofia's eyes cleared, as she regained her composure.

"I have something to add to this story, Jeremy!"

He got up, then walked up and down. He couldn't help feeling that he was going to find out something else that was compromising. He gave Sofia time to explain.

"After our meeting with Cecilia and Rupert, I went back to Spain to tidy up some loose ends. Elizabeth and Samuel had told me about an address they had been given, not long after my mother had died. I was curious to know where it would lead me. I believed there was more to the story of Juan Garcia. I guess I'm like my grandmother, I also have dogged determination. The show must go on!"

Jeremy made himself comfortable to listen. He had a feeling this might take some time.

"I visited the address which was an hour and a half drive from Samuel and Elizabeth's home. It was twilight when I got there. I could just about see a house high up on a hill among the trees.

The area looked quite beautiful as the sun was going down. Shadows from the pines stretching out across the valley, with fine mist starting to gather high on the hill tops.

I parked my car in a small lay-by on the country road. I sat for a while and questioned why I was there, but I knew my curiosity wouldn't be quenched by driving off. For some reason I felt fearful, so I made a phone call. It was a while before I summoned up the courage to get out of the car. I composed myself before I made my way up the hill. I had no idea what I was going to achieve, let alone the danger I might be in. I skirted the house. No one was there.

The house was more of a glorified cabin. It was a one-storey building set quite high above the ground on posts. I walked up the old wooden steps to the front door, not even knowing what I might say.

No one was there, not a soul. I tried the door, but it was locked. There were chickens roaming around, also goats fenced in nearby. So, I guessed someone must have been there at some time during the day."

Jeremy admired her bravery.

"What do you think you would have done, if someone was there?"

"Maybe I thought if I saw someone intimidating, I would be able to bluff my way out of it. All I knew was that whoever owned this place was tied to what happened to my mother! I went around the back and broke in!"

Jeremy looked aghast. His thoughts were *what the hell have I got myself mixed up with, Sofia is just as crazy as Cecilia.* She carried on with the story.

"It was almost dark. I'd had the sense to take a torch. As you know, Jeremy, I had done this before!"

She smiled at him. In some ways, it was if she was telling him about a journey to the shops or a park, it was so matter-of-fact.

"Inside, I looked around in a haphazard way because I wasn't looking for anything in particular. I was just driven by the cause in my head. It was a simple layout and little by way of furnishings. Then I saw lights coming in the front windows, as a car pulled up outside. My nerves were jangling. I immediately thought, *get out of here.* Instead, I sat down in a chair facing the front door, then I sent a text and waited. As the door opened, the figure turned on the light, then stared at me sitting there. At first, she took a step back, as she tried to sum me up. She was a cool customer, because she never uttered a sound. Instead, she stepped back in, closed the door. The first thing she said was, *'Would you like a drink?'*

I said nothing. I didn't want to lose the upper hand by letting her hear the nerves in my voice. She stared at me, expecting a response, then she decided to help herself.

She went over to a cupboard and opened it, then pulled out a bottle of brandy. She then asked me if I was responsible for the death of Juan Garcia! Then introduced herself as Evita Garcia.

Again, I kept my mouth shut. I had no idea what she was talking about, although I had an inkling.

I could see her better now in the full light of the room. She poured herself a drink. She looked quite stunning for her age and had obviously looked after herself. Her clothes were expensive and her hair was perfect in every way. For some reason, her pearl earrings seemed to glint in the half-light. So much so, I felt hypnotised by them. She looked at me strangely, which snapped me out of it. Then she told me that the house once belonged to her parents and she saw it as a place to escape to, especially at this moment in time. It was almost as if I was a friend and she was letting me into her little secrets.

She spoke perfect English with the odd word taking a nod to her Spanish heritage, then she looked at me more seriously and asked,

'By the way, how did you find this address?'

I thought it best to contribute to the conversation. Anyway, I was feeling less nervous by then. I told her that friends had given it to me.

'Who are these friends?' she asked.

Again, I ignored the question. She took another sip of her brandy, then sat opposite me. I wanted answers so I asked her if she remembered my mother, Natalia Neele, and if she'd had her murdered.

She was calm and as cool as a cucumber, Jeremy. She stared at me with her cold dark eyes, then said,

'I've had many people murdered. You don't expect me to remember them all!'

I somehow found the courage to continue. She was a formidable woman. I reminded her that my mother ran down Pacos, her nephew, over twenty years ago.

She looked at me. I could see the recognition in her eyes as she realised who I was.

I sat there with an open mind, waiting for her to speak. A sip of brandy later, she told me that she had had my mother watched then she killed her. She blamed Juan and Pacos for being too soft and not tidying up their mistakes. This was one of many.

She was angry, Jeremy! She kept waving her hands around, as if she was about to strike some imaginary enemy. She moved forward on her seat and looked at me intently. Then said she had met my mother on the beach in Nerja. They swam together, like old friends. Evita then told me that she pulled her down under the water. She added, *'if it helps, it was quick!'*

I snapped, Jeremy, it was red rag to a bull. I immediately stood up and went to go for her, but she pulled out a gun from her handbag that was placed at her side!

'I'm happy that you stood up?' she said, *'We are going to take a little walk!'*

We stood opposite each other, almost waiting for something to happen. As you can imagine, Jeremy, the fear of God spread through my body. I knew that this woman was a fearsome character!

In those few moments that passed, I could feel my phone vibrating in my pocket. So I tried to delay Evita for a little longer. However, I didn't need to. She got angrier and blamed me for taking apart her organisation. She then told me that she would remove me, then go after the Perez's as well as anyone who had helped me!

I was at a loss as to what she was talking about. There was no way I was there to wipe out anything. But somehow, I was at the end of a gun and about to die. The terrible thing was, I had done nothing! I'd killed no one. To be perfectly honest, I was just there to tie up the loose ends.

Evita then told me to move towards the door. I opened it. She told me to keep my hands up, where she could see them.

A bright security light was on outside. I walked down the wooden steps. As I reached the ground, Evita was coming out of the door, following me. I turned to see a long piece of wood hit Evita's legs forcefully, then the gun fell from her hand. The five steps from the cabin didn't seem that high, but Evita fell awkwardly and hit her head on the bottom step. The sound of it was awful, as it echoed over the valley below. Anita came out of the shadows, carrying the broken branch from a tree. I knew immediately Evita had broken her neck.

You don't know how glad I was that Anita had got there. We hugged, not thinking of Evita at all. After a minute or two, I checked Evita's pulse. She was dead.

'*Fuck me, Sofia. She's gone!*' said Anita.

After the cold realisation that the murderer of my mother was now dead, both of us did a triumphal dance. It took some time for the adrenaline to settle. My mind was already on getting away from there. However, Anita was fascinated by Evita's earrings.

'*Can I have them?*' she asked.

I told her that at this moment in time it looked like an accident, but if she took the earrings it would look like murder. So, in no uncertain terms, I said '*No!*' She was annoyed. I then told her that I would split the proceeds of the house in Frigiliana between us, rather than me having three quarters. To be honest, Jeremy, she had saved my life and of course it was right to do that anyway. Satisfied with the deal, we shook hands and hugged.

I took the gun, wiped it and put it back in Evita's bag, cleaned up inside the cabin, then left everything as it was!"

Sofia was now sitting opposite Jeremy sipping coffee. He was digesting what she had said. His mind was a merry-go-round and he wasn't sure when it was going to stop, so he could get off. Truth was, he had never wanted to. Sofia then continued, "Anita and I went back to Samuel and Elizabeth's place. We told them what had happened. It was fortunate that I had asked Anita to come and see them, otherwise, there was no way there would have been a happy outcome to all of this. When I arrived at Evita's house, I called Anita then asked her to come to the address I gave her. She borrowed Samuels truck, so she arrived in time to save my life. I must tell you, Jeremy, that night was wonderful in many ways, but mostly because I felt I had let my mother's soul free!"

There was a moment that can only be described as the culmination of events being settled. Like the ripples on a pond being still or a feather on the wind that comes to rest.

"So, let's sail!" Sofia said.

She was definitive, confident and certain. Then she banged on the table with her fists, almost as if it was the only thing to do.

"Ok!" said Jeremy.

He was shocked by her manner, but knew he would be swept along by her determination. She grasped his hand, then they went back up on deck. Jeremy unhitched the rope fore and aft, then climbed back on the Gypsy's Kiss. Sofia started the engine. A friendly chug chug noise was accompanied by coughing of diesel smoke that spluttered out into the air once more.

"I guess we are joint captains, then?" he said.

"I don't mind being the captain's mate," she said, "As long as the captain wants to play around later!"

She smiled at him cheekily, which made him laugh. Both their hands were on the tiller once more, one on top of the other. Jeremy was reflective, which she picked up on.

"What's troubling you, Jeremy?"

"Cecilia! In all of this, I don't think I can face losing her!"

"Why are you going to lose her?"

"The cancer!"

"Do you honestly believe that it will take her?"

Jeremy thought for a moment and couldn't think of a world without Cecilia.

"No, I don't!"

"If you were a cancer, would you fight Cecilia?"

"I guess you're right!" he said, "She didn't do so well against Covid, though, did she?"

"Maybe not, Jeremy, but she didn't die from that either!"

Like everything that had gone before it, this was at the forefront of his mind, but he tried to let it go. He did realise however that if Cecilia wasn't a national treasure she was a treasure to him.

Sofia looked up into the sky. She looked like a goddess basking in the warm sunshine. He watched her, as her dark hair reached down her back. He couldn't help the urges that such a scene gives to a young man. After all, it was spring and Sofia was a beautiful woman. She caught him staring, then smiled. Knowing what he was thinking, she said,

"I think that, maybe, we should stop before lunch and take a rest!"

Her knowing look was joined by his. Then she said,

"Isn't this wonderful, Jeremy? All this is ours. I think this is a day to die for!"

Although he categorically agreed with her, the words sent a shiver through his body. Certain things were niggling in his mind, in particular the fact that he was party to numerous deaths, carried out by the women he loved. Even though Sofia may not have been guilty of murder, she was involved in Evita's demise.

Jeremy had listened to everything. In the beginning, he was a reporter of what he saw as the truth. As time had gone by he had become engulfed in a family affair that had its tendrils tracing through his thoughts and now his life. He couldn't help but think that he had become a puppet in a show that Cecilia, Sofia and Rupert were all part of. He was also inextricably involved. For some reason, he could hear Cecilia's profound, beautiful voice saying,

But love is blind and lovers cannot see!

There were no more questions. No more words to spoil the feeling that wrapped around them like a bubble of love. The world he was in was all he could ever have wished for. He was in love with it and, what's more, with his Princess!

Of course, there were doubts, but none that would lessen his passion for Sofia. As the Gypsy's Kiss cut through the calm water, onwards to the next lock, Jeremy couldn't help looking over his shoulder, just in case.

The End.

BOOKS BY THIS AUTHOR

The Worriers

Weird & Wonderful - 10 Short Stories

Printed in Great Britain
by Amazon

36013792R00225